THE ICE CASTLE

An Adventure in Music

by PENDRED NOYCE

Illustrations by Joan Charles

JUNIOR
SCARLETTA
An imprint of Scarletta Press
READERS

The Lexile Framework for Reading® Lexile measure® 800L
LEXILE®, LEXILE FRAMEWORK®, LEXILE ANALYZER® and the LEXILE® logo are trademarks of MetaMetrics, Inc., and are registered in the United States and abroad. The trademarks and names of other companies and products mentioned herein are the property of their respective owners. Copyright © 2011 MetaMetrics, Inc. All rights reserved.

Library of Congress Cataloging-in-Publication Data

Noyce, Pendred.

The ice castle : an adventure in music / by Pendred Noyce ; illustrations by Joan Charles.

p. cm.

Summary: "The return to Lexicon begins when thirteen-year-old cousins Ivan and Daphne find their Aunt Adelaide deathly ill. Leaving their aunt to rest, Ivan and Daphne accidentally let their younger cousin, Lila, in on their secret world of Lexicon. Ivan and Daphne must track Lila, who disappears, through the frozen landscape to the Land of Winter where social status and freedom is determined by how well one sings. Fortunately for Lila, her musical talent lands her in the most favorable place. Separated by class now, the cousins face the cold, hunger, poverty, illness, injustice, and the malicious plotting of a power-hungry blind man. Slave, servant, and fine lady, the three cousins must escape their own imprisonment before they reunite, provoke a revolution, and restore spring to the Land of Winter. Book includes discussion questions, challenge activities, and cross-curricular activities. "-- Provided by publisher.

ISBN-13: 978-0-9830219-6-4 (pbk.)
ISBN-10: 0-9830219-6-1 (pbk.)
ISBN-13: 978-0-9830219-7-1 (electronic)

[1. English language--Usage--Fiction. 2. Mathematics--Fiction. 3. Singing--Fiction. 4. Social classes--Fiction. 5. Cousins--Fiction. 6. Fantasy.] I. Charles, Joan, ill. II. Title.

PZ7.N953Ice 2012
[Fic]--dc23
2011053387

Illustrations: Joan Charles
Design & Composition: Mighty Media
Distributed by Publishers Group West

First edition

10 9 8 7 6 5 4 3 2 1

Printed in Canada

Books by Pendred Noyce

Lexicon Adventure Series
Lost in Lexicon: An Adventure in Words and Numbers
The Ice Castle: An Adventure in Music

Other Books
The Desperate Case of the Diamond Chip

For my boys, who love to sing:
Owen, David, and Damian.

Author Acknowledgement
With special thanks to my husband, Leo Liu, and all those who have helped make Lexicon a success: Rebecca, Darcy, Mary Golden, Denise LeBlanc, the staff at Scarletta, and most of all the readers who have joined the adventure.

Contents

Cast of Characters

Daphne

Aunt
Adelaide

Ivan

Lila

Aunt Leonora

Kanzat

Ezengi

Kit

Raibley

Fort

The Hermit

The Diva

Allegra

Itzo

Mr. Silica

Thomas

Lady Nadia

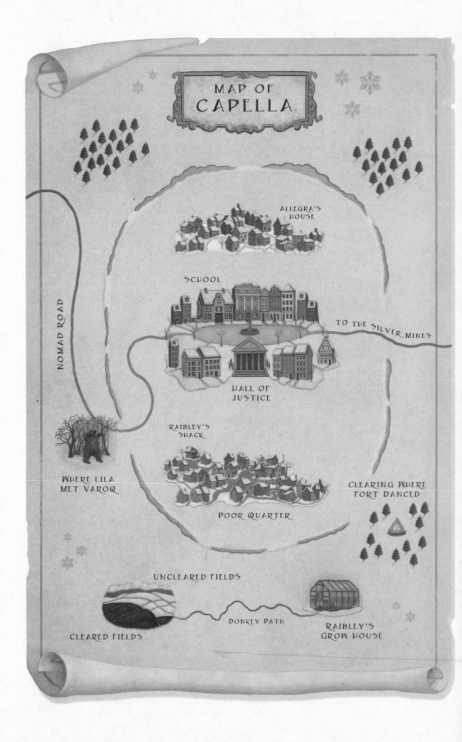

CHAPTER ONE

Great Aunt Adelaide

Ivan looked up into the darkening afternoon sky and extended his tongue to catch a snowflake. It melted as it landed. He reached into the mailbox and pulled out the banded wad of magazines, letters, and oversized envelopes. This was his favorite chore: bringing in the mail after school, while his parents were still at work and his little sister at daycare. He liked sorting through the catalogs and bills, and during this season he liked opening holiday cards and setting them out for the rest of the family to see as soon as they came home.

The only envelope addressed to Ivan was padded, yellow, and heavy. When he shook it, it grated with the sound of something metal sliding around inside.

Ivan carried the mail up the driveway, peering at the yellow envelope as dry snowflakes fell on it and then drifted off like dandelion seeds. His house was low and comfortable, with fading white clapboards and blue shutters and a carved front door that only strangers used. Family and friends used the side door, which stuck so badly that nobody bothered to lock it. Ivan karate-kicked it open and stumbled into the kitchen. He set his backpack on the floor, let the mail slide onto the kitchen table, and poured himself a glass of orange juice.

After a couple of gulps, he set the glass down, inserted his thumb under the flap of the yellow envelope, and tore it open. Slipping his hand inside, he touched a disk of metal so unexpectedly cold it stung his fingers. Ivan knew at once what it was.

He drew it out and let it sit on his palm: a bronze medallion stamped with a tall stool and a telescope. It was the gift he had brought his Great Aunt Adelaide out of the Land of Lexicon last summer. Lexicon, the secret country. Ivan could almost smell the sweet, fresh air of it. He and his cousin Daphne had puzzled their way across Lexicon until they found a way to lead hundreds of children safely out of a collapsing mountain.

He had carried the medallion home as a gift from the elderly Astronomer who had known Aunt Adelaide long ago. Weighing it now in his hand, Ivan remembered the glow of Aunt Adelaide's face when she slipped the medallion on, and how her long fingers had run over the surface as if she were reading its memories. He'd have sworn she never meant to take it off again.

He felt in the envelope once more and pulled out a piece of folded notepaper that read only: "Just in case. Aunt Adelaide."

Just in case *what?* Ivan sipped at his orange juice, but it seemed to have turned sour, and it made his stomach hurt. Something felt wrong.

Ivan dumped out the rest of the orange juice and went to rummage in his mother's desk. In her address book, he found Aunt Adelaide's number. Good thing a telephone was one modern device his great aunt allowed in her cottage.

But there was no answer. And, of course, she had no answering machine.

Nothing to worry about, he told himself. She's probably just out feeding the chickens or gone to the library. But the uneasy feeling in his stomach didn't subside. Aunt Adelaide was so old, and she lived alone.

Eventually Ivan flipped his cell phone open again and called Daphne in Maryland.

Daphne answered right away. "Ivan? What's up? Hey, congrats on that newspaper prize."

He groaned. "How did you hear about that?"

"Your mom called mine."

"It was just a dumb story I did for English class. The editors must have been blind. You know how much I suck at writing."

"Maybe in the old days," Daphne said. "Before Lexicon."

Ivan combed a hand through the bristles of his hair.

"Well, uh, thanks. That's sort of what I'm calling about. Daph, Aunt Adelaide sent me back the medallion."

"The Astronomer's medallion? She wouldn't!"

"She did. With a note saying, 'Just in case.'"

The phone ticked softly, as if he could hear Daphne thinking. Finally she said, "Maybe it's another clue, another adventure."

"Well, yeah. But it gives me a creepy feeling, as if she's ... I don't know, sailing off into the sunset or something. So I figured since she'll be going to your house for Christmas—"

"But she's not! Mom said she was going to be with you guys."

"Great, now she's tricking us." His mind ran over the possibilities. "I don't like this. Something's happening with her. I tried to call her, but there was no answer."

After a pause, Daphne said, "I'll get through, one way or another. I'll call you back."

*   *   *

By suppertime, Daphne still hadn't called. Ivan perched on the edge of his chair, pushing ziti and meatballs around his plate with so little enthusiasm that his mother was reaching to feel his forehead when his cell phone rang in his pocket. His father said, "No phone at dinner, Ivan."

"Sorry, Dad. Just this once, okay?" Ivan said, and he walked over to stand by the window.

Daphne sounded breathless. "She's in the hospital. I couldn't reach her even though I tried five times, but when my mom got home she called that neighbor Mr. Dill and he said she'd gone in, supposedly just for tests. But she closed up the house and she's been gone a couple of days already."

Ivan's mother sang out, "Ivan, have them call back later."

Ivan swung around and told his parents, "Aunt Adelaide's in the hospital." To Daphne he said, "What are you going to do?"

"We're going to drive up first thing in the morning. Mom's skipping work and she says I can miss the last couple days of school because it's all just parties anyway."

"I'll come too," Ivan said. "I can take the bus. Listen, I'll figure things out and call you back."

*　　*　　*

Ivan's father offered to drive him to Pennsylvania.

"But John," his mother said. "Tomorrow's my office Christmas party. You wouldn't make me go alone!"

Ivan's father leaned across the table and touched her hand. "Nina, I promised Uncle James I'd watch out for his Adelaide. Besides, what if Leonora shows up? Jen might not be strong enough to hold her off alone."

Ivan's mother pressed her lips together. "Your brother should have divorced that Leonora years ago. Anyway, there's no reason Ivan has to tag along. He has school."

Ivan broke in. "Not go? Are you kidding me?" He stopped himself. "Sorry. Let me start over. Mom, the school will understand this is a family emergency. They'll let me make the work up after Christmas." He arranged the talking points in his head—his good grades this year, even the newspaper award. But as he started, his voice broke and

17

the words came out with a squeak, which made his mother's face soften as she said, "All right, but just this once."

*　　*　　*

Snow banks lined the highway, and as they entered Pennsylvania, new flurries whirled around the windshield. Ivan had plugged his iPod into the radio, and he sat listening to rap and watching the snowflakes rush by. Next to him, his father drummed his fingers on the steering wheel the way he did when he was worried about work.

The music wasn't making either of them feel any better, so at the end of the song Ivan switched to his father's favorite Afro-pop instead. Some guy from Cameroon started crooning in French.

His dad grunted his thanks. Ivan looked over at him— broad face, light brown hair receding from his temples, big freckled hands on the wheel. Ivan's hair was darker, and his face and frame were narrower, like his mother's. And Ivan had no freckles. At this moment, Ivan thought, his dad looked more like a farmer than a lawyer.

The song changed, and Ivan said, "Thanks for driving me, Dad."

"I'd have come anyway," his father said. "Aunt Adelaide means a lot to me. I spent some fine summers on the farm, working for my uncle James. Cleaning out the barn, fixing the roof, that sort of thing." He glanced at Ivan. "Sometimes I'd take off on my own for a day or two."

He paused as if awaiting a response, and Ivan shifted in his seat. Ivan and Daphne had promised each other not to tell anyone—*anyone*—about their adventure launched from that barn roof last summer. At last Ivan said, "Yeah, Aunt A's pretty cool about stuff for an old lady."

His father started drumming his fingers again. "She left a message at the office last week. Said she wanted to consult me professionally, no big hurry. And darn it, Ivan, it slipped my mind."

By the time they turned into the hospital parking lot, the snow was falling faster than the windshield wipers could brush it away. The visitors' lot was only half cleared. Ivan stuffed the iPod into the front pocket of his backpack and sheltered the pack under his jacket.

A sign behind the front desk said that visiting on the surgical floors was restricted to those fourteen and older. "How old's your son?" asked the woman sitting under the sign.

"Fourteen," said Ivan's father without blinking.

The third floor of the hospital was spacious and gleaming, with an anxious bustle and a hum of goodwill in the background. Ivan's basketball shoes squeaked as he followed his dad down the polished hallway.

Aunt Adelaide shared a room with a plump woman who lay snoring with her arms flung out like clock hands. Ivan's father drew Ivan past her to Aunt Adelaide's lime-green curtain and said, "Knock, knock."

The curtain flew open, and Daphne threw herself at Ivan. Her yellow curls sprang in all directions, her nose was red, and when she hugged him, Ivan felt tears moist against his neck.

"I'm so glad you came." Daphne's voice was hoarse, as if she had a cold. "We've been doing anagrams while we waited, but now ..."

"Ivan's grown again," said his Aunt Jen. She wore jeans, a plaid shirt, and a determined cheerful look that wasn't reassuring. Ivan turned his glance to the bed.

Aunt Adelaide sat ruler-straight from the waist up, half swallowed by the pillows that propped her in place. Her cheekbones stood out, and the fluorescent lights gave her skin a yellowish tint. On the table beside her, she had arranged letter tiles into nonsense words. Ivan wanted to hug her, but she looked breakable. "Hi," he said.

"Good heavens," Aunt Adelaide said in her normal, crisp voice. "How the flock gathers. You'd think I'd pressed one of those 'Help me!' buzzers they supply to the frail elderly." The dents at the corners of her nose whitened as if she were annoyed, but her eyes settled on Ivan's face in a way that made him feel welcomed all the same.

"We're all here now," Daphne said. "Please, Aunt Adelaide, tell us what's happening."

Aunt Adelaide rearranged the letter tiles on her bedside table until they read "MOON STARER." Then she sighed, mixed the letters, and let her frail hand rest on them. "Very well." She looked from one to another of her visitors, as if judging whether they had fortitude enough to receive her news. "It seems this indigestion I've been having is not the false alarm I assumed. Dr. Fortnum tells me I have pancreatic cancer." She checked their faces again. "Since my liver tests are clean, surgery is still an option. While a cure is unlikely, I may gain several months of life, perhaps a year." She turned to Ivan's father, and her voice softened. "So you see, John dear, why it wasn't urgent. Though now that I've questioned the surgeon, I'm glad you've come, since apparently there is no guarantee of surviving the operation itself."

Ivan fell back a step. Perhaps a year? No guarantee of surviving the operation? All at once his stomach hurt again, much worse than yesterday. Aunt Adelaide couldn't die. She was too tough to die. Except—she was old, more than seventy. Ivan closed his fist around the medallion in his pocket. She'd sent it back because she thought she was going to die.

As Aunt Jen asked questions and made soothing noises, Ivan clamped his mouth shut and blinked back tears. Aunt Adelaide would disapprove if he broke down. He stood helpless, his ears buzzing so loudly he couldn't hear properly as Aunt Adelaide took his father's hand and murmured something about "amendments" and "revisions."

"That's settled then," Aunt Adelaide said at length. "You'll come back this afternoon, John, with your legal pad and a nice dark pen. And now, why don't you and Jen leave me alone with Ivan and Daphne for a bit."

"We'll find your doctor," Jen said, wiping a sleeve across her eyes. "I still have a few million questions." She pulled the green curtain around them as she left.

"Well, children," Aunt Adelaide said when the grown-ups were gone, "I have something to discuss with you." She paused for a long minute, her eyelids heavy, and Ivan thought she might fall asleep. But then she shook herself and stretched her hands toward the cousins. Thin and bony, with long fingernails, the hands looked like bird claws, but Ivan and Daphne took hold of them. "Before I talk to John," Aunt Adelaide said, "I need to know if you agree. You see, the farm—"

The curtain clattered open. "I knew it!" sang out a voice meant for grand opera. "I knew they'd congregate the moment they heard!" In strode Ivan's Aunt Leonora, trailed by his shy and lovely cousin Lila.

CHAPTER TWO

Aunt Leonora

Daphne felt herself swept aside as Aunt Leonora swished forward in her green silk and emeralds, her chest cleaving the air before her like a snowplow. Following in her tracks came their cousin Lila, who at the age of twelve was destined for the stage. Ah, Lila, Daphne thought, and her throat felt as if some big half-chewed chunk of meat had stuck in it. Make way for Lila, the talented and beautiful. Adults always admired Lila's shining dark hair, the rosy curve of her cheek and her luminous green eyes.

"How'd you get in? You're way too young," Daphne said. Immediately she bit her lip, because like everything she said to Lila this had come out sounding snarky.

"I *informed* the woman at the counter," Aunt Leonora declaimed, "how Lila had put at risk a promising part in

a famous musical not far from Broadway to rush to the comfort of her beloved and admired, her quite possibly *dying,* great aunt."

Daphne felt as if her aunt's words, swelling to fill the room, pressed everyone flat against the walls. She hated Aunt Leonora for plowing in to say "dying" with such thoughtless relish, and she despised how Lila couldn't answer a simple question for herself.

Aunt Leonora gazed around her with a satisfied smile. "I told that woman I pitied anyone who tried to stand in Lila's way."

Lila scuffed a foot and stared at the floor until her mother, with a shove between the shoulder blades, propelled her forward. Then Lila actually curtseyed. "Great Aunt Adelaide," she said, with an earnest gaze and a voice both clear and musical, "I have come to wish you the quickest possible return to health and happiness." Lila glanced upward at her mother, no doubt, Daphne thought, to see if she had said her lines right. At her mother's impatient nod, she returned to rest her green-eyed gaze on Aunt Adelaide's face.

Aunt Adelaide's glance flickered from Lila to Leonora.

Lila took a breath and said, "I meant to tell you, I just finished reading *The Mist of the Mountain,* and I think it's the best one of all."

Aunt Adelaide winced and studied her grandniece with her eyebrows pulled together. Lila reddened but did not flinch, and Aunt Adelaide's eyes closed for a minute.

"Thank you, dear," she said, in a voice much less crisp

than usual. She offered her hand, and after hesitating in front of the bony thing, Lila took it.

A short nurse with blond hair pulled tightly back stuck her head past the curtain and said, "End of visiting hours, I'm afraid. Heavens, how are there so many of you?" She shooed them from the bedside. "It's time now for our bath and a little rest. Tomorrow's the big surgery day, remember, and we need to save our strength."

Aunt Adelaide's lips pursed in annoyance, but as Daphne backed through the curtain, she saw her great aunt's eyelids drifting down again. She's exhausted, Daphne thought. But she never finished telling us what she wanted to say about the farm.

*   *   *

Three cars made their way down the two-lane highway toward the farm. Once Aunt Leonora had heard that the other relatives meant to stay overnight, she had insisted on joining them. Daphne wondered, where are we all going to sleep? I bet I'll end up sharing that lumpy old pullout couch with Lila.

The snow still fell, but one lane was plowed all the way to Aunt Adelaide's front driveway, over the troll bridge and into the yard. Snow had drifted high against the sides of the barn.

Mr. Dill, with his sheepskin hat pulled down over his ears, was shoveling a path to the door as they drove up. Ivan took a shovel from the back of his dad's car and went to help.

Leonora's high heels sank into the snow. Daphne's mom offered her an arm and said, "I never meant you had to come yourself, Leonora."

Aunt Leonora laughed. "Of course not. Rather keep the coast clear of competition, wouldn't you?" She clutched the offered arm. "It's just a joke, dear. Don't mind me." She leaned on Daphne's mother all along the shoveled walk to the kitchen door.

Competition? Daphne wondered, as she followed the others inside. Aunt Leonora seated Lila at the kitchen table, and Ivan's father bent to light the wood stove.

Ivan said, "Daphne and I'll go check on the animals."

His father's head shot up, and he gave Ivan a searching look. "You can check, but I'm sure Mr. Dill's keeping an eye on them. And don't be gone long. I want to feed you lunch."

Lila popped out of her chair. "I'll come too."

"Not a good idea," Daphne said. "You'll ruin your fancy clothes." And since Aunt Leonora agreed, Daphne and Ivan made it outside alone.

Ivan picked up the shovel leaning outside the door and carried it across the driveway to the barn path, which was filling with snow. Daphne kicked at the snow along the path's edge. "What did my mother go calling them for?"

"She's News Central, your mom."

"Well, of course she is," Daphne said, suddenly defensive. "Someone has to keep this lame family organized. But what's that book Lila mentioned? *The Misty Mountain* or something?"

"Never heard of it."

"And what's Aunt Leonora yammering about? What competition?"

"My dad says everything's a competition with her." Ivan threw aside a shovelful of snow. "A competition starring Lila, poor kid. But it's obvious enough, Daphne. What do you think Aunt Adelaide wants to talk to my dad about?"

Daphne felt her mind shutting something out. "How should I know?"

Ivan paused with the shovel held across his body. "Her will, that's what. And Aunt Leonora doesn't want Lila left out."

Aunt Adelaide's will? So that stuff about less than a year to live ... Daphne turned the thought away. Doctors are wrong all the time. She shook her head. "There's nothing to compete about. It's not like Aunt Adelaide's rich."

"She has this farm. She wanted to warn us about the farm."

"Aunt Leonora wouldn't want a farm."

Ivan stabbed the snow again with his shovel. "So she'd sell it, wouldn't she? And they'd build townhouses or something, and no one would ever go to Lexicon again."

Picturing the cupola knocked down, the other world closed off forever, made Daphne's throat feel tight, and then she thought of something worse. "What if some real estate agent or builder or greedy person fell through into Lexicon by accident, and they told everyone, and some company set it up as a huge amusement park where hunters could go shooting wild thesauri and ..."

"Exactly," Ivan said. He cleared the last foot of the path

and threw down the shovel. Daphne helped him pull on the sliding door until it rolled open.

Inside, dust motes cruised the cold air, and the smell of manure stung the inside of Daphne's nose. She watched Ivan toss a handful of feed to the chickens and, following his example, she went to feed the pig but found it already gorging at the trough. Even with animals present, the barn's interior felt lonely and ancient—like poor Aunt Adelaide must feel, Daphne thought. And all at once the answer to Aunt Adelaide's last anagram, the one she had erased, jumped into Daphne's mind. MOON STARER became ASTRONOMER. Daphne's eyes watered.

"What I'm thinking," Ivan said, closing the grain bin, "is maybe we should talk to my dad. I kind of think he knows something already, the way he keeps dropping hints about working on the barn roof when he was a kid."

Daphne squeezed her eyes shut. "But we don't even know that she's dying. I mean, they haven't even tried anything yet. We shouldn't talk about her like she's doomed."

Ivan gazed at her without speaking—looked down at her, she realized. Well, good for him, he had finally hit his growth spurt. "Stop looking at me that way," she said. "Like you're so superior and wise. You don't know any more than I do." She spun away from him and strode toward the stairs. "Let's go check the view."

She heard him clumping behind her up the stairs to the hayloft on the second level. From among the hay bales, the folding ladder still stretched up to the cupola room. As she approached the ladder, Daphne's stomach clenched and her skin felt strangely alert. According to Aunt Adelaide, the land of Lexicon drifted in and out of view as it chose: sometimes it appeared beyond the cupola windows, and sometimes it hid. If today was like that rainy day last summer, they would find the barn surrounded by a pond, and beyond the pond would lie another world. She and Ivan would be tempted to step through, abandoning Aunt Adelaide and frightening their parents by disappearing for a day. As she climbed the ladder, Daphne told herself it would be much better, really, if the gateway turned out to be closed.

It was closed.

No Lexicon, not now, not today. Through all four cupola windows she saw only the bleakness of the farm in winter: white meadows rising to a wooded slope, the frozen stream with the snow-dusted highway beyond, and Ivan's thin shoveled track to the cottage door. Daphne looked out the window, and her arms and legs felt drained and empty.

"Nothing," said Ivan beside her. In the flatness of his voice Daphne heard the same dull blankness she felt. Aunt Adelaide was dying, and the world had gone gray and flat and bereft of magic.

"Ivan? Daphne?" A musical voice rose from two floors below. With a glance at each other, Daphne and Ivan hastened down the ladder to the hayloft. Ivan still had his foot on the bottom rung when Lila emerged up the stairs into the loft from the ground floor. She came all the way up and drew off her gloves, which were lined with fake fur to match her full-length fake-fur-lined green coat. "What are you doing?" Lila asked. "What's up there?"

"Nothing's up there," Ivan said, and Daphne half-nodded, half-shook her head in agreement.

Lila looked at Ivan, then at Daphne, her gaze full of reproach. Dark, finely arched eyebrows framed green eyes that shone with the start of tears. Her rosebud mouth trembled. "Why won't you guys let me hang out with you?"

Ivan stepped forward, put an arm around her shoulders, and turned her away from the ladder. "Now come on, Lila, that's not fair," he said. "There's nothing to do out here, and it's cold. Let's go inside and play Monopoly."

* * *

By the time Ivan's father called them down to lunch, Daphne already had a monopoly of the orange properties, and her prospects looked good. Lunch was canned tomato soup with bread and butter. Daphne paused before sitting down, looking with dismay at the meager pickings. Then she saw Lila wrinkle her perfect nose, and that made her sit right down, say "Thanks, Uncle John," and start spooning in the soup.

Uncle John wiped his hands on his apron. "I'm off to the hospital again. It's almost time for afternoon visiting hours."

Aunt Leonora pushed back her chair. "I'll come with you."

"No need, Leonora. It's just business. Let's not weary her with a cast of thousands."

"All the more reason to give her another sympathetic ear." Aunt Leonora wiped a napkin across her mouth and stood. "To ensure she makes no hasty decisions in the throes of drugged exhaustion."

So Ivan was right. Aunt Leonora meant to lurk at Aunt Adelaide's bedside to make sure she got her share of the loot.

"Leonora ..." Uncle John sighed and made a gesture of assent. If he gives in so easily in court, Daphne thought sourly, he must never win any cases.

Daphne's mother began to pile dishes in the sink. "I'll come along and buy groceries."

Leonora fluttered her hands. "But who will watch the children?"

"The children can watch themselves for an hour or two."

Aunt Leonora swept her glance over them, her raised eyebrows proclaiming her skepticism. "Daphne, please see that Lila spends at least fifty minutes rehearsing. She does have a lead role, you know. Ivan, you clean up."

Ivan, who had just lifted his bowl to carry it to the sink, set it back down and slowly put his hands in his pockets. Daphne knew he was furious. On the way out, Uncle John ruffled Ivan's hair and said in a low voice, "Come on, be a sport. I've got the diva mom to deal with."

Lila stood chewing her lip, her head lowered like a puppy waiting to be scolded.

"No more Monopoly, I guess," Daphne said. "Since I'm in charge of your practice schedule all of a sudden."

Lila shook her head. "She's right. I'm missing rehearsal."

"What's this big lead part you're playing?" Daphne heard the sharpness in her voice.

Lila lifted her chin. "The show's *Les Miz*, and I'm Cosette. She's sent away as a child and forced to be a servant while this other girl her own age gets treated like a princess. She just has one main song, about dreaming of a beautiful castle, but it's important."

Daphne folded her arms. "Why don't you go upstairs and perform in front of the mirror while I help Ivan, *your* servant, clean up your lunch."

Lila's eyes glistened. "Don't talk that way! I'll help too."

Ivan stepped forward. "Come on, Lila. Don't let Daphne upset you. You go ahead and do what you need to. I'll have this cleaned up in half a sec."

Lila gave him a grateful look and tripped away upstairs, where a moment later she launched into a series of scales. Ivan filled the sink with soapy water. Daphne piled as many dishes in her arms as she could and dumped them loudly into the sink. Ivan jumped back from the splash. Daphne picked up a dishtowel and stood ready to dry.

"You shouldn't take it out on her, Daph," Ivan said.

"That socially immature, mousy little Oklahoma girl, acting so cool."

"Wow," said Ivan. "You know, Daphne, sometimes you really sound like a snob."

"Me?" Daphne couldn't believe the injustice of this. "She's the one who's stuck up."

"Do you think so? I think she's really talented. We saw her in *The Wiz*, and she sure got lots of applause. And she has a horrible mother. You should feel sorry for her."

"Fine then, why don't you marry her if she's so

wonderful." The words felt hateful and childish as she said them, but Daphne didn't care. "Oh no, too bad, I forgot. She's your cousin. You can't."

Ivan let the soapy water drain out of the sink. "It's not like that and you know it. She's just a kid. Yeah, she has a great voice and gets tons of attention, but I don't think she's very happy. It wouldn't kill you to be nice to her."

Daphne threw down the dishtowel, stomped to the door, and shoved it open. She glared out at the white puffiness of the scenery, everything so soft and perfect looking, like the pillows smothering Aunt Adelaide in that horrible, perfectly clean hospital. Tears blurred her vision.

Ivan spoke behind her. "Come on, let's get some fresh air. The dishes can dry themselves."

They put on hooded jackets and heavy boots and made their way down to the troll bridge, where they chucked snowballs onto the snow blanketing the frozen stream. After a while Ivan climbed down the bank and probed at the ice with a fallen pine branch, and soon after that he fetched a shovel and began to clear the ice beneath the bridge. Watching him work in his methodical way, Daphne found her anger dissipating, and she descended to help him. Soon they were sliding around on the ice, playing broom hockey with pine branches for sticks and a pinecone for a puck.

Daphne's nose ran and her throat felt worse than ever, but she kept the score nearly even. After a long time, when they both tumbled onto the bank, breathing heavily, Ivan said, "We should ask Lila to join us. I'm sure she's sung enough by now."

"Okay," Daphne said. Ivan had called Lila just a kid; they could be kind to her.

They threw away their branches, clambered up the bank and crossed the yard to the house. "Lila, come on out!" Ivan called, but there was no answer, no sound of singing.

"She's probably taking a nap," Daphne said. She ran upstairs, feeling uneasy.

She found no Lila in either bedroom upstairs. She ran down again, and she and Ivan said together, "The barn."

The barn door was open, but when they called Lila's name, the sound echoed in the empty expanse. Blobs of melting snow lay on the stairs leading to the loft. "Lila!" they called. No answer. Daphne reached the ladder first and scrambled up it to the cupola, certain that they would find her—but no.

Cold air blew through the open window. Outside, the snow-draped scene stretched across flat land to woods on all sides and high gleaming mountains in the distance. There was no sign of Aunt Adelaide's cottage, or the farm, or the bridge and the highway beyond.

Ivan came up beside her, and Daphne pointed to the marks in the snow on the roof outside the window: a trough, as if someone had slid down through the thick layer of snow and dropped over the edge. Below, a single set of tracks led away to the woods.

Daphne thought she might burst out of her skin with fury at being robbed of their secret world and fear that Lila wouldn't make it back alone. Even in Lexicon, a person might freeze to death.

"We have to go get her," Daphne said. "Right now, while we can see her tracks and before our parents come home." She levered herself up onto the windowsill.

"Yes," Ivan said. "But no, wait … Just in case, we'd better …"

"What?" Daphne demanded. "No delays, Ivan."

"You go ahead. Maybe you'll catch up to her right away. Oh, man, I hope the portal doesn't close too fast. I'll get supplies and be right behind you."

Cautious Ivan. Daphne nodded and stepped precariously out onto the snow. Lowering herself to her seat, she pulled with her heels and scooted down the slanted roof. When she reached the edge she gave herself no time to pause but just took a breath and launched herself through a whooshing eight-foot drop into a snow bank. She stood to beat the snow off her jacket, but her mittens were wet now, and snow filled her boots. Well, fine. She just had to catch up to Lila and get her home, fill her with hot chocolate, and swear her to secrecy before the grown-ups got back from the hospital.

As Daphne searched out Lila's tracks and let her gaze follow them to the dark line of fir trees bordering the clearing, it struck her that nothing looked like last time. This wasn't the pond near the village of Radix in the Land of Morning. It was someplace altogether different, someplace cold and deserted, and the reddish sun was sinking toward the distant mountains.

CHAPTER THREE
The Snowy Woods

Lila crept up the ladder that led from the loft to that funny room at the very top of the barn. Coming out of the cottage, she had heard distant laughter, but now the barn was silent. By sneaking up on them, she would find out at last what Ivan and Daphne were being so mysterious about, with their sidelong looks and their whispering.

But when she lifted her head through the trap door, she found nobody inside, just a smell of plywood flooring and a square of bright light falling from the window. The sunshine cheered her, and she stood up to look at the view.

How the snow made it all look strange and beautiful—field, woods, faraway mountains. She didn't remember seeing such high peaks gleaming in the west. "Mountains," she whispered, thinking of Aunt Adelaide's book about a speechless girl who left home to climb shining mountains and brave many dangers before she found her voice hidden in a valley of sound.

Lila turned to the other windows, looking for Aunt Adelaide's house. She couldn't find it, and a strange excitement stirred inside her.

The countryside looked so exquisite, so pure, that it made her want to do something beautiful and brave, with no one watching, no one directing her. She pushed open the window and took deep breaths of the cold, inviting air. She longed to slide down the roof and jump into the snow, to throw herself into that scene of freshness and beauty. Of course, if she broke a leg, her mother would kill her. She'd miss the musical, and that would end her career and waste all her mother's sacrifices. They'd have to move back to Oklahoma and live with her father again above the bicycle shop and be nobody.

For a moment Lila imagined life back in Oklahoma, riding a jolting bike over cracks in the sidewalk, then jumping off and wheeling the bike into the cool of her father's shop, where spokes and pedals gleamed in the half-shade. She imagined herself hanging up nylon shirts and arranging water bottles for sale while her father whistled and adjusted the brakes on some racing bike that was light as a cobweb.

Yes, but her mother would never be able to tolerate moving back to a place with no prospects. She always said that anyone with Lila's gifts owed it to herself to embrace her talent. Lila's mother would call this desire to jump selfish and suicidal, a slap in the face of a parent who had labored so long for her child's career.

But with snow so deep and soft, surely Lila wouldn't break her leg.

Her coat was so thick it made climbing over the windowsill clumsy work, but at last Lila half-stumbled into the soft snow on the roof. She was so high up! Far across the clearing, the dark trees stretched away, and the sky was vast above her, so vast that it seemed to tilt toward the distant mountains. In haste, Lila sat down to fend off her unsteadiness. She tried pulling at the snow with her mittened hands and managed to paddle and scoot her way down the roof in a slow and bumpy progress, not at all the wild slide she had imagined. The blanket of snow bunched on the slope in front of her and crept inside her coat. Sunlight glinted on tiny snow crystals that rose around her as she slid, making the air glitter. When she reached the edge of the roof, she gathered all her daring to lean forward, topple—and fall on all fours in a snow bank. Tiny grains of ice puffed into her face.

Lila wobbled to her feet, brushed away what snow she could, and looked up at the roof above her, jolted to see how far she had dropped. She needed to find a way back. She took a few steps alongside the barn. Her boots sank deep into the snow, becoming heavier with every step, and she still couldn't make out where everything was. With one hand brushing against the lapped siding, she circled the barn. Still she saw nothing she recognized—no hill, no cottage, no cars in the yard, no slope down to the stream. Somehow the sliding barn door had closed itself. Maybe Daphne and Ivan had followed her inside. She tugged, but couldn't slide the door open, and although she pounded and yelled, neither cousin came to let her in.

Lila trod back to her starting place and gazed up at her track down the roof. Her heart pounded with exertion and unease. Where am I? she wondered. In her head, the echoing question shifted. Where is Lila? Who is Lila? She hugged herself to make the questions go away.

Scenery shouldn't change this way. Cold ran up Lila's arms, and her legs trembled. She imagined herself collapsing in the snow and crying until someone came. But, no. She wasn't the weakling people like Daphne thought she was. Somehow she would face whatever strange thing was happening.

Lila turned her back on the barn and started across the clearing. On the far side, fir trees rustled. At the edge of the forest, the breeze subsided, and as she looked up at the evergreen branches, silence fell over her, soothing as a down quilt on a chilly night. Then, far ahead, she heard a faint, musical tinkling.

She turned to look back at the barn. She should go back; of course she should. But she could never jump high enough to reach that roof. If she stood at the bottom and yelled with all her might, Ivan or Daphne or her mother might come in an hour or two. But she couldn't bear the thought of shouting again, fracturing the quiet that cradled her in this mysterious place, where the smallest sounds reminded her of magical stories and half-forgotten images from old songs.

The faraway tinkling came again, like the sound of fairy bells, summoning her. The music hinted at beauty and adventure. Who is Lila? she thought again. Lila is timid, protected, directed, obedient. But not this time. This time Lila is the girl who takes a breath, turns around, and plunges into the forest.

*   *   *

Lila trekked on. She told herself that she was in a fairy tale and that soon she would reach a hidden castle, or a magical beast would befriend her, or a great queen in disguise would beg her for help. Against the niggling worry that she was wandering into woods where she might freeze and never be found, she held fast to the memory of distant music and the sense of unearthly quiet—no sound of traffic, no planes overhead, just the shush of her boots, her coat sweeping past branches, and snow dropping in great dollops from the trees. She felt herself glide freely through a dream-like world.

But as time passed in the stretching shade of the forest, Lila's legs grew tired and her stomach growled. She was used to a hollow stomach, because her mother kept a tight watch on her diet, but as Lila walked farther and grew hungrier, her bravery faded. She had entered the woods hoping to find something magical, but there was only weariness and cold. She imagined her mother, back by now and searching for her, furious. In the dropping temperature, Lila's feet dragged.

She paused, pulled her fur-lined hood closer around her

ears, and looked up. The sky was fading into grayish purple. She had kept on too long. She had to turn around and hurry home before dark.

But her tracks leading back were not so easy to see. Thick splotches of snow falling from the trees had left the way pitted in all directions, while Lila's own footprints collapsed in on themselves. In the shadows it was hard to make out the difference. And now the snow was graying in the twilight.

Lila started off in one direction, became uncertain, and circled back. With a swooshing sound, a branch above her shed its load of snow onto her head. As she shook it off, biting her lip to keep from crying, she heard the music again—a faint tinkling of wind chimes no longer quite so far away. She tilted her head to try and catch the direction of the sound. Off to the left, she thought. Bushes and low branches blocked her path, but she ducked and pushed her way toward the music.

Far off behind her rose a long, wavering moan. Lila's scalp prickled. She had heard the sound before only in movies—a wolf's howl. Two other voices answered, crying out cold, hunger, loneliness. A shiver took hold of Lila, and she could hardly walk straight. She wove toward the chimes still faintly sounding over her own footsteps and her thumping heart. She pawed at branches that tried to block her path. With the same motion, she pushed away the sense of some creature tracking her, until a low growl and footfalls sounded at her back. Lila gasped and stumbled forward as fast as she could. In the bushes beside her, heavy feet padded. Surely the wolves could not have caught up to her so fast. Branches cracked and crashed.

Lila ran until her breath came in stabs, and she had to pause, gasping. A huge, pale form hurtled past her in the woods, turned, and reared up to face her. It was a bear, enormous, the color of sand. Steam blew from its nostrils. Lila froze, and a whimper escaped her.

The bear settled onto all fours. Stand, Lila told herself. Stand and face it. But instead she whirled and flung herself back along the way she had come, lurching from one deep footstep to the next. Behind her came panting and the crash of underbrush. She pictured the beast raising a huge claw to tear at her. Like a rabbit she darted sideways, only to trip and fall facedown in the snow.

The fall took her breath away. She squeezed her eyes tight and lay rigid, closing her hands as if she could cling to the snow. She braced for the feel of claws ripping into her back or teeth crunching her skull. Heavy breathing sounded above her, then sniffling and a low growl. She smelled musk and sour milk. A drop of what must be slobber fell on her neck, and she pressed her mouth against the snow to keep from sobbing aloud.

Padding footsteps receded. Above her, like a breeze running through a wheat field, music rippled: the tinkling of a hundred tiny bells, a sound like a new beginning. The cold soothed her, and in time, her breath calmed. The strange notion struck her that maybe the bear had chased her over some border into a place of peace and beauty.

If she kept lying in the snow she would freeze to death.

Lila lifted her head and tried to peer upward in the darkness. When her heartbeat slowed, she got to her hands and knees and stood.

She had almost gathered her courage to turn and look behind her when a thick arm caught her about the waist, and a gloved hand clamped across her mouth.

CHAPTER FOUR

Rescue

Upstairs in the cottage, Ivan dumped clothes and schoolbooks out of his backpack and began filling it again. He threw in extra socks, a knit hat, and the algebraic compass from Lexicon. He added a notebook and pencil, then hurried downstairs to rummage in a drawer for a flashlight. He tossed in packets of cheese crackers, a small jar of peanut butter, and a box of raisins. He couldn't shake the feeling that he was responsible for the girls and had to think of everything they might need. At the same time, if he dallied, the window to Lexicon might close and the girls would be left alone in the bitter snow. What else? Band-Aids, extra mittens, a scarf. He scooped them into the backpack. At the last minute he threw in a packet of matches in case they didn't get back this afternoon.

On the way to the door he remembered he should leave a note. What could he say to reassure the grown-ups while they were gone? With luck he and the girls would be back before they were missed, but usually, Aunt Adelaide had told them, visitors to Lexicon arrived home about a day after they'd left. He ripped out a sheet of notebook paper and wrote,

Dear Dad,
Something came up and we had to go somewhere. It's important, but don't worry, we'll all be back tomorrow at the latest. We're off to see a friend of Aunt Adelaide's. If you ask Aunt A, I'm sure she'll tell you not to worry.
Don't worry, we'll be back soon,
Ivan

He read it over. In spite of saying "don't worry" three times, he had a sinking feeling the note wouldn't be enough to stop Aunt Leonora and Aunt Jen from calling the police and tracking them to the barn until their tracks led through the window and vanished. He crumpled up the note and started over.

Dear Dad,
We've decided to camp out in the barn tonight. Don't worry, we have everything we need. Please do not interrupt us, because we're really bonding as cousins. Lila is doing her rehearsal for us and we're having a great time. This is really important to us. We're supporting each other through

49

Aunt Adelaide's surgery. It's like a ritual. We'll come back tomorrow. PLEASE DO NOT INTERRUPT!
   Your responsible son,
   Ivan

There, he thought, that would give his dad a better chance of bottling up his aunts' anxiety. He grabbed his backpack, slung it onto his shoulder, and headed out the door.

As he crossed the yard, he heard the sound of a car engine pause and resume. He looked over his shoulder, and yes, there was Aunt Jen's SUV turning off the highway onto Aunt Adelaide's driveway. As the car rumbled over the troll bridge, Ivan sprinted across the yard and dove into the barn. As the car parked, he rolled the barn door shut. He'd made it out of there just in time.

Two stories up, the cupola window still stood open and still looked out on Lexicon. With one foot on the roof, one on the windowsill, poised between worlds, Ivan dug the algebraic compass out of his pocket and took a bearing. Distant mountain ranges, edged in gold, lined the horizon in two directions, and the needle of the compass swung to point at a spot where the two ranges intersected. With a shock Ivan saw how the horizon dipped into a gap at the juncture. At Origin, the center of Lexicon, a mountain had collapsed at the end of their last visit, and there it was, a hole in the landscape. But the mountains rose in the wrong direction, and the countryside didn't look familiar to Ivan. Even a cover of snow shouldn't change a pond and surrounding meadows into this flat clearing surrounded by forest. What if they were being led into another world and not Lexicon at all? All the more reason to retrieve the girls and get out fast.

Ivan slid down the roof in pinkish-gold afternoon light that poured over the distant mountains. At the edge he stood and leaped, landing in a drift far beyond the trampled snow where the girls had touched down. Deep blue tree shadows stretched across the snow. Cold as it was, the air still had that freshness he remembered—a smell of snow and sky and trees with nothing industrial mixed in, but something else, an invitation to adventure. He shook it off. There was no room for adventure, not this time. He had to find the girls and get them all home before they were missed.

He pulled up his hood, settled his pack, and took off as fast as he could, stepping in the tracks Lila and Daphne had left. He tried to jog, the backpack thumping on his back, his breath coming short.

At the edge of the woods he hoped he might see Daphne, but that was foolish. She must be way ahead by now. Tree branches closed like quiet curtains above him, letting in only a few sparkling glimpses of sky. In the thinner snow beneath the trees, he leaned forward and jogged again, keeping his eyes on the tracks. Once he called out, but his voice trailed off with such a sound of loneliness that he decided not to try again for a while.

Evening fell fast in the forest. Already the woods had darkened enough that he was finding it hard to follow the tracks. He paused to pull out his flashlight, and when he turned it on he swept it in a long arc around him, lighting the trunks of tall firs on all sides, an occasional slim oak or birch slipping upward through the shadow. Then from the side of his eye he saw a deer leap away, and far away he heard what sounded like the howl of a wolf.

He shuddered and started forward again, wondering if a flashlight could scare off wolves the way a fire can. No, of course not. Find the girls.

A dark form burst from the shadow beside the path, and Ivan raised the flashlight to defend himself. "Hey, don't hit me," said Daphne's voice. She stepped into the light. "A flashlight, you're a genius. Aargh, my throat. I can hardly talk." She shuddered. "It's getting really dark. What do you think she's doing all by herself in the woods?"

Ivan wished he'd taken the time to search for a second flashlight. "Here, take the light. I'll follow."

He didn't mention the wolves, and neither did Daphne. He focused on the light shining on the pitted snow before them, and the two of them swished on as fast and steadily as they could. He had done this with Daphne before, a rescue in the forest at night, and a grim sense of purpose stifled what might otherwise have become fear. Ignore the cold, his annoyance with Lila, the fatigue, the ghostly silence. Don't listen for howling in the distance. Just keep walking.

Daphne said, "The track's mixed up."

He came up beside her, took the light, and shone it in all directions. Lila's boot prints turned and looped, crossing over themselves. To one side her small tracks led away, but a second set of broad tracks crossed hers, fell on top of hers, crushed them. The tracks were two long padded feet and two shorter ones, but huge. Bear tracks?

Daphne gave a sob of fear and Ivan caught hold of her elbow. They crept forward, Ivan shining the light low, hoping somehow not to be seen. The bear tracks left Lila's and disappeared into the woods, but by some miracle Lila's continued. And now there were other footprints obliterating Lila's, prints of booted feet—where had they joined the path?

Ivan and Daphne came into a clearing of trampled snow among the silvery trunks of some new kind of tree. It seemed to Ivan that the silence had changed, that all the forest held its breath. Daphne touched one of the smooth trunks. A sound like sweet bells tinkled overhead, and Ivan turned the light upward. On silvery branches above them, bell-shaped yellow leaves shivered in the breeze and let fall a shower of notes.

A movement caught the corner of Ivan's eye, and he whirled around, thrusting Daphne behind him. Three large men wearing dark furs stepped out of the forest, their drawn bows aiming at his chest.

Fear took Ivan's breath and his knees quaked, but he didn't try to run. Whoever these guys were, they probably had Lila, so he had to stay and negotiate. He shifted position to try and block their view of Daphne, but she stepped up next to him. He felt her straighten her shoulders and shake her hair back so she could look whatever was coming straight in the eye.

A broad man with a full black beard and flashing teeth parted the archers and stepped forward. He wore a light-colored pelt over his shoulder and he had the air of a leader. "More runaways," he said, grinning and wiggling

his eyebrows. "Woods is full of you today, skedaddling this way and that. But as you're all rotated round and bemildewed, youngsters, you should fall down on your knees in gratefulness we caught you prior to them wolves."

Daphne, standing at Ivan's shoulder, kept her silence, so Ivan said, "We're not runaways, but we're looking for one. A small girl, dark hair, younger than us, named Lila. I think maybe a bear was chasing her. We came to take her back."

The bearded man cocked his head to one side and squinted at them. "You did, did you? And envoyed from which commune, shall I ask?"

"Not one near here," Ivan said. "Off a ways. Afar."

But the word "afar" didn't seem to hold the explanatory magic it had wielded on their first journey to Lexicon. The man shook his head and grinned. "You're mendacious. You haven't journaled far, not without tents nor furs nor weapons." He waved at the men behind him, and they lowered their bows and stepped forward, while five others, armed with long clubs, emerged from the woods and stood in a circle around the cousins. "No more entertainments," the chief said. "You're from Capella. Tell me your class."

"Class?" Ivan had no idea what he meant. "Um, eighth grade."

"Eighth?" The man threw back his head with a shout of laughter. "Come on, younger, no one's that low-down debased. If you infuse to reveal your grade, we won't know what to sell you for, now will we? So give us a song, boy."

A song? Now Ivan was really confused. He glanced at Daphne, who shrugged and shook her head.

Ivan turned back to the bearded chief, who made an

impatient gesture with his hand. What could he sing? He was the world's worst singer, the only person he'd ever heard of to be cut from middle school chorus for never producing a single in-tune note. But the chief was tapping his booted foot. Ivan decided to try the school fight song.

"Ride on, you Warriors,
Swinging your swords,
With your heads high,
Your eyes fierce—"

The chief raised his hand, wincing. "Stop! Decease! I hear why they revented a new grade for you. So you're a laborer, nigh worthless. And her?"

He gestured to Daphne without looking at her, something Ivan knew would make her furious. When the chief continued, "Is she a first class miracle, like the little one?" Ivan saw Daphne's jaw clamp shut, and he was sure the chief wouldn't get a note out of her.

"She can't sing," he said, and then, fearing Daphne's anger, he added, "She has a sore throat."

"Mute, eh?" the chief said, and leaned toward Daphne with his lip curled and a glint in his eye. "Speakless but spoke for, I take it? Servant to the little one?"

Ivan decided to ignore this. "What have you done with the little one?" His voice, which he meant to keep level, came out in an accusing squawk.

The chief regarded him sidelong, one eyebrow raised, a look of injured benevolence on his face. "Done nothing. Enwrapped her up and fed her and transposed her into shelter. Same as I'd do with you if you was straight and rectitude with me."

"But I am being straight with you. We came a long way to get her back and take her home where she belongs."

"I see," said the chief, as his men shifted impatiently around him. "And you cogitate you have enough ransom in that pack of yours? Looks mighty skimpified to me."

Ivan hesitated. "Ransom" suggested he could buy Lila back somehow. It didn't make sense. Surely this kidnapper could hit him on the head and grab the backpack as he pleased.

He tried to sound confident. "Take us to see Lila. Then we can discuss whatever you like."

Half an hour later Ivan caught the scent of woodsmoke, and soon he and Daphne, surrounded by the men in furs, stepped into a clearing lit by a large campfire. About the clearing huddled a scattering of domes covered in snow, like igloos or snow-covered yurts. From far off where the clearing faded into darkness came a chorus of grunts and low growls. Dogs, maybe.

The chief bandit laid a hand on Ivan's arm. "In there rests your Lila, and I remit she sings receptionally clear and lovely, and weeps recedingly pathetic, and begs me, Kanzat, to take her home though she can't dismember to what town, nor why she ran off in the first place. Gaze on her and then come trade."

Ivan guided Daphne to the dome Kanzat had indicated. Ivan pulled aside a pelt hanging over the door, and he and Daphne stepped inside.

CHAPTER FIVE

Barter

Ivan entered the smoky dome, with Daphne just behind him. A small central fire lit curved walls made of bent branches. Ivan's eyes smarted from the smoke, and he blinked to see in the flickering light. Animal skins carpeted the floor. Beside the fire, Lila sat wrapped in a blanket, her face pale and her eyes large. When she caught sight of her cousins, she scrambled up with a cry and darted around the fire to hug first Ivan, then Daphne. "You came! You found me!" Her voice trembled. "I was so scared. How did you find me?"

Before Ivan could answer, Daphne spoke up, her voice rasping. "We followed your tracks." She glared at Lila. "How could you do something so stupid and dangerous?"

"I didn't mean to," Lila said. She lowered her head and

looked up at them from under long eyelashes. "I wanted to have an adventure." She hiccupped and began to cry.

Ivan felt himself melting into sympathy, but Daphne rolled her eyes and said, "Stop whimpering. We've come to rescue you."

Ivan unslung his backpack, and Daphne rummaged through it, saying, "Not much here. I suppose you can trade the flashlight. They don't seem to have one of those. Just don't mention how batteries run out."

"Yeah," Ivan said. He felt vaguely guilty, and he didn't know why, until he remembered the iPod in the pack's front pocket. He knew he didn't want to give it up. Downloading and arranging the songs had taken him months.

He squared his shoulders. "I'll just go bargain with Kanzat, I guess. Come with me, Daphne. Help me convince them."

Daphne said, "Lila, you stay here, or the sight of your beauty might make Kanzat remember how much he wants to keep you."

Ivan let Daphne walk ahead of him as they exited the dome. At once the cold struck them, and Daphne started shivering.

Beside the fire, fur-clad men stomped and sang a song so deep and resonant Ivan could feel it through the soles of his boots. As he and Daphne approached, the voices stopped, and Kanzat stepped forward.

"Check out this pack," Ivan offered. "Very useful, made of strong nylon, padded straps, double zippers." He demonstrated, and the chief nodded, frowning. Ivan lit

a match and tossed it into the fire. Then he drew out the other objects from the backpack and laid them on the snow, trying to gauge from the bandit's eyes how he valued them. "Some food, as you see—raisins, crackers, peanut butter. Socks. Extra mittens. A hat. Paper and pencil."

Kanzat took the food and clothes, but tossed the paper and pencil aside. Ivan picked them up and stuffed them in the pocket of his jeans. "So what do you say?" Ivan asked. "Do you let Lila go?"

Kanzat laughed. "What, no gold, no satin, no jewels? A few camp supplies and fire sticks in return for a singer? You consult me!"

Ivan switched on the flashlight and handed it to him. "Very useful for trips through the forest at night."

Kanzat took it but scoffed. "We have our eyes and our ears to guide us. Our torches cast more light than this."

The bottom of the backpack was empty. Ivan considered offering the algebraic compass in his pocket, but he would need that to find their way home. The Astronomer's medallion around his neck? He wondered if this was what Aunt Adelaide had meant by "Just in case." But instinct warned him to hold onto it.

He zipped up the backpack, which still weighed heavy in his hand.

Then he remembered. He raised his face to Kanzat. "I have music," he said. "I have music that you can carry with you, many different voices, and you can play it so you're the only one who hears."

Kanzat snorted. "You want to sing to me?"

"No. I can give you real music playing in your ears. If I give it to you, will you let us go? Will you take us back to where you found us and set our feet back on the path to home?"

Kanzat raised his eyebrows. "Through the forest in the deep well of night?"

Ivan considered. He was hungry and cold. Daphne's feet dragged, and her eyes had a feverish glint. Lila was small and not that strong. How many hours could they keep walking through the night? And what if the flashlight went out? A trip to Lexicon always lasts about a day on the earth side, he reminded himself, no matter how long you stay. Tomorrow would be as good as tonight—better, walking in the light and sunshine, with the wolves dozing far away.

"Tomorrow will be fine," he said. "Tomorrow I'll give you the gift and you'll set us free."

"Show me the gift now."

Ivan unzipped the front pocket of the backpack and pulled out the iPod. He approached the chief, gestured for him to bend down, and reached to fit the ear buds into his ears. As he pulled back Kanzat's thick hair, he got a shock—the chief's ears were unusually large, furry, and cupped outward from his head. When the wire brushed against one, the furry appendage swiveled back out of the way. Ivan jumped, the chief jumped, and then Ivan bit his lip and finished settling the buds into place.

Better start at low volume with ears like that, he thought. He chose one of his father's Afro-pop songs and slowly turned the volume up from zero.

He thought Kanzat's eyes might pop out of their sockets. Ivan put the box in Kanzat's hand and guided his other hand to change the song. Kanzat's eyes narrowed; he winced; a slow smile started across his face as he moved from song to song.

"I will keep this," he announced. "I will use it tonight."

"No," Ivan said, and he switched it off.

Kanzat looked so baleful that Ivan added, "During the night I'll fill it up with more songs."

As he and Daphne walked back to Lila's dome, Ivan looked up at the sky. Bright-edged stars showed around the borders of the clouds. A smattering of snowflakes floated down in the firelight to waltz with the sparks flying upward. The deep, reverberating music started up again, and Ivan felt certain the next day would be clear.

CHAPTER SIX

The Sled

Daphne woke in a sweat with her throat afire and her head throbbing. She untangled herself from Lila, who had clung to her in sleep, and crept out from between the deerskin blankets. She stuck her head out the door of the dome. The cold eased her headache but stung her cheeks. Snow had fallen during the night, spreading an extra layer of quiet over the camp. Daphne remembered feverish dreams of wolves and cracking branches.

The snow on the ground looked four inches deep at least. All their tracks would be filled and their pathway home concealed. Last night they had seemed so safe, with the deep songs rumbling outside like thunder rolling among rocks while the cousins sheltered in the cozy dome. But today they had to get home.

She shook Ivan awake and told him, "It snowed." Her voice reminded her of windshield wipers scraping over ice. As he sat up and rubbed his eyes, she added, "It's been snowing all night. I hope you have the compass."

He gazed at her with bleary eyes, but once her words penetrated he staggered up and went to look out the door. His shoulders slumped, and then he dug in his pocket and pulled out the algebraic compass. She came to look over his shoulder.

"I know the general direction," he said. "But one little clearing in the middle of this huge forest! What if we can't find it?"

Daphne's voice wavered. "I bet these guys are good trackers. They might help."

"If we can trust them." Ivan sounded doubtful. "Have you guessed where we are?"

"The Land of Winter," Daphne said. They had glimpsed it last summer from the mountain at the center of Lexicon: the Land of Winter, with a thick pelt of forest and a cloak of snow.

*   *   *

They found a young woman turning cakes on a griddle. Kanzat crouched by the fire, and when the woman flipped him a pancake he caught it and cursed, laughing, tossing it from one hand to the other. Then he gulped it down and stood to greet the cousins.

"You sleep late, youngers." He pumped Ivan's hand. "This

is a fortunate day. I inquire a music box, we collect the leaf harvest your Lila showed us, and you return homebound."

Daphne didn't know what he meant by a leaf harvest. She waited for Ivan to ask, but he just handed over the iPod and demonstrated once more how to use it.

The chief stood back with the ear buds in his ears, swaying and bobbing his head. Ivan lifted one of the ear buds and asked, "How will we find our way home? Our tracks are gone."

"Ezengi will glide you." Kanzat spoke in the loud voice of someone trying to hear himself over music. "Ezengi can track a squirrel through the trees, a swallow through the air. Varoq with his nasals helps Ezengi find the way."

Kanzat swung his arm to indicate two figures at the far side of the clearing. Daphne tensed. A skinny man stood with one hand on the shoulder of a huge, sand-colored bear.

"Varoq," Kanzat said with satisfaction. "Chief of our brothers the bears. He daunts the wolves away from our herds, and he it is who dislocated your Lila among the music trees."

Ivan asked in a wary voice, "So the bear's tame?"

Kanzat winked. "Tame for us, because we raise him on reindeer milk and sing his language. Tame for you, because we tell him so. To enemies, fertrocious! Now eat, fill your abdomens, nutriment your little singer, so this fortunate day can begin."

* * *

With a shambling gait, Varoq, chief of bears, drew a

sled through the snow. Beside him, one hand on the bear's shoulder, strode Ezengi the tracker, who had a long, limp mustache and furs that seemed to drip off him. Lila, wrapped in furs, rode with her back against a huge basket. Her pale face looked rearward toward Ivan and Daphne trekking behind her. Lila the oblivious, thought Daphne. Lila the spoiled, who attracted special treatment wherever she went, even after leading them into this mess, even when Daphne was the one so sick that her head ached and her voice broke while her throat burned.

Ivan walked beside Daphne, consulting his compass. So far he seemed satisfied with what he saw. Daphne focused on following the track of the sled. Behind her paced three of Kanzat's men, and at the end came the chief himself, weaving his head in time to his private iPod music.

The tinkling of chimes broke into Daphne's thoughts. Varoq hauled the sled into the grove of silver trunks and yellow leaves she remembered from the night before. In daylight, Daphne wondered how the trees retained their leaves in the middle of winter.

Ezengi eased Varoq to a halt, and to Daphne's surprise, the bear splayed out all four legs and collapsed on his belly. Ezengi unhitched him. The three men behind Daphne filed around her, lifted the basket down from the sled and drew out a net, which they spread under the largest tree. Then they stationed themselves around the trunk and struck at the tree's branches with long clubs. Branches shook, and yellow leaves fell with a quivering of notes.

When the men with clubs could beat no more leaves free,

they shook the leaves from the net into the basket. Kanzat watched, smiling, his head bobbing to his own music.

"Not enough," Ezengi said. "A light person must climb up." He looked at Daphne.

No way, Daphne thought. I'm sick, and I don't owe you anything. Then, to Daphne's surprise, Lila struggled free of her furs and jumped out of the sled. "I'll climb," she said in her sweet voice.

With a frown, Daphne stepped forward to join her.

The men cupped their hands to raise the girls into the branches. They offered clubs to the girls, but instead of taking one, Lila scurried to the top of the tree, where the branches were thin and the trunk itself so supple that it swayed under her weight. Daphne, trying to climb along a lower branch, had to drop her club and hold on with both hands.

Lila shook the tree, making yellow leaves drift down, tinkling and ringing in a scattering of tones. "Do you hear it, Daphne?" Lila said. "It's like being in a cloud of music!"

Daphne closed her eyes and imagined herself inside some magical instrument that sprinkled music as it swayed.

Daphne's balance wavered, and she opened her eyes. On the limb in front of her, a furry yellow caterpillar humped its back. Daphne lifted it and held it in the palm of her hand. Quick as a flutter of feathers, a bird settled on her wrist, pecked at the caterpillar, threw back its head, and swallowed. Then the bird took two steps and turned to face her. It was the size of a mockingbird, but with yellow

highlights among its brown feathers. It gazed at her through a shiny black eye.

"Look there, she's got a yellowkin," one of the men below shouted. "Girl, close your hand on it!"

Daphne started, and the bird fluttered up. As it left the shelter of the tree, one of the men threw a second net at it and cursed when he missed.

"Get more leaves," one of the men called to Daphne. But the bird's near capture had annoyed Daphne, and instead of obeying, she climbed down and poised to jump into the leaf pile. As she leaped, Kanzat caught her around the waist and swung her aside. "Are you crazed?" Indignation swelled his cheeks, and his oniony breath puffed on her face. "If you stample the harvest, you steal food from our mouths."

*   *   *

When the basket was full and Kanzat had coaxed Lila down from the tree, Varoq the bear gave a noisy yawn, lumbered to his feet, and stretched. Kanzat removed his earphones long enough for detailed, muffled instructions to Ezengi, and then he and the three other traders set off back the way they had come. Only Ezengi remained to escort the children home. "Ride on the sled," he told Lila.

"I think it's Daphne's turn," Lila said.

Daphne started forward, grateful, but Ezengi shook his head. "The servant walks. Your voice must go home safe." He lifted Lila to her seat, packed her in furs, and wrapped a second scarf around her neck.

Lila's voice, Daphne thought bitterly. Lila's precious voice. Wait till she gets my flu.

As Varoq started to pull, Lila snuggled in among her furs and placed her ear against the basket. The sled rocked with Varoq's pace, and a blissful look crossed Lila's face as she listened to rustling of the yellow leaves.

*   *   *

Daphne trudged behind the sled. Her throat burned, her legs ached, and she felt disgusting. Her nose ran, and if she didn't wipe it fast enough with the back of her mitten, the mucus froze on her upper lip. Back in the grove of musical trees she had felt almost warm; now the temperature was dropping fast and the cold air hurt to breathe.

Beside her, Ivan dug the compass from his pocket and studied it. "We're going the wrong way," he said.

Plunging into the deeper snow beside the sled, Ivan lurched along in Ezengi's footprints. When he caught up to Ezengi, Ivan began to question him. Ezengi held out a hand for the compass and examined it without stopping. Varoq stepped along at a fast and steady pace. It occurred to Daphne that with Ivan up ahead and Lila huddled next to her basket with that idiotic look of bliss on her face, nobody would notice if fatigue overcame her and she collapsed in the snow. She put down her head and plowed forward.

Ahead, Ivan gave a cry of dismay. The sled pulled past him, but Ivan remained in one place, and when Daphne reached him she found him pawing at the snow. "The compass," he said. "Ezengi threw it away." He tore off his glove, probed the snow, and pried the compass from beneath one of the sled tracks. "No," he said. He shook the compass, peered at it, and turned it over in his hand. "No."

Daphne held out a hand and Ivan passed her the compass. Its metal face was dented, and the arrow lay stuck in the dent, so that no matter which way she turned and tilted it, the point didn't move.

Ivan looked sick, staring at the snow as if he wanted to throw up. Daphne took his hand and without a word folded it back over the broken compass.

The sled was pulling farther away. She pointed after it.

Ivan's head snapped up. "You're right. Wherever he's taking us, it has to be better than here." He grasped Daphne by the elbow and urged her into a jog after the sled.

*   *   *

After that, Ivan kept his grip on Daphne's elbow, half supporting her. Snow fell again, in thick heavy flakes that lined Daphne's eyelashes and blocked her view. She hunched her shoulders, ducked her head, and kept treading. Snow slid down her collar, her toes were freezing, chunks of ice clung to her hair, and her cheeks felt raw. Even Lila looked miserable now, perched on the sled like a huddled snow cone. Daphne remembered with a sick feeling that Aunt Adelaide was having surgery this morning somewhere in another world.

All at once she bumped up against the sled. Ezengi had called a halt. He walked back to join them.

He smiled through his mustache and pointed off to the side. "Just there. Just ahead, your home. Here I leave you."

Daphne stood shoulder to shoulder with Ivan. Behind them lay the woods; before them stretched a rolling expanse of snowy meadow. It was hard to make out shapes through the falling snow, but she thought she spied the humped roof of the barn. Beyond it she saw nothing—no mountains, no trees, nothing but falling flakes merging into solid gray-white.

"It looks right," Ivan said, with doubt in his voice. "Wait here, I'll check it out."

"You go, too," Ezengi said to Daphne, but she shook her head and sank to the snow in exhaustion.

No tracks remained from the day before, and Ivan slogged off through deep snow until he was only a shrinking, stubby-legged shadow against the gray-white background. Daphne stretched her neck to watch him, to discern by his pace, by the set of his shoulders, whether he saw the way home.

Through the blur of fatigue, something nagged at her. Why had Ezengi wanted to send her with Ivan, while Lila stayed? Why, unless he meant to keep Lila after all?

She struggled to her feet and lurched toward the sled. "Lila, get off!" she shouted.

Ezengi whirled to look at her, his smile gone.

"Lila, jump!" Daphne cried.

Lila, looking puzzled, put aside her fur blanket and got to her feet. At the same moment, Ezengi sprang onto the sled runners and shouted a guttural order to Varoq.

The sled jerked forward, and Lila toppled among the furs. Daphne lunged for the sled, but it drew out of reach, swaying wildly as Varoq tore across the snow.

CHAPTER SEVEN

Lila

Lila gripped the railing as the sled careened across the snow. Had Varoq, chief of bears, gone crazy? Daphne had told her to jump, but how could she jump when Ezengi was glaring at her and they were sliding so fast? Just to look over the side at the ground whizzing past made her dizzy. Surely any moment now Ezengi would get control, turn, and take her back to her cousins. Together they would find the barn and Ivan would lift her to the roof.

Ezengi slowed Varoq down, but instead of turning back, he continued to steer the sled straight ahead.

"Wait," Lila said. "My cousins."

Ezengi smiled. "They will follow, little song-princess. I take you home now."

For the first time since her cousins' appearance, Lila worried. "No, no, we need to be together."

Ezengi laughed, blowing his mustache out. "They steal a magical voice. I return you. Reward comes to me, punishment to them."

Lila thought of her cousins stranded in the snow while she rode packed in furs. She couldn't remember why she had given in to Ezengi and accepted a ride while her cousins walked. A new, unpleasant feeling gnawed inside her chest. She tried to disregard it. She was the youngest: that was why she had been allowed to ride. But no, she knew it wasn't that. The wild men treated her differently, better, because she could sing. "Talent brings rewards," her mother always said. Lila rode because she was talented, special—because she deserved to.

The unpleasant feeling gnawed harder, and Lila squirmed, trying to get free of it. All this was her cousins' fault for keeping secrets. Their secrets had lured her into the barn and off the barn roof. For an instant Lila tasted that moment again, that sense of teetering on the verge of wonder, then falling into freedom. But still Ivan and Daphne treated her as the outsider. They never asked her opinion on anything.

Not that she had answers. She didn't know what she thought, about being lost in the snow, about anything. She was a blank, waiting for something to happen—always in rehearsal, waiting to be directed. Lila waited patiently for other people to figure things out, to fix things, to tell her what to do.

But just last evening she had been different. How she had

75

trembled, surrounded by those wild men in furs with their long bows and weird clubs, when they asked her to sing. But she had lifted her head and sung it out, defiant, her shoulders back—"Castle on a Cloud," Cosette's song of hope. As she sang, their gazes fixed on her and she felt the way she always felt when performing—real. Real, substantial, someone who came into focus instead of fading into the background. She sang, and those rough men listened. She overwhelmed them. When she finished, they turned to one another muttering their amazement. She was a star.

Even now, riding through a snowstorm into an unknown place, Lila felt the glow. If only Daphne and Ivan had seen her! Then they would see why people treated her as special.

As soon as Lila formulated the thought, shame seeped into her. She had no reason to be proud. Her cousins had come to rescue her, and now they were stranded. Daphne was sick, abandoned in the snow.

Lila wasn't used to standing up to anyone. But if there was ever a time to start, this was it. She said to Ezengi in as firm a voice as she could muster, "Turn around. We must go back for my cousins."

Ezengi laughed.

"Turn around or I'll jump!"

"Jump if you like, little one, but I'll catch you with my net and drag you after me."

Trembling, Lila stood and looked over the side of the sled. Varoq was pulling more slowly now. She could jump off and roll in the snow. But if she escaped Ezengi, she would be alone in this great expanse of whiteness. What if she couldn't find her cousins? She imagined herself left behind, a small figure wandering and calling, until the falling snow smothered her in silence.

Lila sank back onto the fur blankets with a whimper. She hid her face.

"Don't worry, little one," Ezengi said. "We're almost there. How glad they will be in Capella, to have your voice returned to them."

And then she knew what to do.

*   *   *

No barn greeted Ivan. Nothing but snow-covered hummocks scattered across the plain. Ezengi was an incompetent idiot after all, he thought. He turned and retraced his footsteps in the falling snow. By his estimate the barn should be north-northwest of here, and Ivan wished bitterly that he had never tried to show Ezengi the compass.

Surely he should be able to see the sled by now. Wait— there was Daphne, sitting in the snow, alone. Ivan broke into a lumbering run.

"Where's Lila? Where's Ezengi?"

Daphne lifted her pale face. Her voice rasped. "He stole her again. I tried to stop them. It was all a trick."

Ivan beat his head with his fists. "I can't believe I let this happen. We should have left last night. We could have followed our tracks. I should have made Kanzat—that cheat—come along before he'd get his iPod. What an idiot I am."

"Yes," Daphne said in a toneless voice.

It was so unlike her that Ivan turned to give her a hard look. Two red spots glowed in the middle of her white cheeks, and she stared, unmoving, into the falling snow.

"Let's rest," she said, her voice little more than a whisper. "Rest and then go home."

Fear sparked through him. Daphne was fading, giving up. Left to herself she'd sit here and freeze to death. Ivan grasped her wrist and pulled her onto her feet. "No, Daphne. We follow Lila. We came to bring her home and we're going to do it." He tugged her hand. "Come on, Daphne, no slacking now. I need you."

She nodded, staggered, then lowered her head and plodded forward once more in the sled tracks.

"You're a hero, Daph," Ivan said as he fell into step beside her.

*   *   *

Ivan was half dragging Daphne with his arm around her waist and her arm draped over his shoulder when he heard a grunting and swishing sound. He looked up. The great bear loomed out of the snow like a dream creature, magnificent in his coat of fur and ice. He took a pair of long strides toward the cousins. Daphne didn't lift her head.

Ezengi came around Varoq's side.

"You dirty rat," Ivan said. "Where did you take her?"

"The young singer is on the sled. I tried to rescue her from you kidnappers and sorcerers. But she swore she'd never sing again until I came for you." Ezengi tilted his head, a look of hurt on his face. Lila burst from behind Ezengi and ran toward Ivan and Daphne with her arms wide. Ivan shielded Daphne and caught her with one arm.

"I wouldn't let him abandon you. Daphne's really sick, isn't she? Let's get her on the sled so she can lie down."

"Where is he taking us?"

Ezengi narrowed his eyes. "To Capella town, of course. Where you came from."

"But we didn't!" Ivan's eyes stung with frustration. "We told you, we came from Afar, another land."

Ezengi shrugged. "I don't know another land. Find it yourselves."

But Ivan couldn't find it, not in the snow, not without the compass. And Daphne couldn't take much more. They needed shelter. Ivan ground his teeth. "Fine. Deliver us to the town ... Capella."

Ezengi grunted, but he helped Ivan boost Daphne onto the sled and pack a fur blanket around her. Then he placed Lila on top of the covered basket of leaves and told her to hold on. Lila sat wide-eyed and stiff with her legs hanging down.

"You ride on the runner," Ezengi told Ivan.

Ivan perched on the runner, holding on to the sled, and said, "I bet you can't drive fast."

Ezengi glowered at him, jumped up beside him, and growled to Varoq. The sled jerked forward so hard Ivan almost lost his grip. The sled jolted and swayed wildly, as Daphne's wrapped body rolled and Lila gripped the edges of the sliding leaf basket, her mouth pulled back in a grimace.

79

Varoq's huge feet raised clouds of snow that billowed around them as they whooshed across the plain.

A long time later, Ezengi spoke, and the sled creaked to a halt at the edge of a snowy field bounded by a low stone wall. Just ahead, the roofs of a town rose through the mist. Stomping toward them through the snow came a husky young man with a scanty mustache and a dark green bandana looped around his throat.

CHAPTER EIGHT

Capella

The young man with the mustache stopped ten yards from the bear. Ivan stepped off the sled runner to greet him, but Ezengi thrust himself between them.

"Traders?" the young man asked.

"With runaways," Ezengi said, puffing out his chest. "Which we rescued as the wolves came closing in. We expect a reward."

The young man raised his eyebrows and nodded, looking impressed. "I'm Raibley. I'll help you unload. Get the kids back to school, too. They look half frozen. As for a reward, you'll have to talk to folks at the school."

Ivan stepped around Ezengi. "But we're not—" He checked himself. School sounded warm, at least.

Raibley, carrying the basket of leaves, led them across

empty fields. Ivan supported Daphne, and Ezengi kept a close eye on Lila. They made their way through winding lanes where stuccoed cottages projected overhead, until finally they passed through a gate into a walled courtyard where blue school uniforms hung drying stiffly in the cold air. Raibley set down the basket and led the cousins and Ezengi up a stone stairway, where he knocked and pushed open a door. "Kitchen entrance. Sorry," he said to Ivan. The five of them stepped into air steamy with the smell of vegetables. At the table a tall girl with a kerchief and blondish braids stood chopping carrots. She looked about eighteen. When she saw Raibley, she dropped the knife and came over, wiping her hands on her apron.

"Trader bought home some runaways, Kit," Raibley said. "They're cold and all worn out. You know them?"

"We're not runaways," Ivan said.

Kit stepped forward, looked in their faces, and said, "I don't think they're ours, but we can feed them. Take them into the refectory, Raibley. I'll fetch Mother Cadenza."

Raibley led them through the kitchen, past smells of soup and potatoes, into a tall, arched room paneled in dark wood. He clomped across the wooden floor to a long table, where he pulled out chairs to seat the girls. Ivan sat beside Daphne, whose head drooped almost to the table. Ezengi sauntered over to lean against the wall.

A door opened on the far side, and the sound of children singing accompanied a tall, dark-skinned lady into the refectory. She glided toward them, looking regal despite her close-cropped gray hair and her plain woolen dress. Behind her, Kit turned to catch the door so it closed silently.

The dark-skinned lady examined them with sharp eyes, and turned to Ezengi. She spoke in a resounding contralto. "You have brought a delivery of music leaves. You may see Brother Dorian for your payment."

Ezengi pulled himself from the wall. "Ho, I brought you these runaways, too. We could have sold them to the next town for plenty of silver. My chief demands a reward."

Mother Cadenza gazed down at him. "These are not our students."

Uh-oh, thought Ivan. He stood to speak. "Please don't send us away with him. My cousin's sick." He pulled back his shoulders, trying to look strong and reliable, worth keeping.

The lady raised her eyebrows and twitched them, as if he had no business speaking.

Ezengi continued as if Ivan hadn't spoken. "All the more reason you owe me, then. I've brought you new voices. Wait till you hear the little one."

The lady lifted her nose in the air and peered down it at Ezengi. "Capella does not pay for children. Parents move here voluntarily to enter their children in our school. Now be gone before I confiscate your leaves and send archers after that idiotic bear of yours."

Ezengi scowled. He turned a baleful glare at Ivan, blew out his mustache in an exaggerated sigh, and strode away.

Mother Cadenza smoothed her dress and turned to the children, replacing her stern look with a tired smile. "I am

Mother Cadenza, children, director of this school. Welcome to Capella, choral champion town. I congratulate you on your safe arrival. You look exhausted. Kit will feed you, and then we'll find you places."

*　*　*

Lila dipped her bread and sucked the soup out of it, feeling the warmth seep into her fingers and toes. Beside her, Daphne dragged the spoon to her mouth and sipped, hardly eating anything. Kit and Raibley stood against the wall, their hands behind their backs.

On Lila's other side, Ivan guzzled his second bowl of soup. When the far door opened, admitting Mother Cadenza again, he set the bowl down with a hollow thump. He stood, and Lila watched.

Ivan said, "Excuse me, Mother Cadenza, I need to explain. We're only here by accident. Our cousin Lila—this one—got lost in the snow and we came after her, and now we can't find our way back."

Mother Cadenza studied him with her lips pressed together. "You're runaways from somewhere," she said. "Ambitious ones. I don't judge you. People will do anything to give talent room to grow."

That's what my mother says, Lila thought. She sacrificed everything, even my father, to give my talent room to grow. Then why do I always feel so squeezed and tight? She glanced at Daphne, who drooped over her soup, not looking ambitious at all.

"We're not runaways," Ivan said. "Do you know Origin, and the mountain that fell down?"

Mother Cadenza thinned her lips further. "Yes. Some of our children barely escaped with their lives."

"Us, too," Ivan said. "We made it out just in time." His glance flickered to Lila.

Why didn't they tell me all this? Lila wondered. We could have had fun if not for their oh-so-special secrets.

Mother Cadenza said, "That was two years ago. Surely you haven't been wandering since then."

"Two years ago?" Ivan shook his head. "No, it was just last summer."

Mother Cadenza's voice grew cold. "You're mistaken. You need to get your story straight if you expect to deceive people."

Lila surprised herself by speaking up. "He's not deceiving you, ma'am. We go to school really far from here. In a place with no bears and not much snow."

Ivan nodded. "Beyond the mountains. Afar. Time ... runs differently there."

Mother Cadenza put a hand to her cheek. "*Aus der Ferne?*" She peered at them, lowered her hand, and babbled a string of guttural phrases.

Lila thought she recognized a couple of words from the German *lieder* her singing coach made her memorize. But she wasn't sure, so she didn't say anything.

Ivan spread his hands. "Sorry, I only speak English."

Mother Cadenza frowned. "I see that you are impostors, weaving a fantastic tale. According to the new rules sent out to us provincials by the Composers, you should be thrown out in the snow. But in Capella, we don't let children—even impostors—freeze to death. In winter, as you should know by now, only the nomad traders can find their way through the blizzards, and they'd as soon sell you as guide you."

"We noticed," said Ivan.

"We'll have to keep you until Spring Festival, that's all there is to it. Then if you've earned it, you can tag along to Melodia, where you'll find people from every town, even from other countries."

Ivan asked, "When's Spring Festival?"

Mother Cadenza frowned. "At winter's end, of course. When the Ice Castle melts and the goddess returns. But mind you, boy, even strangers and visitors, so long as they eat our food and sleep in our beds, pitch in and live by our rules. Is that clear?"

Ivan nodded. "Just tell us what we need to do."

"That depends on your placement. Are you ready to sing?"

Ivan cast a desperate look at Lila. "I can't sing."

Mother Cadenza clucked her tongue. "Nonsense, I'm sure you can, a fine-looking boy like you. Though I admit you're unlikely to have had the training *we* provide." She smiled. "Now stand straight, young fellow. Shoulders back. Sing after me." She sang a simple five-note phrase in tones that rang high and clear.

Lila gave Ivan an encouraging smile. Anyone could manage a simple tune like that.

She could see that Ivan tried. He opened his mouth and

attempted to copy what he'd heard, but he was so flat Lila winced. Mother Cadenza gave him another phrase, and another, but he didn't begin to reproduce it, couldn't match even a single note when Mother Cadenza sang it for him, not even when she signaled with her hand whether he needed to go up or down.

A look of pity crossed Mother Cadenza's face, along with something else—distaste, Lila decided, as if someone had promised her hot chocolate and instead had served cold lemon juice. "I see," Mother Cadenza said. "So you are not of our class at all."

Ivan shrank into his chair, but Mother Cadenza spoke sharply. "On your feet in the presence of your betters. Go stand with Raibley."

Ivan slunk off to stand against the wall with the young gardener. He looked smaller than he had a few minutes ago, Lila thought with surprise.

Mother Cadenza nodded at Daphne. "Now you."

Daphne pushed herself up from the table. She looked awful, with her red, dripping nose, her tangled hair and hollow eyes. She croaked, "Please, Mother Cadenza, I'm sick and have hardly any voice at all."

Mother Cadenza drew back a step and observed Daphne with eyebrows drawn close. "And I suppose you can also not sing a note?"

"I sing in my school chorus."

"A singer, yet you run off in the snow with no scarf? Foolish girl. You will go to the infirmary for plasters and concoctions. We'll wait for you to recover your voice before your evaluation." She turned to Kit, who curtseyed and stood wide-eyed, awaiting instructions.

"Take this child to the infirmary and help Sister Glissanda attend to her throat," Mother Cadenza said. "And Kit, no mixing with the students until she's healed. We can't let the contagion spread."

Kit nodded and took Daphne by the hand. Lila felt strangely hollow watching her go, but the servant girl looked kind. Head sagging, feet scraping the floor, Daphne followed Kit out of the room.

"And you, little one," Mother Cadenza said above Lila, in a cold voice. "I suppose you have some other excuse for not singing?"

"No, please," said Lila. Now it was up to her to earn them all a warm place with food and shelter. She stood. "I can sing."

"Try this, then." Mother Cadenza sang her first phrase; Lila echoed it. Then another, and another.

Lila's shoulders relaxed, and she let the music carry her.

Mother Cadenza raised her eyebrows. She offered a long and complicated phrase of wordless, tumbling notes, like a stream coming awake in springtime. Lila took a deep breath. Light fell from the high windows, and Lila breathed it in, let it fill her inside, then opened her mouth and sang, a silvery tumble with glitters and splashes all its own.

Mother Cadenza closed her mouth, opened it, and closed it again. "I see," she said at last. "Well, I don't know where you came from, child, or how your companions brought you here, but there is no place better in all the Land of Winter for

musical training than here in Capella." She stepped forward and pushed a strand of hair out of Lila's face. "Here we recognize birth and talent. We will surround you with the refinement you deserve." She laid a motherly hand on Lila's shoulder. "Come with me."

Ivan tried to fall into step behind them, but Mother Cadenza whirled on him. "Haven't you done enough, dragging this child through snowy wastes and sneaking in here among your betters? I should have you jailed! Stay right there, boy, until I decide how to dispose of you."

As Mother Cadenza swept her toward the door, Lila twisted around to look back at Ivan, who stood stunned and motionless.

"Come along, child," Mother Cadenza said.

"Please," Lila said. "He came after me to save me. Please don't send him away."

Mother Cadenza's eyes narrowed. "He can't stay in the school. A boy like that shouldn't come near you. But I'll give him a test. If he proves his worth, Raibley can find him work in the fields."

*   *   *

Ivan waited at Raibley's side until Mother Cadenza returned. She scanned him up and down as if trying to find any value in him at all. Finally she said, "Well, boy, I'm glad you brought us two young ladies, though you did it with little care for their health. Clearly there's no place for you in school. Since you have no sense of music—"

"But I like music," Ivan said. "I just can't sing."

"An ear but no voice? I doubt it." She sighed. "Still, I promised to give you a trial. Sorting the leaves is always such a chore. If you succeed, I'll let you serve as assistant to Raibley here. Would you take him, Raibley?"

Raibley nodded.

"Show him to the courtyard and get back to your work. Sort the leaves by note, boy, low to high, if you can."

Raibley made a slow pivot and led Ivan through the kitchen and out the back door. They descended to the cobbled courtyard. Wooden wheelbarrows leaned against the wall. In a tall pile in the corner, on a ground cloth under a lean-to, lay the yellow leaves they had gathered in the forest.

Raibley gave Ivan sidelong glance. "Can you do it? Sort the notes?"

"I don't know," Ivan said. "I'm so tired I probably can't do anything. And to tell the truth, I'm pretty tone deaf."

Raibley nodded. "Me, too. Born that way and never educated out of it." He looked worried. "Don't know why you need to sort leaves to become a gardener's helper. But give it a try or you might get thrown out of town. Inspectors figure there's too many like you and me, who have no music in us." He paused, his brow furrowed. "Even though we do all the regular work. Anyway, you sort those, low to high like, onto those different mats, and then knock on that door and they'll wrap 'em up and bring 'em inside. I'd help you if I could, but I can't much hear the differences myself, and I have to fetch the suppertime vegetables."

"What do they use the leaves for?" Ivan asked.

"They brew a tea," Raibley said. "Helps their voices, they say. Makes them strong and true."

When he was alone, Ivan walked over to the pile of leaves and picked one up. Snowflakes swirled overhead, but here within the walls of the courtyard the air was strangely still. The leaf Ivan had chosen stayed silent until he flicked his finger against it, and then it emitted a clear, pure tone, very soft. What note it was Ivan didn't know, but he laid out a cloth and set the leaf on it. He picked up another leaf and flicked it. A tiny peal rang out, lower than the first one, he was pretty sure. But with the next one he couldn't tell. Did it belong between the first two, or was it the same as the first one? He put them both close to his ear, flicked them in turn, and decided they might be different.

He hadn't made the slightest dent in the pile of leaves, and already there was a good chance he'd made a mistake.

He had placed a few more leaves when the door opened and Lila crept down the steps. "Oh Ivan, I'm glad they didn't send you away. I saw you from my window. That's it way up there." She pointed to a window high on the fifth floor. "They put me in the top class, Ivan."

"Wonderful," Ivan said. "As for me, I'll be thrown out of town unless I can figure out how to sort these stupid leaves."

Lila stepped closer. "I saw you were doing something. I love these leaves. I came to help."

Of course! She was the one who could help him. Ivan explained, and laid out the mats along the wall near the leaves. Lila picked up leaves, shook them next to her ear, and placed them without hesitation. She even switched around a couple Ivan had already placed.

How did she do that so easily? But still she had made hardly a hollow in the pile. This would take days, and she couldn't help him for days. He had to learn to do it himself. He stood among the piles, lifting the leaves she had placed, shaking and flicking them, examining them, trying to hear the differences.

"Hey," he said. "The low ones are thicker. A tiny bit heavier. More dense."

"Really?" Lila asked. She didn't even turn to look, just kept lifting and listening.

Ivan sat back on his heels and thought. After a minute he boosted himself to the top of the wall, where he felt a smooth, steady breeze. He dropped back down and turned to Lila. "Stop. I have an idea."

"But I have to hurry before they notice I'm gone."

"I know. Let's just try something."

Lila placed a leaf and turned to look at him. She had a little color in her cheeks, Ivan noticed, and she looked determined instead of meek.

He scooped a small pile of unsorted leaves onto a cloth, and told Lila to lift two corners while he took the other two. "Now," he said, "we toss them up. Lightly, lightly. The wind will carry the lightest ones farther. Here, toss a little higher than the wall."

Lila, with a look of doubt on her face, followed his timing as they bounced the leaves in a cloud, higher, higher, until the breeze caught them and they swirled. The denser leaves spiraled steeply downward while the lighter ones stayed aloft longer, letting the breeze carry them farther downwind, farther into the courtyard, before they fell into the still air of the walled space and settled to the ground. The leaves fell in piles that curved in arcs around the point where they had first caught the wind.

"Let's check," Ivan said. They dropped the cloth and hurried to test the fallen leaves.

"Yes!" Lila said. "A high C. Another one. And here just short of them is a B. Back here an A, and between them a B flat. Each band of leaves its own note. Ivan, it's like hundreds of leaves are sorting themselves!"

"I hoped so," Ivan said. "Is it good enough? Can we count on it?"

Lila shook her head, then nodded, and then bustled around, testing the stray leaves that had fallen between bands. "I just have to check these ones on the edges of piles."

Lila placed the few stray leaves, and then they tossed another set. The leaves caught the breeze, and it carried them as they fell, quickly or slowly, until they landed in bands that matched their notes. If only the lovely perfect wisp of wind continued exactly like this, so smooth and steady, and if nobody noticed Lila missing—he still needed her to help him toss, and to serve as quality control—they might finish the job.

They tossed larger and larger piles of leaves, racing against the dropping sun. Just before it got too dark to see what they were doing, Lila placed the last leaf on a pile. "Middle C," she said. "Just as it should be." Her eyes shone in the faint light from the windows. "Ivan, I better go inside before you show Mother Cadenza."

Ivan nodded. "Thanks, Lila ... I couldn't have done it without you."

"It was your idea." She turned and skipped up the steps.

Ivan waited a few minutes. Then he took one leaf from each pile and stuck them in his pocket before he went to knock at the kitchen door.

CHAPTER NINE

The Infirmary

The infirmary had four beds, all fresh and white and empty. Kit the servant girl led Daphne to the bed by the window and helped her into a clean, loose nightgown. Daphne hadn't realized how very sick she felt, how close to collapse. Now that they were safe for at least a while, how lovely it was to slip between these cool sheets and let her throbbing head sink into a pillow. The servant girl's fingers were cool on her forehead.

"Thank you," Daphne managed.

The girl shook her head. "No talking, miss, you know better. My name's Kit, and if it's talking you need, I'll be the one doing it. Now you lie quiet and I'll bring Sister Glissanda."

Sister Glissanda turned out to be a broad woman with

a soft, slack face and thinning curls, who peered down Daphne's throat, pulled down her eyelids, thumped her chest, and squeezed her ankles. Then she sat by Daphne's bedside and hummed a lullaby that seemed to lift the pain in Daphne's throat as it drew her toward sleep.

Some time later Daphne woke with a smelly linen bandage cooling on her chest. On a brazier beside her, a boiling pot filled the air with moisture and the scent of pine and lavender. When Daphne stirred, Kit appeared beside her. Hushing her, the servant girl peeled off the bandage, showed her a chamber pot, and helped her climb back into bed after she used it.

Daphne slept and woke and dozed again. Each time she woke, Kit was there to spoon soup into her, to wash her face, to renew the bandage on her chest.

When darkness came, Kit made a nest of blankets on the floor beside Daphne's bed and prepared to lie down. Daphne managed to lift herself on her elbows and object. "You can't sleep on the floor! Look at all those empty beds."

Kit pushed Daphne back down in the bed, smoothed her blanket around her, and scolded in her sweet low voice. "Now, miss, hush. You know those beds are for students. Besides, this way if you need something in the night you can just reach down and shake me."

*   *   *

On the second day, Daphne spiked a fever and alternated between sweating and shaking. Kit was always beside her, and through a mist of weariness Daphne often heard singing—first Sister Glissanda, and then a younger voice like a cool waterfall.

On the third day, she woke to a light, sweet chirping. A bird hopped on the sill outside the window at the head of her bed. The bird was round and light brown, but as it turned in the sunlight its feathers glinted yellow, like the bird from the forest. Daphne glanced around the room—no Kit, no Sister Glissanda. She reached up to the casement, turned the handle, and drew the window open. Cold air swept inside and the bird flew away, but Daphne scattered crumbs of leftover bread on the sill before closing the window and climbing back into bed to wait.

Today she would tell Sister Glissanda how much better she felt. She needed to get out of this room and find out what had happened to the others.

The little bird alighted again on the windowsill, its feathers fluffed. It marched along the sill pecking at the breadcrumbs. Daphne knelt on her bed and watched.

"Good morning, miss. I've brought your breakfast. Eggs today. Now turn around and sit up proper, miss, so I can give you your tray."

"Look at the bird," Daphne said. Her voice wavered.

Kit set down the tray. "Why look at that! A yellowkin, so early in the season. What's he eating? Oh, you didn't, miss, that was very bad of you, a draft is the worst thing for a throat."

She's forgotten to scold me about talking, Daphne thought. She said, "Why's it called a yellowkin when it's mostly brown?"

Kit shook a finger. "No talking! But they turn full yellow, so they do, when the sun stays longer and the days are warmer and they start singing full songs again. Midsummer they're like flashes of sunlight swooping over the fields, and such pretty songs glimmering down."

"Midsummer?" Daphne asked. "Does it actually get warm here?"

"As long as we have a good Spring Festival, the snow melts all around for miles and there's lovely mud everywhere. Streamlets bubble up, and good crops, and the children run around in short clothes."

"What happens at Spring Festival?"

"Now hush, miss, or you'll have me thrown back to the kitchen, and I do like nursing work so much better. I'll talk all you want, and you can just nod if you want me to go on, or shake your hand at me if you want me to shush, but don't let Sister Glissanda catch me letting you talk, do you promise?" Only when Daphne nodded did she continue.

"Where can you come from, that you don't know Spring Festival? That's when all the towns send wagonloads of their best singers to the capital, and they have feasts and contests of singing for three days, and at the end they melt the Ice Castle and dedicate it to the goddess to make the warm days and sunlight come again. That's what we train for all year. I say 'we' though of course a servant girl like me doesn't add anything with my voice. But I serve you ones who do, just like the farmers help feed us, and the carpenters make the wagons and all, so we each have our part. Am I boring you, miss?"

Daphne shook her head and said, "Why is it so horrible if I talk? So what if my voice takes a bit longer to heal?"

Kit shook her head with such vigor that her braids slapped her cheeks. "Oh, no, no, no, it can be much worse than that. We had a scholar here once, a boy named Fort, almost grown, with the most beautiful deep, resounding voice, and he ruined it. He had some kind of lump on his throat, but he kept talking, and it swelled with fever until he was almost choking, and then Dr. Fugue came in and pierced it from the side with his lancet. Pus ran everywhere, and Fort seemed to get better, but he talked too soon. He wouldn't stay quiet, he kept talking to me"—she blushed—"and he even kept teasing Sister Glissanda in his creaky odd voice. The strain made it scar up wrong, red coils like a rope down his neck, and his voice broke for good. At the end he could talk well enough, just a little rough, but he couldn't sing at all, so he lost everything."

"Lost everything?"

"He got expelled from school of course, and then his family couldn't keep him, because they had a beautiful daughter who sang so sweetly they couldn't have him around to corrupt her, so then—"

"Corrupt her? Because he lost his voice?"

"Well, people do say the voice is the echo of the soul, don't they? They said it was corruption hid deep in him that came bubbling out in all that ugliness, but Sister Glissanda says it was just bad luck and infection, and ... and I know if I had just managed to keep him quiet ..." She gulped and backed away from the bedside, wiping at her eyes with her apron.

"What kind of family would throw out a son just for losing his voice? Where is he now?"

"Oh, but they're a very high and proper family, miss. And now their son is banished. They condemned him as a Dissonant, but I don't believe that, he was so lighthearted and kind to everyone ..." She caught up the edge of Daphne's sheet and blew her nose, then looked horrified and pulled the sheet off the bed.

Troubled, Daphne said nothing. Once Kit had stopped sniffling and changed the sheet, she gave Daphne a grateful look.

"You're doing so good, miss, not talking. I know it's hard, but if you promise to keep on, I can let you have a visitor, someone who's been asking for you."

Daphne nodded eagerly. Ivan! Now she could learn what was going on—now they could make a plan.

But when Kit returned half an hour later, the person who slipped in after her was not Ivan but Lila. She wore a sky blue dress with a yellow scarf around her neck, and as she entered she looked behind her and quickly shut the door, as if to make sure she wasn't seen. She crept toward the bed, her eyes wide and alert. Daphne tried not to let her disappointment show. After all, Lila couldn't help not being Ivan.

"Daphne, are you all right? They let me sing for you once when your fever was high. I wanted to come back sooner but they said students mustn't visit the sickroom, and even now they think I'm in study hall, so ..." She stopped and looked over her shoulder at Kit.

"I won't tell," Kit said. "I'll even let you talk alone, but Miss Daphne's not to speak, or at least hardly at all, and I'll be watching by the door. If you hear me thumping and fumbling with the latch that means we're coming in, Sister Glissanda and me, and you'll just have time to hide under that bed there." She nodded at the one next to Daphne, which she had arranged so that its coverlet fell all the way to the floor. She curtseyed and slipped out the door.

What a conspirator she is! Daphne thought. She sat up among her pillows and gestured for Lila to sit at the foot of the bed. "You're in school?" she asked. "What about Ivan?"

Lila shook her head. "They sent him off to work in the fields. I helped him sort those yellow leaves. I tell everyone he's my cousin, but they just shake their heads and say distant family connections are of no importance, and I shouldn't advertise connections to the laborer class, not if I want the fame I'm entitled to." She looked at Daphne with wide eyes, which made Daphne feel crowded and uncomfortable. Lila looked as if she were asking for something.

She wants me to tell her what to think about Ivan, Daphne realized. Not just what to do, what to think. An image came to mind of Aunt Leonora, so large and loud and certain, leaning over Lila and instructing her in how to hold her spoon. Maybe Lila grew up never having room to think things out for herself.

"How are classes?" she asked.

Lila looked down at her hands. "It's practically all singing.

They do a little bit of reading and history but mostly it's singing and learning songs all day. And then there's public service where we're supposed to go out and sing to the crops and things, but I don't get to do that until I've been here a month, and—"

"A month!"

"Yes, and Daphne, the funny thing is, there are no pianos or instruments of any kind, no accompaniment, and everybody in the upper classes has perfect pitch. And—and I've made a friend!"

She said this with such wonder in her tone that Daphne peered at her. Lila's eyelashes trembled. She made it sound as if a friend was something remarkable, unprecedented. Daphne wondered uncomfortably whether maybe friends didn't fit in the world Aunt Leonora had built for Lila. Maybe that was why she came trotting after Ivan and Daphne all the time.

Lila continued, "Her name's Allegra, and she's the best singer in this school but she doesn't act high-and-mighty at all. She's kind to me and explains how everything works and wants to know all about my life and—"

There came a fumbling sound at the door, and Lila whirled. The iron handle jiggled as if it were stuck. Quick as a bird's swoop, Lila dived under the bed beside Daphne's.

Kit opened the door. "I don't know how it got stuck, Sister," she said as Sister Glissanda swept past her.

"Go and get some kitchen grease for it, there's a good girl." Sister Glissanda came to lean over Daphne. "And you, child, stick out your tongue."

Sister Glissanda examined her throat, prodded her stomach, and thumped her back. Then she rocked back on her heels. "So, can you speak today? Give me a sentence."

"I can talk a little," Daphne said, and for good measure she added, "ma'am."

Sister Glissanda nodded. "Better. Talk a little is what you shall do. Ten sentences today, short ones, that's all I'll allow." She raised her eyebrows at Daphne as if to say, and don't think I don't know you've already begun. She turned to look out the window. "Why, look, you have a yellowkin visiting, such a good omen! Humph, I wonder how these crumbs came to be on the sill." She gave Daphne a look obviously meant to be stern, with her eyebrows pulled down and in, but a twitch at the corner of her mouth gave her away. "Tell you what, I'll have Kit bring in the birdcage. Sometimes we let a songbird stay while a patient is healing, but it must be contained. I'll have no bird mess on my floor."

Daphne nodded, trying to look as obedient as possible. But she decided to use one of her sentences. "About my cousin Ivan, who came with Lila and me ..."

Sister Glissanda shook her head. "Raibley took him away as instructed. He'll be staying with the workers now."

"May I send him a message? Write him a note?"

Sister Glissanda held up three fingers. "You're using up your sentences, child. So that boy knows how to read? I can never convince anyone in this town that teaching them is worth our trouble. 'What does a laborer need with reading?' they ask. Still, best not get in touch with him, child." She leaned over Daphne again and smoothed a curl away from her face. "Just give it a moment's thought. A foreign boy of his class! If the Inspectors learned he not only tried to weasel his way into our school but also knows how to read and write—well, what could they think him but a Dissonant? And the new Composers in Melodia are clamping down harder than ever. It would be the silver mines for sure." She shook her head. "Forget him, child. I know at your age that rough, physical type can seem romantic, but I assure you there's no future in it. None at all."

Daphne sank back, momentarily struck dumb by the description of skinny, brainy Ivan as the rough, physical type.

Sister Glissanda pulled the blankets around Daphne's shoulders and patted them down around her. "Now I'll go see about that birdcage."

When she was gone, Lila poked her head out from under the adjacent bed, her eyes and mouth round with excitement. She crept out and crouched by Daphne's side, ready to dive again if Sister Glissanda returned. "It would be so much better if Ivan could sing just a little," she said. "We could have a lot of fun here."

"But we have to go back!" Daphne said, and her voice thinned and snapped. Her next sentence came out a croak once more. "Remember Aunt Adelaide and everyone. We have to go back as soon as we can."

Lila's smile erased itself. "I guess," she said. "I was only imagining."

A rustle sounded at the door, and before Lila could hide again, Kit came in carrying a wicker birdcage half her height. "Sister Glissanda told me about the bird, miss. And you, miss—" she nodded at Lila—"study hall is almost over, so you'd best hurry back."

Lila leaned to hug Daphne. "I'll come again," she promised.

Watching Lila cross the room and slip out the door, Daphne found herself smiling. What a strange little person she is, she thought. She made hiding under that bed look like the biggest adventure she's had in her whole life. I'm glad she came. But how do I get in touch with Ivan?

CHAPTER TEN

Allegra

Five days later, Allegra hung over the back of Lila's chair, watching her color the map that lay on the table before her. Lila liked to stay in the classroom when the other girls went to the library during study hall, because it gave her time to sneak off and visit Daphne. But today Allegra jiggled the back of her chair and made impatient noises. "Aren't you ever going to finish?"

"I want to get it right," Lila said, tracing a town boundary. She always wanted to get things right.

"But it's just dumb old geography, it doesn't count for anything. Besides, if you don't stop, I won't tell you my surprise."

Dumb old geography, but so different from the geography in the atlas at home! Capella and the other towns floated like islands in a sea of forest, and to the north lay the snowy wastes, and far to the south the ocean stretched away. Lila sketched the paths the trading nomads took, and the road to the capital, which she traced in yellow because she imagined it paved in yellow brick. As she bent over the map, she could picture it all, bear caravans making their way through the forest, the glittering Ice Castle her teachers lectured about, and maybe, far away, ships sailing on the distant sea.

Daphne kept saying Lila must learn all she could about this place to help them find their way home. Daphne was being nice to her now, maybe because she was going crazy in the infirmary, with no one but Kit to talk to.

Daphne. It was time to sneak out and visit Daphne. Though how she was going to do it with Allegra hanging over her this way, looking as if she was about to burst, Lila didn't know.

Then Allegra's last words penetrated. "Surprise?" Lila lifted her head.

Allegra turned Lila's chair around. "Yes, a surprise. Today's Fa-day, middle day of the octave. On Fa-day, the day students are allowed to take boarders home to dinner. And Mother Cadenza and my parents say you can come home with me!"

"But I'm not ready," Lila said.

Allegra pulled her out of her seat. "You look fine. You don't have to dress up, your school uniform's good enough."

That wasn't what Lila meant. She knew she should be excited. It was the first time a friend had invited her anywhere since—well, since before her mother moved her from Oklahoma to New York to cultivate her talent. What Lila meant was that she wasn't ready to try out her newfound popularity, her happiness, on the world beyond these school walls. "What if your parents don't like me?"

"Of course they'll like you, silly. They have very good taste." Allegra pursed her lips. "Just don't tell them that story about another country, Lila. They don't really understand fairy tales and all that."

Whenever Lila tried to tell Allegra about life in the real world, the older girl laughed in delight at Lila's descriptions of cars and airplanes and television. "How do you think these things up?" she asked admiringly, to Lila's confusion.

"But what shall I say if they ask where I'm from?"

Allegra shook her head. "Let's just tell them the truth, you were dropped off by nomads, and change the subject."

Lila recalled her manners. "Thank you very much for inviting me, Allegra. Are we leaving right now?"

"At the end of study hall. I'll meet you by the front steps. Don't worry, you don't have to bring anything, just yourself. Now I have to go pack up my homework."

As soon as Allegra had gone, Lila retrieved her fancy green coat, rolled up the map, and stashed it in her pocket with a couple of pencils. She felt in her other pocket to make sure the orange that Raibley had handed her at breakfast was still there. Then she slipped out the side door of the classroom and snuck down the stairs to the third floor, where the infirmary was. The door was open an inch, and she heard only a peeping sound, so she slipped inside.

Daphne sat on the bed with the yellowkin perched on

one finger. The two of them huddled beak to nose, making whistling sounds at each other.

"Allegra says whistling warps the mouth," Lila said. "It stretches the cheeks wrong and ruins your resonance."

"Allegra, Allegra, that's all you ever talk about," Daphne said. "What a bunch of nonsense." Her hair was messy and she looked particularly discontented today. She shook her hand, and the yellowkin flew to perch on the windowsill. "Did you find out any more about Ivan?"

"Yes, I did." Lila stood up straighter. "And I even brought you this." She pulled the orange out of her pocket. "Raibley brings the vegetables, and he gave it to me. He says oranges are very precious in winter." She didn't tell Daphne the orange was supposed to be for Kit.

"Raibley?" Daphne said. "The one who took Ivan away?"

Lila nodded. "Ivan's staying with him and working as a gardener. Raibley comes here every day to deliver vegetables, and he has a crush on Kit."

"Good job, Lila," Daphne said. "Hurry, give me a pencil."

Lila fished a blue pencil from her pocket, and Daphne looked around wildly.

"I need to write Ivan a note, Lila. Don't you have any paper?"

"Here," Lila said bravely, and she handed over the map, face down. Now she would get detention tomorrow for sure.

Daphne scribbled. "If Kit will help us, and we manage to

reach Ivan through that Raibley, we'll be all right—we can start planning how to get out of this country."

Lila wondered why Daphne was in such a hurry to leave. Lila liked it here. She could sing and learn about singing and have friends at the same time. But as usual, no one had asked her opinion.

Daphne looked up and seemed to notice something on Lila's face. "Good job, Lila, really," she said, and then she bent over her letter again, filling it with blue words.

"Well, off I go, then," Lila said.

Daphne, her pencil scratching at the paper, didn't even look up as Lila slipped out the door.

*   *   *

With a tumble of laughter and chatter, schoolchildren poured down the steps into the plaza. Lila and Allegra flowed with them until the groups of children diverged into separate streams leading down every street of the town. Allegra held Lila's hand, which surprised her, but she liked it; she remembered walking down the sidewalk with her father, the two of them swinging their clasped hands and singing at the top of their lungs.

Already the sun hung low, casting an orange glimmer on the sides of the buildings. Snow sifted from the sky, melting as it struck the cobbles. Food vendors with handcarts called as they passed, and Lila saw the haggard face of an old lady huddled in a blanket against the wall. Lila turned and looked back at her as Allegra chattered about her favorite sweet, sugared plums.

The flat white façade of Allegra's house loomed over them. Narrow steps led to the entrance, and a brass musical staff hung on the door where a handle should be. "Let's see," Allegra said. "Key of F." Her fingers tapped out a pattern on the staff, and the door swung open.

"How ..." Lila began.

Allegra looked at her. "Oh, don't you have these yet where you come from? They're the newest thing, but they cost a lot. You tap out the notes of your family song in the key of the day. It keeps the riffraff out."

Allegra's family was rich; Lila could see that. The wooden floors shone, candlelight flickered in heavy chandeliers, and portraits lined the hall. The maid wore a uniform much lacier than Kit's, and she kept her eyes down as she took their coats. Allegra drew Lila up a sweeping staircase to her bedroom, where they kicked off their shoes and wiggled their toes in a light green carpet spotted with color, like a meadow with wildflowers just emerging. The walls were painted with rainbows, and three pear-shaped prisms dangled from the window frame, fracturing the last of the sun's slanting rays.

"It looks like spring," Lila said.

Allegra bounced on her bed. "I'm glad you like it. Mother worked so hard on our rooms, to make them just right for us, so we'd grow up with music in the air. She says the right start is everything."

"You said 'our.' Do you have a sister?" Lila didn't want to share Allegra, not even with a sister.

"Not a sister. I have—had—an older brother." Allegra looked down and fumbled her hands together.

"You have a brother?" said Lila.

Instead of answering, Allegra said, "Did your mother fill you with music, Lila?"

"Oh, yes, starting with Baby Mozart."

Allegra jumped up from the bed and grasped Lila by the hands. "What? Are you saying Zart visited you? And he was a baby? Did you tell the teachers? Wait, wait, wait, this is just another one of your stories, right?"

"I don't know what you're talking about," said Lila. "They were tapes, you know, music tapes. And I had lullaby tapes, show tunes, classical music playing at dinner ..."

Allegra dropped Lila's hands, shaking her head, and Lila broke off. She looked around the room. No books, no speakers, no musical instruments of any kind. "But where's your music, Allegra?"

Allegra sat back on the bed and gestured at the painted walls. "The rainbows, of course. They're like scales, seven colors and then back to the one you started with, just like the seven notes of the scale. Don't they teach you that in the town you come from? Red is always C and orange is D and ... Even toddlers know that!"

"Oh," Lila said. "I mean, of course." To cover her confusion, she reached her index finger and gave one of the prisms a spin. The colors played across her hand and spilled against the opposite wall. If she concentrated, she could almost imagine the notes ringing up and down the scale.

*　　*　　*

Dinner was a starched affair. Lila sat to the left of Allegra's father, who had polished black hair and a villain's curlicue mustache. On Mr. Cantabile's other side sat his wife. With her pinched face and sharp, darting eyes, she appeared to be calculating Lila's worth. Her orange hair swept up and back from the sides of her face like the wings of a bird poised for takeoff.

"We're so glad Allegra has a new friend," Mrs. Cantabile said as she lifted the lid off the soup tureen. "Now where did you say you come from?"

"Oh, Mother, let me do the soup!" Allegra bounded up from her seat and came around the table to take the bowls. Her father frowned, but her mother sank back in her chair and let Allegra take over. "See, Lila, these are real truepitch bowls, an old family heirloom. Listen!" She struck one lightly on its metallic rim, playing a D, pure and clear, before filling the bowl and passing it to her father. The next bowl was E, the next one G, and the last one A.

"You skipped the F sharp," Lila said brightly, showing off. She wanted them to know she had perfect pitch and knew her D scale.

Allegra almost dropped the bowl she was filling for herself, and her mother hiccupped.

"One got smashed," Mr. Cantabile said. His mustache quivered. "It was an F, not F sharp. Minor key."

During the soup, and all during the second course, a fat roasted goose, Mr. Cantabile talked about his work as Inspector of Schools and Music. He praised the Composers for issuing new, stricter rules from Melodia. "Now at last we'll have a stronger hand over the curriculum," he said.

"About time, too. Do you know some schools let students graduate with a vocal range of less than three octaves?" Lila's voice had a range of two and a half octaves, so her stomach fluttered as she kept her head low and concentrated on her food.

When the goose had been carried away and they were all soaking their fingers in lemon-peel water before the last course, Allegra's mother spoke again. "But you never told us where you're from, dear."

Lila shot a look of appeal at Allegra, but her friend seemed to have no more tricks. Lila decided to act the orphan. "I ... I can't remember, ma'am. I was brought here by nomads who found me in the forest."

"But Allegra says you truly sing. You're not a wild child. Someone has taught you."

"Hush, wife," Mr. Cantabile said. "Don't press the child. It's birth, I tell you, birth and blood, nothing parents do."

"I don't believe it, dear. What would all my work as a mother mean if I believed that? Tell me, child. Surely you remember some training, some way you started."

"Oh, yes," Lila said, wanting to comfort this lady with her strange nervous intensity. "My mother taught me. I'd stand by the piano while she played out the notes, one by one, and—"

"Piano?" Mr. Cantabile asked, mustache trembling. "What's that?"

"Why, it's a—" Lila paused, confused. "It's a keyboard instrument with 88 keys and—"

"Preposterous!" Mr. Cantabile cried, slapping his napkin onto the table.

Lila swallowed. He glared at her, his hands clutching the table edge.

No one said anything. Lila struggled to recapture her train of thought. "Yes, she'd play scales and intervals, and I—"

Mr. Cantabile thrust himself to his feet. "Instruments! Props and crutches." He turned on his wife. "Wife, I can't think why the school doesn't screen for such fraudulent entrants! This is how mediocrity worms its way into the bloodline." His eyebrows bristled. "I'm all for meritocracy. No one can say I hold out for hereditary privilege, but this kind of scrambling and scraping, of *cheating* to climb into society—I will never—"

Allegra burst into tears.

Mrs. Cantabile, her face paler than ever and her hair wings all a-flutter, cried, "Husband, please!"

Allegra's father stood with his chest heaving, his cheeks puffing in and out. "Where does it lead, wife? All this whining for special privilege, for *instruments* and compensatory education?" Veins bulged on his forehead. "I'll tell you. It leads to perfectly respectable families taking in, adopting, out of the goodness of their hearts, some *counterfeit* child, with sweet sounds on his lips but discord in his heart—no patriotism, no true devotion, just hunger to bring disgrace on those who nurtured him."

Allegra tugged on Lila's hand. "Let's go," she said. "Please let's go."

All the way up the stairs Allegra gulped as if she were swallowing sobs. "I'm so sorry. I thought he was over that, I thought ..." She pulled Lila into her room and shut the door behind them. "But why did you have to talk about an instrument?" She said it with shock in her voice, as if it were something shameful.

"I don't understand," Lila said. "What's so bad about a piano?"

Allegra shuddered. "I don't know what a piano is, but it doesn't matter. If we allowed music made with instruments, just anyone could do it. Oh, Lila, don't you see? They wouldn't have to be pure of heart like you and me. The lower classes would think they were just as good as we are. They'd clatter and bellow and sing off-key, offending the goddess. Without us to guide them they'd bring anarchy and suffering, and even their children would die of hunger, and winter would come back and smother us all."

"Oh," Lila said, and she started to cry. Nothing made sense, and everyone seemed so angry, and now her only best friend ever wouldn't like her any more.

But to her surprise, Allegra pulled her over to her bed and put an arm around her shoulders. "Don't cry, Lila, you didn't know. Lots of good families try to find ways to give their children a head start. I suppose it's not that different from my prisms and rainbows, really. It's just that Father—ever since—you really don't know about our family, do you?"

Lila shook her head.

"We don't talk about it, but everyone knows. My brother—I told you I had a brother?"

Lila nodded.

"He was adopted. My parents kept trying to have children, but they didn't, and my mother wanted one so badly, and the nomads brought this boy—they said his parents were peasants, but he tested so well musically my parents thought he was a special child, one who could rise. So they took him in, and my mother did everything for him. He was—I don't know—her experiment."

She looked pleadingly at Lila, who nodded again.

"And then I was born, and my father was sorry they hadn't just waited. Fort loved to play tricks and talk back to teachers, and he got in trouble a lot. But he was funny and a wonderful singer, and he was always good to me. Two years ago he led the whole chorus from our school to Spring Festival, and he won a prize and so did the chorus, so it's because of him that we won the most territory ever, and he was a hero.

"But one night he was out too late in the cold, and he got sick, some terrible infection in his throat. Sister Cadenza couldn't heal it and neither could Brother Angelo, so in the end Dr. Fugue came and operated, and I swear he cut something, because after that my brother could never sing again."

She looked down at her hands as if that were the end of the story, but Lila said, "And then?"

Allegra sighed. "So of course he had to drop out of school and go work in the fields, but he didn't take to it well. The school kids called him Frog because of his croaking voice, and they threw mud at him. He kept tracking mud into the house until my father pointed out it really made more sense for him to go live with the other workers. My father was running for Chief Inspector then, and it wasn't proper for someone with no music to live in a house like ours. They had a huge fight and that's when the bowl got broken ... So Fort moved out of our house."

Allegra paused again, then took a deep breath and hurried on. "The next thing we heard Fort was arrested. He was caught telling the peasants they were just as good as us, that the music in their hearts was truer than what came out of our mouths, and worse, that the goddess didn't even care who sang to her. He was tried for heresy and treason, but my father intervened and he got off lightly—banishment, not even the mines. He said good-bye to us outside the prison door. He kissed my mother and swung me around in his arms, but he just looked my father in the eye and didn't even shake his hand."

She sat dry-eyed, turning her own hands over in her lap.

"That's a terrible story," Lila said.

Allegra shook her head and wiped at her eyes. "It's more than a year ago now. I thought we were back to normal. Some of my old friends are coming back, not avoiding me so much anymore. But you were new, you just took me as I was, and now that you know all this ..."

"Now that I know all this," Lila said, giving her a quick hug, "I'll love you even more."

*　　*　　*

A knock came on Allegra's door, and Mrs. Cantabile entered. She had dried her face and put on blush and somehow glued her hair back into place. "Allegra, dear," she said, "your father will walk your friend home now."

Allegra bounced up from the bed. "I'll come, too."

Mrs. Cantabile shook her head without even a glance at Lila. "No, dear, I want you to take a bath. And the night air, dear. You know."

Allegra went to her closet and pulled out another yellow scarf, this one wool. She knotted it around Lila's neck and whispered in her ear. "Don't be afraid of my father. Really, he's just sad. My brother broke his heart."

She stayed in the doorway while Lila followed Mrs. Cantabile downstairs to where Allegra's father stood waiting in the front entry. He wore a red scarf around the turned-up collar of his overcoat.

Lila followed him out the door and trailed after him along the walk. Then a surge of indignation took hold of her and she trotted up to walk beside him. Her breath steamed at the thought of him throwing his son out on the street. Her own father, like Ivan, could hardly sing a note, but he was a good person who loved her no matter what. If Lila lost her voice and ruined all her mother's plans, her father would hug her tight while she wept and then take her for a bike ride. Just the thought of pedaling beside him made Lila hold her head high.

Flame from the street lamps sent orange shimmers rippling across the puddles. Mr. Cantabile spoke in a gruff voice. "Mother Cadenza says you seem to be of good character."

Lila didn't answer.

"I won't report this 'piano' business if you don't mention it again. I'm glad you befriended my daughter. She's been lonely."

"She's the best friend I ever had."

"Well!" he said, as if the notion of a best friend was something he'd never considered. Then he held a hand to his ear and frowned.

Lila heard it, too. From beyond the buildings, from far off where the fields must be, came the sound of drumming, low and urgent. The sound made her feet twitch, and she wondered if people were dancing out there, if maybe Ivan was out there, too, dancing.

"Deep down, they're savages," Mr. Cantabile said. "We can tame the lower classes with fine music, but only until some agitator comes and works them into a frenzy. Then they'd tear through the streets and rip our houses down if we didn't have police." He peered into Lila's face to see if she was paying attention.

Lila thought of Raibley, the gardener boy who came to the kitchen every morning and dawdled on the lookout for Kit. She gave the tiniest shake of her head.

Mr. Cantabile straightened with a grunt of annoyance. "What do you know about it, a child like you? In winter the cold keeps them humble, but if the police don't put an end to this drumming, we'll see riots by summer."

He spoke not another word all the way back to school.

CHAPTER ELEVEN

Planting

Someone shook Ivan by the shoulder. "Come on, get up," Raibley's voice said in his ear. "We plant today."

Ivan groaned and rolled over. For days now he'd done nothing but shovel snow and move rocks, and every part of him ached. Only the faintest light glimmered under the cabin door. He groaned again and pulled the blanket over his head.

"Already been up two hours, making deliveries," Raibley said. "I brought you something."

Ivan threw back the blanket. "From Daphne?"

"Guess so."

Raibley fumbled in his pocket and handed over a curled page, which Ivan smoothed on the plank of his bed.

Ivan, how are you? I'm so worried about you. Lila and I live in comfort. She's a top student and she's made a friend, which seems like some big huge deal for her. I'm bored to death in the infirmary except for a yellowkin who sits on my finger and sings to me. My flu, or whatever, is finally better and I'm going to have to sing to find out what class I'm in, or whether I get thrown out of the building like you, ha-ha, not funny I know. But I keep thinking maybe I should get booted on purpose so I can find you because I can't stand not knowing how you're doing, so if Raibley finds you with this, PLEASE WRITE BACK.
Daphne

Ivan still had the notebook and stub of pencil in his jacket pocket. He said, "Quick, Raibley. Let me write an answer."

"Won't be going to the school again till morning delivery tomorrow," Raibley said. "Leave that, I want to show you something."

True, he could write the note tonight. Ivan folded Daphne's letter, and for the first time took note of what was on its reverse side: a hand-colored map, with neatly lettered names of towns, pictures of forests and mountains, and "The Land of Winter" inscribed across the top. How had Daphne gotten hold of this? She was brilliant. He wanted to study it, but Raibley shifted from foot to foot, eager to get back to his dirt and his little green plants. Ivan folded the map and slipped it into his shirt pocket.

He pulled on mud-encrusted boots and crossed to the door, stepping carefully among Raibley's houseplants and neatly stacked boxes of seeds. They shared this room in the middle of the workers' quarter, a warren of low cabins at the southwestern end of the city. From here each morning, servants took off for the fine houses of the town, craftsmen walked to their workshops, and agricultural laborers spread in work brigades to the fields. People who had no livelihood begged or waited in the tangle of streets, keeping an eye on dirty children at play in the gutter, sweeping garbage away, and hoping their neighbors would share some food at the end of the day.

Ivan knew he was lucky that Raibley had decided to befriend him. Raibley had given him a green bandana and told everyone Ivan was an apprentice gardener. Though he didn't know how to read or write, Raibley had a way of making things grow. He was happy as long as little green shoots kept poking their heads above the dirt in his pots. Still, Ivan had never risen early enough to see where Raibley got the vegetables he delivered: as far as Ivan could tell, nothing grew in the frozen fields.

"I'm starving," Ivan said.

Raibley looked him over. "You eat a lot for a skinny fellow." Raibley himself was slightly rounded at the edges; he looked soft, but Ivan had seen him work. "Get you something on the way."

They stopped at a cart where an old lady stood frying fat pancakes. "A sweet one, please," Raibley said, passing her a coin. She spread jam on one of the pancakes, folded it over, and handed it to Ivan.

Ivan stuffed the pancake in his mouth as Raibley guided

him through the streets. "You're always asking what's so good about the upper classes. Today you'll see."

They passed the last shacks of the workers' quarter and stepped into open fields. The sky was a glassy blue, and the cold came like a slap in the face. Here the fields that they had cleared of snow all week—all "octave," as they called it here—sported a new dusting of snow, and Ivan saw a team of workers sweeping the snow into piles to be shoveled and carted away. Next to one pile a brown donkey stood with its head low, waiting for its cart to be filled.

Ivan sighed and stepped forward to seize a shovel. Inside his gloves, his hands were covered in blisters, but at least shoveling kept him warm and kept his mind off worrying about the girls and Great Aunt Adelaide.

Raibley caught his arm. "Plenty here doing that," he said. "Today we borrow the transport for planting." He stepped forward and took hold of the brown donkey's halter.

Surprised, Ivan stationed himself at the donkey's other side, and they urged the little animal forward. The wide cart yawed and tilted as its two wheels rolled over frozen ruts. Ivan didn't know much about farming, but he couldn't see how Raibley meant to plant in hard-frozen soil.

"I'm going to show you my invention," Raibley said. He led the donkey along a trampled walkway, but the cartwheels kept getting stuck in deep snow on either side of the path. More than once, Ivan set his shoulder to the wheel to get it going again.

"Here we are," Raibley said.

Ivan came around the cart to see. What he saw was a huge, low greenhouse in the middle of a patch of snow.

"I call it a growhouse," Raibley said. "Come inside. It's nice and warm."

Ivan gave the donkey a final pat and followed Raibley down the steps and into the greenhouse, whose moist, warm air smelled of fresh-turned earth and oranges.

"Built it myself," Raibley said. "I was doing a lot of deliveries at the school a few winters back, and I kept noticing how warm it was by the window. So I thought maybe windows have a way of letting just the warm in, not the cold. And I tried it. Got a frame of wood around a pane of glass and laid it on the snow, and the first sunny day the snow melted below the glass but not next to it. So then I built a little house of glass and tested it, and now I have this big house where I can get the sproutlings started. Last year I even saved up and bought this orange tree."

"Do you use glass to warm the fields, then?" Ivan asked. "So you can plant?"

Raibley shook his head and laughed. "Oh, no, I don't have enough glass for that. Besides, the singers don't like us showing off new-fangled ways, though they like the oranges well enough. Now come on, Ivan, help me load." He handed Ivan a flat wooden box of tiny sprouts, and Ivan carried it up to the cart.

They kept carrying flats until the back of the cart was filled. "But I don't see the point," Ivan said. "These things'll all die if you stick them in frozen ground."

Raibley just grinned and clucked to the donkey.

As they approached the field, they saw laborers leaning on their shovels, waiting. Along the path from town streamed a long line of schoolchildren in blue uniforms and yellow scarves. The children, who ranged from kindergarten age to several years older than Ivan, parted to flow around the edges of the field, where they stopped, facing inward. The laborers climbed over stone walls to stand in silence behind them, outside the circle. Then an instructor raised a baton, and the schoolchildren began to sing.

Their song had no words, at least none Ivan recognized. The children sang and swayed, dipped and waltzed, moving toward each other until their bodies and voices seemed to make a pool of warmth in the center of the field. Then they receded like a tide pulling back, and the song that had come together in unison swirled into different themes. In and out they sang and danced, the song taking form and color. When Ivan closed his eyes he imagined a team of weavers passing skeins of colored wool, pulling the lengths of yarn past one another in an elaborate pattern. With his feet planted on the earth and his toes warm for the first time in days, Ivan swayed to the music.

The song faded away, and the children fell back. Raibley made his way among them and squatted down to feel the ground. "It's ready," he called, and the workers let out a cheer. They swarmed to the cart, laughing and talking as they passed the flats of seedlings down, across the low wall, and into the field.

Ivan carried one of the flats and set it down on ground that was suddenly soft. He took off his glove and laid his

hand on the warm earth. Around him workers slid their spades into the butter-soft dirt, loosening the soil.

Raibley walked around directing the planting. Ivan knelt among the other workers, pressing sprouts into the earth and packing soil like a warming blanket around them. He didn't know what to make of what he had seen. He wondered if all those children's dancing feet had broken through a layer of ice to a warmer layer of dirt below. But no, he had heard it and felt it himself. The song warmed the air as well as the ground, and even his ears felt warm.

All day long Ivan helped Raibley carry flats from the growhouse and planted seedlings in neat rows. Some of the other laborers worked in the next field, shoveling snow off the ground in preparation for the singers' next visit. Whenever he got the chance, Ivan took off a glove and pressed his hand to the warm soil. I don't understand it, he thought. How does it work? Is it something about sound waves? How does it turn into heat?

He felt as if he had entered a new world. Well, of course. But he had always taken food for granted before, not thinking much about where it came from or how somewhere hard human labor scratched it from the ground. We all eat, we all give back, Raibley liked to say. Ivan thought, Up to now I've been getting a free ride all my life.

At dusk they made their way back from the fields. Ivan dragged with fatigue. Raibley traded herbs from his growhouse with one of the old ladies cooking omelets over a fire. As soon as he had finished eating, Ivan lit a candle, tore a page from his notebook, and took himself into a corner to write to Daphne.

... I've talked to R. and a lot of others, and they say it's not safe to travel north until after their Spring Festival, which won't come for a few more months. We have to get back, but if the blizzards all winter stay as bad as they say, I don't think we can risk it yet. Thanks for sending the map, though. Now if only it had the barn marked on it!

Two boys around Ivan's age stuck their heads in the doorway. "Come on Raibley, let's go. You have to see the dancing."

Raibley, sitting on his bed and poking at a seed with his pocketknife, shook his head. "Don't think so, lads. No drumming parties for me."

"Oh, come on, why not?" One of the boys came inside and pulled at Raibley's sleeve.

"Now quit that. Too much drumming, too much cider, next thing you know people are trampling the fields and throwing up in ditches. I don't like it."

"But Raibley, we had planting today. You have to celebrate. And besides, there's this fellow in a scarlet cloak and a black mask, and he dances like fire and tells us such things."

Ivan lifted his head. A dancer in a scarlet cloak? That sounded like better entertainment than sitting here in the dark. But Raibley sat stolidly, shaking his head.

The boys departed, and Ivan didn't follow. The truth was, he was too tired for dancing. He turned back to his letter.

It's so weird to be living here in the workers' quarters instead of traveling from place to place with you. I'm glad to hear Lila's doing so well. Sometimes at night I lie in bed shaking the last of those yellow leaves and listening, trying to hear what Lila hears. She got so excited about those stupid leaves. It really makes me wonder. I hate to say it, Daphne, but did you ever think that maybe this one is Lila's adventure, and we're just along for the ride?

Ivan

CHAPTER TWELVE

Letters

Dear Ivan,

My audition placed me in the third grade (third from the top). Pretty good considering I haven't been studying music my whole life like the kids here. At last I'm well and out of the infirmary, but I had to let my yellowkin go.

Here's my school day. After breakfast, the day students arrive and we head to class. Mostly we sing and study harmony and music history and health, which is all about taking care of your voice. Our classroom clock is a circle with letters for notes instead of numbers, starting with C in the 12 o'clock spot and C# at the 1 o'clock, going all the way around to G# where 8 o'clock should be and then back to A B C. At B o'clock, during reading and writing period (I tested out), I get to help Sister Glissanda in the infirmary. At lunch I sneak into the kitchen to see Kit.

After lunch we have this awful class of memorizing verses in some ancient language they use in prayers and hymns. Sometimes it sounds like there's a German phrase thrown in. Then we have games and musical movement (we're not allowed to call it dancing), then study hall and evening chorus. After supper we read in the library or gather in classrooms to sing with friends. And that's it. Lights out at A o'clock.

We don't study any math or science. "We finished adding and subtracting ages ago," they say, and "Science is for mechanics. People of our station don't bother with such things."

I see Lila at meals and in the evening. Her friend Allegra is tall and lovely with flame-colored hair. When can I see you? Can't you help R. with his morning deliveries?

Write back,
Daphne.

Hi Daph,

R. says I may not come with him on deliveries. They only let him go because he has a "nice speaking voice." My voice cracks in the middle of sentences. Therefore I'm not good enough to carry vegetables to your stupid school.

Don't they ever let you out?

Everybody's freaking out about the weather. The winds and blizzards out of the northwest got fiercer when the mountain fell at Origin two years ago (four months our time), but this winter is worst of all. All kinds of choruses come out to walk the perimeter of the city and "sing back the cold." Then they skip on home to their fancy houses while the poor people here shiver in little hovels. The police come through at night telling people to put out their fires, because smoke settling over the town would harm the singers' voices, and we have to put our faith in music, not firewood.

Listen, my candle's running out. I wanted to tell you about the drumming, but no time. Come visit. We get a half day off on Fa-day.

Ivan

Dear Ivan,

It's crazy that we're living in the same town and can't figure out how to see each other. The simplest way would be if I could go out on one of the singing crews, but apparently I'm not good enough yet.

Singing is the heart of their religion here. It gives me shivers just to write about it. Mainly I think it's all superstition, but two nights ago the brothers and sisters prayed and chanted all night, and then just before dawn all the students gathered in the great hall and sang. Somehow from all our voices blending and mixing in the arches of the ceiling, there seemed to be a new voice descending, singing a note that none of us were singing. The hair stood up on the back of my neck.

Then it was gone, and we crept out of there and went to breakfast. Nobody talked. But in history class, Brother

Legato told us the ceremony goes back to the creation of this land, and it's the bond between us and the goddess. If we sing well enough, she'll touch down among us to sing along, and her song, which we're generally too debased to hear, is what makes everything happen, the sunrise and the crops growing and pure water flowing down from the mountains.

So I guess that's why they're so serious about singing.

Something helpful has happened. My roommate here, a very proper girl named Partita, has decided to go back to being a day student. She's much too polite to say so, but I think she got tired of my clumsiness and questions. Anyway, I've convinced them to let Lila move in with me, so, even though Lila can be a pain, at least two of us will be together, which will make planning lots easier.

I'm working on how to get out of here, but with the weather as bad as you say, I think you're right. We'll have to wait for spring.

Your cousin,
Daphne

Dear Daphne,
You sound good. Say hello to Lila. It's discouraging out here. Last night it snowed again, and snow piled up even on the fields we'd already planted. You should have seen Raibley on his knees trying to clear the snow from around all his little shoots. Some of the plants were so brittle with cold their stems just snapped in two, and there were tears running down Raibley's face. He says the cold has never returned before to settle on a field that's already been cleared

and song-warmed. It's kind of a scandal. The workers grumble that the upper classes have grown too fat and lazy and corrupt to protect the town.

Daphne, I keep seeing little kids with snotty faces and cracked hands and big eyes looking hungry and cold. In their shacks at night the parents try to teach them to sing. Every once in a while, Inspectors come through the slum here and ask children to sing for them. If they find one with talent, they take him to be brought up right in your school with some rich family sponsoring him. The real parents are supposed to give up all contact to give the kid a chance at a better life. I saw it happen when I came back for lunch break yesterday. A man took a four-year-old girl right off her mother's lap. The little girl clutched her mother and screamed, but the man and his helpers just peeled her fingers loose and carried her off. Other women crowded around the mom, patting her shoulder and telling her what a blessing it is, what fine food the child will eat and what pretty dresses she'll wear. But the mom just kept bawling.

Darn—I meant to tell you about the drumming, but Raibley's about to leave. Love to you and Lila both,

Ivan

PS. Sometimes I think the reason we were sent here was to start a revolution.

Dear Ivan,

That's terrible, that story about the little girl. We'll keep an eye out for her in the nursery class. Ivan, I'm writing in a hurry so Raibley can take this right back to you. The *sisters say the extra snow and cold make an emergency, and all of us, even the newest, need to go out and sing today. (We are not fat and lazy and corrupt, we're all fired up with patriotism.) We're starting in the north and marching counterclockwise around the whole city. Lila will be there, too. Try to see us.*

    Daphne

CHAPTER THIRTEEN

Public Service

The students marched in ranks of three, singing one of their interminable prayers in the language Daphne didn't understand. The wind keened around them, and although the sky was clear except for a few high wisps of cloud, ice crystals blew off the snowdrifts in small tornadoes. The wind stung Daphne's cheeks, and she was glad of her long school cloak and the yellow hat and scarf she wore.

She wished her voice didn't sound so puny and wavering. Up at the head of the line, where Lila walked with Allegra, the song had a sweetness that seemed to turn the cold aside, and behind her the smaller children sang out with such gusto that they drove the snow away. But here in the middle, she thought her classmates sounded unsure of themselves.

Peasants and workers stood lining the paths as they

marched. Daphne tried to see in their faces what Ivan saw. She saw no spark of rebellion. Mostly the people looked dull and brutish, hunched against the cold, gripping their shovels or carrying bundles on their backs. Half of them shifted from foot to foot, swaying in time with the music. The others stood planted to the ground, their eyebrows gathered in and sullen scowls on their faces. If they were so miserable, why didn't they do something for themselves? Go gather firewood or—or start a bakery or something? Why didn't they at least wrap scarves around their children?

Now the schoolchildren turned past the corner of the town wall and marched along the west side. Here a few of the fields had already been planted, and a men's chorus had stayed out last night to protect them. Daphne still saw no sign of Ivan or Raibley.

Lila ran back along the line and stepped in beside Daphne. "I'm to help your section because you don't have much experience," Lila said. Her eyes shone; tiny snowflakes paused on her dark hair for an instant before melting. Her cheeks were flushed, and Daphne thought she had never seen her cousin look happier. That withdrawn, above-it-all Lila—the stuck-up one that Daphne had always resented—had disappeared, and instead here was this lively, eager girl. When she sang she looked all around her, joyful, glad to be of use. Daphne could see that the peasants and workers along the path responded to her. They lifted their chins and looked more hopeful. I wish I could do that for them, Daphne thought, and she struggled to keep the wish free of resentment.

Where Lila stepped through the snow, she left steaming footprints behind her. Like Good King Wenceslas in that old Christmas carol, Daphne thought. I have to admit it: she has a gift. As soon as she articulated the thought, Daphne felt lighter. Lila hadn't asked to be gifted at music, any more than Ivan had asked to be tone deaf. Daphne wished her other letter hadn't called Lila a pain.

The children sang, and the air shimmered. The singers swung toward the south side of the village, where the houses of the workers huddled out of the direct path of the wind. More fields here were planted, and looking ahead, Daphne saw Raibley standing with his legs wide and fists resting on his hips. He had thrown his cloak aside, as if he had a warmth all his own. Beside him, copying Raibley's stance but now raising his hand in a wave, stood a vigorous-looking young man in a patched brown cloak. He threw his hood back, and with his hair standing up every which way, he was unmistakably Ivan.

Daphne nudged Lila and raised her voice, trying to blend her tones with her cousin's. She wanted Ivan to see how hard they were working to infuse the ground with warmth. As he watched them, a grin broke out on his face, and he said something to Raibley at his side. He had a stature about him, a pride she hadn't seen before. Daphne stumbled and fell out of line. Lila paused to reach a hand to her, but Daphne said, "It's nothing, just my ankle. I'll catch up. Don't stop singing. Lila, go." She waved the line of singers forward, and the children parted around her, looking down at her but not faltering in their song. She clutched her ankle until they passed, and then she crawled toward the row of spectators, where Ivan hurried to her side with Raibley trailing him.

"Are you all right?" Ivan asked, bending over her.

"Of course I am," she said in his ear, so that even Raibley wouldn't hear. "How else was I going to get some time with you? Here, help me back to your place."

She threw her arm around Ivan's neck and groaned convincingly as he hoisted her to her feet. "Quick, before anyone asks questions," she said, and he supported her as she hopped and grimaced across the uneven ground toward the line of shacks that marked the southern border of Capella.

As they passed between the first shacks, Daphne straightened and began to walk normally.

"You even had me convinced," Ivan said, dropping her arm. "I was practically carrying you."

"Good thing you're strong from all your shoveling," Daphne said. She meant to tease him, but it was true that he felt very solid, all muscle and bone. "It's good to see you."

Ivan bought hot chestnuts from a woman in the alley outside his cabin, and they sat on his bed, which consisted of a few planks stretched between stacks of bricks and covered by a couple of blankets. How miserably cold his room was, Daphne thought, with its dirt floor and the door that didn't sit tightly in its frame. In spite of her cloak she pulled one of the blankets across her lap and tried not to shiver. Ivan sat with his sleeves rolled partly up his forearms as if it wasn't that cold at all.

"You're right, it *is* spooky," Ivan said. "When all the

singers come by, you can actually see the snow pull back, and the little plants kind of lift their heads. But then you pass by, and the cold seeps back in, and it seems like a losing battle."

"Too bad not everyone can sing," said Daphne. "No, wait. That sounds bad. I didn't mean it like that. I meant that way you wouldn't be so dependent on ..."

Ivan put on a snobbish accent. "Aren't poor people *such* a bother?"

"That's not fair. I didn't mean that. Don't look at me that way. What's your great solution? You think a revolution will help. Barricades and songs and people dying like in *Les Miz*."

Ivan studied his fingernails full of dirt. "Not like that. But it doesn't seem right, that some people are born to hardship and hunger and cold."

"It happens in our world too, Ivan."

"Do you think I don't know that?"

"At least here there's some purpose to it," Daphne said. "Division of labor to keep everything running, so everyone can survive. Everyone plays a part."

"So that's the story they tell you. Raibley believes it, too. But there's something twisted about it, something basic that's just wrong. I can't get a grip on it. At home you and I live in the privileged world. You even go to private school. And you still live in privilege here, so I can't expect you to understand."

Daphne said, "That's not fair. I'm not blind."

Ivan gave a laugh. "Yeah, but your school inspector is.

So's the mayor and the chief judge. Haven't they told you how blind people are the most revered citizens, because their hearing is so refined? Except they don't wander down here to hear things like children crying from hunger and women crying out as their drunken husbands wallop them."

"I'm not responsible for drunken husbands," Daphne said. "Don't be so high-and-mighty, Ivan. What exactly are you accusing me of?"

Ivan stood and began pacing up and down. "I don't mean to accuse. But Daphne, I can't believe we're supposed to just sit here meekly in our separate compartments until summer comes and we can walk away. Don't you remember last time? We had a job to do. Listen, there's this drummer in scarlet and black who shows up at night, and the people come alive. Raibley doesn't like it and tells me to stay away, but I want to see what it is. I want you to come with me, Daphne."

Daphne's mouth felt dry. "But Ivan, if I don't get back to school by dark, I could get expelled."

"What, and then you'd have to live out here with us lower classes, is that it? Poor little you."

"Don't be sarcastic. I just got over being really sick. I could get sick again."

Ivan sighed and ran his hand through his hair.

"Besides," Daphne said, "drumming? How could drumming matter?"

Ivan dropped his hand and turned away. "All right. Let's get you home."

It's the cold, she wanted to tell him. I just can't stand

the cold. But Ivan, with his back turned and his head bent, looked so lonely that instead she stood and let the blanket fall from her shoulders. She had so looked forward to seeing him. When she imagined him delivering her to the warm safety of the school and then returning to this cold, bleak place, it didn't seem right. For the sake of their old comradeship, she stepped forward and touched his arm. "Oh, Ivan, of course I'll go with you."

CHAPTER FOURTEEN

Dancers

Waiting for the drumming to start, Daphne huddled on the bed, and Ivan made porridge in a blackened pot pushed to the back of the hearth, where a few coals smoldered. Just as Ivan pulled the pot off the coals, Raibley stepped through the door. Raibley looked askance at Daphne but didn't ask questions. He just took two wooden bowls from the shelf, went out, and returned with a third bowl and a handful of walnuts. Raibley gave the walnuts to Ivan, who tossed them in the bowls and spooned porridge over them. The three of them sat with bowls perched on their knees. Ivan passed around the last of the raisins he had kept back from Kanzat, and each of them took just a few to sprinkle over their supper.

"Why don't you build yourselves a table?" Daphne

asked. She was still angry with Ivan for suggesting that the poverty around her was the fault of the rich people in town, and she wanted to point out that they could do better with a little effort.

"We have a wood quota," Ivan said. "We're allowed barely enough for a little fire, and not even that some nights."

Raibley gestured with his broad hands, "You see how it is. The woods around here are all that breaks the wind when it comes tearing down from the mountain or across the plain. We can't just go cutting down trees. As for warmth, well, if we all labor in harmony, our town will produce the finest music, and that will be enough to warm us all."

Ivan caught Daphne's eye, gave his head a shake, and jerked his chin toward Raibley in a way that said, You see how brainwashed he is.

Daphne liked Raibley. He was loyal and innocent and hardworking, and she had seen the looks he gave Kit while she bustled about the kitchen. Raibley had provided Ivan with a home; he'd made Daphne welcome, even though he obviously didn't approve of her presence. She began to ask him about plants, about what vegetables to plant when, and what he knew about medicinal herbs.

As darkness dropped over the town, the sound of drumming reached them. Ivan stood and pulled on his cloak. Daphne sat for a moment longer, warm from the porridge, tapping her feet on the dirt floor. Then she pulled up her hood and stood also.

Raibley said, "Come, now, Miss Daphne, that'll be no

place for a lady. It's not safe." He turned to Ivan. "You should be ashamed, taking a lady to wild dancing."

"I'm not a lady," Daphne said. She twirled once and took note of Raibley's bewildered expression as she followed Ivan out the door.

They didn't have a torch, but they followed the glow of distant firelight as they wound through the alleys, heading east. Villagers materialized from the shacks and shadows around them, and at one point Daphne nearly stumbled over a toddler chugging after his mother on stubby legs. They emerged into snow-covered fields on the eastern side of town, where the feet of eager villagers had stamped pathways through the snow. From a hillock a few hundred yards ahead, where a bonfire burned, the urgent throb of drumming pulsed through the air.

They walked faster. As they left the town behind them, Daphne felt her spirits lift in a kind of wildness. The stars shone high and clear in the cold air, and the scent of burning fir gave a sweet tint to the night. Her feet felt light as she and Ivan pushed through the jostling crowd.

The drums were stumps, hollow logs, upturned bowls, or horseshoes. The drummers included men and women and children, even a girl tapping out a rhythm on her brother's back. At their center, weaving and dipping like some maniacal composer, swirled the figure Ivan had spoken of—a tall man in a scarlet cloak and hood, with a black scarf pulled high over his mouth and nose. Slung over one shoulder he had a long drum with a skin drumhead, which he tapped and pounded with rapid hands. Beneath the cloak, his clothes were also black, and other than his hands, only his eyes flashed in the firelight. Daphne's heartbeat quickened in time with his drumming. As more townspeople converged on the fire, the scarlet figure nodded to a man by his side who tossed drumsticks to anyone who held up a hand.

The scarlet drummer lifted his knees high and stamped on the ground, and soon people who weren't drumming began to echo his movements, until they stamped and jumped and reeled in a wild dance. The beat was urgent, angry, and yet a celebration, and as it sped faster, the drummer began to chant in a rough, grating voice.

Now who gets to sing when the winter comes?
Who has to dance when the sun goes down?
Who dines at home in a house of stone?
Who huddles in mud while the children moan?
Why have they stolen your music?
Why have they stolen your music?

The day comes, goddess, when your people rise,
When all of your people rise and sing,
When they dance and they drum and they stand their ground,
And all the stone houses come tumbling down.
Stand up!

The people roared with him. "Stand up!"
"And dance!"
"We'll dance!"

The rhythm of the chanting and the wild energy it awakened swept Daphne into the dance, and she spiraled toward the bonfire with the workers. The people jumped and bobbed and whirled, separating her from Ivan as the drumming continued, new drummers picking up the rhythm and changing it. It was wild, barbaric, Daphne thought, almost a war dance. How often the villagers missed the beat and stumbled! How far their dancing was from the measured beauty of movement to music she studied in school! Yet Daphne felt a strange elation at their rowdiness, mixed with a sense that the mob was about to burst out of control.

She turned to look for Ivan, but when she located his face in the crowd, he had a glint in his eye and a tilted grin she didn't recognize. He threw back his head and shook it, letting out an ululation that she couldn't believe came from him. He sounded like some creature both fierce and primitive. Overwhelmed by the press and noise and savagery of the crowd, she shrank away from the dancers, only to find herself surrounded by drummers, whose urgent beat made her clap her hands to her ears even as she kept dancing.

Then someone caught her hand and laughed with such joy that happiness caught hold of her, too. It was the scarlet drummer, and he spun her around, caught her waist with a firm hand, and rocked her into a high-stepping, wild dance that carried them through the crowd. She sought out his eyes above the black scarf covering half his face. They were deep brown, warm, laughing, regarding her in a way that made her feel she could do anything.

Just as she decided she would follow the scarlet dancer

anywhere, he twirled her around again and let go of her hand just in front of Ivan, who caught hold of her. Daphne felt the air go out of her. The dancer had rescued her and then deposited her like a child back to the care of her cousin.

Well, Daphne thought, taking a breath, she would just have to show them both, Ivan and the dancer, that she didn't need a caretaker. In middle school dances at home, she kept an eye on what the other kids were doing and tried to match them. Here in the fire-lit darkness, even old people and toddlers danced. Here she could be free. Daphne's feet wanted to leap and fly. She loosed herself from Ivan and sprang away from him, shaking arms and hair. She danced for joy. She danced to release the people from their fatigue and discouragement, and when she saw them lift their knees and shake their arms, she danced faster. Why, Daphne thought, as she shimmied and jolted and let herself go, this is life, this is happiness!

She toppled into Ivan and balanced against him, panting. He took the edge of his cloak and wiped the sweat from her neck and forehead, and then pointed to the outskirts of the circle, where jugs were passing from hand to hand. Daphne noticed how thirsty she was and how her chest was heaving. Ivan drew her to the edge of the circle, where he caught onto a jug as it passed. He gave it to Daphne, who took a swig of something sour and fruity. She gasped, and Ivan drank, and then Daphne reached for the jug again and glugged down what she could until Ivan wrested the jug from her hand and passed it on.

The drink settled like a glowing coal in Daphne's

stomach. She looked around and saw people with sweat glowing on their faces. "Look, they're hot," she said, and Ivan nodded and gestured toward the ground. The pounding feet had melted the snow, but the circle of mud seemed to be expanding even beyond the place where the people danced, and Ivan bent close to say in her ear, "There's a circle of cleared land from each night he's been here. The people are clearing the land without the singers."

"Without the singers?" Daphne shook her head to clear it. "But then ... do the people need the singers? And class divisions ..." She looked at Ivan.

"They mean nothing," Ivan said with such force that Daphne took a step backward and stumbled. Ivan reached out to steady her, and then he steered her back into the crowd. The smoke made her eyes sting, but she danced again. She threw off her hood to cool the sweat trickling down her temples. Bodies crashed and spun and rollicked around her, and Ivan held on.

"I think he's leaving," Ivan shouted. Daphne looked toward the fire and saw the man in scarlet lift his drum under his arm and turn away toward the distant woods.

"But he can't leave now!" She pulled Ivan toward the fire, toward the drummer. How could he slip in and out like that, stir everyone up and just disappear? She wanted to know more about him and ask him questions. She wanted to dance with him again.

Someone else reached him first. A long arm seized the dancer by the shoulder, and three more figures in blue ranged themselves around him. A murmur, then a gasp ran through the crowd. Daphne pivoted. On all sides, men threw aside their patched cloaks to reveal blue uniforms with gold markings. She recognized them now: police.

The crowd began to waver at the edges, then to melt away. People drew their cloaks over their heads and fixed their eyes on the ground as they shrank and scuttled back toward the dark alleys of the lower town.

The drummer in scarlet shook off the policeman's hand. He took a step forward, but three others closed on him.

"I arrest you for treason and sedition!" the first policeman announced. He held up a pair of handcuffs. "Give me your hands!"

The man in scarlet turned in a circle. "I'm no citizen of this town, and I refuse your laws." He stood almost a head higher than the policemen, and as he turned he cast a look across the field at the fleeing villagers. "Stand up!" he shouted, and the first policeman struck him across the face with a whip handle while another brought a club down on his shoulder.

The scarlet drummer went down. A section of crowd close to him surged forward, as if to protect him, but then it fell back again, leaving the cousins in front. As the police converged on the fallen man, kicking and punching, Ivan jumped like a crazy man to yank on the coat of the policeman nearest him.

"Ivan, don't!" Daphne cried.

A policeman struck Ivan in the face with his fist and slashed with a whip that curled around him as he fell. Ivan landed on his hands and knees, and the policeman kicked him in the ribs. Ivan collapsed, and Daphne threw herself to her knees beside him. He sprawled face down in the dirt, his torn cloak in a swirl around him. She rolled him over. "Ivan."

He groaned, clutching his side.

"Let's get out of here, Ivan. Everyone's running away. There's nothing we can do."

Ivan rolled over again and with a grunt of pain pushed himself to his knees. There he paused to watch two policemen drag the drummer to his feet. Daphne looked with him, and when the injured drummer raised his head, her eyes locked on his. The policemen had ripped away the scarlet cloak, which lay in a tumble in the mud. They had torn away the black scarf. Daphne saw dark hair and a pale face, swelling now along the jaw. Most notable of all, now that the scarf no longer concealed it, she saw on the drummer's neck a writhing scar of angry red.

CHAPTER FIFTEEN
The Dissonant

Daphne got Ivan back into the workers' quarter without encountering any more police. Ivan set one hand against the side of a shack and doubled over, retching so hard Daphne feared his stomach would tear. But finally he straightened, wiped his mouth on his sleeve, and reached for her shoulder again.

She supported him through uneven alleyways all the way back to Raibley's cabin. Instead of knocking, she leaned her free shoulder against Raibley's door, gave it a push, and then steered Ivan to the corner where his bed should be.

Only one glowing coal remained of their fire, and it was so dark she couldn't see Raibley, but she heard rustling from his corner of the room.

"What happened?" Raibley's voice was soft.

"Police. Everyone ran away. They arrested the drummer, and Ivan got beat up."

Raibley let out a sound like a hiss through his teeth, and then he was a bulk beside Daphne in the dark, helping her settle Ivan in his blankets, pulling off his boots. Without saying anything, Raibley drew away, fumbled near the fireplace and blew on the coals until he lit a candle, which he brought to Ivan's bedside.

In the circle of candlelight, Ivan looked up at Raibley. "I know, you told me not to go," he said. "Sorry to mess up your house." It was hard to see his expression through the mud on his face, but Daphne thought one corner of his mouth turned up in a half-smile. She let out a sigh of relief.

Ivan turned toward her as if surprised she was still there. "You have to get back, Daph."

She shook her head. "Not in the middle of the night. There's no way."

"There's got to be a way, right, Raibley?"

Raibley frowned. "Depends. There's the kitchen cellar. The door might be open."

"Take her home, would you, Raibley? I'd do it myself, but ..."

"Raibley, don't listen to him," Daphne said. "I'm sure the police are still out. I don't want you getting into trouble."

Raibley hesitated. Then he set the candle on the floor and with both large hands felt all over Ivan's limbs and torso. Ivan grunted and ground his teeth, but apparently Raibley found him whole.

"Right. Back soon," Raibley said, and he picked up the candle and led the way to the door.

"Take care, Ivan," Daphne said. She bent to give him a kiss on the cheek. At the door she turned and said, "I'll try to help the drummer."

All the night's festivity had been swallowed into silence. Raibley made his way through the alleyways like a hulking shadow, and Daphne followed as quietly as she could. Dark buildings and murky forms loomed on either side, and her ears rang in the stillness. She remembered the whirling dance, the scarlet drummer's eyes, the sense of joy she had felt. She remembered how Ivan had pushed forward to help the drummer, while she had pulled back. She followed Raibley, but the ground felt unsteady underfoot. She couldn't forget that sudden ugly face of brutality. Nothing in Capella looked the same.

As they approached the central square, they heard bursts of laughter. Raibley ushered Daphne to the left, around a massive block of buildings, into the pathway he had taken when he first brought them to the school. At the back courtyard, he tried to open the gate. The latch clanked, but the gate didn't open. Instead, a shout sounded from the square, and boots clattered on the cobbles. Raibley made a stirrup of his hands and heaved Daphne to the top of the wall.

Taken by surprise, Daphne lay flat atop the wall, clutching the stones, watching Raibley run into the shadow. Torchlight approached, and in its glow, a policeman swaggered, swinging his large head, peering into alleyways and slapping a whip against his boot. Gulping down fear, Daphne swiveled and hung her legs over the inside of the wall, feeling for a foothold among the stones. One step down, another, until her foot slipped and she fell, crashing onto the cobbles. She scrambled up and ran across the courtyard. A curse and clamor of boots rose from the street as Daphne flung herself down the stairs to the cellar door and grabbed the handle. Locked. No. Stuck. It groaned and turned as the policeman yelled and rattled the courtyard gate. Daphne pushed open the creaking cellar door and slipped within. She leaned back against the door, catching her breath and listening for a policeman with a whip slapping his boot as he strode across the courtyard.

But he must not have seen her. No footsteps approached. "Thank you, Raibley," Daphne whispered to the dank air.

Maybe she could hide all night in the cellar and find her way up to the kitchen in the first light of morning. But the cellar was clammy and smelled of mildew, and Daphne longed for the warmth of a bed. She felt her way forward, identifying by touch the wood grain of barrels and the yielding burlap of sacks of grain. Finally she banged her toes against something that proved to be, when she bent to feel it, a step.

She crept up the stairs on all fours until she felt a door in front of her. She paused to remove her boots. With a knot in her stomach, she pushed the door. The sisters must have missed her at dinner. They would be lying in wait for her, and she had no good story to tell them.

From the windows opening on the courtyard, the faintest

hint of moonlight slanted through the empty kitchen. Carrying her boots, Daphne made her way across the stone floor and through the refectory to the front hall. Nobody patrolled the hall. Daphne crept up the stairs, shivering as she remembered the drummer's pale, handsome face, the haunted look in his eyes as the workers fled, and that ugly gash along his neck. She was certain he was the boy Kit had told her about, the one who had been a singer until his voice was ruined in a botched throat operation. Scratchy and rough his voice might be, but he had held the workers mesmerized.

Third floor. Daphne turned down the hallway, took a right, and counted doors. She set her hand on the knob and hoped Lila wouldn't scream.

She half-expected a hand to fall on her shoulder, but instead Lila, ghostlike in a white nightgown, leaped from bed to embrace her. "You're back!"

Daphne asked, "How much trouble am I in?"

"You're not," Lila said, drawing her deeper into the room. "I told them at dinner you'd come home miserable with your hurt ankle and were asleep upstairs. Sister Glissanda said she'd go check on you, but Kit jumped up and said she'd do it. They wouldn't let me go along, so I thought you were done for. Then Kit came back and said you were sleeping soundly and didn't wake up even when she wrapped your ankle. So they sent her to take dinner upstairs to you. Careful, don't step on it. It's there on the floor by your bed." She bent down and handed Daphne a plate. "The food's all cold now," Lila said in apology, but

Daphne carried the plate to the window where she could see a roll and vegetables and slices of meat.

"I had a little porridge," she said, and thought of Ivan and Raibley in their cold cabin. "Lila, you're wonderful. You've saved me. And Kit! I wonder if she helps everyone break the rules."

Lila shook her head. "She says if a yellowkin likes you it means you're a good person."

A good person? Daphne thought about how sharp she'd been with Lila sometimes—Lila, who had no idea what was going on or what Lexicon really meant to Daphne and Ivan; Lila, who had that horrible mother to frighten away all her friends; Lila, who had covered for her tonight. Daphne set the plate beside her bed, changed quickly into her nightgown, and crawled under the covers. "Come on in next to me, Lila. I'll tell you what happened while I eat."

Between bites of cold meat and carrots, she told Lila about her visit to Ivan, about the poor part of town, and about the drumming and dancing. "It's funny," she said. "I never really noticed, but with all the focus on music here, nobody seems to just sing for fun, you know? But those villagers, dancing, they were really having fun."

"Only fun?" Lila said.

Daphne tried to quote the drummer's chant.

"He sounds like some kind of rapper," Lila said.

"Sort of," said Daphne. "And then police rose up out of nowhere and broke it all up. They beat up the drummer and arrested him."

Lila huddled with her knees held tight to her chest.

Daphne said, "Everyone ran away except Ivan, so they knocked him down and kicked him."

"No!"

"Yes. They were vicious. But I got Ivan home. And one other thing. They pulled away the drummer's mask, and Lila, he had a huge scar down the side his neck, just the way—"

"Fort," Lila said.

"What?"

"Fort. Allegra's brother. They kicked him out of school when his voice got wrecked in an operation."

"Kit told me about him."

"What did she tell you? Allegra said he got rebellious when he couldn't sing, and his father kicked him out of the family and sent him away."

Daphne said, "He doesn't look like Allegra. His hair was really dark."

"He's adopted." Lila shivered, and Daphne put an arm around her. Lila asked, "What will they do to him?"

"I don't know." Daphne shuddered, too, and squeezed Lila closer. "In the morning we'll figure it out, okay? Meanwhile we should rest, but since I'm too worked up to sleep, let me tell you the story of our first trip to Lexicon ..."

*   *   *

Allegra arrived late to school, and as soon as she walked into class, Lila saw from her smudged and swollen face that she'd been crying. Sister Gavotte, the chorus mistress, nodded to her to get in the second row behind Lila, but

Allegra's voice trembled and faltered on the high notes. Normally Sister Gavotte would scold someone who stumbled so badly, but this time she pressed her lips together and kept conducting.

At break, Lila took Allegra's hand and drew her over to the window. "Tell me," she said.

Allegra looked both ways and leaned close to Lila's ear. "Fort came back and he's been arrested. Nobody would have told me, but during the night my father was yelling at my mother as if it was her fault. I know I should cut Fort out of my heart, but I'm so scared for him, Lila."

"Where is he now?" Lila asked.

"In a cell under the courthouse. He'll have a trial day after tomorrow."

"Can he have visitors?" Lila asked.

"Oh, Lila, I couldn't! My father would kill me. He says our only hope is to let people forget we ever knew him."

Lila took a step back. Not go see her brother? Why, if Lila had a brother, she'd stick with him through fire and rain, through hurricanes and landslides. "I'll go see him," she said.

Allegra stood with her mouth open. "You? But he's *my* brother."

"You can come if you're brave enough," Lila said. Sister Gavotte called the chorus again, and Lila swept away from Allegra, like the heroine in a play.

In history class, Lila rushed through her written work and brought her paper to the desk to speak to Brother Legato.

"Please, I'm sorry to disturb you, but there's so much I don't know about how things work here."

He regarded her over his spectacles.

"I heard there was a drummer arrested last night. What happens to him now?"

"Sit down, Lila," he said in his slow way. "Gossip doesn't become you." But well before the end of class he went around collecting everybody's papers, and then he sat on the edge of his desk to address the pupils.

"Rumors are spreading in a way unworthy of this school about the young Dissonant who was arrested last night. You should know he is a cowardly agitator from outside who has stirred our workers with wild rhythms and animal-like grunting. We can all see the danger—it snowed again last night, and if the cold settles in for a long stay we'll have shortages of everything before summer."

A boy raised his hand. "But it snows every night."

Brother Legato looked at him in such long silence that the boy began to squirm in his seat. "All the more reason for concern. The line between civilization and savagery is a thin line of melody. This disturbance has been building for some time."

"What will happen to the prisoner?" someone asked.

"The penalty for treason is one of the four Grim Sanctions." Brother Legato enumerated them on his fingers. "Exile, slavery, deafness, or death. One way or another, he will be rendered harmless."

Allegra gasped, and Lila raised her hand. "Sir, don't we believe that music can tame even the wildest heart? What if a few of us went to see him, to sing to him? Maybe we could change him."

Brother Legato frowned. "Lila, you have a most unfortunate obsession with this miscreant. Now, class, you are dismissed."

*   *   *

At lunchtime, Daphne hobbled up to the infirmary to look for Kit. A small boy lay sleeping in the bed that had been Daphne's, and Kit sat on another bed, deep in conversation with Sister Glissanda. They both looked up as Daphne limped across the room. Kit's face was blotchy as if she'd been crying, and Daphne's heart sank.

Kit hauled herself up and came to meet Daphne. "Did you come for help with the bandage? I can see you made a mess of it during the night."

"Thank you," Daphne said, trying to put extra meaning into the words.

Sister Glissanda stood, wiped her hands on her apron, and watched as Daphne climbed onto the bed and let Kit unwrap her perfectly sound ankle.

"That prisoner," Daphne said, trying to wince at the right moments as Kit probed her ankle. "I heard he's ill."

Kit's hands trembled, and Sister Glissanda's eyelid twitched. Why, they were talking about him when I came in, Daphne thought. That's what was going on.

"Did you know the lad?" Sister Glissanda asked suddenly, and she made a jerky gesture with her arm, taking in everything outside of this room. "Out there, before you came here—did you know him?"

Daphne looked from one to the other of them and spoke with caution. "I saw him ... yesterday. He didn't seem so terrible. He seemed to ... care about people."

Kit nodded vigorously, her eyes fixed on Daphne's face.

Sister Glissanda clucked her tongue. "Misguided, that's all he is. We never had a finer boy. And that doctor, what had he been drinking that day? But Fort looks at everything through the glass of his own misfortune ... of course they don't feel hardship the way he does, the lower classes, because they were born to it. That's what he doesn't see."

Instead of disputing this, Daphne leaned forward. "Will you go see him, to check on his scar and treat him?"

Sister Glissanda bit her lip. "I suppose I might. And Kit, you might come with me."

"And me, too," Daphne said. "I'll carry your basket. Anything."

Sister Glissanda shook her head, but Daphne said, "I know there must be some way to help him." She jumped up from the bed, her fake injury forgotten.

Sister Glissanda gazed down at her ankle with eyebrows raised. Then she looked Daphne straight in the eye and nodded.

CHAPTER SIXTEEN

The Prisoner

Daphne tried to close her ears. "No. They're not going to let four of us visit."

"Please," Lila said. "That way I can tell Allegra I saw with my own eyes how he is."

She was acting like the old, annoying Lila, who wanted to tag along everywhere. Daphne formed her mouth to say "No" again, but then she took note of Lila's shining eyes, and remembered how her cousin had covered for her last night. "I guess we can try," she said.

At the infirmary they met Kit and Sister Glissanda, who were wrapped in two cloaks each as if contemplating a great journey. Sister Glissanda carried a basket on her arm, and Daphne wondered for a wild moment if it contained tools to help Fort escape.

"What, another?" Sister Glissanda asked, leaning down to look at Lila.

Daphne put an arm around Lila. "My cousin. You never know, Sister, beautiful singing might comfort him, and no one sings more sweetly."

"Humph. Cast of thousands," Sister Glissanda said, but she turned and walked down the corridor, and the girls filed after.

Down the stairs, across the entry hall, down the granite steps, and into the square they marched, Sister Glissanda with her basket, then Kit swallowed in her two cloaks, and finally Lila and Daphne with their hoods pulled up. They crossed the square and climbed the steps of the Hall of Justice and Inspection. Sister Glissanda led them into the building and straight to the front desk, where a meager man sat hiccupping and writing with a fine quill pen.

"Business?" he inquired.

"We have come to see the prisoner," Sister Glissanda said.

"No visitors, madam."

"Of course not. We are not visitors. We are singers."

"But—" he said. At that moment, double doors at the top of a short, wide stairway opened, and down the stairs tripped Allegra's father, Mr. Cantabile. His mustache sat cockeyed as if someone had twisted it, and his eyes and cheeks were red. His glance swept over them without settling.

"Squinch," Allegra's father said, "I need you to set up the signs."

"Yes, indeed, Inspector," the little man said.

"Not deafness," Mr. Cantabile said, his voice trembling. "Don't set up deafness. That I won't allow."

"No, sir. These visitors, sir."

"I am removing myself, Squinch. I know nothing of the order of the gates."

"No, sir. The visitors."

"You can attest, I in no way interfered."

"Of course not, sir. Can you advise me ..."

Mr. Cantabile threw back his head, pivoted, and disappeared through the outside door. Mr. Squinch threw up his hands, told Sister Glissanda, "Wait here," and climbed the steps to the double doors.

When he had gone, Sister Glissanda turned toward the others. "What's that he said? 'Right here?' It's so hard to understand him with all that hiccupping. He must have meant to go down these stairs over here, don't you agree?"

The four of them continued down two levels to where a guard sat with his legs thrust out. Before he could open his mouth, Sister Glissanda said, "We have a pass," with such authority that he pulled back his legs to let them through.

But at the bottom of the next stairway, from behind a locked gate, another guard, this one with thick brown whiskers, stood and said, "Your pass."

"We come as nurses to the prisoner," Sister Glissanda said with dignity.

"Your pass." He stuck his hand through the bars and gave it an impatient shake.

Acting on a hunch, Daphne pulled a half-finished homework paper from her pocket and handed it to him. He frowned at the close-written words, turning the paper this way and that. "Where's the signature?" he demanded.

Daphne grabbed the paper from his hand and turned her back to him, blocking his view of Lila. "Lila, where's the signature?" she asked, trying to keep panic out of her voice. Lila stared, then reached in her pocket, pulled out a pencil, and drew a treble clef with a couple of sharps and a three on top of a four. She took the paper from Daphne's hand. "Are you both blind?" she said, shaking the paper in the guard's face. "Here it is, a key signature to let us in. And a time signature, too, see? Right here, for three-quarters of an hour."

The guard studied the paper, his chin thrust out, and then he nodded and opened the gate. Empty cells, with bars stretched floor to ceiling, lined the corridor. "Down that way," the guard said, pointing.

"We'll need a key to get in and examine him," Lila said in a sweet voice.

The guard glared at her, and although she fluttered her eyelashes at him, he shook his head. "Examine him through the bars."

They proceeded down the corridor, Sister Glissanda marching straight forward with her eyebrows high, Kit casting looks of admiration at the two cousins.

The young man sat on a bench at the side of the cell, his head in his hands. His dark hair fell forward, concealing his face. His scarlet cloak was gone, and he was clad all in black.

"Fort," Sister Glissanda said.

The young man's head jerked up, revealing dark eyes and dark eyebrows, a hawk-like nose and the beginnings of a beard. As he got to his feet, he shook his hair away from his face, uncovering the scar that twisted like an angry snake down the side of his neck.

"Kit, Sister, it was good of you to come," the young man said in his grating voice. His glance moved over the other two, and rested, questioning, on Daphne.

"Two of our newest students," said Sister Glissanda. "Daphne and Lila."

"Oh, Fort, why did you come back?" Kit asked. She clutched the bars of his cell, her hands almost touching his.

Daphne thought, Oh, I see. Poor Raibley doesn't stand a chance.

Kit gave the bars a shake. "You said you were leaving for good."

Fort's teeth flashed in a smile. "Well, it was for the good I left. I learned a lot out there. And now I thought it would be for the good to come back and stir things up."

"But the risk," Kit said.

He shrugged. "I thought if I stayed outside town limits, and didn't keep anyone from work, I might be allowed to entertain the poor."

"Entertain?" Daphne said. "It was more than that." She was angry with him—angry that he seemed to focus only on Kit, angry to see him shrug at what he had done out there beyond the fields.

"Yes, it's more," he said. He studied Daphne. "What

happened to that boy? The one who came to help me, and got hurt."

Daphne felt Sister Glissanda's sharp gaze and winced. She'd given herself away. First forgetting her injured ankle, now this revelation that she'd been out with that rough, physical type. Some spy she'd make. "He's okay," she said.

Fort spoke again, as if Ivan's sacrifice meant Daphne deserved a full answer. "I wanted to inspire the workers, challenge them, make them question. Give them hope. They're not beasts, just because they can't sing. You, Kit, you know how some of the students treat you. Beautiful singing voices don't guarantee goodness."

Kit hunched her shoulders and looked at the floor. "You shouldn't say such things."

She's like Raibley, Daphne thought. She believes in this system. She asked, "What happens now?"

Fort shrugged again and gazed toward the ceiling. "The gates. I get to choose at random—banishment, slavery, deafness, or death."

"Not deafness," Lila said. "Your father was upstairs, and he said not deafness." They all turned to look at her, and she added, "I know your sister. She, um, couldn't come, but she sends her love."

Fort barked out a laugh. "So, my sister stays away, and my dear not-real father will let his fellow Inspectors kill me or send me into slavery, but not deafen me." He bent forward and shaded his face with his hands. "The funny thing is, he's right. To be exiled from sound—that would break my heart."

Before Daphne could ask about the gates, the guard came striding down the hallway. "You said you was here for an examination," he said. "Not for plain old chattering. We don't allow visitors."

"Of course not," Sister Glissanda said. "Fort, come close and tip your head so I can see that scar."

Fort glowered but obeyed. He stepped close to the bars, knelt down, put his head back, and leaned toward Sister Glissanda.

Lila let out a soft moan. "Oh, I can't look," she said. "I feel faint. Someone let me out of here."

Fort's mouth twisted in a grimace, and the other three visitors shot Lila looks of disapproval. Lila grasped the guard's sleeve. "Please. I'll wait upstairs."

His face softened. He led her to the end of the hallway and opened the gate for her.

She was so eager to come, Daphne thought. Who'd have thought she'd be so squeamish? But at least she got that guard out of our hair.

*   *   *

Lila scampered up the stairs to the front hall. "Set up the signs," Allegra's father had said. What if they were signs for the gates Fort had to choose from? What if there was some way of knowing which gate he should choose?

Little Mr. Squinch was back at his desk, scribbling with his head down. Lila tried to tiptoe past, but he lifted his head and demanded, "Where are you going now?"

"To see the signs," she blurted. As he rose from behind

the desk to stop her, she added, "I hope you didn't put up a sign for deafness."

"Of course not!"

"Inspector Cantabile asked me to check," Lila said.

"What?" He turned around, as if trying to see where the inspector and Lila could have met. "He's never questioned me before."

She lowered her head, looked both ways, and leaned close to him. "The Inspector's not himself. His only son, you know." She shook her head in sympathy. "Such a shame, such a shame."

"His *adopted* son," the clerk corrected. "The Inspector indulges that soft-hearted wife of his. Many's the time I warned him. 'Blood will tell,' I told him. 'Blood will tell.'" Shaking his head as Lila had, he let her pass.

Lila tripped up to the double doors through which Allegra's father had come. Inside, the room resembled a theater, with long semicircular rows of chairs looking down on a stage. A simple wooden chair, its back to the audience, stood stage front, facing a long table and five chairs at the back. The prisoner's place and the judges', no doubt. Ranked between them stood three easels. Each was painted like a gate, and each gate had a paper sign pasted to it. How could she be so lucky? Lila hurried down the aisle and stepped close enough to see. Her excitement fizzled. The lettering of the signs made no sense—unless they were clues or were hiding something.

Lila climbed onto the stage to look behind the easels, and to lift the paper signs and peer under them, but there were no other labels on the gates. She hurried to search the judges' table, but it had no drawers and nothing on top but a pile of blank paper and a pencil with bite marks all around it.

The only possible clues were the paper signs. Maybe Daphne could make something of them. Lila grabbed the chewed-on pencil and copied the letters down as fast and as carefully as she could. Her hands shook, and the letters came out wobbly. She folded the sheet of paper and stuffed it up her sleeve, then ran for the door before someone found her spying.

She exited the courtroom and paused outside its doors, gazing down on Mr. Squinch just as Sister Glissanda, Daphne, and Kit emerged up the other stairway from the jail below. Sister Glissanda gaped at Lila. At his desk Mr. Squinch turned his head back and forth between the two parties.

Lila flew down the stairs and approached the desk. "Fine job, just right. I'll make sure to tell him." She leaned close so only he could hear. "I dusted the judges' table and swept up that pile of mud under the chair. I won't mention anything if you don't."

Mr. Squinch gave a little shudder and pushed back from the desk, looking stunned. Lila nodded pleasantly at him, twirled, caught hold of Daphne's arm, and pulled the visiting party out the door.

*   *   *

Once they were down the steps, Sister Glissanda swung around to face Lila and Daphne. "The two of you, with your limping and your key signatures and your fainting! What did you take from that room?"

Lila lifted her hands. "I'm not a thief, Sister."

Sister Glissanda, her lips pulled into a frown, examined Lila's hands and made her turn her pockets inside out before she pulled away, apparently satisfied. "What did you see in there?'

"Three gates. They had signs on them that didn't make sense."

"What did the signs say?"

Lila screwed up her face, then let her shoulders drop and shook her head. "Sorry, Sister, I can remember tunes, but not writing."

Daphne, who had caught her breath, let it out in a rush and turned away.

Sister Glissanda studied Lila and then turned away. "You know the penalty for spying, I suppose. I'd hate to see another fine voice go to waste." There was a sound like disappointment in her voice as she said, "From now on, no more snooping, do you hear?"

* * *

Lila took hold of Allegra's hand at the end of evening chorus, and as the students filed out of the Great Hall, Allegra bent her head to listen. "I saw Fort, and he's okay," Lila said. "But you have to find out from your father how the trial works. If Fort needs witnesses, I know Daphne would speak up for him."

Allegra jerked her head up as if the idea startled her. "Speak up for him? What good would that do?"

Lila stopped short, and the exiting class parted to pass around them. "Look, are you ready to just give up on your brother? Because that's what it sounds like."

Allegra reddened. "My father says ..."

"Did you ever think maybe your father is wrong about this?"

As she spoke, Lila heard an echo in her head. It was Aunt Adelaide, when Lila announced that her mother was taking her to New York to launch her career. Aunt Adelaide had held her arms, looked her in the eye, and asked, "Did you ever think maybe your mother is wrong about this?"

Lila remembered twisting away, angry with her great aunt for trying to plant doubt. What did she mean, wrong? Lila's mother was so sure, so excited for Lila. Besides, what could Lila do? She was only ten at the time.

Allegra turned her head away. "My father's an Inspector," she said, as if that explained everything.

Lila waited.

"I'll find out how the trial works," Allegra said.

CHAPTER SEVENTEEN

Three Gates

Lila set the candle on the windowsill and waited for Daphne to change into her nightgown. Daphne had been quiet all evening, and Lila knew she was thinking about Fort. Now, as Daphne climbed into bed, Lila pulled out the piece of paper she had kept up her sleeve. "Do you want to see what it says on the gates, Daphne?"

Daphne whipped her head around and stared. "You know what it says? Lila! Why didn't you tell me?"

"It's just letters," Lila said. "It's hard to figure out what it means."

They knelt on the floor, smoothing the sheet of paper on the stone between them. Lila had drawn a sketch of the three gates.

I.	S	II.	B or E	III.	B or S

"It looks like one of those logic problems," Daphne said. "You know, where they tell you what's behind the door." She furrowed her brow. "Unless there's a trick. Did you look behind the gates, Lila?"

"There was nothing back there. And I looked around for a translation but I couldn't find anything."

"All right. So, let's see, he's choosing between death, exile, or slavery. Then E is exile. S is slavery. But what's B?"

"E could be execution," Lila said.

"Or enslavement. Rats, we're nowhere."

Lila thought. "B could be beatings, S could be sent away."

"Banishment!" Daphne said. "Not exile, Banishment. S is still slavery, of course."

"And E is execution, as I said," Lila pointed out.

Daphne looked at the drawing again. "Why, this is easy! He wants banishment. Gate I is slavery, he doesn't want that. Gate III is either slavery or banishment, but we already have slavery, so it must be banishment."

"So Gate II is execution," Lila said.

Daphne glared at her. "Do you have to keep repeating 'execution' in that happy voice?"

"But I am happy," Lila said. "You figured it out."

"But it's so easy. How could they make it so easy?"

"Maybe ... maybe his father is protecting him. Or maybe ... when you're standing there in court it's not so easy to do logic."

Daphne considered. "I guess. So we just have to send him a note telling him to choose Gate III."

"Yes!" Lila pulled Daphne into a dance. "We've done it. We've saved Allegra's brother."

Daphne pulled away. "Let's get to sleep, Lila."

"Daphne," Lila began, but Daphne shook her head and climbed into bed.

Lila folded the paper and blew out the candle. Why was Daphne being so cold again? Lila got into bed, snuggled under the covers, and turned to say good night. But her cousin was staring at the ceiling, her eyes wide open, and it looked as if she was still thinking hard.

*   *   *

Allegra caught Lila's sleeve at the classroom door, and they let the other students file down to lunch without them. "I asked my father, Lila. He didn't like telling me. I told him I'd been chosen for an oral report in history. I told him I thought they were singling me out because they suspected me of having sympathy for the victim." Allegra half-swallowed the last words, looking down at her feet, her face splotched with red. She would be a terrible actress, Lila thought. On the other hand, looking troubled and ashamed like this fit the part she had played for her father perfectly well.

"And?" Lila asked.

"There are no witnesses or anything like that. The judges just read out the charges and tell him the goddess will help him choose his punishment. They usually set up four gates, but Fort will only have three. My father begged the judges not to let the shame of deafness touch our house, and they granted him that. There's a different punishment behind each gate. They put clues on the front of the gates to help the prisoner choose. The only thing is ..." Her lower lip trembled. "... Not everything the clues say is true."

"Not true!" Lila felt a shock run through her body.

"Some of them might be true. Just when the prisoner's about to make his choice, they tell him how many are true and how many are false. My father says doing that weeds out the ones who are just clever. It throws them off balance, and then only the goddess can save them. It's up to her."

Lila bounced on her toes. She had to intercept Daphne before her cousin sent a message to Fort. "How many clues will be true this time?" she asked.

Allegra shook her head. "My father doesn't know. No one will know until the last moment. And ... he ordered me to sit beside him at the trial. He made me promise not to cry—I have to look stern and unmoved the whole time. He says it's the only way to convince everyone I'm completely pure and free of bad influence. Lila, how can I do that?" Her voice shook, and she gulped twice.

"You'll do it for your brother," Lila said. "You were brave enough to ask your father, and you'll be brave enough for this. One way or another, by the way you look at Fort you'll show him you still love him. You will, Allegra."

Allegra used the ends of her red hair to wipe her eyes. She nodded.

"I'm going to the kitchen," Lila said. "Tell them ... tell them I went to complain about a fly in my porridge this morning." She grabbed a few sheets of paper from her desk and made for the exit before the teacher arrived.

*   *   *

Lila knocked on the door of the third grade classroom and pushed open the door. Some of the children stopped singing, but others kept on in wavering voices as Brother Largo turned with slow menace, his baton still waving vaguely in the direction of his chorus.

"Please, sir," Lila said in a loud whisper. "Daphne's needed to help in the infirmary."

Brother Largo scowled and waved Daphne out without a word.

Lila drew her into the hallway. "Daphne, you were right, there is a trick."

Daphne looked swiftly up and down the hallway. "What kind of trick?"

"At the last minute, they tell the prisoner how many of the signs are true. They could all be false."

Daphne groaned. "No way. What makes you think that?"

"Allegra's father told her, and he's an Inspector."

"This is terrible. I can't do this. Logic isn't my thing. We need Ivan."

"We don't have time. The trial's tomorrow. Besides, I'm sure you're smarter than Ivan anyway."

Daphne looked at her, and then suddenly pulled her into an empty practice room. The two of them knelt on the floor with Lila's sheet of paper between them. Lila drew the three gates and their labels at the top of the paper.

I. Slavery	II. Banishment or Execution	III. Banishment or Slavery

"Okay," Daphne said. "Let's say they're all lies. Then Gate I is not Slavery, and Gate II is not Banishment or Execution, so it's Slavery. And Gate III is not Banishment or Slavery, so it's Execution. So we already have Execution and Slavery, which means Gate I has to be Banishment." She looked at Lila, her eyebrows raised.

False: Slavery	False: Banishment or Execution	False: Banishment or Slavery
Not slavery or Execution. Must be Banishment	Slavery	Execution

"Too easy," Lila said. "They won't give him that one."

Daphne's face fell. "You're right. Okay, so say one of the signs is a lie. But we don't know which one. Say it's Gate I, then Gate I is really either Banishment or Execution, the same as Gate II, which means Gate III has to be Slavery." She chewed on the inside of her cheek. "But that doesn't help with Gates I and II. I'm worried."

"He'd have to guess," Lila said. "Would they do that?"

Daphne shook her head. She wasn't sure of anything. "Let's say it's Gate II that's the lie. That means it's not really ... wait ... I'm losing track."

"We have lots of paper. We could write down the possibilities to keep track."

"How?" Daphne asked.

Lila drew a neat grid of lines across the paper. Daphne bent close, and the two girls argued, wrapped their fingers in their hair, moved some lines, and tried some labels. When they finished, their paper looked like this:

What the gates say	I. Slavery	II. Banishment or Execution	III. Banishment or Slavery
If all are true	Slavery	Execution	Banishment
If two gates are true	True (S)	True (B or E)	False (not B or S)
	Slavery	?	?
	True (S)	False (not B or E)	True (B or S)
	?	?	?
	False (not S)	True (B or E)	True (B or S)
	?	?	?
If only one is true	True (S)	False (not B or E)	False (not B or S)
	?	?	?
	False (not S)	True (B or E)	False (not B or S)
	?	?	?
	False (not S)	False (not B or E)	True (B or S)
	?	?	?
If all are false	False (not S)	False (not B or E)	False (not B or S)
	Banishment	Slavery	Execution

Daphne talked her way through the possibilities, and Lila marked the page. When a certain possibility yielded a result that didn't make sense—two gates leading to the same fate, or an answer impossible to decide, they discarded it.

In the end, Daphne lifted her head. "This might be okay after all, Lila. For each number of gates that are telling the truth, there's only one answer that makes sense."

"But it's a different answer for each number of gates— no, All True is the same as Two False." Lila shuddered. If Fort made the wrong choice, he could die.

"I bet they're going to use One False," Daphne said. "But we have to give him all the possibilities, so he can memorize them."

"How will we get the message to him?"

"Kit will do it," Daphne said. "I think she'd do it even if it meant knifing the guard in the heart."

"Really?" Lila rocked back on her heels. "Would she use a big kitchen knife, do you think?"

"I was exaggerating," Daphne said. "Write down the answers."

Very carefully, checking their page and speaking aloud as she did so, Lila wrote in neat round letters,

If all the gates are True, choose Gate III.
If one is False, choose Gate II.
If two are False, choose Gate III.
If all are False, choose Gate I.

Daphne moved her lips, silently repeating the conclusions. At last she nodded. "I'm sure we've done it right. I'll get these to Kit and she can go check his wound. I just hope he trusts us."

"I hope he can learn it," Lila said. "It looks so complicated. What if he messes up?"

"He'll learn it," Daphne said. "If he wants to stay alive, he'll learn it." But she wasn't sure. What if Fort froze at his trial and his memory didn't work? What if he decided to rely on instinct or the goddess instead of logic? Worst of all, what if the judges changed the signs or lied to Fort about how many were true or false? Her stomach spun itself tight as she folded Lila's paper into a small rectangle and hid it in the palm of her hand. She pushed Lila into the hallway and headed down to the kitchen to look for Kit.

CHAPTER EIGHTEEN

The Trial

"I'm to go to the trial," Sister Glissanda told Daphne, looking down at her hands. "As one who was responsible for his care, I'm to learn from what he's become, so I won't make the same mistakes again."

"Mistakes!" Daphne said. "In that case, I hope Dr. Fugue will be there."

Sister Glissanda shook her head. "He didn't spend much time with Fort."

"He botched his operation, though."

Sister Glissanda looked shocked. "You mustn't say such things."

"You said he'd been drinking."

The corners of Sister Glissanda's mouth turned down. "I'd like a companion."

Daphne's stomach felt as if a fish was flopping inside it. "I'll come with you."

*　　*　　*

Sister Glissanda and Daphne sat on the stage itself, along one side, among members of the school. Opposite them, against the far wall and beside her father, sat Allegra, her face pinched and white. The three gates, each covered by a sheet, stood before the judges' table.

Daphne waited with her hands folded in her lap. Kit had delivered the note. Everything would be all right. She sat trying to look calm and meek as the courtroom filled with onlookers. Tall ladies with hats and fur-lined cloaks sat in front, resting gloved hands on the arms of red-faced gentlemen with mustaches. Craning their necks to see over them sat the tradespeople of the town in colored cloaks and earmuffs. At the rear of the room, a few bearded men in broken-down boots filed into the back seats, followed by women in worn dresses hushing children with newly scrubbed faces. Daphne tried to see if she could recognize any dancers, but these people looked too weary and timid ever to dance.

In filed the judges, four pompous-looking men whose bellies made a swelling in their long, black robes. Two of them, clearly blind, sat with tilted heads, their eyes closed. Amid the four seated judges stood an empty chair, which, Daphne guessed, Allegra's father usually occupied.

A jail officer escorted Fort, who was chained at the ankles and wrists, through the crowd. Fort held his head high, and above the scarf that hid his neck, black stubble lined his chin. He shuffled and rattled his way down the center aisle and up three steps to the table that faced the judges. There, the guard shoved him into his chair and took a station beside him. Daphne shifted her chair for a better view of him, and the teacher next to her gave her a brief smile.

One of the judges stood and cleared his throat. "Stand and hear the charges against you.

"You returned to this town from which you had been banished. You stirred the lower classes with Dissonant sounds and filled their heads with Dissonant ideas. You plotted to upend the order of this town. For these crimes, we charge you with treason. What say you?"

Fort shook his hair out of his eyes and spoke in his grating voice. "I did not enter this town. I stayed outside it. Your guards dragged me here. I brought the people a form of music—rhythm—which all of them can understand. I let them enjoy themselves as night fell after their weary days."

He closed his mouth, and for a moment no one said anything. Then the prosecuting judge spoke again. "And what of your plot to overthrow us?"

Fort hesitated. "I came with no specific plan to overthrow anyone."

"Aha!" The judge slammed his hands down on the table. "A general plan! He admits it! And now that you have confessed, young man, do you beg forgiveness?"

Fort tipped his head back. "I beg the goddess to forgive you for your arrogance, your ignorance, and your oppression of the poor!"

The audience murmured, and perhaps to frighten them, the guard beside Fort reached and dragged the scarf from his neck, revealing the jagged scar, which seemed to shout out anger and bitterness. Daphne felt the audience on the side that could see the scar draw in its breath.

The prosecuting judge clenched his jaw. He stood rigid until the judges on either side of him pulled him down, and the four of them consulted in low tones. The audience stayed silent.

After a minute the youngest-looking judge went to a door at the back of the room—a closet, apparently—and pulled out a fourth gate, this one, too, covered by a sheet. Daphne's chest hurt. At a signal, the guard dragged Fort around to face the audience while the young judge placed the new gate among the others.

The guard turned Fort back to face the judges. The prosecuting judge rubbed his nose and said, "Your father requested that you be spared the possibility of deafness. But your defiance is so absolute, your depravity so evident, that we regret to say we think it a highly suitable punishment. Nevertheless, it is not up to us, but to the goddess, to decide."

Daphne's heart thumped loudly as she did her best to shut the judge's voice out of her mind. If only she could see through the sheet on this new gate! Then at least she could start thinking. But what use would it be anyway? The new gate would change everything. She needed quiet, pencil and paper, and time to figure. Fort would just have to pray and guess after all. Chance was all he had left. She saw the whites of Fort's eyes, the sweat starting out on his forehead.

The judge had finished explaining the rules. Now his younger colleague undraped the gates. Yes, they said what Lila had told her, only written out in words this time, and with the new gate inserted into the third place among them.

I.   Behind this gate lies Slavery.
II. Behind this gate lies Banishment or Execution.
III. Behind this gate lies neither Execution nor Deafness.
IV. Behind this gate lies Banishment or Slavery.

The prosecuting judge said, "You have two minutes to pray for guidance. Oh, and I must tell you, three of those statements are untrue."

Fort stared at the gates, his lips moving in silence.

He's trying, Daphne thought. He's not giving up, and neither should I.

What if the only true one were Gate I? That would be easiest, because then that would be Slavery. So Gate IV would have to be Banishment. No, no, Gate IV would be false. It could be Deafness or Execution. II would be Slavery or Deafness—Deafness, obviously, because Slavery was taken. So Fort should choose III. But III couldn't be Banishment, because III was a lie.

Unless she had mixed herself up somehow.

Daphne felt like sobbing. How much time had passed? She couldn't keep track, and she didn't have time to try them all. A roaring sounded in her ears, and she thought of Fort condemned to deafness.

Deafness. Wait.

The third gate was Deafness. It had to be. That was the new gate, the one they put in when they added Deafness.

So that meant ...

It meant Gate III was false, and with three false in all, so were two of the other gates. She racked her brain, trying to remember what she had written down for Fort to memorize.

If two gates are False, choose III. But the old Gate III was now Gate IV.

She had no time to check her answer. She looked over at Fort, willing him to see it. His face was white, his mouth moving as fast as ever.

"Two minutes are up," said the youngest judge.

The clamor in Daphne's ears grew louder. She could be wrong. She could be wrong about Deafness being behind the third gate. The judges might have planned it ahead of time after all.

Fort swallowed. His manacled hands pressed the table in front of him. He opened his mouth, and no words came.

Daphne rose from her chair. All eyes turned to her, and she wavered. There was no way to tell him. Unless ... she could try Lila's trick. She swiveled toward Sister Glissanda, moaned, "I feel so ill," staggered backward toward the prisoner's chair, and collapsed in a faint. She threw one arm over her head as she fell, and she raised four fingers on that hand as it hit the floor not far from Fort's feet.

Hubbub sounded in the courtroom. The guard peeled Daphne from the floor, and she clung to him, letting her knees wobble. Over the guard's shoulder she glimpsed Fort's face, pale and set. Had he seen, had he understood? Sister

Glissanda helped lower her into her chair and pushed her head down between her knees.

"Prisoner?"

Daphne held her breath.

Then came Fort's voice, rasping but steady. "The goddess bids me to choose Gate Four."

The goddess! Daphne thought giddily. That makes me a goddess with my head between my knees. Except I'm so nervous I really do feel sick. What does this silence mean? She licked dry lips.

The prosecuting judge said, in a stiff voice, "You have chosen Banishment."

A collective sigh rose from the audience. Maybe they hadn't wanted a more terrible punishment, after all, for this young man who had once played with their children.

There came a sound of whispered consultation among the judges, and the same voice spoke again. "You chose Banishment, but you have rebelled against banishment before. This time we banish you to the mines, and to make sure you go where you are told, we send you as a prisoner in chains."

"But that's slavery!" Fort cried. Daphne lifted her head. Fort stood, his eyes wild, straining to pull his hands free of his chains. "That's no different from slavery!"

The judge placed his hands on the table before him and leaned forward with a smile. "Just so."

The guard wound Fort's scarf twice around his neck, yanked it tight, and led him from the courtroom.

CHAPTER NINETEEN

Return of Varoq

Ivan swung out of bed, thrust his feet into his boots, and stomped over to give the coals in the fireplace a kick. No good—the fire had long since burned out. He wrapped a blanket around his shoulders, pulled bread and cheese from the shelf, and carved hunks of them onto two plates. Today he felt well enough to work for the first time since his beating. And today Raibley would bring news of the drummer's trial. Yesterday rumors had flown around the workers' quarter: the drummer had begged for mercy, he had knifed a judge, he had been executed on the spot, he had been set free.

The door opened, and Raibley kicked the mud from his boots before he came in from his morning deliveries. He didn't meet Ivan's eye as he handed over a folded letter.

"What's wrong?" Ivan asked. "What happened at the trial?"

"No one would say."

Ivan unfolded the letter and read aloud:

Ivan,

I helped our friend. I can't say more. In the end he chose the gate for banishment but they cheated him anyway, and he goes to the silver mines in the next load, maybe even this afternoon. I hear it's backbreaking work and most people don't come back. I wish I could remember the words he chanted.

I had to spend last night in the infirmary for "fainting" at the trial yesterday. I'm not allowed to go field singing today.

Daphne

Raibley let out his breath in a spray. "But that's not right! Once the goddess picks, folk should obey. Even judges should obey."

"I agree," said Ivan. He turned Daphne's letter over to write on the back, trying to remember the words Fort had chanted.

Who has to dance when the sun goes down?
Who huddles in mud while the children moan?
Why have they stolen your music?
...
And the houses of stone come tumbling down.

Most of the lines were missing, but he could ask around and see what some of the other workers remembered. It was the only thing he could think of to do, and somehow it seemed important. Ivan folded the paper and stuffed it in his shirt pocket with Daphne's other letters.

* * *

Lila held hands with Allegra as they hurried along the path that led around the western edge of Capella to the fields that needed warming. Allegra's eyes were red, and she sang in a wavering voice. Lila sang steadily, to cover for her friend, but she felt like singing off-key and ruining the song. That handsome Fort, cheated of his freedom, after all she and Daphne had done! It would serve the Inspectors right if the whole school went on strike and refused to sing until he was freed. Lila had tried to talk to some of the girls at breakfast, but their looks of horror had convinced her they would never do it. They believed what their teachers told them, that Fort was a dangerous Dissonant and traitor.

Up ahead, girls from the second class screamed and fell back toward Lila's group. Allegra clung to Lila, who stretched to see what had frightened the girls. One girl fell in the snow and lifted her face, crying in terror. Lila heard a growl. Around a hillock, shambling after the fleeing children, came a huge, sand-colored bear.

Lila unlatched Allegra's hand from her arm and stepped forward to shield the other girls. "Varoq, shame on you," she scolded. "This is no way to behave."

Varoq stopped with a grunt and swung his head back and

198

forth, sniffing. "You know me," Lila said. "And I'm telling you to stop."

Out from behind the bear came Ezengi and Kanzat, one on each side. Kanzat spread his arms wide. "Ah, little singer," he said. "The very one we inspected to find. She displays her curvage, she faces our brother bear and feels no flight."

Up from the back of the line of singers came Brother Dorian, the rotund accounting brother who stood little taller than Lila. He trembled as he said, "For shame, to bring your wild beast here, so close to the walls, to frighten our children."

Kanzat shook his head, looking aggrieved. "It is not my wish to terrorate children. But we have a letter, a missile, straight from the Palace, and it conserves one of your girls, Brother, that one right there." He pointed at Lila.

Lila stepped back and felt for Allegra's hand. Kanzat said, "Our errand is urchin. We dare not ignore it. My bear master, Ezengi, will calm the chief of bears as you recompany me and the child straight to the people who run your school."

* * *

Ivan leaned on his hoe and stretched his back. It was good to be working in a field already cleared, with warm ground underfoot. He could actually smell the earth, and not just the clean, blank smell of snow. All around him workers bent over, hoeing weeds away from thin, green blades of grain.

From time to time Ivan passed among them and asked them to help him remember lines from Fort's chant.

From the northwest, down the path the school singers followed, poured a rush of schoolchildren. The farm workers turned together as a gaggle of schoolgirls in blue uniforms hurtled toward them along the path, and a girl with flame-red hair ran into the middle of the field and asked loudly, "Which one is Ivan?"

Ivan passed his hoe to the man working next to him and stepped forward. "I'm Ivan."

"It's Lila," the red-haired girl said. "Two men came with a bear, and everyone screamed and ran, but Lila stood up to them and scolded the bear." The girl shuddered. "They told Brother Dorian they had a letter about her, and the four of them went back to school. Lila said to find you and tell you."

Ivan looked around. Girls spread over the fields, squealing and exclaiming, as their teachers tried to rank them in singing order.

Ivan thanked the red-haired girl. She began to cry and said, "I'd do anything for Lila. She tried to save my brother."

Without stopping to comfort her, Ivan pulled away. He found Raibley directing field workers to take pitchforks and stand guard along the edge of the field, in case the bear came. Ivan pulled him aside. "The girls are in trouble. I have to go find out what's happening."

Raibley shook his head. "No. Keep your head down. Do your work. The police are looking for troublemakers.

There's too many folks nervous, too much talk of spies and treason keeping winter so long."

"I have to go," Ivan said. "I'll be back when I can, but if I disappear, you don't know anything."

Raibley bent his head in assent.

Ten minutes later, Ivan entered the leaf courtyard and crept down the steps to the cellar door. It creaked open. He made his way through a space smelling of cider and onions and crept up the stairs toward the kitchen. At the top of the stairs he paused and listened until, hearing a light footstep he hoped was Kit's, he opened the door.

Kit jumped back, putting a hand over her mouth to stifle her cry of surprise.

He put a finger to his lips. "Kit, what's happening to Lila? I heard the nomad traders are back and talking about some letter."

Kit stood frozen. Her eyes, like Allegra's, were red from crying. It seemed a day of general disaster. Kit pulled Ivan into the middle of the kitchen, opened a closet door, and handed him a broom.

"Here, take this," she said. "Put up the hood of your cloak, and wear it low over your eyes." She adjusted his cloak and led him to the kitchen door. "They're in the refectory. Keep your head low and keep sweeping. No one takes notice of servants."

Grasping his broom and peering out from under his hood, Ivan shuffled into the refectory. There at the end of the room stood Kanzat, hands on hips, broad and boastful in his furs. Melting snow puddled around his boots. Facing him stood Mother Cadenza, unrolling a scroll he had obviously handed her. Lila stood close against Mother Cadenza's skirts, and in the background, Daphne waited, squeezing her hands together. Only Daphne looked up at Ivan; she drew her head back in surprise, and he lowered his head and fell to sweeping.

"And you say this is from the Palace?" Mother Cadenza asked.

"Undoubtfully." Kanzat jabbed a finger at the scroll. "The Diva's seal. I can't read, madam, but I know that seal. One of her courtiers, the Lord High Chamberpot or whoever, gave me this and disclaimed it most urchin to deliver."

Mother Cadenza furrowed her brow and studied the document.

"It discerns the little singer," Kanzat said helpfully.

Mother Cadenza frowned, read on, rolled up the document, and placed it in a pocket of her gown. She examined Kanzat's face. "How did they know she was with me?"

Kanzat spread his arms. "Such a rare find in the forest. Who wouldn't spread the tale of her rescue? Word got to the Palace."

"And how do I know this isn't a forgery?"

"A forgery, madam?" Kanzat's voice was all injured innocence. "From a man who can neither read nor scribe? Tell me what the missile says."

"It says," Mother Cadenza said, turning to look down at Lila, "that this young child is the runaway goddaughter of the Diva and must be returned at once."

Ivan swept furiously, coming closer to the group. Lila drew back from Mother Cadenza, her mouth an O until she said, "But I've never even met the Diva."

"Of course you have, a singer like you. Tell me, why did you run away? Is the new Composer so fearsome as that?"

Lila shook her head, and Mother Cadenza put an arm around her. "Dear girl, the pressure of living in the Palace must sometimes be great indeed. But each of us in this great land has a role to play. You have no more right to refuse your place of honor than that working boy who brought you here has a right to crawl into our school."

Ivan jumped and swept backward, but apparently Mother Cadenza was speaking generally and hadn't noticed him. Daphne, meanwhile, stepped forward and said, "But Mother Cadenza, we really don't know the Diva. We came here from across the mountains. We're strangers here, and the nomads captured us to sell to you. Now they want to take Lila and sell her again."

Mother Cadenza turned on her. "Indeed? What of this letter then, with Her Highness's own seal, brought to me by an illiterate man? People across the mountains do not sing like this child. At least now I know where she got her training and her voice."

Daphne looked across at Ivan, eyes wide with distress. He lifted his shoulders and shook his head. He had no idea what to do. If he spoke, he'd be the one accused of kidnapping. Daphne bit her lip, then shook herself and addressed Mother Cadenza again. "Lila will need a servant for the long journey. Let me go with her."

Mother Cadenza peered at her. "You who stole her the first time?"

"But she didn't!" Lila broke in. "She helped me when I was lost, even though she was sick. I need her, Mother Cadenza."

Mother Cadenza frowned again. "All maidservants in the Palace must be deaf and dumb, as everybody knows."

Daphne said, "Let me go with her as far as the Palace, and then I'll come back or find a job. Just let me go that far."

Mother Cadenza studied her. "Yes, go. Keep her warm. I won't have it said we neglected her. It's best we put all this behind us. And that boy. I'll tell Raibley that boy must be ejected."

"Rejected, yes, that's it," Kanzat said with satisfaction. "Seized and boxed and rejected out into the snow."

Head low, Ivan swept backward as fast as he could until he backed through the door to the kitchen. Kit stood there, her hands twisting her apron. Ivan pulled her closer to the broom closet. "The nomad chief, that liar, that Kanzat, he says he'll take her to the capital—" he began, but footsteps at the door interrupted him. Kit opened the closet and stuffed him inside as the kitchen door opened.

Daphne's voice blurted, "Oh, Kit, I need to speak to Ivan."

Pushing back his hood, Ivan opened the closet door. Daphne said, "What are we going to do? They gave us two hours to pack and go. I couldn't let her go alone, Ivan. I couldn't."

"Of course not." Ivan fumbled in his pocket, pulling out

a sheaf of Daphne's letters. "Daphne, I meant to give you this. It's the words to the drummer's chant." He handed it to her. "And here's the map you sent me." Daphne shook her head as if she didn't know what he was talking about, but he pressed on. "The capital, Melodia, it's back the way we came, but farther west and south. It might be a little warmer there, and it won't be that far away from where we left the barn, which I think must be about here." He put his finger on the map. "So we'll go, that's all."

"But you can't come, Ivan. Kanzat hates you. The iPod batteries must have run out."

"I'll follow after, in your tracks."

"You'll starve. You'll die of cold."

Kit came up behind Daphne. "I can give him a brazier to carry coals in, and he can bring lots of blankets."

Daphne turned to her. "And food, Kit? Can you pack him lots and lots of food?"

"I'll put it in a pillowcase," Kit said, and Ivan felt his knees go weak at the thought that he was really going to have to live up to his words, tracking a bear-drawn sledge for days and nights across the snow.

He straightened his shoulders. "All right." To his horror, his voice broke, and he hastened on. "The more food the better. But what's that noise?"

They turned to look out the window. Snow drifted down over the gray, leafless trees in the courtyard. Beyond, from the direction of the town square, came the sound of shouting and stamping feet.

CHAPTER TWENTY

Prisoners

Kit grasped the edges of her apron. Even before she spoke, Ivan knew what she was going to say. "It's the prisoners. They're bringing out the prisoners to load them for the silver mines."

"Fort," said Daphne. Her face had turned as white as Kit's. "Fort, going off to slavery. Oh, Kit, we have to go out there and let him see us. Let him see that there's at least one or two who care what's happening to him."

Kit stripped off her apron and took a cloak from the broom closet. Daphne touched Ivan's arm. "Ivan, you stay here and start packing food."

"No way," said Ivan. He wanted to see the drummer again, to see if without his scarlet hood and drum he still had that lordly stance, that way of drawing every eye. Ivan pulled his hood low and followed the girls.

They descended into the courtyard and rounded the school into the swelling sound of jeers and stamping feet. A surge of people jostled for viewing position around the plaza. Kit paused at the back of the crowd, but Daphne squirmed her way through, and Ivan ducked his head and followed.

Amid the circle of spectators, two horses stood hitched to a wagon, flicking their tails. Guards flanked a line of three prisoners as they descended the steps of the justice building. The prisoners were chained together at the waist, and the first two, their clothes crumpled and hair dirty, shuffled with their heads bent low. Last in line, Fort strode with his head high, his long hair glowing and his glance sweeping the crowd. Ivan felt that glance cross him in swift appraisal, then swing back to settle again on him and Daphne. Ivan met Fort's gaze and nodded.

The guards jerked the chain to make the prisoners turn toward the wagon. Prodded by a club, the first prisoner jumped up, caught on to the high wagon siding, and tried to wrench himself over. Just as he teetered on the edge, swinging his leg up, the guard thrust his club into the belly of the second prisoner, who recoiled, jerking the first man back onto the cobbles. The crowd roared with laughter.

A policeman patrolled the front of the crowd to keep it in line. Ivan craned his neck to see over Daphne as the fiasco of loading played itself out twice more. Then Fort organized the other two prisoners so that all three of them jumped at once, caught on and levered themselves over the side. The first two prisoners slumped onto the wagon floor, but Fort drew them to their feet. He stood surveying the crowd as the driver gathered his reins to roll away. Fort shook the hair out of his eyes, took a breath, and spoke out in his rasping voice.

"Keep dancing, citizens! Keep drumming. Music belongs to you all."

The guard standing behind him jabbed a stick into Fort's ribs, and he doubled over.

The crowd erupted, some of them booing, some cheering, and Ivan couldn't tell who was shouting for what. He turned in a circle, sweeping both arms upward. "Stand up!" he shouted. As he faced the crowd, someone grabbed his cloak by the scruff of the neck. Ivan pulled at the cloak's tie to loose it, but before he could free himself, his captor yanked him into the open between the crowd and the cart. The policeman who had grabbed him pushed back his hood. "I got him!" he cried. "Look at his face, mates, this is him. Assaulted me the other night." He yanked Ivan around so that all eyes could see him. "This filthy peasant jumped us as we were securing the prisoner. Those are my marks on him. See!" He jabbed his thumb at Ivan's black eye and the yellowing bruise on his cheek.

The crowd rumbled. Ivan couldn't tell which side they were on, but then someone shouted, "Send him along!" and the policeman holding Ivan's collar laughed and shook him.

"A good idea," he said. "The mines can always use more miners. Anyone else want to go?"

Daphne shouted, "That's not fair!"

Ivan squirmed half toward her and shook his head. In case she hadn't seen, he shouted, "Keep quiet!" In response, the policeman struck him savagely across the face, knocking him to his knees. Ivan struggled to stand. He had never been a fighter, but he fought now. He kicked and punched, punched for Lila stolen away, Fort cheated, Aunt Adelaide fighting for her life in a hospital far beyond the horizon. He fought to give Daphne a chance to melt away.

Other policemen converged on Ivan. Knocked to the ground, he tried to roll aside, covering his head, but they grabbed his arms and legs and lifted him. Laughter mocked him, and he felt himself carried, then swinging high. He flew into the wagon, landing hard at the feet of the prisoners.

"What about a trial?" Fort's sandpaper voice barked out. "What about justice?"

A boot rolled Ivan over; with his arms still protecting his face, he heard the clank of a chain, and something cold and hard cinched tight around his waist. Chained, he dragged himself to the edge of the cart to scan the crowd. He saw a few men shaking their fists, women with their hands to their mouths, others slinking away. Nowhere did he see Daphne.

Good, he thought, she got away.

But when he fell back in the wagon and stared at the grey and empty sky, he had never felt more abandoned.

* * *

Beyond the shouts of the crowd, Daphne heard the clopping of horses' hooves and the clatter of wheels as the prisoner wagon pulled away. She stood pressing her hand against the corner of the school as if the cold stone could steady her. What should she do? Ivan had warned her off, she understood that. Kit stood behind her, pulling on her sleeve, urging her back to the kitchen.

With Ivan carted away, a prisoner, their trio had shattered. Daphne felt panic beating behind her ribs, making it hard to think. We'll never get home, she thought. I can never go home without Ivan. I can't leave Ivan. I can't go tripping off to the capital without Ivan.

The crowd broke up around her, people walking back to their shops or houses, shaking their heads and talking among themselves. Even Kit slipped away, back to her kitchen. Only a small group of ragged boys still jumped about, laughing and chasing. When the police tried to disperse them, they darted away and ran after the receding wagon.

In her head Daphne imagined Ivan urging her to go with Lila. They had come into this Land of Winter to rescue Lila. Ivan was tough and smart; he'd manage somehow. Lila was young and trusting and eager to please, without the sly toughness she would need to free herself. She needed a protector.

The thought of the wagon carrying Ivan and Fort away made hot tears spring to Daphne's eyes. I'd rather go with Ivan, she thought. I need him to help me. I can't handle this kind of trouble without him.

She blinked the tears away. And Fort, too. I want to follow Fort, to be his loyal friend. I want him to look at me and think I'm brave and smart and special. But I can't. I have to let them go, while I watch over Lila in Melodia. Ivan will know where to find us.

Daphne pulled her cloak closer around her and made her way back toward the kitchen.

CHAPTER TWENTY-ONE

The Silver Mine

Ivan lay on his back in the rattling wagon with the chain around his waist clanking and biting into his backbone at every jolt. Overhead, low clouds moped their way across a sullen sky. The taste of humiliation was bitter in his mouth. To think that he had longed to return to Lexicon. Coming here was the stupidest, most backbreaking, most pointless thing he had ever done. He had no quest, no reason to be here. The land didn't want him; it flouted him at every turn. His only excuse for coming had been to rescue Lila, and at that he'd failed. Now he was riding into slavery.

Nobody in two worlds was as useless as he.

He touched the light chain hanging around his neck and pulled it around until the medallion came into his hand.

Closing his eyes, he fingered its contours, picturing it—a telescope, a tall stool.

"What is that?"

Fort sat across from him, arms around his knees, regarding him with interest. Ivan dropped his hand from the medallion, and Fort leaned close to look, his dark hair falling forward until only his nose showed through the curtain. Ivan shifted in discomfort. To him the medallion represented the Astronomer, Aunt Adelaide's childhood friend. Ivan struggled to sit up. "A gift from an old man," he said. "He was always trying to figure things out, to make them better."

"And did he?" Fort asked. "Did things get better?"

Ivan considered. "Some things. Once he really screwed up, and a mountain fell down." He thought of the Astronomer sitting by the chasm under the mountain, full of self-blame, weeping.

"I remember that day," Fort said. "The earth shook, and the sky filled with dust." He chewed on his lip, nodding.

At the edge of town, the clatter of wheels gave way to a swishing sound as the horses strained to drag them along a snow-covered lane. The wagon hissed to a halt, and the three guards prodded the prisoners. "Jump down! Time to attach the sliders."

They tumbled over the side, the length of chain between them too short for grace. The guards threw down broad wooden skis and directed the prisoners to fasten them under the wagon, fixing the wheels so they no longer turned. A wagon on skis, Ivan thought—now the ride would be smoother. The prisoners stood back as the driver urged the horses forward. They leaned into the harness, and the wagon, top-heavy and awkward, slid forward.

"Let's keep it easy on the horses," the driver said. "Prisoners can follow after."

At that the guards tossed down more skis and directed the prisoners to attach them to their feet so that their forefeet were tied on and their heels swung free. They were cross-country skis, Ivan realized, though they seemed heavy and awkward. One of the guards pitched him a pair of poles too flimsy to use as a weapon.

Two guards climbed into the wagon facing backward at the prisoners with their bows at their sides, and the third skied behind them. "Follow the wagon," he told them. "It's got your food, your blankets, everything. You'd be fools to fall behind."

In his years of exile, Fort must have learned how to ski. He was the only one of the prisoners who could glide forward with long smooth steps. Fort kept running up on the heels of the prisoner in front of him, or jerking on Ivan's waist, making him lose his balance and fall in a heap, so that the guard behind ran into him and all the prisoners, yanked awry, toppled like dominoes. The fifth time Ivan got up to the curses of the guard, he burst out, "Well, free us, then, or at least lengthen the chain, you idiot. Can't you see it's not long enough between us?"

Instead of answering, the guard prodded him with a pole. Ivan decided he'd be better off skiing beside Fort rather than behind him. He pushed forward, looking right and left, trying to see if there was any chance of rescue or escape. Nothing; the landscape was blank, white, and blurred at the edges. They slid after the wagon in the middle of a snowy plain, as whirlwinds of snow rose in the north.

Ivan struggled to get the knack of the skiing: push and slide, push and slide. Fort, beside him, said, "You're the one who jumped in at the dancing, when they were clubbing me." He added in a lower tone, "The only one."

Ivan said, "You danced with my cousin Daphne." He kept his head down, sliding in rhythm, but he was glad Fort recognized him.

"She's your cousin? She saved me at the trial. She fainted and raised four fingers for the fourth gate." Fort gave a laugh and shook his head. "What courage, what spirit! Her hair spilling all over like golden leaves, and those fingers pointing at me for anyone to see!"

"So that's how she did it." Ivan felt shaken for a minute, missing Daphne. He stared at the snow stretching toward the creaking wagon. "Why did you come back?"

Fort lowered his head and pushed forward, almost running up on the fellow ahead of him again. His voice came out a croak. "The poor can't sing. I was raised to think that meant they were stupid or lazy or dirty somehow. To think that my lost mother was lower than the stiff, anxious people who adopted me. Now my voice is the worst of all, but I'm the same man inside. Or I was, until I saw how vicious the powerful can be to people with bad voices."

"But still, why come back?"

"To see for myself, to see if the poor had music in them,

if they could be roused to noble things. If they could take hold of their lives, of music, even. To see if they were ready to break free from their chains." He gave Ivan a rueful look. "And look, here we are. In chains ourselves."

"I can't sing," Ivan said. He was breathing hard to keep up. "I tried to learn, but I gave up. Got kicked out, actually. They said I had no talent. You can't just suddenly give people talent."

Fort shrugged. "The ones with talent get training from before they can talk. They get the most accomplished parents, the best teachers, time, leisure, and companions who sing. If you switched them in the cradle, the ones with talent and the ones without, who's to say who would sing better in the end?"

Ivan pondered this notion for a while, and then said, "Where did you go, when you were gone?"

"I wandered with the nomads for a while. What voices they have, singing two notes at once, taming the bears! They track game with these fantastic ears that hear three octaves lower and three octaves higher than ours—and yet we consider them backward. After I left the nomads, I moved from town to town, working here and there. Do you know in some towns they let all the children sing? But that's changing. Inspectors from Melodia sweep into town, talking about standards, sorting the children, sending some out to work and closing some inside to learn their scales."

"I don't really understand," Ivan said. "Why does music have to be so perfect? Why can't just anyone sing? Why can't you? Where I come from, you could still be a rock star with a voice as scratchy as yours."

Fort barked out something that might have been a laugh. "A rock star, sure enough. Three days from here, we start mining silver, chained together in the dark, our ears ringing with picks striking stone. Rock stars, all of us." His voice grew harsher. "No deafness, my father said, but the mines will destroy our hearing soon enough."

Fort's words trailed away, and his face closed down. He skied like a man already defeated.

Well, that sure didn't cheer you up, Ivan thought. I guess you've never heard of a rock star. But I'm here because of you, because of your voice and the things you said. Because I jumped in. No way you're pulling out on me now. His arms ached from the poling, and the horizon stretched ahead without feature. If Fort gave up, nothing would be left but dreariness and labor and cold.

Ivan thought of the Astronomer, kindly, full of questions, like a small mammal sniffing here and there, always curious, hungry to learn. "What about me?" he suggested. "You could try teaching me—the musical moron, the tone-deaf idiot—as an experiment. You could teach me about scales and flats and sharps and all that stuff. There was this game my cousin described to me, where the little kids throw a ball around a circle, singing out notes. What was that about?"

Fort looked at Ivan and his eyebrows twitched. He knows I'm trying to cheer him up, Ivan thought.

"That was the circle of intervals," Fort said. "The kids drill on that when they're, oh, seven or eight years old."

His face, turned toward Ivan, looked serious and intrigued. "Think of a circle with twelve positions, in a pattern like a clock, for the twelve half-notes that make up a scale. The kids stand in the position of their own assigned note, and they throw the ball in a pattern, for example to every fourth kid or every seventh kid, and each one who catches the ball sings his own special note and then tosses it on. That's how they learn their intervals."

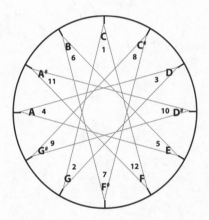

In late afternoon, the guards pulled up the horses at the foot of a wooded hill. They threw down a bale of hay from the wagon, scattered it, and then loosed the horses to let them eat. They even unchained the prisoners, figuring, Ivan guessed, that they were so far from any town none of them would take the chance of fleeing. The other two prisoners squatted in the snow as the guards built a fire and cooked up a kind of gruel with bitter vegetables thrown in. But Fort led Ivan to the edge of the firelight and made a circle of twelve deep footsteps in the snow. "Here's our clock," he said. "You're standing at the top, at C o'clock. To get to D, you jump a whole note, which is two places, like ten minutes. Ten minutes more to get to E. But only five minutes, a half note, to get to F."

Fort bounded around the circle, saying the names of the notes and then singing them in his croaking voice, as the guards watched, grinning.

"But I don't get it," Ivan said. "If there are twelve steps, why do we only use seven letters? Why have all these flats and sharps?"

Fort stopped. "That's how Zart told us to do it, when he showed us how to write music."

"Who's Zart?"

Fort shrugged. "Who knows if he was even real, or just a myth? They say

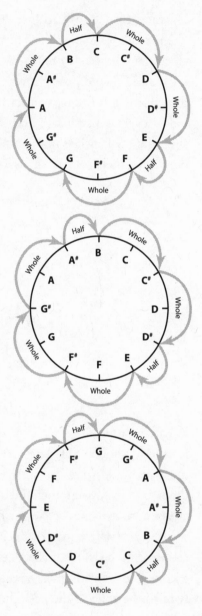

he was a boy prophet who appeared and disappeared four times. Our people were already singers, but he taught them the names of the notes and how to put them together, and he told them music was the most important thing in the world. So we do it his way. Now come and learn your major scales."

"Okay," said Ivan, still wondering about the mysterious Zart. He leaped through the snow after Fort. No matter what note they started on, the pattern of jumps around the circle was the same: ten minutes, ten minutes, five, ten, ten, ten, five. Sometimes the jumping led them to sharps or flats, the spaces that fell between letters. If Ivan started at C, the pattern came out C, D, E, F, G, A, B, C. If he started at G it was G, A, B, C, D, E, F# (F sharp), G. But if he started at B, it was B, C#, D#, E, F#, G#, A#, B.

"No more tonight," said Fort. "I don't want you getting dizzy. Tomorrow we'll go after some flats."

After supper the prisoners climbed back into the wagon, where the guards chained them to bolts on the floor. A length of canvas thrown over the wagon made a kind of roof, and the guards lay down just beyond the prisoners' reach.

Ivan's arms and legs ached, but even after Fort was asleep, he repeated his lessons under his breath. "Twelve half-steps in an octave, like twelve numbers on the face of a clock. But only seven letters to represent them. Put the C on top because it's easier to see that way. Only half a step between E and F, and half a step between B and C. Like how on a piano keyboard you have pairs of white keys with no black keys in between. I bet there are no black keys between the

B and C or the E and F." In the little bit of moonlight that made its way through holes in the canvas roof, he traced a twelve-step circle in the hay dust on the wagon floorboards. "And wherever you start, to make a major scale you jump along in the same pattern. Whole step, whole, half, whole, whole, whole, half. Ha, I'm learning music. They can't stop me." He pulled out the faded yellow leaves from his pocket. The sound of the leaves when he flicked them was fainter now, but he listened and tried to arrange them in a circle. He tested himself, starting with different letters, working out the patterns, until the letters all whirled around one another and he fell asleep with his cheek on the leaves.

* * *

On the afternoon of the third day, an escarpment rose before them, and the snow ahead was trampled and stained with stone dust. Horses huddled in a corral on one side. Wagons stood about the yard, and chained men without cloaks hoisted baskets of ore and piles of silver ingots.

The prisoner wagon pulled to a halt across the yard from an entrance like a gaping mouth in the face of the rock. On command, the four prisoners jumped down, and the guards escorted them through the mouth and into the cave. There, a dozen uniformed soldiers lolled about, playing cards and drinking from leather bottles. One, a man with stripes on his sleeve and a squared-off haircut, stood up from his table and stretched.

"New batch, eh? Where from, and what charges? Let's see their papers."

A guard shoved them forward. "From Capella, Captain. Two thieves and a Dissonant, and this one, a ..." He looked at Ivan, fumbling for a label. "A rabble-rouser. A ruffian."

The squared-off officer took their papers and marched up and down the line of them, prodding their chests and feeling their biceps. When he came to Ivan, he fingered the Astronomer's medallion and gave it a tug, trying to break the chain. Ivan pulled back, and the chain held firm.

"What's this?" the officer demanded. "Where'd you get this?" He called another fellow over, a leathery man with a thick beard and black dust engrained in his fingernails and

the creases of his face. "Look here, Rocco, what kind of metal do you reckon this is?"

Rocco slouched forward and stuck his face next to the medallion. Ivan smelled weeks of dried sweat in his tangled hair. Rocco lifted a broken, dirty fingernail and flicked it against the medallion. A note rang out, clear like the notes of the yellow leaves but stronger, lingering.

"A," Fort said. "That's a perfect A."

Rocco gave Fort a swift look and returned to Ivan. "'Ere boy, let's 'ave that," he said, and he tried to lift it off Ivan's head.

Ivan ducked his chin to hold onto the chain and pressed his forearms to his head to keep Rocco from pulling it off. He felt Fort shifting closer. "It's mine. You can't have it."

Fort spoke in his gritty voice. "Don't you think you'll learn more just by asking the boy?"

There was a moment when Ivan thought Rocco's grip on the chain would break it, but then the pull loosened. "Speak up, boy," Rocco said. "Where'd ye get that thing? Where'd the metal come from?"

"It was a gift." Ivan rubbed his neck. "From beyond the mountains."

"Time was they used to mine metal like that 'ere in these 'ills," Rocco said. "Back before my day. Veins of pure notes, melted down to ring out in bells and such all over the land. And then the veins ran out. Nothing but mixed ore now, all jumble and cacophony. So we moved to mining silver. Serves men's greed, it does, but it don't feed their souls." His black eyes glittered as he put his face close to Ivan's. "They say metal calls to metal. I bet you know more than you say. Find us a vein like that and I'll make ye a free man."

Ivan looked around. The soldiers stood back at attention, and he realized with amazement that this filthy old miner was the true boss here.

But I can't find a vein of metal in a mine, he thought. That's crazy! I don't even know what I'm looking for. This guy's a miner, and if he can't find it, how can I?

Still, it was the first opening he'd come across, and he wasn't going to pass it by. "In fairness, I should be free already," he said, jabbing a thumb toward the guards who had brought him. "They don't have any papers for me."

The square-head officer riffled through the papers in his hand. "Only three," he said, with a frown.

Rocco twirled a finger in his beard. "Free, sure, go on out and take a walk, young fool. Ye'll get out about half a day till the wolves or a snowstorm swallow ye. Else lead us to a new vein and ye'll be a rich man and an 'ero."

"And my companions, too," Ivan said. "You'd have to set them free also."

The two thieves, who hadn't talked to Ivan all journey, lifted their heads and gazed at Ivan in amazement. Fort stood facing straight ahead, letting not even an eyelid twitch to betray his thoughts.

The miner allowed his gaze to flick back and forth between the square-headed officer and the band of prisoners. Then he shrugged. "If ye succeed, why not? For then we'll all be rich. As long as them criminals don't show up in their 'ometown again."

By now, a group of mining slaves, linked together at the ankles, gathered close around Ivan and his little band. Around the end of the line came a man, skinny, barefoot, and unchained. He leered at Ivan. "The mine will grind you with stones and spit out your bones."

"Pay no mind to Lupo," Rocco said. "Stuck behind a rockslide once—came out crazy."

The crazy man, who had bowlegs and bits of spittle clinging to his wispy black beard, stuck his face close to Ivan's. Ivan recoiled and said to Rocco, "Where have you looked up to now?"

"We've scoured the mine," Rocco said. "But there's cracks and crannies no one's crawled along. Ye can try there."

Ivan had already made his way through the tunnels of one mountain. The thought of rocks teetering over him and walls pressing close made his skin prickle. He said, "I'll need someone to help me. This guy next to me will do." He jutted an elbow toward Fort.

One of the guards who had brought them in the wagon objected. "Not that one. He's a dangerous Dissonant, he is, and a redivicist—a revidicist—a guy who's committed his crime more than once, besides."

Rocco kept his eyes on Ivan, paying no attention to the blustering guard. "Too big," he said. "We need a little thin one, like you."

Ivan bristled. Little thin one! A low blow. But that meant the cracks and crannies must be narrow. He felt sick.

The line of watching miners clanked close around him. "Let Lupo take him to the Monster," one of them suggested.

"That's it," another said. "The Monster could tell him the secret or else eat him."

Ivan swiveled around to look at them. They were laughing, elbowing each other and pointing from Ivan to the crazy man. Ivan turned back to Rocco. "Who's the Monster?"

"Naught but a legend," Rocco growled. "Some call him the Hermit. Ghost of a fellow who ran the mine in the old days. He took off when the vein ran out and went exploring other mountains, where he died in a rockslide, so they say."

Lupo jigged side to side. "Dead, but hungry. We feed him 'cause we need him."

"Where does he live?" Ivan asked.

Rocco shook his head and twirled a finger by his temple.

Lupo rolled yellow eyes and said in a singsong tone, "Deep at the end of the darkest hall, where folk run away for madness' sake, where the streams run down to the big dark lake, where the water waits to swallow us all."

Ivan shivered. Rocco growled and pushed Lupo aside. "Will ye do it or no?"

Beside Ivan, Fort croaked, "I'd give my left arm to find a pure vein. Once at school one of the brothers read us a story of a golden age, when all the people jingled their bangles of music metal and carried their own songs with them. Mother Cadenza was furious. She said the story was blasphemy, and she sent the brother away. What if the people had that power again?"

Ivan heard the hope in Fort's words. He said to Rocco, "Release me, give me a torch, and I'll go looking."

CHAPTER TWENTY-TWO

Melodia

Varoq drew the nomads' sled along a snowy track through the forest, and Lila sat cozily among the furs, clutching her knees to her chest, where she felt butterflies flitting about. "Melodia," she said under her breath for the fiftieth time.

Daphne, who crouched wrapped in a blanket at Lila's feet, glanced up and then quickly away. The nomads had decreed that if the girls were going to stay together, Daphne must stay in the role of servant, and practice being deaf and dumb, because otherwise everyone would get into trouble from the Composers. Daphne wasn't very good at mute servitude. She reacted to sounds, and whenever she had to serve Lila she scowled and stuck out her lower lip.

Lila wished they could just be friends working together

the way they had in Capella, but the best she could do was try to be a thoughtful mistress. She insisted that Daphne be allowed to ride on the sled with her, and she shared her fur blankets. At dinnertime she set aside some of the best morsels of the food Daphne served her, so Daphne could eat them while clearing up.

"Melodia," Lila said again. She wanted to talk to Daphne, to cheer her up. "They used to talk about it in class, back at school. Did you hear stories about Melodia?"

Daphne made no sign she was listening.

Lila continued, "Allegra says every singer dreams of visiting Melodia. They say music runs like rivers through the streets. They say music washes the windows and carries away old people's aches and pains. It's like a fairy tale."

Daphne just stared back the way they had come. Lila knew Daphne was worried about Ivan. Once they had encountered a wagon on its way to the mines to collect silver ingots, and Daphne had begged the driver to take Ivan a note, even trading away her yellow school scarf. Lila missed Ivan, but she was in no hurry to leave this place. At home, it would be back to acting classes, voice lessons, gymnastics, coaching, makeup, tutors, rehearsals, and auditions. Every moment scheduled, and her mother's urgent whispers that Lila could do better if only she showed a little more *feeling*. Lila could wait.

"This is how it is in Melodia," Lila said to Daphne's back. She let her voice fall into a storytelling rhythm, the way the geography master told it in class. "Each year all the towns send their sweetest singers and their strongest choruses to

Melodia for Spring Festival, to help the Diva sing winter back into its cave, and to coax forth sunshine and warm breezes. Each year the Diva and her Council of Composers award prizes, and the towns who have sung the most beautifully receive silver, land, fine furniture, and delicacies. Above all, they bring home honor." She considered, and dropped back to her normal voice. "That's what they say, Daphne, rolling it out like that, as if it's the greatest thing in the world: Honor! But Allegra says singers take bribes to abandon one town and join another.

"Allegra says the most talented ones get to stay in Melodia for special training in the Palace. The boys can grow up to be nobles and Composers, and the girls become ladies-in-waiting to the Diva."

Daphne scowled. "No female Composers?"

Before Lila could answer, Ezengi called a halt. The sled ran against Varoq's heels, and the bear gave a low growl.

"What's going on?" Lila said. Daphne glowered in silence again, so Lila jumped down from the sled.

They had stopped at a dip in the road, and Ezengi pointed to a stream running down a wooded hillside toward them until it dove into a culvert that ran beneath the road. "Melted already," he said. "Chief, we check it?"

Kanzat directed one of the nomads to stay with the bear and sled, while he and Ezengi scrambled over a pile of stones and strode upstream. Lila trotted after, eager to stretch her legs. Like a good servant, Daphne followed along behind. A shelf of ice still spanned the stream, but water ran over and under it. Lila wondered what could make water melt in this bitter cold. Then they pushed past a stand of young firs and she saw what Ezengi had suspected—a grove of yellowleaf trees straddling the stream, their roots toeing the water.

"Yup," Ezengi said, stretching his back and looking up at the leaves. "Look at these, nice and healthy. What do you think we'd get for those leaves in Melodia? And a bird, too—look!"

Kanzat shook his head. "Notify it for our next journey, not this one. The sky foresays a storm tomorrow. Don't dismember, profit this trip comes from the little girl."

Ezengi scratched his head. "I suppose. Not much room to carry leaves anyway."

Daphne approached a tree and reached her hand toward the yellowkin flitting in the branches, but when the bird paid her no attention, her shoulders slumped. Lila turned to Kanzat and jumped up and down like a child. "Oh please," Lila said, "Let us climb up, just for a minute!"

The men looked surprised, but Lila noted Daphne's look of gratitude. Before Kanzat could object, Lila moved to the nearest trunk, where Ezengi held his two hands like a stirrup. Daphne selected the tree with the yellowkin in it, and Kanzat, shrugging, hoisted her up. "Here we shall pause for our repasture," he said.

The men sprawled on the forest floor beneath the trees, while Lila, above them, rustled the yellowleaf branches and listened to the tinkling music.

She watched as the silent Daphne, perched in her own tree, examined the branches and picked off caterpillars, which she stowed in her pocket. How strange, thought

Lila, but then Daphne held a caterpillar out in her palm. With a flutter and a sweet arpeggio, the yellowkin landed on Daphne's finger and fed with quick delicate nods. Lila wrinkled her nose, took a breath, and pocketed a caterpillar from her own tree.

*   *   *

The evening of their arrival in Melodia, capital of the Land of Winter, they halted outside the northeastern entrance. Travelers, traders, and caravans camped in an area of campfires and trampled snow. Ahead of them the city walls were only a few feet high, and the road passed through an archway that contained an iron gate shaped like a grand staff, with bass and treble clef in curlicues of metal. In the distance beyond the gate, banners fluttered from towers edged with orange in the setting sun, and Lila turned Daphne to see them. "Look, that must be the Palace of Music."

Kanzat left them to make camp while he talked his way through the gate. Lila approached Ezengi where he stood feeding Varoq from a flask of reindeer milk. She asked what she had been wondering all through their journey from Capella. "Is it true they want me at the Palace?"

Ezengi laughed. "Who would know you at the Palace?"

Lila felt as if he had slapped her. "You brought that letter."

"Bought from a clerk in the next town. Plenty of towns hate Capella for its high-and-mighty ways. You cheated

Kanzat in a trade. This time he'll make sure and collect his reward."

Lila swallowed. She had believed in the power of her singing, believed it had made the nomads revere her and care for her. Her voice wavered as she asked, "Then what will happen to us in Melodia?"

Ezengi weaved his head from side to side. "A good price, we hope. A good home. Or a bad price and a bad home. But a price, sure enough. And a little extra for your servant."

*   *   *

In the morning, Kanzat and Ezengi flanked Lila and Daphne as they entered the city. Kanzat had furnished Lila with a long, pink robe and a pink feather boa, but he made Daphne wear her school uniform inside out so it looked gray and nondescript. The yellowkin from the forest rode in Daphne's hair.

"Restrain from contemplation of escape," Kanzat said as he led them through the gate. "I plan to match you with top households, but if you define me, no one will welcome you."

Ezengi added, "You'd end up eating rats in the gutter for sure."

Lila took small steps in her fancy dress, holding up the hem and trying to convince herself Melodia had no rats to bite her ankles. Within the city gate, the streets were clean and the air cool without being freezing. From alleyways and doorways drifted musical sounds of morning—a spoon scraping the bottom of a wooden bowl, ceramic milk jars slung onto doorsteps, footsteps running down stairs. Doors opened, and children in uniforms and boater hats with trailing ribbons clattered down front steps and hurried off to school.

Kanzat halted at a shop front marked, "Furnishings and Antiques." A bell rang as he pulled the door open and ushered the girls inside. Ezengi waited, peering in the window.

"Here she is," Kanzat said to a plump little man with half-moon spectacles, who emerged from behind a counter to inspect them. "I prevent to you Lila, the young singer I promised."

The little man nodded and walked around the girls, tugging at this or that part of their dresses. Lila stood patiently. It wasn't that different from standing still while the costume mistress fitted her for some theatrical role. Daphne, on the other hand, jerked away from the little man's pinching hands, and the yellowkin flew up to the rafters. The costume master loosed Daphne's hair and let it flow over her shoulders. "There," he said. "A servant, but indulged. The little mistress is fond of her. That appeals to them, you know. The nobility like to see kindness all the way down the social line. It makes them feel benevolent."

Kanzat mouthed the word "benevolent," storing it away, Lila thought. "Sit in the window, sweetie," the shopkeeper said to Lila, and he led her to a rocking chair. "Some domestic sewing will occupy your hands. Call back the bird. We'll have it pecking at crumbs. And signal your servant, for she's truly deaf, yes? Signal her to sit devotedly at your feet. Just so, such a picture. When someone approaches the shop, young lady, sing in soft tones as you rock. The three of you, perfect, all innocent and unconscious of your charm.

"As for you, my friend"—he turned to Kanzat—"come back for your share this evening. No one wants to see the traders. The girls must just *appear*, you know, no past to interfere. I assure you I'll get the best price I can. Indeed, if she can really sing, and if the bird stays with them, I have high hopes for this trio."

* * *

All day Lila sat in the shop window, pretending to embroider. She dipped her needle but didn't actually prick the cloth, which was already half-adorned in threads depicting a vase of blue and purple flowers. Lila glanced up after every few non-stitches to look around the shop at the furniture piled in shadowy heaps. The antique business didn't seem to be flourishing. It was much more cheerful to look out the window. When she peered through the faintly colored diamonds of window glass onto the street, blurred pedestrians floated by in pastel colors.

Daphne sat at Lila's feet, making vicious stabs at the lower-class sewing the shop owner had given her. A pile of mending grew beside her: buttons re-attached, tears patched, socks darned. The yellowkin, perplexed by this activity, pecked at the buttons and declined to sing.

Lila was impressed, because she would have guessed Daphne didn't know anything more about sewing than she did about embroidery. Every so often Daphne sucked in her breath and shook her hand as a drop of blood formed on the finger she had punctured this time.

Whenever one of the passers-by paused at the shop door, Lila sang an old Oklahoma lullaby. She folded her hands over her embroidery and rocked, trying to feel as serene and dreamy as she meant to look. "Why, how sweet!" the fine ladies said, while the demure younger ladies following gave Lila sour looks. Then the matrons' glance passed to Daphne with her mouth all a-twist as she stabbed at her work. "How useful, too. I shall have to speak to the mister when he comes home. How much did you say? Come, dear." Each lady swept up her skirts and, followed by the now-sulky girl Lila might displace, brushed her way back into the street.

In mid-afternoon a man in a dusty black coat and trousers all bunched at the knees came in, looking worried and rushed. "What's all this, then, Synchrony? Worth my consideration?" He listened to Lila's song. "Yes, yes, sentimental as kittens, but has she nothing to show me her range?"

Lila set down her embroidery, stood, and prepared her stance. An audition. The good thing was that all her old favorites were new to people here. She sang "Somewhere over the Rainbow" and a French chanson.

Looking unhappy, the hurried man pulled his coat tight, muttered, "Duties, the Palace, must go," and bustled out the door. Disappointment pinched Lila: her first clear rejection of the day.

An hour later the hurried man was back, accompanied this time by a tall, completely bald companion who wore

dark glasses and tapped his way with a cane, and by a still taller woman whose blue veil hung from a velvet hat. The threesome paused on the threshold of the shop, and Mr. Synchrony hurried to open the door, bowing and murmuring humble greetings.

The lady entered first and glided over to stand by Lila. At Mr. Synchrony's anxious gestures, Lila jumped to her feet and made a curtsey. She dragged Daphne up beside her, although now Mr. Synchrony shook his head, gesturing that it wasn't necessary, no, Daphne didn't matter. As Daphne rose, the yellowkin, unsettled, flew upward. It fluttered toward the lady, stalled not far from her face, then swooped left and right, like a salute. Instead of starting back in fright the lady nodded as if she were receiving applause.

The bird returned to Daphne, who stood behind Lila's shoulder, resting one hand on the small of Lila's back. It was good to feel Daphne's support.

The bald man in dark glasses—he was obviously blind—turned his head side to side without looking directly toward them and said in a pleasant voice, "Another foundling. So seldom anything to get excited about. Children without proper training ..."

A shudder passed through Daphne, strong enough that Lila felt it through the light touch of Daphne's hand on her back. Daphne retreated a step and slid gracefully to the floor behind Lila as if she were hiding, although it made no sense, Lila thought, to hide from a blind man.

"Sing, child," the lady said, and she pulled back her veil enough that Lila could see her long, furrowed face, her full lips, and the shadows about her blue eyes. For the first time all day, Lila hesitated. Such a noble face, so sad. No little show tune could be fine enough for that face. Lila trembled with a longing to sing something truly beautiful.

She closed her eyes and sang the song she had improvised in imitation of Mother Cadenza the day they came to Capella—no words, just a tumble of notes, like the stream that flowed from the yellowleaf grove.

When she finished, she stood with her hands folded and her eyes downcast.

"Yes," she heard the Diva say. "Yes, she will do."

CHAPTER TWENTY-THREE

Monster of the Mine

Every day, Ivan took a torch, tucked a hunk of bread and cheese into his jacket pocket, and carried a long ball of string to unroll behind him as he walked. Thus equipped, he explored the dark reaches of the mine. The cave branched in every direction around him, and all along the cave walls, miners had hacked their way into cracks, reinforcing them with timbers as they tunneled into the mountain. Parallel to the ancient corridors that had followed the music metal, miners now delved for silver. As he felt his way in semi-darkness past entrances to tunnels, Ivan saw faint glows of distant torchlight and heard the harsh clang of metal on rock. But when he crawled deeper into the mountain, those sounds receded into faint echoes. He heard instead the scattering of pebbles when his foot brushed against them, the gurgle of water far away, and a kind of sighing, deep and lonely.

Each day he came back empty-handed, but he drew what he remembered of his travels on the back of discarded lists he picked up from the square-headed officer, whose name was Captain Igni—lists of food supplies, weights of silver sent out in wagons, and records of prisoners coming in. Ivan worked to construct a map of the mine, measuring out lengths of string and marking them so he could get the dimensions right. He stretched thousand-foot spans of string between distant stalagmites and left them in place as guide wires. Once he stumbled and dropped his torch, which rolled aside and extinguished itself in a puddle. In utter blackness, he felt about on the floor for the string. When his fingers finally brushed against it, he seized it with such relief that he gulped, and he ran both hands along the string as he crept back to the mine entrance.

In the evenings Ivan sat beside Fort, who was caked in sweat and stone dust from his mining. Fort pulled from his ears the earplugs Ivan had made him from a torn shirttail to protect his hearing from the clangor of picks and breaking rock. "Explain to me," Ivan said. Fort protested that his muscles ached, that he wanted only sleep, but eventually he drew a stick from the fire and traced circles in the dust. Ivan placed his dry leaves around the circle, and Fort worked on teaching him to hear how much distance there was between notes. Slowly Ivan progressed. At singing itself Ivan was clumsier, his voice still giving out in sudden squeaks. "But that will get better," Fort pointed out. "Not like my voice."

Sometimes other men sat watching and listening in the firelight, their faces drooping with weariness, their heads nodding as they listened. But if Fort tried to ask a question about music or draw the men closer so they could learn, they recoiled like turtles hiding their heads.

*   *   *

It bothered Ivan to be moving around freely while his companions were still in chains. Not that he was really free. A platoon of soldiers lounged in the cave's broad anteroom and outside its mouth. And of course there was nowhere to go if he escaped. The mine held men from other towns besides Capella, but all of them had traveled two or more days to get there. They were four days from the capital, Melodia, and other towns were farther. Ivan worked to redraw the map of the Land of Winter he had left with Daphne, and in consultation with different prisoners he tried to place the various towns correctly.

One day when he came back from a long fruitless day of cave scouting to drop by the fire of his companions, Fort handed him a folded bit of paper. In a frenzy he unfolded it. It was a note from Daphne—they were on their way to Melodia—could he somehow get to Spring Festival? In the damp, cold, darkness of the mine he had almost forgotten that somewhere it could be spring, and soon.

"Fort," he asked. "How long until Spring Festival?"

Fort stretched out his legs to the fire. For the first time in days he looked almost happy, and Ivan realized he must have received a letter, too. "Six octaves, I should think," he said. "Maybe forty-five days."

"We have to get there," Ivan said. "We can meet the girls there. Your sister will be going, won't she? Fort, figure out how to get us there."

Fort pulled in his legs and swung his head around to gaze at Ivan. "You're the one who has to free us, with your upcoming great discovery."

"I'm working on it," Ivan said. "But I'm stuck. I must have walked and crawled a hundred miles, and I'm getting nowhere." He pounded a fist into his palm. "You're the one with the golden tongue. Not your voice, your words. I heard you, back in Capella, persuading the people. Now persuade the guards. I don't know, talk them into having us help transport silver to the Festival, or something."

Fort rested his forearms on his knees, gazing into the fire. After a minute he wiped his sleeve across his face, clearing a white trail through the grime, and said, "Maybe you should talk to Lupo."

Ivan shivered, remembering the filthy man who had tried to scare him. "But he's crazy."

Fort said, "Never dismiss the lowly people. Lupo's so crazy he's had free run of this place for twenty years. He knows byways the miners haven't heard of."

"I don't know where to find him," Ivan mumbled.

*   *   *

But apparently Fort knew, because the next morning Lupo appeared by the breakfast fire, scratching his belly and burping, as Ivan rolled up his ball of string. "Ready for the Monster?" he asked Ivan. "Not scared of coming back without a head?"

Ivan stopped winding. Lupo, encrusted in stone dust, wore nothing but a pair of ragged trousers and a sleeveless rag of a shirt, but he looked less crazy than before.

Lupo grinned, showing yellow teeth. "The Hermit, folks used to call him, till he gobbled up a few of them. Now they call him Monster of the Mine, and I feed him to keep him tame. Ghost of the mountain, he is."

"I don't believe he's real," Ivan said.

Lupo shrugged his narrow shoulders. "Real or not, he takes the food I leave him. Real or not, he keeps the mine from falling in."

"So how come I haven't seen him?" demanded Ivan.

Lupo scratched one leg with the long first toenail of his other foot. "I can take you where I leave his food. Soon's I clean up."

I don't want to do this, Ivan thought, as he helped Lupo tidy the sleeping site and carry dishes to a basin. What a waste of time. This guy's crazy. But ... Fort expects me to go.

Lupo heaped leftover porridge, dried apples, and biscuits on a plate he balanced on one hand. He seemed willing to start off without a torch, but Ivan pulled one from the fire, and it cast a flickering glow across the rocks ahead of them as they set off along one of the corridors.

Lupo moved with a light, sure quickness that put Ivan with his maps and measuring to shame. At the edge of the torchlight, with one hand balancing the plate, Lupo darted

left and right through passageways that he appeared to recognize by the touch of a hand or the unevenness of the ground beneath his bare feet. He slipped through crevices Ivan was certain were too narrow. Ivan squeezed after him, with tight rocks compressing his chest until he pushed through.

Deep in the heart of the mine, they climbed a tilted slab and slid on their bellies under a low overhang. Like letters through a slot, they dropped to a ledge suspended high above a gurgling stream.

Lupo took the torch from Ivan and waved it at a rock shelf a little way downstream. "That's where I leave the food," he said. "And there's been no cave-ins for three years because of it. You go leave the food and fetch back the empty plate."

Ivan took the plate and sidled along a narrow walkway, his back against the cave wall. Below him the stream sank into darkness, but its gurgle swelled into a gush, and he knew he didn't want to fall. In the faint light from Lupo's distant torch, he fumbled at the space beside him until his fingers encountered an empty wooden plate swinging in the air. When he peered closer he saw that it sat on a tray hanging from the near end of a long horizontal pole that swayed above him. The pole hung suspended at its middle from a rope that spanned the gorge, and at least at this end, where Ivan could see it, the rope was fastened to a bolt drilled into the rock.

Ivan replaced the empty plate with Lupo's full one and gave the pan a half-hearted push that sent it swinging partway out over the gorge until it reversed and swung back to his hand. Well. The apparatus, clearly a device for feeding the Monster, certainly looked human-made. Ivan squinted into the darkness, trying to see movement on the opposite bank. He saw nothing. Empty plate in hand, he stole back to Lupo.

"So?" Lupo said. "You going to wait for him?"

Ivan shivered. "When does he come out?"

"When no one's here."

"I need the torch."

Lupo passed it over. "Ha! Good luck. Maybe tomorrow I'll find your bones picked clean." Clutching the empty plate and laughing to himself, he withdrew, scuttling up the tilted slab with the swift movements of a lizard.

Ivan watched Lupo go, and darkness crept closer around him. He knew at once he'd been a fool. There was a good chance Lupo had led him into a trap. Ivan had never ventured so far without a length of string to lead him home. Even with a torch, he'd never find his way alone through the maze behind him. If Lupo never came back, Ivan would sit here waiting until the torch burned out, and then he'd hear the snarls of the Monster drawing near.

With unsteady hands, Ivan wedged the torch into a crack in the rock beside him and braced for a long wait. This was one time he could do with less imagination. The rig for the food suggested that the Monster was human and kept to his own side of the underground river, but Ivan kept imagining a slimy creature with long claws and teeth, stretching up from the river chasm to grasp him the moment his light failed.

Yellow torchlight played on the gray rock behind him and probed the black void before him. From time to time, a drop of pitch from the torch popped and hissed. The stream gushed below. Ivan couldn't tell if time was passing at all.

To entertain himself, he began to sing. In a sandy voice he sang songs by Green Day, Big Country, Bon Iver. Then he swung into some of his father's favorites: Pink Floyd, Bob Dylan. The sound caromed off the rocks, out of tune, almost as painful to the ear as the blows of the miners' picks. After a while Ivan began to sing more softly, trying the scales and intervals Fort had taught him. He listened hard, trying to hear what Fort heard, modulating his voice until it sounded right. Now he sang folk songs, old songs his mother sang in the evenings, trying to find the right sound. His mouth dried out, but he didn't dare make his way down to the water for a drink. He closed his eyes and imagined that the water in the stream, cooling his throat, could give him the pure, steady tone the singers of Capella carried when they sallied forth to clear the fields.

His stomach growled, and he eyed Lupo's plate of porridge and vegetables.

To stop himself from stealing the Monster's food, which seemed like a bad idea, Ivan pried the torch loose from its crack and crept farther along the rock shelf. Below him the dark stream plunged lower, rushing through a wide crevasse. The dim, yellow torchlight wavered along the rough wall opposite. Nothing promising in this direction. He returned to sit by the food, trying to ignore its smell wafting against the underlying reek of damp rock. Again, he began to sing.

A distant light bobbed, disappeared, appeared again. Ivan moved away from his own torch into shadow.

The torch opposite flared up, lighting a broad-chested man of middle height with wiry gray hair springing from his head and chin. One of the man's eyes appeared to be half shut, and the other had a white cast, a scar that covered the pupil. Blind, Ivan thought. But blind men don't carry lights.

"Cease that horrible mewling!" the man bellowed, in a voice that shook the air. "Do you think your puny voice can tame me? Get away from my food, or I'll come make a meal of you!"

CHAPTER TWENTY-FOUR
The Palace of Music

Hurrying along the corridor with muffled steps, Daphne carried a pot of tea for Lila to serve to the Diva. These days she always tiptoed, paused outside doorways, melted into the background, and tried never, never to be heard. This Palace of Music, washed in pastel light from a hundred colored windows, seemed to Daphne full of shadows. Always in the background now, Daphne, who was supposed to be deaf and dumb, felt as if she had become all eyes and ears. Beneath the peals of music that rang like laughter through the corridors, Daphne heard malicious whispers, whispers of sweethearts slipping into the Palace and murmurs of Lady Nadia and Lady Dominica stealing each other's songs.

She heard whispers about the blind man who so often closeted himself with the Diva. Daphne had glimpsed him only that one brief time in the shop, but she remembered his bald, gleaming head and his thin, brown mustache. The memory of his smooth voice still made a shiver brush along her spine. He was a Composer, of course, Lila told her during one of the rare moments when they could actually talk. Master Thomas was a fine Composer, new, pure-hearted, a visionary bent on reforming the schools, and the Diva loved the songs he brought her.

Thinking of Master Thomas, Daphne carried the teapot down a corridor where tiles shaped like fish paved the floor of the long hallway. Tinted windows glimmered in the candlelight. The yellowkin that she had befriended in the forest clung to her head, holding onto her scalp with tiny claws.

Lila had never met the Nomologists of Origin, regal men and women with white hair and silvery voices who persuaded everyone that they knew the best way to raise children and the best way to govern. So eager were they and blind to danger in their pursuit of social harmony that had Daphne and Ivan not interfered, they would have held hundreds of children inside a collapsing mountain. When the mountain fell, the Nomologists emerged from their utopia wearing dark glasses, dazzled by the sunlight.

But sunglasses didn't make a man a Nomologist, and a smooth voice didn't make him a liar. Besides, since Master Thomas was blind and Daphne was silent, they would never have anything to do with each other. Yet something about Master Thomas's closeness to Lila and the Diva made Daphne uneasy.

Lila was now the Diva's favorite among all her Ladies, the maiden she chose to sing her to sleep at night. "You may find that others resent you," she told Lila once, while Daphne stood in the background. "That will always be true, my dear. Many with no talent will adore you, but those with talent almost as great as yours will long for your downfall."

Daphne mounted the broad stairs to the third floor balcony, crept along a hallway, and climbed a winding staircase to the Diva's bedchamber halfway up the west tower. With a nod to the guard at the threshold, she slipped through the door.

The Diva sat in front of an oval mirror, while Lila brushed a coloring paste into her long, golden hair. Lila turned to greet her. "Daphne!"

Startled, the yellowkin fluttered up from Daphne's hair. Without turning around, the Diva reached for a cookie on the plate beside her, crumbled it, and held the crumbs flat in her hand until the little bird landed to eat. She did this every evening; like her Ladies, she thought it amusing that a deaf girl should own a songbird.

Unlike the bird, Daphne made no sign that she'd heard Lila, though she lifted her head when Lila turned. Often the young Ladies spoke to their deaf servant girls in bright cheery tones as if they could hear. The older nobles, on the other hand, treated the servants as if each was only a pair of hands and feet. Any duties they failed to understand, the Diva and her Ladies explained in flourishes of sign language.

Daphne poured out two cups of tea. Lila carried the first one and knelt by the Diva's chair to offer it.

"Why, thank you, child," the Diva said, reaching down to stroke Lila's head. Her voice held a weariness, a quaver. It was the whisper of the Palace: could this be the Diva's last year? Would her voice, trained and nurtured all these decades—her great voice that patrolled the land, driving winter away—fail her at last? The Ladies of the court jostled, eyed one another, walked in whispering conference with their favorite Composers, and locked themselves in their chambers to perfect their solos. Who would succeed the Diva? Lady Nadia's name came up most often, though people often shook their heads as they spoke. And if the Diva proved too stubborn to step down, who would convince her it was time to go?

The Diva took a long sip of tea and lolled on the chair, her head and arm thrown back in a picture of relief.

"You're the apothecary now, young miss," one of the cooks had said, the day she taught Daphne to make the tea. "Though you can't hear me say it and can't never say you heard it from me." She grinned, and Daphne stared at the gaps in her teeth. "Folks say it's the tea makes the Ladies slaves to their art, but I don't hearken to that. Probably just helps them sleep, if you ask me."

People talked around Daphne. This was what she had learned: gaze at people with the mute pleading look of an intelligent dog, and they will tell you things. She was a spy in a Palace that feared spies above all. That was why only deaf girls were allowed to serve the Ladies: deaf girls couldn't betray secrets. They couldn't sell a Lady's new songs to her rivals or overhear conspiracies. Daphne gathered secrets on all sides—secret romances, envious whispers, and everywhere phrases of new songs headed for the Festival— but she drooped in the loneliness of having no one to tell. Evenings, like now, she lingered, hoping the Diva would forget to send her away, so she could talk to Lila when the Diva fell asleep.

"Child," the Diva said, "I am so weary. Help me to bed."

Lila stepped forward while Daphne remained in the background by a tapestry in the corner. Lila helped the Diva out of her heavy gown, wrapped her newly dyed hair in a towel, and led her to the high, canopied bed

"Sing to me, child. I am so hot."

"You practice too much," Lila said, smoothing the sheets over her. "You'll wear yourself out."

"Practice too much?" The Diva shook her head. "There is no such thing, my child, and you know it. You serve me, but I serve art and the people, and neither is ever satisfied. As long as the voice holds out ..." She lifted her head. "Have you heard talk, child, about my voice?"

"No, no," Lila soothed her. "It's more the other way. Your voice is too strong. The warmth of it overheats you. You don't see how you look—your face like a furnace until people fear for you—and you're still too hot even hours later like this."

"Hush and fan me, child. See if you can get the bird to sing."

Lila fanned the Diva with a long peacock-feather fan, and she coaxed the yellowkin with soft arpeggios, but it wouldn't sing.

The Diva turned restlessly on her pillow. "The voice is not as strong as it was, child. Never betray me, never tell anyone I said so. The problem is not its weakness—I can fight that—but something else. As you say, the heat stays too much with me. Every day I work on it. I stand in front of the mirror and try everything. The breathing, the ribcage, my gestures, how the sound echoes in my head."

Lila stroked the Diva's hair, but the Diva pulled her head away and continued. "All the old knowledge that never failed me before is no longer enough. I have sung with pneumonia, did you know? One year I brought spring only a day after my father died. I have always found a way. Yet my knowledge fails me now. I sing, and the heat bottles up inside me instead of emanating outward. I can't direct it properly. What will become of the people if I cannot bring the spring this year?"

"Hush now," Lila said, and Daphne was surprised by the tenderness in her cousin's voice. "Hush now, my lady. Let me sing to you."

"Yes, child. Sing me cool. Sing the light winds over me until I sleep."

Lila began to sing Christmas songs. The songs sent such a wave of homesickness through Daphne that she shivered. Christmas should have come weeks ago. She and Ivan and Lila should have scampered down the stairs of their own homes, amid their own families, to open their stockings, eat turkey, and sing carols by the fire. But Lila's songs weren't cozy. Something in the way she sang them made them cooling, as if a breeze played among the branches of pine trees. Lila added embellishments, and the breeze seemed to set the branches swaying and sparkling, while the Diva nodded off to sleep.

Lila sat by the sleeping woman until Daphne crept forward and touched her shoulder. Lila started and turned around. "Oh! I almost forgot you were there."

"Are you all right?"

Lila nodded, her cheeks pink. "Oh, yes. She's teaching me so much, Daphne. She teaches me ancient songs and shows me how to breathe and how to enunciate and—oh, I've had lots of singing lessons, Daphne, but she's the only one who puts in so much of her own heart. And I'm not worth her time at all, except that when she's teaching me she stops looking so hot. I think I actually help her a little."

"Until Ivan gets here and we go home."

Lila's eyes lost their eagerness, and she gazed at the floor.

"You don't want to go home, do you?" Daphne accused her. "For you, everything's perfect. No matter what happens to anyone else, you're the Diva's favorite."

Instead of denying it, Lila said, "Have you heard from Fort and Ivan?"

Daphne deflated. "No news from the mines. Just the usual rumors getting louder. They say rebellion's stirring in the south, and the Composers want the Diva to crush it."

"She won't. She says the soldiers are her children and she won't send them into danger. Instead, when the rebels come she'll tame them with the terror and beauty of her music."

"Well, that's great," Daphne said, "as long as they decide to hold the revolution in a concert hall." She didn't know what to make of the rumors of rebellion—they might just be another ploy to make the Diva look weak and out of touch. She hesitated. "I hear the Ladies don't like you, Lila. They say you're proud and won't take advice."

Lila tossed her hair. "You heard what Her Highness said. They're jealous. They try to put their advice between me and the Diva. They're envious because she chose me out of all of them to be near her."

Daphne sighed. She doubted the stirrings she'd heard of were envy of Lila's talent. All the Ladies had talent. What they resented were Lila's youth and prettiness and most of all her access to the Diva at a time when she might be choosing her successor. "Just don't offend them too much, Lila. I hear dark tales of assassination and intrigue."

"From the old days, Daphne. Hundreds of years ago."

"Still. The Diva protects you, but she won't always be here." Hearing herself, Daphne thought for a brief, bleak moment of Aunt Adelaide and death.

"Don't say that," Lila said, shaking her head "Please don't say that."

CHAPTER TWENTY-FIVE

The Hermit

For a monster, he looked pretty unimpressive, Ivan thought. Scruffy and a bit loony, maybe, but not monstrous.

"I don't want your food," Ivan shouted across the chasm that separated them. Great, he'd started off with a lie.

"What are you here for, then? Prophecies? Sorcery? Want me to put a hex on your rival in love? Speak up or get lost!"

Ivan shook his head. "I want to know about the music metal and where to find a pure vein."

The man cackled. "And what do you want that for, foolish boy?"

"To earn my freedom. And—for other reasons, too." The other reasons were murky in Ivan's mind, but he remembered Fort's tale of a golden age. Maybe somehow beauty and fairness could be restored to this country if only the metal were mined again.

The Monster, or Hermit, or whatever he was, reached up and gave a push to the end of the balance hanging above him. The apparatus swung, and the plate of food Lupo had prepared swiveled across the deep chasm and thwacked against the Hermit's hand. He lifted the plate down and sat cross-legged.

"Find your way across by the time I finish and I'll talk to you," he said. He filled a spoon with glop and stuffed it into his mouth.

"But how do I get over?"

The Hermit jerked his head to the left. "Down that way. E major scale, that's safe enough." He licked his lips.

E major scale? What was the old loon talking about? Ivan eyed the swivel overhead, wondering if he could swing on it, but it definitely looked too fragile to carry his weight. All right, then. The Hermit had gestured downstream. Ivan picked up the torch and edged his way again along the narrow rock shelf.

Only a little farther than he had ventured last time, he rounded a corner and found where the stone pathway broadened into a landing. From two stone pillars anchored in the rock floor, a suspension bridge swung across the crevasse into darkness.

Ivan brought his torch lower to examine the bridge. It was constructed of thick ropes, two above as handholds and two below crossed at intervals by wooden planks. As he bent closer, he saw that each plank was inscribed with the name of a note: C, D flat, D, E flat, E, F ... dipping into darkness. The planks lay on the supporting ropes with gaps yawning between, and some of the planks looked unreliable.

What is it with me and bridges? Ivan thought. It didn't look safe, not safe at all. What did he want from the loony old Hermit, anyway? The best idea would be for Ivan to turn back right now.

"E major!" the Hermit called. "Better hurry!"

He's lonely, Ivan thought suddenly. He wants me to come over. The notion encouraged him, and he tried to think. E major, E major, what did he mean? Yes, the scale. Maybe those were the only planks safe to step on.

If only Ivan could remember the E major scale. He dragged up the memory of his lessons with Fort. Whole, whole, half ... Ivan visualized the circle of notes on the stone in front of him. If he put the E at the top and then moved the minute hand ahead ten minutes, ten minutes, five ... E, F sharp, G sharp, A ... He held the torch high, but as far as he could see, there were no sharps marked on the planks, only flats. His neck prickled. No, wait, G flat meant the same as F sharp.

Ivan turned to the bridge and took hold of one rope. He would have to leap over the first four planks to land on the E. The waters roared far below, beyond the torch's light. If he fell, he would be swept away into tunnels of sloshing darkness.

He leaped, and as he grabbed for the rope, he dropped the torch. The plank beneath his feet rang out a note, the bridge bucked, and the torch rolled through a gap between planks and plunged into the chasm. The orange light dropped away, shrinking, and after an unnerving gap of time, it went out with a splash.

In utter darkness, all thoughts of music having fled his mind, Ivan clung to the swaying bridge.

Eventually, the swaying slowed, and so did the heaving of Ivan's stomach. E major. He was starting on the E. Now he needed to step whole, whole, half ... He couldn't see a thing in the inky darkness, but he felt his way with his foot past one plank onto the F sharp plank. A note sounded, and it held. Next was G sharp, the same as A flat. Of course he couldn't see it, but he took the step. The note sounded as if it made sense underfoot. Next a half-step onto A. He felt more sure now. He had done whole, whole, half. Now it was whole, whole, whole, half, and he stepped with more confidence in the darkness: B, C sharp, D sharp, E. Well. So far, so good. He supposed he would just have to repeat it, although the bridge had begun to slope upward, so he must be nearing the end. Whole step, whole step, half—but instead of another A plank his foot encountered rock.

Ivan lurched forward and stumbled onto hands and knees. Rock, solid rock, beneath him; he felt like kissing it.

"I made it!" he shouted.

"Not yet." The Hermit smacked his lips. "Good food. I'm almost done."

Ivan turned toward the voice, feeling his way on all fours toward the flickering shadow of the Hermit's torch. Once he could see clearly, he walked.

Up close, the Hermit was uglier than ever, with long, yellow fingernails and dirt ground into all his creases.

"Here I am. I made it."

"Sorry." The Hermit licked his fingers. "I just finished. You're too late."

"Not true." Ivan indicated the Hermit's dirty shirt. "There's a spoonful sitting right there on your chest, not to mention crumbs in your beard."

The Hermit glanced down, not blind at all. "Why, so there is." He scooped up a blob of porridge with two dirty fingers and plopped it into his mouth.

"Now will you tell me where to find a pure vein of music metal?"

The Hermit grinned through broken teeth. "There isn't one. The only pure music metal you'll find in this mine are the old bolts holding the planks of that bridge in place."

Ivan sank to the ground. No pure vein. Of course not. No ticket to freedom, no way out of the labyrinth. He ground his teeth. "You lured me over here. You better show me something useful."

The Hermit raised bushy eyebrows. "Useful? Art is not meant to be useful."

"Art?" Ivan got to his feet. "Art and music are too good to be useful? What about the songs that clear the fields? And I may be a terrible singer, but at least singing kept me company while I waited over there. Where I come from, even people who sing badly are allowed to try, and even if they don't sing, they can play instruments and join bands and make up new songs in their garage, like punk rock or grunge or hip-hop or anything."

The Hermit's eyebrows rose. "Just so," he said in a soft voice. "Just so." He stood, picked up the torch, and brought it close to examine the medallion that hung around Ivan's neck. "Where you come from, eh? You'll have to tell me more. I'm glad you happened by, boy. Follow me."

He loaded his empty plate onto the balance that crossed the gorge and gave it a shove. Then he turned away and walked along a track worn into the rock. Not sure what to think, but sure he didn't want to wait in darkness for Lupo's return, Ivan followed.

After about three hundred yards of winding tunnels, light gleamed ahead, and they emerged into a rock chamber lined with torches anchored to the walls. Ivan saw to his amazement that the chamber was furnished like a room. A bed stood on a rock platform, and planks arranged over another platform made a table. There was a chair, and even a rag rug, and a kind of fireplace against the wall. Water dripped from a stalactite into a pool at one corner, and the walls, between torches, were lined with laden shelves.

"Well, what did you think?" growled the Hermit. "That I live in a crack like a blind salamander?"

"No ... What happened to your eye?"

"A rock chip flew up and hit it, back when I was prospecting in the Exponential Mountains with your friend Gorgle there."

"Gorgle?"

"Calls himself something else now, no doubt." The

Hermit came close, fingered Ivan's medallion, and flicked a long fingernail against it. The sweet note rang. "Yep, that's his. Best of us all, he was. Not after riches or fame, just wanting to understand things. Always curious." He peered at Ivan. "Are you like that?"

Ivan considered. The single beady eye probed at him, and it seemed unwise to lie. "I'm lazy sometimes. But lately I really want to figure things out. Like here. Why your winters are so long, whether this world is really—well, the Astronomer"—he tapped on the medallion—"told me your world wraps around mine like a spiral. How would that work? I might want to be a physicist." Ivan stopped. It was the first time he had voiced the thought aloud. He pictured himself scribbling, working out a theory to explain how the two worlds worked, and whether there might be more worlds winding through the universe.

The Hermit shook his head. "I have no idea what you're talking about, any more than I usually did with him. Is he gone, then?"

"Gone? Oh, no, I saw him a few months ago." The idea that the Astronomer was mortal, too, like Aunt Adelaide, shook Ivan for a moment, and he floundered. "He's teaching mathematics now ... a traveling teacher."

"I can believe that."

"And you, sir, what's your name? Next time I see him ..."

"My name? I hardly remember. Don't they call me the Monster?" He showed his teeth.

Refusing to give him satisfaction, Ivan shook his head. "They call you the Hermit, but you must have a name."

"Hermit's good enough. Now I'll feed you and we can talk."

The Hermit led Ivan to the chair, where he brought him a plate of nuts and a cup of water from the pool. Stalactite water, Ivan thought. Must be full of calcium, good for the bones.

The Hermit hung over Ivan, shifting from foot to foot as he ate. "Hurry up, can't you? I have something to show you."

Ivan stuffed some nuts into his pockets and stood. "Ready."

"This is just my living room. Next door is the workshop." The Hermit guided Ivan ahead of him through a low stone arch. Ivan stepped into another room, one with a higher ceiling and fewer furnishings. It was colder here with no fire in the fireplace. On wooden tables scattered about the room lay a collection of what looked like odd musical instruments. Strings stretched in random directions, holes pierced long wooden tubes, and shards of pottery hung suspended like a mobile.

The Hermit pushed past Ivan into the workshop to wander among his creations, plucking here and blowing there. Curious notes resounded through the cavern. "I invent things," the Hermit said. "Right now I'm trying to invent music. Instruments, you call them. Instruments of music. I have ancient descriptions, which I try to translate, and mathematical formulas, which I try to understand, but no pictures. Not even, to tell the truth, a very good ear."

"Why do you do it?" Ivan asked. "And why here, hidden away?"

"Why hidden? Boy, are you ignorant of politics? To build an instrument is a crime. Instruments of rebellion, they're called, and the punishment is banishment, deafness, slavery, or death. I selected banishment preemptively, and found this place to continue my studies."

"But why?" Ivan repeated.

The Hermit gave a helpless gesture. "I don't know. To understand. To figure it out."

"I see," Ivan said.

"So, boy, have you appeared out of nowhere to be my apprentice? Will you labor beside me? Help me with the mathematics?" The Hermit tilted his head, peering up at Ivan with his one good eye.

More distraction and delay. How was he ever going to get to Melodia if he stuck himself in a cavern here? Ivan fingered the medallion, feeling the raised figure of the stool and the telescope. He flicked it with his fingernail and heard the clear note. No vein remained of the music metal. Fort's crazy hope was doomed. But there might be another way, with instruments. Knowledge is freedom, he thought. Maybe somehow instruments can free the people. Free me. And what more does this old man know? Where does he find nuts underground?

"My name is Ivan," he said. "And I'll stay and help you for a while."

CHAPTER TWENTY-SIX

The Glass Shop

Daphne walked through the streets of Melodia, a basket on her arm. On top of the basket, perched on a plain blue cloth, sat the yellowkin. His feathers were beginning to droop, just as the other bird had when he was captive in Capella. She had hoped freedom would keep this one vibrant, but now she wondered if it was just exile, being away from his forest home, that made him droop so.

In her plain gray uniform with the blue trim, Daphne commanded the sympathy of the citizens. "Look, there goes one of those poor deaf girls from the Palace," she heard them say sometimes. "I hope her mother got a good bounty."

Lila spent most of her time with the Diva now, and as long as Daphne avoided the kitchen and the cleaning crews, she had a lot of free time. She spent it like a spy, learning the streets of the city, mingling among women in shops, and listening. She didn't know what she was listening for—word from the mines, perhaps, or a hint of spring.

There was a shop window in a side street where she loved to stop. The window was decorated in lozenges of pale color, the glass faintly stained. Through the shop window she saw prisms and globes of glass. She would love to hold them, but she couldn't think of any plausible reason for a Palace serving girl to step inside such a shop.

Daphne pressed her nose against the window, and in a corner of the window display she saw a collection of silver jewelry. Silver. Surely she hadn't seen that last week. Maybe she could learn when the last shipment of silver had come. After hesitating for a moment at the door, she slipped inside and tiptoed over to look at the display: bracelets and a locket cast in the shape of a bird. The bird looked like her yellowkin. She reached for it.

"Can I help you?"

Daphne whipped around, then immediately realized her mistake. How could a deaf girl have heard him? A man, short and stout and bowlegged, stood looking at her with friendly interest. A fluff of hair ringed his head, and two buttons had burst off the front of his shirt, exposing a strip of pale pink undergarment.

"Can I help you?" the man repeated.

Daphne made a helpless gesture behind her at the silver.

"You want to know the cost, is it? My dear, I'm afraid ... But what's this? A yellowkin, here in the city? With no cage, no strings attached?" He reached his finger to the bird and

did something Daphne hadn't heard from anyone else in all the Land of Winter: he whistled three sweet notes.

The bird hopped onto his finger. "There you go, there you go," the man said, stroking the bird's head with the finger of his other hand. "What a fine fellow you are, to be sure."

"But he's fading again," Daphne said. "He's fading and I don't know what to do."

She clapped her hand to her mouth.

The man looked at her, the folds around his eyes crinkling. "Not dumb after all," he said.

"Oh, please." She found herself reaching to pull on his coat in appeal. "Don't tell. There's someone I have to watch—keep safe—at the Palace."

He stroked the bird's head. "Why would I tell? This obsession with silence in the Palace is a lot of nonsense, if you ask me. Now what's the trouble with this fellow?"

She bit her lip. "I have one idea, but it's probably wrong."

He stood before her, no taller than she was, stroking the yellowkin and waiting for her to speak.

"You know the birds live on the yellowleaf trees, and the nomads catch them when they collect leaves to sell."

He nodded, smiling.

"And then the nomads complain that when they come back next year, the trees aren't as good and the leaves are full of holes. So I looked—and the trees have caterpillars, big fat golden ones. I saw a yellowkin gobble up a caterpillar, and what I thought was, the caterpillars eat the leaves, but the birds eat the caterpillars, and when the birds are gone the caterpillars just take over."

The man nodded. "It might be so. Indeed it might."

Daphne lowered her head. "I gathered a bunch of caterpillars. That's why he stays with me. People think it's because of my yellow hair or because I have a special way with animals—"

"You do have a special way with animals," he said. "You noticed about the caterpillars."

"I fed him one every day, but a couple of days ago I ran out."

"Oh," he said. "I see. Have you told him it's time to go home?"

She looked at him, then took the yellowkin from his finger and carried it to the door. "Go home!" she said, flicking her hand. "Be free. Go home!"

The bird flew up to the eave just outside the door and perched there.

"Hmm," said the man. "It's a start. Maybe he'll go the rest of the way in a minute." He drew Daphne back inside. "Now, you wanted to ask about the silver."

"Yes. Where does the silver come from? Do you get shipments from the mines? Because I have another friend— my cousin, really." She inspected his face to see which way his sympathies might lie. "A prisoner, to tell the truth, but he didn't do anything wrong. He doesn't know where I am, and I want to send him a letter."

He raised his eyebrows. "You can write?"

"Yes." She surveyed his face, wondering how much to

tell him. He was the first person in so long to pay her any attention that his interest made her suspicious. But the yellowkin had trusted him. She said, "Where I come from, which is Afar, everyone learns to write."

He studied her, then nodded. "I see. Then Afar must be a lovely country, and someday you must tell me more. But first, let me answer you. The silver is old, brought to me to sell by a family that has come on hard times. Nowadays the silver from the mine is used only for money, which the Palace spends left and right on luxuries and armies." He scratched his head. "But there are other shipments, side shipments of raw ore, the matrix the silver lies in. I use it—my son uses it in the manufacture of colored glass. But you're not interested in that."

"Yes, I am," Daphne said. "I'm interested in everything. The glass is so beautiful."

He smiled. "One day, then, I'll close up the shop and take you to meet my son. He's a master of technique. Why, he can blow the glass into bubbles so fine you can hardly see them. But for now ... yes, a shipment of ore is due. Write a note, dear, and I'll ask the wagon drivers to carry it to your cousin."

He led her to the back of the shop, where there stood an old desk whose front was riddled with drawers and compartments. He pulled out an inkwell and laid a sheet of paper before her.

She sat at the desk, and he nodded and withdrew.

A friend, Daphne thought. I have a friend. She let out a long sigh, and it occurred to her to wonder how many in the Palace felt the way she did—as if they had to guard every move, stay alert, and betray nothing. Here at last was someone who listened but didn't pry.

She lifted the quill, and great splotches of ink dripped onto the paper.

* * *

Though she tried to shoo him away, the yellowkin followed Daphne back to the Palace. She couldn't tell him aloud to go home, but each time she threw him into the air, he rose and circled before settling back on her hair or shoulder. At the servants' entrance, she beat the heavy knocker against the wooden door, and the bird flew up just as the guard opened up. Daphne could have darted inside and pushed the door closed, locking him out, but instead she held up a finger and waited for his claws to curl around it before she went inside.

He's not ready to leave yet, she told herself, and she traipsed down to the kitchen to prepare Lila's evening tea. "There you are," the cook said. For the first time, Daphne noticed how ugly the cook's voice was, scratchier even than Fort's. "A new batch of tea has come in special just for your lady. Delicious. I took a snuff myself. Ha, ha. Good thing you can't hear me, or you'd report me, wouldn't you, you sweet-faced innocent thing." She pulled out a small wooden chest, gave it a shake, opened it, and thrust it toward Daphne. Daphne inhaled the heady scent of fresh herbs.

She accepted the box from the cook's hands and proceeded

to brew the tea. It was a time-consuming procedure: two steepings at different temperatures, then careful mixing.

Daphne carried the pot along the corridor, her thoughts on Ivan. She had sent word, and she wondered where he

would be when he got the letter. He might be a miner by now, covered in dust. Perhaps he was finding treasure, the way they had thought they might on their first trip to Lexicon. Or he could be solving some problem, inventing something, making himself respected among the men. Once again she had begged him to keep up his spirits and most of all to find a way to Melodia by spring.

She nodded to the guard at the door and entered the Diva's chamber.

Lila posed in front of the mirror, singing scales. The Diva stood behind her, holding Lila's shoulders straight, reaching a finger to tilt Lila's chin upward. Lila's tone, Daphne noticed, though still as sweet, was fuller than before. She sounded less like an orphan, more like a girl who could take charge if she had to.

Seeing Daphne in the mirror, Lila started to turn, but the Diva twisted her back into place, and she kept singing scales. Daphne took two cups from the cupboard and poured them full of tea.

The last note quavered, and the Diva let go of Lila's shoulders. "Never stop in the middle of a practice," she said.

Lila nodded and came to collect the tea. She took two sips herself, gave Daphne a nod, and carried the Diva's cup to her. The Diva set it on a small table and took Lila by the sleeve. "Do you understand, child? No more interrupt a practice session than you would break off a performance. Practice is something we who live in the Palace dedicate to the goddess, and to our people. Do you understand?"

Looking embarrassed, Lila murmured, "I understand."

The yellowkin, who had stayed on Daphne's shoulder until now, fluttered over and landed on the lip of the Diva's cup. He tipped down and bobbed his beak into the tea, taking a series of small sips.

"Oh!" Lila cried, shooing the bird away.

The Diva laughed. "Look, another slave to music, as I am! Don't worry, child. I'm flattered he wants to drink from my cup."

Lila shot a look at Daphne, who removed the cup and poured a new one, which Lila set again at the Diva's elbow.

"Send your servant away, child," the Diva said. "I have a song for you to try."

Lila reached an arm toward Daphne and fluttered her fingers.

Daphne stuffed down the feeling of resentment these silent dismissals always gave her. After all, if she was playing the part of a deaf servant, she should expect people to treat her as one. She placed the dirty cup and the teapot onto a tray. The yellowkin flapped down to resume drinking from the cup. Daphne lifted the tray and glided out of the room. If she had to be a servant, she was going to be a good one.

On the way to the kitchen she examined the bird. He looked more bedraggled than ever. She could swear his feathers were turning from yellow to brown in front of her eyes. Perched on the teacup rim, he cocked his head to look at her with his bright, round eye. Then, all at once, he staggered and splashed into the cup.

Daphne scooped up the bird and set the tray on the floor with her free hand. She knelt and cradled the bird against her. He lay panting in her hands, his little heart beating a furious scherzo. Then a shudder ran through him, and he fell still.

Just like that, the little life was gone. A sob filled Daphne's throat. He had been failing, but to have death come so suddenly at the end—she hadn't been prepared for that. He had looked so jaunty, drinking the musical tea.

The new tea.

Daphne jumped up and ran, clutching the bird's dead body. Panic churned within her as she raced along the corridor, screaming in silence, Stop, Lila, stop! Don't drink!

CHAPTER TWENTY-SEVEN

Length of the String

"But this is some weird other language," Ivan said. "I can't read a word of it." He threw the yellowing papers aside.

The Hermit gave him a hopeful smile. "But it has numbers, doesn't it?" He nodded at Ivan's medallion. "*He* used to say numbers worked across any language."

"Not if they're surrounded by words," Ivan said. He pushed back the chair, stood up, and paced. "I can't stand much more of this. Living in a hole, getting nowhere, eating glop, and sleeping in the dirt." It had only been four days, and already he was going bonkers. Four days of drawing and describing every musical instrument he could think of, trying to answer the Hermit's questions. Four days of humiliation, because it turned out he didn't know enough about any instrument—hadn't *noticed* enough—to be able to show how it worked. A flute, for instance. It had holes, and pads to cover them attached this way and that—why? A trombone looped back on itself, and something slid—how? What did the shape of a violin have to do with anything? How did the keys of a piano work? He felt stupid and useless, and now even The Hermit's prized ancient manuscript turned out to be meaningless.

"Apprentices are meant to be unhappy," The Hermit said. "Deprivation is part of the learning. With true dedication you'll cease to notice."

"I never said I'd be your apprentice. I resign. Right now."

"You'd leave me?" The corners of the Hermit's mouth drooped.

Ivan looked around him at the oddly shaped instruments scattered throughout the workshop. He had plucked, blown, pounded them all, and listened to strange combinations of sound. None of them were right, but still, there was something here. Some crazy scent of hope. Compared with the dank air of the mine, the air had a whiff of possibility.

He flung himself back onto his chair. "I'll stay, but not as an apprentice. I'll be your consultant."

The Hermit squinted at him. "What's a consultant?"

Ivan tried to remember what he'd heard his parents say. "Someone really expensive who comes in to give you advice. He tells you what to do and doesn't stick around to see if it works."

"Humph." The Hermit scratched his head. "I don't think I like it."

"Here's some advice. First: you need to serve better food. Second: you need to clean yourself up."

The Hermit looked down at himself. "Clean up? What's wrong with me?"

"Work on it," Ivan said. "And I'll take another look at this manuscript."

Muttering, the Hermit withdrew into his living quarters.

Ivan turned over the crackling pages. The writing didn't even use regular letters. How was he supposed to make head or tail of it? On the fourth page, he came across a fraction that looked like this:

$$1 + \cfrac{1}{1 + \cfrac{1}{2 + \cfrac{1}{2 + \cfrac{1}{3 + \cfrac{1}{1 + \cfrac{1}{5 + \ldots}}}}}}$$

Ivan's heart sank. He didn't even know where to start with a fraction like that. He turned over more pages.

He found some more familiar fractions: ½, ⅔, ¾, ⅘, ⅚ ... Well, those looked more hopeful. But what was the text around them saying? He scrutinized it, hoping to crack the code. There seemed to be a few large letter-symbols that stood out and were repeated often. Could those be the names of notes?

He turned the pages until he found one where a string of letters stood alone. Were there seven letters, like the seven letters of the scale? No, too many. So much for that. He brushed the quill feather against his cheek, thinking.

Wait, there were twelve. Twelve letters, each with a one beside it, and then they repeated again in the same order, with twos beside them this time. Twelve letters, like the twelve numbers on a clock, just like the number of notes in an octave when you counted all the sharps and flats. Yes! He had it! He could break the code.

Well, not break the code exactly. Not read the text. But he could match these symbols up to the steps of the scale. Where should he start? Which of these letters was A, and which one was C?

After a long time of thinking, and after sketching out a labeled clock face, Ivan convinced himself it didn't matter, as long as the letters followed one another in the same order every time. Carefully, he copied out two cycles of symbols and placed the letter names of notes, with A the lowest, beside them. Now back to the page where pairs of symbols were matched with numbers and fractions. He replaced the symbols with their corresponding letters.

A1 A2 = ½, he wrote. A2, he guessed, might be an octave higher than A1. So moving twelve half notes higher, once around the clock, gave you ½. He wrote out the rest of the fractions and counted the steps.

A1 E1 = ⅔   7 steps
E1 A2 = ¾   5 steps

C1 E1 = ⅘   4 steps
A1 E2 = ⅓ 19 steps

Ivan stopped, rubbed his forehead, and stood up to pace. What could it all mean? He sat down and drew out his circles of notes, and then he put the fractions next to them in order of size: ⅓, ½, ⅔, ¾, ⅘. The larger the fraction, the smaller the number of steps between the two notes. It was confusing.

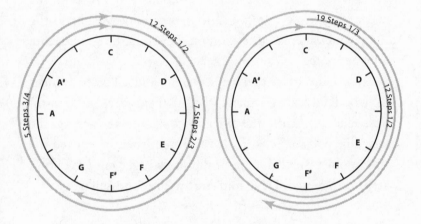

Ivan turned the page and found a drawing.

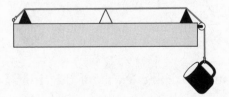

The picture seemed to be saying that if you plucked a string and got a certain note, and then you interrupted the length of the string to make it half as long, you would get a note an octave higher. That must be what was meant by the ½ next to C1 C2. But Ivan had to try it to make sure.

He rummaged through the strings and bolts and boxes and lengths of wood in the Hermit's workshop until he found everything he needed except a pulley. In its place he used a smooth dowel of wood that the string slid over easily. For a weight he hung a mug full of nails and screws on the end of his string. He found that by adding weight to the mug, which increased tension on the string, he could create a higher note.

Eventually he settled on a weight and adjusted wedges of wood under the string, sliding them back and forth. Sure enough, with the weight constant, shortening the string he had to pluck made the note higher. He flicked the Astronomer's medallion and slid the wedges until the notes seemed to match. He would start with A and call it A1.

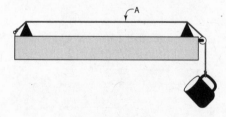

He measured half the length of the string between the two wedges and inserted another wedge. He got a higher note, but was it an octave higher? He played the two notes over and over until he convinced himself they matched so well there must be an octave between them. He had found A2.

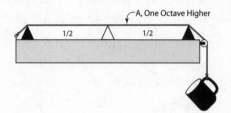

Now what? He moved the wedge so that it divided the string into ⅓ and ⅔ of its initial length. According to the chart, the short length should be 19 steps higher than A1, which would be E2. The two-thirds length should be 7 steps higher than A1, which would be E1. And look, because ⅓ was half of ⅔, the E2 string was half the length of the E1 string. And E2 was 12 steps, or exactly one octave, higher than E1. It worked! The contraption gave consistent results, and they matched the text.

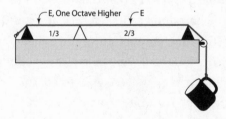

Immersed now, Ivan didn't notice the time pass. He worked from the notes and intervals he knew to figure out the others. He marked where along the string he placed his wedges, and when he removed them, he found he could play the notes just by pressing the string down to the board at those marks. He had created a one-string guitar. He practiced playing a scale: whole, whole, half, whole, whole, whole, whole, half. He was trying to pick out "Mary Had a Little Lamb" when he heard the Hermit's footsteps in the next room.

Ivan stopped playing. His fingers tingled, and he wanted to dance. He had done it; he understood. He stood looking at his beautiful one-stringed instrument, too full of his news to speak.

The Hermit said from the doorway. "I brought us some better grub."

Ivan turned see an old man with combed hair, clean face, trimmed beard, and brushed pants. He even wore a bottle-green vest. "Wow! You look great," Ivan said.

"Balderdash," said the Hermit. "Come try the food."

On the table plank he laid out roast chicken, boiled carrots, and a loaf of warm bread. The aroma made Ivan's stomach rumble. He hadn't realized how hungry he was. He jumped into a chair and grabbed a fork and knife. "Where'd you get this stuff?"

The Hermit coughed. "I visited my people. I'd been neglecting them, and they were glad to see me."

"What people?" Ivan bit into a drumstick.

"There's a village in the grove at the back of the hill where you entered the mine. Bet you never saw it. Fissures in the cave give off warm vapors, enough for a little farming village even in winter. The villagers keep to themselves, but

I stumbled across them when I was exploring the cave one day. A little boy saw me rise out of the rocks and called his family, who thought I was some kind of god. Well, I convinced them I wasn't, but they still think I'm a prophet." He rolled his one working eye at Ivan. "A blind prophet, of course. So they lay out food for me, and sometimes I appear to answer questions."

"What kind of questions?"

"Should so-and-so marry, when will spring come, that sort of thing."

"You don't know if people should marry!"

The Hermit shrugged. "If they bring me good food, I tell them what they want to hear. Don't look at me like that, boy. No one listens to advice anyway, not even from a prophet."

"But that means ..." Ivan said. "That means there's a way out of here."

The Hermit bit into a drumstick and chewed slowly. Even his fingernails were short now—a little ragged, but short and clean.

The Hermit said, "There is a way out. I didn't mean to tell you, but I've decided you can leave if you want. One twisted Monster in this cavern is enough."

"Leave? Not yet. After dinner I want to show you something."

"You found something?" The Hermit stood so fast that his chair fell over. "Show me now!"

*   *   *

They spent the next few days refining Ivan's discovery,

adapting it to multiple strings on a board, thinner and thicker strings, and to the distance between holes in a woodwind instrument. They tuned the instruments as best they could to the perfect A of the Astronomer's medallion. Ivan pulled the yellow leaves from his pocket. Turning brown now and curling along the edges, the leaves still emitted a faint tone when flicked, and Ivan used them as best he could to check the notes he and the Hermit created.

By the fourth day Ivan was restless. Now that the Hermit was cleaner, Ivan noticed how much his own clothes stank. His fingertips were raw from plucking too many strings, and his neck ached from leaning over instruments. He rocked back on his heels and watched the Hermit pick out a tune on the zither-like instrument they'd built. "I'm finished," he said.

The Hermit looked up, but didn't stop playing.

"I got you started," Ivan said. "My consulting job is done. I hope you make a hundred instruments and crawl up through that hole in the roof and teach the villagers how to play. I hope music spreads over the whole country so the singers can't monopolize all life's good things anymore." He tried to put firmness in his voice. "But I need you to show me the exit. I'm moving on."

The Hermit strummed. "Giving up, eh?"

"I have to find the girls and get them home."

"Running out on your friend, what's-his-name."

Ivan clenched his fists. "You know I can't do anything for Fort. You're the one who told me to quit looking for the music metal, because it's not there."

The Hermit laughed to himself. He seemed to have slipped back from working partner to nasty, mad old Hermit again. "I never said that."

Ivan glared at him. "Liar!"

The Hermit slapped his hand against the wall. "Fool! It's here, don't you understand? Trapped in here. Not pure, no. Everybody wants a pure vein. But there's music metal all around you, bound in the rock. It can't get free, any more than pure notes sound when dogs bark and the wind moans and shovels clank against rock, understand?"

"This?" Ivan said. He stood and ran his hand along the black rock.

"The notes are all there. But no one can hear them unless they're separated one from another."

Like the leaves in the school courtyard, Ivan thought. He had winnowed them with Lila's help. He had separated them by weight—no, by density. The lower note leaves fell more rapidly through the air while the higher notes floated longer downwind. Could he do the same thing with the ore?

The idea filled him, making him stride around the workshop, slamming his fist into his hand. "We could smash the rock. Grind it up really fine, and then try to float the flakes ..."

"They'd sink," The Hermit said. "What do you think? They're bits of metal, they'd sink."

"But if they could float on something really dense, something like molten silver—wait—" Some notion lurked at the back of his mind.

"They'd melt." The Hermit shook his head. "Do you think no one's thought of these things?"

Deflated, Ivan turned away. Who was he, to think he could solve a problem that so many others with more experience had tackled? Of course the metal in the rock would melt. At some temperature, it would melt. At some temperature ... Again, the idea just beyond consciousness prodded at him.

"They're pure substances?" he asked. "The different music metals? Each one is its own thing, its own compound, not some mixture?"

The Hermit shook his head. "Compound, schmompound, I don't know what you're talking about. But yes, each one's pure. It has its own tinge of color, its own sound, its own density ..."

"Its own melting point," Ivan said.

The Hermit's mouth dropped open.

"Am I right?" Ivan demanded.

The Hermit scratched his head, muttered to himself, and blew his nose on a rag. At last he said, "You might be. But we can't build a fire hot enough to test it."

"They melt the silver into ingots in the mine. I'm going to go try it. Want to come?"

The Hermit grimaced, pulled on his beard, and took a step backward. "Not me. They'd slaughter me. I'm the Monster of the Mine. I'm not coming out."

The beauty of the idea skimming through Ivan's mind made him want to leap up and run all the way back to tell Fort. "I have to get over there to meet Lupo next time he brings your food. E major scale on the bridge, right?"

The Hermit shook his head, his good eye wobbling. He pulled his mouth into his old evil grin. "Not on the way back. G minor harmonic scale, descending."

Wicked old man! How had he fixed the bridge so that some planks were safe in one direction and different ones were safe in the other? Then Ivan understood: the bridge was safe. Every plank was safe. The Hermit had been playing with him all along.

Ivan thought, he's lonely. He doesn't want me to go. He even cleaned up for me.

He took the Hermit by the hands. "Thank you. Make your instruments. Give them away. Come out in the world and start an orchestra. People will love you."

"Bah!" the Hermit said, shaking his hands free. "Lousy consultant. Get lost. And tell them in the mine I still eat human flesh."

"Good-bye," Ivan said, and for the sake of the Hermit's pride, he racked his brain and made his way across the bridge along the G minor harmonic scale, descending.

CHAPTER TWENTY-EIGHT

Tea for the Diva

Lila let her head fall back on the satin pillow. She felt the cooling damp as Daphne, silent and exhausted-looking, sponged her sweaty brow. During the night Lila had vomited more times than she could count. Her throat felt as if it had been torn apart, and the next time she threw up she expected to see her stomach itself goggling back at her from the basin

The door opened, and the Diva looked in. "I have had my physician prepare a potion, my dear."

The Diva's voice, hoarse and wobbly, made Lila cringe. She thought again of that moment when Daphne came bursting through the chamber door, a guard holding her by the scruff of the neck because she looked so crazy. Wild-eyed, her mouth open as if she were about to burst out shouting, Daphne held up the body of the dead bird. Oh, too bad, Lila thought, until she saw Daphne's frantic gesture swoop across the teapot toward the cup the Diva was just then lifting to her lips for another sip. "Stop!" Lila had cried, her voice suddenly no more than a croak, and as the Diva raised her eyes in disapproval, Lila knocked the cup out of her hands.

Now the Diva credited Lila with saving her life, when of course it was Daphne who had saved them both, Lila after half a cup of tea, the Diva after less.

Lila leaned over the side of the bed as another swell of dry heaves rolled through her. She thought she'd rather be dead than suffer any more of this nausea. And here was the Diva, bringing another brew. Swallowing brews prepared by strangers didn't seem like that great an idea right now.

Daphne accepted the drink from the Diva's hands, took a couple of sips and waited. The Diva had made Daphne their taster for poison. Daphne might die for them because Lila sang better, and the injustice of it sent another wave of nausea through Lila.

After a few minutes, Daphne passed Lila the bowl of potion. Fighting to control her heaving stomach, Lila sipped, gagged, sipped again, and gagged some more.

Before long she felt a tiny bit better. A few sips more and she could turn over in bed without becoming seasick.

"Thank you," she said, clutching Daphne's hand. It hurt her to hear her own voice, not just hoarse but ugly.

The Diva bent over her and croaked, "Oh, child, your poor voice. Tell no one. I trust we will be better soon, both you and I. I have sent my physician for the one person we dare consult—my personal Composer, Master Thomas."

Lila felt Daphne stiffen. The name, the Composer himself, made Daphne act so strangely. Once Daphne had said she didn't trust people in dark glasses. As Lila recalled, it had to do with the Nomologists, the misguided villains under the mountain in Daphne's first visit to Lexicon.

Lila rasped, "Let my servant stand in the shadows. Such a grand personage might frighten her."

"And I do not?" The Diva smiled.

Lila waved her hand, and Daphne withdrew to stand among the folds of a great crimson curtain that hung by a window.

With a knock, the Composer entered. He was bald—hadn't Daphne told her the Nomologists of the mountain had silvery hair and mesmerizing blue eyes? This old man was bald and blind. He cocked his head, and when the Diva said, "Enter," he hurried to greet her, missing her by just a fraction, his hands held out in appeal.

The Diva caught his hand. "Here I am. Do you recognize my voice?"

"Sadly altered, my dear Lady, sadly altered! And yet, when I think what might have happened—where is the child? Does she live?"

The Diva guided his hand to Lila's. His hand was cool and dry as paper. Lila shivered.

"Tell Master Thomas you are well."

"I am well, sir." Then, mustering her bravery, she said, "Please, Master Thomas, if I could only see your eyes."

He hesitated for a moment, no doubt because her request was so odd.

"It would comfort me," Lila said.

Without saying a word, the Composer removed his glasses. Deep brown, almost black, his eyes flitted around the room in an aimless way, not settling on Lila. There. Dark eyes, not blue. Lila hoped Daphne had seen.

"How do you find the child?" the Diva asked in her tremulous voice.

He replaced his glasses and shook his head. "A fearful change. She is so small—how much did she drink?"

"Half a cup," the Diva said. "And she knocked mine away before I drank more than a few sips."

"A blessing, to be sure."

Lila had the unpleasant feeling that his eyes were still flicking back and forth beneath his glasses. That happened sometimes with blind people, she thought. As if their poor blind eyes were searching for lost images. Could he still sense light at all?

Master Thomas, with his face turned toward the warmth of the window, suddenly stiffened. He turned back toward the bed. "I have made discreet inquiries. No one else in the Palace is ill. Who brought you the tea?"

"Lila's servant girl. What is her name, child? I have forgotten."

Daphne, standing in the shadow of the curtain, gave her head a shake.

Lila cast about for an answer. "Annie. Her name is Annie."

Master Thomas frowned. "I will take her for questioning."

The Diva took Lila's hand. "Oh no, Master Thomas, that would be hovering over the wrong nest. It's the servant girl who stopped us from drinking more."

His forehead furrowed. "A miscreant can change her mind mid-deed. How else would she know to stop you, if she didn't know it was poison?"

Lila raised herself onto her elbows. "Her bird died, Master Composer. That's how she knew." She wondered how to convince him of Daphne's innocence. "Have you checked the kitchen? I bet the bad tea's just sitting there, and she just brought it up as usual. Maybe you could ask the kitchen staff."

He turned his face toward her. If he could see, Lila thought, I would tremble under that gaze. "I will question the kitchen staff, of course. But I must also question the servant."

Daphne, white-faced by the curtain, gave her head another shake, and Lila sent the Diva her most wide-eyed, pleading look. The Diva responded with the slightest nod and said, "When next she comes, the servant shall be sent to you."

The Composer's nostrils flared as if he could smell the deception.

The Diva fanned herself, and her voice wavered. "Who would attack me in this way? You must find out for me, Master Thomas. Why would someone do this, so close to the time of the Festival?"

He took her hand and bent over it. "You are mistaken,

Your Highness. The target was undoubtedly the girl Lila. Nobody knows that you share her tea. She is not widely loved for the way she has wormed herself into your heart. Some jealous rival ... one of the other Ladies, perhaps."

The Diva drew her hand away. "I won't believe it. What business is it of theirs whom I hold close to my heart? These intrigues, these jealousies! They are unworthy of our great house and our great duty." She fanned herself, panting, and her voice grated. "Surely not, oh surely not. You break my heart. And yet ... perhaps you can speak to them, Thomas. Gently. Explore their minds for malice. Let me know what you find."

"Yes, Your Highness." Thomas bowed again over her hand, then backed away, turned, and made his way from the chamber.

When he was gone, Lila beckoned to Daphne and said, "Thank you for protecting my servant, Your Highness."

"Ah." The Diva studied Daphne and shook her head. "They always want to blame the lowly. But Lila, have you made yourself very much hated? It would be wrong of you to hold yourself so high you drive my other Ladies to jealousy."

"Is it my fault I've become your favorite?" Lila asked. She knew the horrible hoarseness of her voice only made her sound more innocent. Yet doubt niggled at her. She knew how to be charming, how to win an older person's affection— how to lend her rapt attention to the Diva's words, how to insert special sweetness into her questions, how to make little gestures of devotion. She liked being the favorite, the special one, the one who wouldn't be cast aside. She thought of her father left behind in his bike shop, looking up from repairing a gear to answer some old customer's question about where his wife and child were living. Favorites didn't get abandoned.

The Diva stroked Lila's hair and sighed. "I fear you must find a new servant, child. For I told Master Thomas that when this one, Annie, comes again, I will send her to him, and you know the Diva cannot lie."

CHAPTER TWENTY-NINE

Questions

Daphne clutched the body of her dead yellowkin, wrapped in one of the Diva's handkerchiefs. At the door of the Diva's chamber she took a breath and darted through. She hunched over the little bird's body as she slipped along the walls, wondering if she was a wanted criminal. She had no faith in Master Thomas's investigation. Exhausted though she was after watching at Lila's bedside all night, Daphne wanted to show the little bird to the cook and see if it made her jump with guilt.

One of the assistant cooks stood over the stove, stirring a sauce, while two kitchen maids chopped vegetables. Daphne crossed to the shelf to lift down the box of tea. It was gone.

She prodded one of the kitchen maids, gestured at the empty spot on the shelf, and made questioning motions.

"Your tea, is it? A lady came and took it away." She acted it out for Daphne, a fine lady sweeping her gown aside and standing tiptoes to reach for the box. "Wasn't it Lady Nadia?" she asked her companion. "Not that I can make this one understand, poor thing."

Lady Nadia had taken the tea—Lady Nadia, who lifted her nose and sniffed whenever Lila's name was mentioned! But resentment was one thing, murder another. Daphne pulled on the assistant cook's arm and mimed a stout figure, then made another questioning gesture.

"You're wondering where the cook is? She's sick." The kitchen maid pantomimed vomiting and wiping her nose, and she pointed to the corridor that held the servants' quarters.

Daphne checked different doors along the corridor until she came to one where she heard moaning. She pushed the door open and entered.

The cook lay groaning with her face to the wall and a pillow clutched to her stomach. The room smelled like vomit, but someone had cleaned it up, and the cook wore a clean white nightgown. Daphne crept forward and shook her by the shoulder.

The cook whipped over and stifled a scream. "You! At least it's not him again. No right, he has, to bully me like that. No right to threaten me. Says he'll have me up for murder if I speak."

Daphne couldn't stand it. "Who?" she whispered.

The cook's eyes flew wide. "A spy, are you? Spying on

me, trying to trick me into confessing something. I'll tell them all you're a spy. Then you'll be sorry."

Uh-oh. Daphne made the questioning gesture again, hands turned up, her mouth an O. She tried to look as stupid as possible. "Who?" she said. "Who?"

"Can't you say anything else? You sound like him. 'Who brought it to you? Who?' As if I knew! 'Some dirty little delivery boy,' I told him. Then he smiled, didn't he, like he was glad. 'If I knew anything about it, do you think I'd be sick like this?' I told him. 'Do you think I'd have taken the tiniest pinch of snuff if I knew?' And then he warned me not to tell anyone how sick the Diva is. How she probably won't be able to sing at the Festival, can you imagine? Last time that happened, with the old Diva before this one, winter lasted all year. There were poisonings and stabbings at the Palace then, I can promise you, though they hushed it all up. Imagine him warning me not to tell. As if I were a loose-mouth like those foolish kitchen maids."

Daphne unwrapped the body of the little yellowkin, and said in a mournful tone, "Who? Who?"

The cook flinched away from the dead body. "I don't know who, you poor little fool, but whoever it was, Master Thomas'll root them out, and then I pity them, whoever they are." She shuddered and clutched her blanket, and Daphne withdrew.

*　　*　　*

So Master Thomas had questioned the cook and warned her not to say anything. But how could she have spread rumors about the Diva in the first place, if he hadn't told her? Telling the cook was like publishing headlines in a newspaper. Even when she thought Daphne might be a spy, she couldn't stop herself from babbling.

Daphne paused outside the kitchen, wary of stepping into the open again. Malice hung in the air. A scruffy boy had brought the new tea. The cook had taken some as snuff, and had become ill. Daphne had brewed the tea and taken it to Lila. Lady Nadia had come to the kitchen and removed the tea, either to hide a crime or to fortify her own voice with Lila's tea, in which case someone ought to warn her.

Daphne stood helpless in her silence. She could track down Lady Nadia or follow her strong impulse to sneak back to Lila's bedside and watch over her. But then the Diva would keep her word and turn Daphne over to Master Thomas, who thought her a murderess.

Could it be true that some jealous rival wanted to see Lila dead? Even with a guard at the door and the Diva's power of protection spread over her, Lila must be frightened, hearing her own awful voice whenever she spoke. If Lila's voice stayed ugly, like Fort's, not only would she be an outcast in the Land of Winter, she would lose everything at home, too—her singing career for sure, and most likely her mother's love.

Through the door to the kitchen, Daphne heard the high, excited voice of one of the kitchen maids. "Oh, my, something is going on for sure. Master Thomas is locked in a room with Lady Nadia, and he's sent word we're to grab hold of a servant girl named Annie and send her along as soon as we see her. I don't know an Annie, do you? Unless he means Lady Lila's servant, but doesn't her name start with D? Should we nab her anyway, next time she passes through?"

Daphne backed down the corridor as fast as she could, grabbed someone's cloak from a hook, and slipped out the servants' door.

* * *

A chime made of cut crystal tinkled when Daphne opened the door to the glass shop.

"Here you are again. But so tired looking. My child, are you well?"

Daphne tried to speak, gulped, and erupted in tears.

The man waited until the torrent slowed, then offered her a handkerchief. She shook her head, reached into the pocket of her apron, and brought out the wrapped body of the bird.

He unwrapped it gravely and ran the side of his finger along its feathers. "A shame he didn't listen to you and go home."

She said, "I don't even know your name."

"My family name is Silica. And you?"

"Daphne," she said, and then wondered if she was right to trust him.

"We should bury him, don't you think? Though I suggest you keep a feather. The feathers are remarkable even after death. They still gleam yellow in the presence of fine music, did you know?"

"I didn't know. I'd like that." She winced as he pulled a

wing feather loose from the little body and handed it to her. She slipped it into her pocket.

Mr. Silica led her through the back of the store to a snug, walled garden with a glass roof. The garden overflowed with daffodils just starting to bloom. Daphne felt the solar heat on her neck.

"I know I'm beginning the song before the baton is raised," Mr. Silica said. "But the sun is higher these days, and I get so impatient waiting for color. So I built this glass room. Shall we bury him here?"

Daphne nodded, and Mr. Silica took a trowel from against the wall.

Tears filled Daphne's eyes again. "There's something worse than my bird," she blurted. "Someone tried to murder my cousin, the one in the Palace."

He whistled. "No. Tell me."

She told him about the tea, the mysterious delivery boy, Lady Nadia, the cook, and Master Thomas's investigation. He listened, nodding, as he dug among the daffodils.

"Do you ever drink the tea?" he asked when she finished.

"No. Servants aren't allowed to."

Mr. Silica leaned back from the hole. Daphne knelt to place the bird, still wrapped in the Diva's handkerchief, into the grave. Both of them sat in silence for a moment, and then Daphne took the trowel from Mr. Silica's hand and filled the grave.

"And the cook said that particular tea was for your cousin?" Mr. Silica asked when she handed back the trowel.

"Yes, but I don't think the cook's the guilty one, because

she stole some for snuff and got really sick. I think she told me the truth, you know. Why would she lie to a deaf person? Some boy brought it to her."

"Someone sent the boy. And that someone meant to harm either your Lila or our Diva."

"People don't know the Diva drinks Lila's tea," Daphne said.

"How can you be sure of that?"

"Master Thomas said so." As soon as she spoke, Daphne remembered that of course Master Thomas knew. He could have mentioned it to anyone. Maybe he had let it slip to someone, and now he was covering for his own carelessness. "I don't trust him," Daphne said. "His voice reminds me of someone I knew in Origin, under the mountain."

Mr. Silica raised his eyebrows.

"He lured children away from their parents to live there and be schooled," said Daphne. "He seemed to be good and kind. But he would ..." She shivered. "He would manipulate people's minds to make them agree with him."

The glassmaker considered. "I've heard this Master Thomas, the new Composer, praised for his ideas about order and harmony. They say he's redesigning the school curriculum. He wants higher standards and less variation from town to town. The Diva embraces the notion."

Daphne knelt in the dirt and traced her finger around the lip of one of the daffodils, pondering. "The man I knew was named Timothy, and he could see, but he might be blind now." She didn't want to go into the whole story, about how all the Nomologists seemed blinded by the sunlight when they emerged from under the mountain. "He had silvery hair, but he could shave it. He had blue eyes, but Master Thomas has dark eyes. Eyes don't change color."

"No," said Mr. Silica. "Eyes don't change color. Unless ..." He peered at the ground.

"Unless?"

After a pause, he shook his head. "Unless you're misremembering. When did you know this man?"

"Just last summer."

He brightened. "In that case, my dear, it's not the same man. Master Thomas arrived two years ago, and has resided in the Palace ever since."

Daphne let out her breath. "I knew he couldn't be the same. Still, it's a relief."

Mr. Silica gave Daphne a hand and pulled her up. "But Master Thomas could still be the guilty one. You say he knew Lila shared her tea with the Diva. It doesn't make sense for him to hurt a child, but would he have reason to hurt the Diva?"

Daphne considered. Much as she mistrusted Master Thomas, she couldn't think of a motive. "I don't know."

"Who benefits?" Mr. Silica said. "We must always ask ourselves, if the plan were to work, who would benefit? The Diva favors Master Thomas. She's the source of his influence. I don't see how it would help him to have her dead."

"But I didn't tell you. First the poison ruins the voice. Maybe the poisoner never even meant to kill anyone."

Mr. Silica pulled on his lower lip, "And who would benefit if the Diva's voice were ruined?"

Daphne sighed. She hated to reach the same conclusion Master Thomas had. "The next Diva. I can't exactly ask around, but I hear the talk. I think it would be Lady Nadia."

"And anyone who wanted to advance with her," Mr. Silica said gently. "Don't forget, it could have been done for her sake without her knowing."

"Or maybe someone else did it to get her in trouble," Daphne said. "One of the other Ladies, next in line, like Lady Dominica."

Mr. Silica pursed his lips and nodded. "Possible, very possible."

"But Lady Nadia's the one who came and took the evidence away." She rubbed her aching forehead. "The worst thing is, Master Thomas wants to question me, and I'm afraid of him."

"Question a servant who is deaf and dumb? How very odd. Worrisome. Perhaps you should hide out for a while. Oh dear, I wish I could go to the Palace for you and find out what the talk is, but ..." He shook his head, and then brightened. "Itzo! My son Itzo, who runs the factory! We must go talk to Itzo."

Daphne didn't see the connection, but Mr. Silica looked so pleased with his idea that she felt cheered. She said, "I'd like to meet your son."

Mr. Silica clasped his hands over his ample belly and rocked back, a pleased smile on his face. "Itzo is a master craftsman. Anyone with vision problems consults him for spectacles, and he can blow globes of glass so fine you can hardly see them. I can't wait to show you. Come along. I'm afraid it's quite a little trek through the city."

He opened the garden gate and led her into a back street, then through a warren of alleys, little shops, houses, and storehouses. They passed a stable with its strong smell of wet hay, and a blacksmith's shop, and a stinking tannery with vats of dye and stacks of cowhide piled in a yard. Finally they crossed a wide snow-dusted lot to a brick warehouse, where a giant letter G hung lopsided from the roof. Mr. Silica gestured at it. "Silica Glass. The S fell off in a storm." He opened the door for her.

Within, Daphne stood in warmth and heard the windy sound of a furnace. Piles of white sand stood along the center of the barnlike building, and smaller piles of black gravel rested nearby. Bottles of every color hung on pegs, and thin sheets of colored glass leaned in the corner, waiting to be cut.

"Itzo!" Mr. Silica called.

Out from behind a cauldron stepped a younger version of Daphne's friend, but a little taller, with a pointed beard and black hair a little neater than his father's. He wore goggles, and when he pulled them off, Daphne was disappointed that he didn't have Mr. Silica's blue eyes with the merry wrinkles at their corners. Instead, his eyes were brown and worried.

"Son, this is my friend Daphne. Can you give us a tour?"

"Father, I would love to," the young man said. "But I've been invited to the Palace to talk about a big order."

Mr. Silica raised his eyebrows. "Your *rapprochement* with the Palace goes so well as that?"

Itzo nodded. "It does."

Mr. Silica said, "In that case, son, I wonder if you might make a few inquiries on behalf of my young friend. You see, there has been a scandal, a case of poisoning, and we need to know if it has been settled beyond doubt, or if people are still being questioned."

"What are you talking about?" Itzo took a step backward. "I don't need to hear these things. You know I can't go snooping into Palace business."

"A few well-placed questions ..."

"Father, I'm sorry, but no. You know our family is still suspect. What you don't understand is how I've worked, what discreet commissions, what delicate, intricate work I've done to win the Palace's favor. An order like the one that's coming could mean our return to fortune. Every rich house in the city will want to imitate it." Itzo shook his head. "To tell the truth, much as I regret to say so, I think it would be helpful if you stayed away from the factory for now."

Mr. Silica seemed to shrink a little, Daphne thought, and then he nodded. "You're right, son. You've suffered long enough the effects of my foolish pride."

Itzo's shoulders relaxed. "Thank you, Father. I won't do anything you wouldn't do. Only the highest quality work. And Father, if your friend's in trouble, just tell her to keep her head down. By spring, whatever it is will pass. Hurry, now. Please go."

*   *   *

They walked away. Mr. Silica looked deflated. Why, the way he looked now, he could even button those last two buttons across his stomach, Daphne thought. "Why doesn't the Palace approve of you?" she asked.

"It goes way back," he said. "Years ago, when they confiscated bells from all the towns and melted them together, my grandfather helped people save some. He melted them into little bells that people could take into their homes, so they could keep some pure notes just to themselves." He took Daphne's arm and steered her around the puddles in the vacant lot. "That put our family on the blacklist for a while. Eventually we gained favor again, but whenever I worked in the Palace, repairing windows or installing stained glass, I used to whistle at my work. It was a habit, but whistling is frowned on, you know. 'Weak imitation music that the unskilled can take up to mock their betters,' that's what they called it."

"They banished you from the Palace for that?"

He wrinkled his nose. "There was a little more to it. Multiple warnings, and then a matter of a fistfight with a guard. I was young and foolish in those days, but a few months in prison changed my tune."

"Was it terrible?"

He marched beside her up the street. "It was gloomy. No music, no colored play of light across the wall. The screech of every closing door echoed for hours. A person could go crazy down there. When the Diva pardoned me, I thanked them very much and asked them never to call me for glass work again."

"Good for you!" Daphne said, and she patted him on the back. The story of her friend's small defiance gave her courage. "I think I'll go back to the Palace," she said. "I think I'll be safe. Nobody even really knows me there. If I need to, I can stay out of sight. Master Thomas probably has the culprit now, and if not, then I have to figure things out myself. I have to keep Lila safe."

"You are a good and faithful servant," Mr. Silica said.

Daphne turned on him to see if he was mocking her, but he only nodded, his face grave.

CHAPTER THIRTY

Molten Ore

Ivan reached a gloved hand and opened a vent into the humped brick oven. Two miners leaned on the great bellows, pumping air under the coals that lined the bottom of the kiln, heating fifty pounds of crushed rock that lay softening in a crucible within. "First melt," Ivan called. "Time to pour."

Two more miners grabbed hold of the wooden ends of an iron bar that ran through the oven. They turned the bar, the cauldron tilted, and molten ore ran into an iron pan with disk-shaped indentations, like a muffin pan for very low muffins. Rocco, the head miner, drew the pan out of the oven and replaced it with another.

It was hard to get the pours at just the right time, when one note had completely melted and another had not yet softened. A thermometer would help, but Ivan hadn't figured out how to make one for temperatures this high. Still, they were making progress. D had the lowest melting point, then D sharp, then E, then all around the scale to C sharp, after which the iron crucible itself began to glow and soften.

Today Fort's job was to check the metal disks once they had been poured and hardened, to make estimates of their purity. He was free of his chains, as Rocco had promised, but neither he nor Ivan would be allowed to leave until they had perfected the melting process. And right now Fort didn't even want to leave, Ivan could tell. The idea of bringing back the music metal had captivated him.

"How do I know if it's pure?" Fort had asked.

"Just listen to it," Rocco growled. "You're the one with the high class ears."

All morning, Fort had been hanging finished metal disks from strings and striking them with a stick. Now he came to report to Rocco. "Not that great," he said, giving Ivan an unhappy look. "You can tell the notes, but they're ... muddy. E's the best, and it goes down from there."

"Not good enough." Rocco shook his head. "Never get there this way. Not good enough."

Fort ran his stick along the string of hanging disks. "Why not melt them again?" he suggested. "Throw in all the E's together, melt them again, and pour them off quick before the impurities melt, too."

Rocco narrowed his eyes. "We'll be wasting a lot of ore."

Fort laughed and waved his stick toward the dark walls on all sides. "I don't think you'll run out anytime soon."

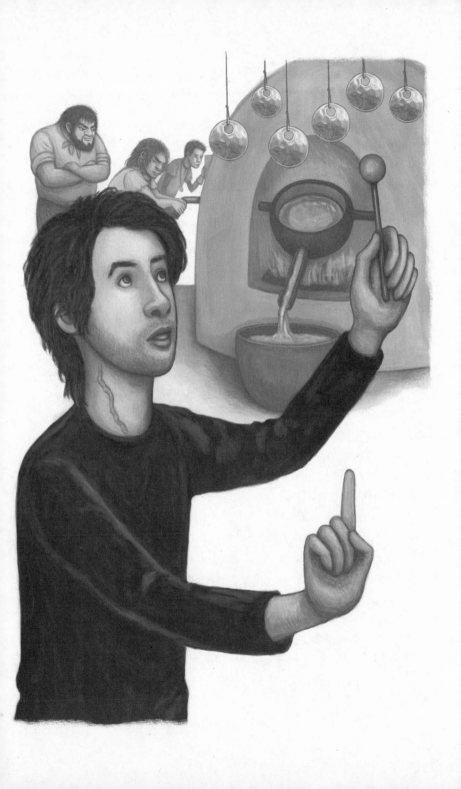

Rocco considered, grunted, and went off to organize more work teams.

Fort threw an arm over Ivan's shoulders. "Do you see how this place is changing? Slaves, at least in this room, out of their chains. Masters listening to their former slaves' ideas. Fewer poor fellows lying twisted in a tiny tunnel, hacking away at a bit of silver and hoping the tunnel won't collapse. And all because of you. You're brilliant, Ivan."

"Thanks," Ivan said. "But there's still a lot of work to do before we get the metal pure."

"Sure." Fort raised his arms, jabbing both fists into the air. "And then our revolution!"

"How do you mean?" Ivan said. Talk of revolution made him uneasy. He knew Fort talked to the other condemned men at night about freedom and justice, but he also heard whispers and muttered curses and talk of slicing arrogant throats and silencing proud voices for good.

"Every person will be able to make music, that's what I mean. They'll have sample notes to teach their children by, so everyone will have an equal chance to learn to sing. Power will be shared evenly." Fort's eyes had their old glow.

"But Rocco and the soldiers just want to get rich. They're supposed to be mining silver, but they've found something better. Who will they sell to?" Ivan rubbed his thumb against his fingers. "Rich people, because they pay more. You think the rich are going to start giving away music metal to the poor so poor kids can grow up musical and elbow their own privileged children aside?"

When Fort didn't answer, Ivan flipped open the kiln

window, saw that he'd waited almost too long, and said, "Second melt. Pour."

Rocco returned with his new band of workers, a weary-looking work crew still chained at the ankles. He said, "Fort, use these men to get that empty kiln working,"

Fort took a stand in front of Rocco and folded his arms. "Nobody in this room works in chains, Rocco. You know that."

Rocco ground his teeth and dug the key from his pocket.

*   *   *

After the evening meal, Fort leaned close to Ivan and spoke in his ear. "I'm not counting on the goodness of the rich. Have you looked around this place lately? Have you felt the change in the air? Listen!"

Ivan listened. He heard men talking by the fire and guards setting down their mugs of beer and laughing.

Fort leaned close. "Do you hear that buzz? You're right. It's the sound of greed. It's Rocco and the guards counting up how rich your discovery is going to make them. With just what they can steal on the side they can be rich. But what if they take over the mine?"

"Take it over?"

"They're just workingmen like everyone else. Every ingot goes to Melodia, to the Palace, which is why we pay taxes in songs instead of money. But I've been talking to the soldiers, Ivan, late at night when you're off in dreamland resting that great brain of yours."

Ivan shifted. There was a glitter in Fort's eye he didn't like. "Saying what?"

"Why should all the music go to the powerful? We need a rebellion, a mutiny. Set the prisoners free, I tell them, but offer them a chance to stay on as miners of music. Sell the music metal to anyone, but charge the rich extra. As for silver, we'll keep mining that, too, for a price—and we'll send enough coins to the poor people in the towns that they can buy decent food. Can you imagine, Ivan? Food enough and music enough for everyone!"

Ivan remembered the crowded lanes and ragged people of Capella and the haughty faces of the judges when Fort came to trial. But he also remembered bits of things he had learned of in his own world—rebellions crushed, protesters shot down like mad dogs, successful revolutionaries who set themselves up as dictators and enriched themselves by robbing the people.

Ivan said, "You're assuming everyone will act out of goodness. You think people will share—here in the mine, out there in the villages. People never share unless they're forced to." He felt with despair the inadequacy of his words. Fort had music in his tongue; Ivan had only a mix of uncertain ideas.

Fort looked down at his hands. "I know I'm an idealist. When I was young, I thought anyone who made beautiful music must be good. Now, well, it's hard to think people like my false father will ever change. But we have to do something. Listen, Ivan, there are men here, men from the south condemned for stirring up rebellion. They want to destroy everything, tear down the houses—"

"Like your poem," Ivan said, and he quoted, "All the stone houses come tumbling down."

Fort stopped. His Adam's apple bobbed, and the scar along his neck stood out bright red. He made a choking sound, as if words had caught in his throat. "I don't want violence, Ivan. I thought—I thought if the people just had music, the walls would tumble down on their own. It was a metaphor, Ivan. Don't you know what a metaphor is? Walls between people, the structures of privilege ..."

"I know what a metaphor is," Ivan said. "But the villagers listening, they didn't hear it as metaphor."

"We have to act. You haven't heard what the people of the south are planning. They want to tear down everything. They think killing music is the only way. Do you know what they talk about doing to rich people, Ivan? People like my sister? Deafness, every one. Hot sticks drawn from the fire and jammed into their ears. We'll be a country of deaf people, and music will die out altogether."

Ivan drew back, but Fort gripped his arm. "We have to rise first, don't you see? We have to bring hope to this country. Your molten ore, Ivan, that's what's going to save us. Are you with us?"

"I'm not a revolutionary," Ivan said. "No matter what you say, I'm afraid I'll end up with blood on my hands."

"Doing nothing will leave blood on your hands."

Ivan groaned and rubbed the sides of his head.

Fort said, "Listen. No blood. You have to trust me. We'll

perfect the melt. We'll arm the people with music. The next two or three wagons that come for silver, we'll commandeer them and fill them with music metal. Then we'll drive to Melodia for Spring Festival, and we'll challenge the order of everything. We can change the world, Ivan."

Ivan touched the pocket that held Daphne's letters, most so soiled and tattered they were almost unreadable now. Among them were two new ones, telling him about life in the Palace and urging him to find a way to come to Spring Festival. It all comes together, he thought, and he knew he'd do almost anything to find the girls again. "How long now until the Festival?"

"Just under three octaves," Fort said.

"Twenty days."

Fort tossed the hair out of his eyes. "Say seven or eight days to perfect the process, six or seven more to manufacture all the metal we can. Four days to travel there. Three days of Festival."

"I'll help," Ivan said, and at once, having committed himself, he felt Fort's words seep into him, filling him with hope and a sense of purpose. "But you can't just show up with wagonloads of metal, Fort. There has to be some way of involving the people, like when you had them dancing outside of Capella." Ivan thought of the Hermit's bridge, the tones ringing out as he leapt across. Excitement grabbed him. "I've got it, Fort. I know what to do, and it won't even take that much ore."

CHAPTER THIRTY-ONE

Glass and a Prisoner

Daphne slipped into the kitchen and, with her head meekly lowered, waited close to the door, ready to flee again if anyone challenged her. In the minute before anyone noticed her presence, she took note of the fact that the snuff-taking cook was still absent, that the kitchen was cleaner than usual, and that all the staff were attending to their chopping and scrubbing and kneading far more diligently than usual, as if they had been scolded.

One of the kitchen maids caught sight of her and said, "There's that Annie. Do we grab her?"

One of the assistant cooks shook her head. "Master Thomas doesn't want her anymore." She drew Daphne over to a chopping board and showed her a pile of potatoes to peel. "We might as well make use of her in the kitchen," she told the others, "now that Master Thomas says the lady Lila's to have no servant anymore."

When Daphne finished peeling a great pile of potatoes, she helped prepare tiny jam sandwiches for the Ladies' afternoon tea. As the Ladies' deaf servants began to arrive to prepare their tea, she went to take her place among them. After all, no one could expect a deaf servant to know any better.

The assistant cook took the teapot out of Daphne's hands and shook a finger in front of her nose. "No, no, no. No more going to the Diva's chamber." She took hold of Daphne's hand and gave it a little slap as if admonishing a child.

Daphne whimpered and put the hand to her mouth, trying to look puzzled. The other servants stared.

Then the kitchen door opened again, and Lila herself stepped inside, pale and weary-looking with dark circles under her eyes, carrying a teapot as if it was too heavy for her. She looked around the steamy kitchen, caught sight of Daphne, and croaked, "Can somebody show me how to make the tea?" She raised one hand and summoned Daphne.

Daphne stood beside Lila, showing her the motions of tea-making, drawing the leaves from the large common tea box. One of the kitchen maids dropped a pile of cups, and in the din, Daphne whispered, "Are you all right?"

"Yes, but I'm not allowed a servant any longer. Master Thomas says it's best if the Diva sees nobody, not even me, but the Diva won't give me up. She says I can be my own servant and that will help cure me of pride."

It's sure helped cure me, thought Daphne. But she whispered, "How will I watch over you?"

The door banged open once more, and all the kitchen staff stood back against the walls as the Lady Nadia swept in, escorted by a guard and followed by Master Thomas. Daphne pulled up the hood of her cloak and melted behind Lila.

"You have no proof," Lady Nadia said wildly. Bedraggled strands of dark hair trailed from her headdress, and tears dribbled down her cheeks. "You, cooks and kitchen maids, tell these gentlemen. It isn't right to treat me so. I'm not the one who brought you that new tea. I'm not the one who mixed it."

The cook who had scolded Daphne spoke up. "That's right, Master Thomas. Lady Nadia never brought that tea. Why, she's the one who took it away."

"To hide it," Master Thomas said in his smooth voice. "To hide the evidence in her chamber, and when I sought to question her, she had fled into the city to swear her accomplices to secrecy."

Lady Nadia's face was red now, and she glanced right and left in the crowded kitchen and made little grasping motions with her hands as if appealing for someone to speak on her behalf.

Master Thomas gave a deep sigh and turned around slowly, speaking to all the inhabitants of the kitchen. "Henceforth, I expect much greater vigilance from all of you. Lady Nadia will be housed in a cell befitting her station until I determine the full truth. No one is to see her except to leave meals at her door. Do you understand?"

The deaf servant girls stood mute and wide-eyed, but the cooks and kitchen maids nodded their heads.

Lady Nadia wailed as the guard took a grip on her arm and led her away.

The assistant cook turned to Lila. "Tell your servant, miss, if you please. I don't know how you talk to them that are deaf, but however you do it, tell her she'll be working in the kitchen and serving the prisoner from now on."

*   *   *

Daphne waited in Mr. Silica's glass shop, fingering the little glass animals, until his customer left. Then he came to greet her, surveying her face. "Itzo said there was only one arrest, Lady Nadia, so I hoped you were safe."

"I'm safe. Even Master Thomas has stopped looking for me, but no servant is allowed near Lila and the Diva. I serve Lady Nadia in the dungeon now. I just came hoping ... Is there a letter from my cousin?"

Mr. Silica shook his head. "Nothing. It's strange, the silver shipment is late this octave. You know they usually unload at the treasury and then bring the leftover bits to me. But this octave they're four days late. Winter must be whirling hard along the road."

Daphne nodded and tried to keep smiling. She had so hoped for a letter from Ivan before the Festival. Probably he was still a prisoner, unable to answer. It was asking a lot to think he could free himself and make his way here.

324

"Don't be downhearted, my dear." Mr. Silica touched one of the prisms in the window and it turned, projecting a rainbow onto Daphne's apron. "If the Festival is a happy one, the Diva issues pardons afterward. For the cousin of faithful servants like you and your singing cousin, surely she would be merciful."

"Really? How can I get a pardon for Ivan?"

"We write a letter, a formal request. I can show you. That's how I got out of prison that time, after all." He smiled at her, and went to his little desk.

The tinkling glass that hung at the door interrupted him. Mr. Silica looked up, and in walked his son, brow furrowed and hat in his hands.

"Father," Itzo Silica said. "I need advice."

Something in his voice sounded so humble, so private, that Daphne withdrew to a corner of the shop.

"So happy to see you, my boy," Mr. Silica said, taking his son by the hands. "So happy. My advice, such as it is, is yours for the taking."

Itzo settled on the chair where his father had sat the moment before. "The order is for five large sheets of glass. A rush order, to be delivered before the Festival. They want it perfectly clear, and at least an inch thick."

"An inch thick, I see. Who, son?"

Itzo looked confused. "Who what?"

"Who sent in the order? Who told you the specifications?"

"The Palace." He looked aside. "A messenger. I don't know who exactly."

His father studied him. "And did you send word that an inch thick is more than we can do?"

The young man shook his head. "That would be commercial suicide, Father. I decided to make do."

"To make do?"

"Yes. To develop a technique. Just like I did for the thinnest of thin glass. And you know, I'm very nearly there. With just a touch of impurity—a little touch of ore melted in at just the right temperature ..."

"What color does it give you?"

"I keep experimenting with different colors. The tiniest bit of rose, a hint of yellow. A touch of pure color, almost too faint to see."

"Yes, I understand." Mr. Silica nodded.

"The problem is I'm left with a weakness. You know how it is, Father. The right note, sung loud enough—I tried layering the glass in, with different impurities, different colors, for reinforcement. But the layers didn't anneal correctly. Bubbles, flaws, internal cracks ... I think a single color's going to work best, Father. Anywhere else I'd be confident. But the Palace of Music! What if some concert, some aria—well, what if the wrong note cracked it somehow?"

Mr. Silica rubbed his chin, considering. "Where is it to go?"

"A new chamber, the messenger said, someplace where breakfast is served. A morning room, a gift for the Diva after the Festival. I thought maybe a rose color would work."

"Well, son, they won't hold a concert at breakfast.

And an inch thick, you say? I doubt a note, however pure, however loud, could crack a pane of glass an inch thick. Even at the Palace. Let me come help you, son. With the two of us working together, we can make sure."

Itzo stood up and made a little bow. "Thank you, Father, you relieve my mind. But it's best to keep the separation. You run the store, I run the business. We can't risk any ... displeasure." He saluted and left.

Mr. Silica looked crumpled when Daphne emerged. He said, "He's a fine craftsman, my Itzo. And a fine son. Just a little too eager to please."

"I didn't know they were building a new room at the Palace," Daphne said.

"Apparently it's a surprise for the Diva, and that's why it's all happening so quietly." The glassmaker peered at Daphne. "Does her Highness still improve? And the little girl?"

Daphne ducked away from his gaze. "Once or twice Lila's snuck down to find me in the kitchen. It's like she's pleading with me. Lila says it's important for the people to have faith in the Diva—she thrives on their faith. Lila says the Diva sings, she sweats, she works all day to strengthen her voice, but I'm not sure how well it's working. Lila's voice still sounds wobbly. And there are rumors in the Palace—do you hear them out here?"

Mr. Silica picked up a tiny glass bear and began to polish it. "Yes, there are whispers, and they didn't come from me. Rumors say the Diva is getting old and vague." He squinted at the bear. "There are whispers that she's infatuated with a young girl and neglects her duty."

"Oh." Daphne felt ill. "Mr. Silica ... no one's told me exactly how it works at the Festival. Does the Diva always have to sing?"

"Oh, my, I keep forgetting you're from Afar." He replaced the glass bear and peered at her over his spectacles. "Yes indeed, she must sing. First there are two days of Festival. Food, singing contests among the towns. Even the Ladies sing, and the Composers judge. Meanwhile, laborers will have built the Ice Castle. They use blocks of ice from the lake southeast of here. Ice cutters are at the lake already, and the nomads haul the blocks in on sledges drawn by bears, great sand-colored bears."

Daphne nodded. "But how can they build a castle of ice here in the city, where music warms everything above freezing?"

"They set up on a hill just west of the old city walls, in a place never used the rest of the year. It's cold there, all right. The evening of the third day of the Festival, the Diva climbs the ice stairs into the room at the top of the tower, and the inside steps are chopped away. She's sealed off in there, in the cold of winter. When dawn arrives, she begins to sing. She summons all her training, all her strength to the task. She sings as the people outside sing also, waiting. In a matter of hours she sings herself free. A doorway melts in the tower wall, and she steps out and comes sweeping down the outer stair. And spring comes. That's it, Daphne, that's the great mystery of the Land of Winter."

"What if she doesn't melt her way out? I bet spring comes anyway."

"Oh, no." Mr. Silica looked shocked. "A couple of times in the past—once when I was a boy—the Diva failed, and the snow on the fields and in the forests didn't melt all year. By the next year, with a new Diva, the snow was all that much thicker and the air that much colder, what with the sunlight reflected away all year by the snow. It took years before the crops were back to normal. We were hungry." He shook his head. "No, no, that can't be allowed to happen again. It's the Composers, now, who give their approval in the end and decide if the Diva should go forward. If not, well, there are always other Ladies lined up ready to assume her duties. That's why we call them ladies-in-waiting."

"Oh," Daphne said, thinking of the Diva rehearsing in front of the mirror, trying to restore her voice in time. Then there was Nadia, the Diva's most aggrieved lady-in-waiting, fuming in a well-furnished prison cell.

Late afternoon light, slanting through the prisms in the window, threw rainbows against the shop's back wall. It was time to get back to the Palace. Daphne touched Mr. Silica's arm in thanks and slipped out the door.

*   *   *

Daphne prepared a plate of food to carry down to Lady Nadia in her prison apartment. At first, delivering the meal had been her only duty, but over time Lady Nadia had charmed the guard at the door into letting Daphne in long enough to tidy the room and brush the prisoner's clothes.

Lady Nadia was housed in the most comfortable part of the dungeon, more a basement apartment than a cell. Daphne descended the kitchen stair and waited for the guard to let her through a thick wooden door into the one furnished room. Lady Nadia sat at her desk near the tiny high window that looked out on the ankles of passersby. A long curtain screened the lady's washbasin and chamber pot. Lady Nadia bent low, writing her protestation of innocence, which she worked on every day, though she didn't seem to make much progress.

Daphne set the plate and a mug of beer on the small table behind the lady. Then she neatened the lady's bed and rearranged her brush and comb beside the basin where she washed. She was glad to see that the chamber pot was empty.

The lady put down her quill and stood, glancing up at the barred window.

"Maybe if I give up eating I'll slim away until I can slip out there," she said. "I could live among the beetles and butterflies instead of here among hypocrites and liars."

Daphne raised her eyebrows and cocked her head to one side in her intelligent dog look. So far the look had never worked on Lady Nadia, but this evening might be the time.

"Yes, liars and hypocrites! Toadies, telling that old woman she still has what it takes to summon the spring. Who among them has prayed as I have, listened as I have, begged the goddess for guidance as I have?" She leaned down and put her puffy face next to Daphne's. "She is too old. Don't they hear it? Too old!"

Daphne recoiled.

The Lady laughed. "Yes, well may you start back in fear, though you don't know what I'm saying. Some would whimper that just to say these words is treason—just to listen to me say so, ha-ha!"

She stomped over and sat at the table, where she seized a chicken leg and waved it in the air. "It weakens the voice, he told me, that's all. Do you know what I was doing, girl? I was making the truth more obvious. So here I sit writing my confession—my justification—but if I put down the truth they'll execute me for treason! Even though I was trying to save my country. So instead I deny everything. What else can I do?"

She chomped into the chicken leg, and Daphne reflected that all these weeks since the poisoning, while the Diva worked so hard to restore her voice, Daphne had not seen Lady Nadia rehearse once.

Lady Nadia waved the chicken leg. "All that nonsense about it being poison. More like truth serum. No one died, did they? No one was going to die."

Daphne gazed at her. My yellowkin died. And who put you up to it? she thought, trying to send the question into the Lady's brain.

Instead of an answer, Daphne heard footsteps in the hallway.

"Oh, heavens, it's him!" cried the Lady. "He doesn't like me having visitors, not that you're a visitor, but—Oh, listen to me, explaining to a deaf person. Quick, behind here!" She thrust Daphne behind the curtain.

Looking down, Daphne saw that the curtain reached

only to her ankles. She hoped the person about to enter was not very observant.

The door opened, and Daphne heard the tapping of Master Thomas's cane.

"Sit down," Lady Nadia said, dragging a chair across the stone floor. Daphne risked a look. Nadia had turned the chair so that the Composer would sit turned away from the window and Daphne's feet.

If he's the one she expected, Daphne wondered, why bother to hide me? Who hides from a blind man? A shiver ran along her spine. She wished she could pull up her feet.

"The Festival approaches," he said in his pleasant voice.

The very sweetness of his voice grated on her. It sounded so much like the voice of Timothy, honey-tongued head of the Nomologists of Origin. All at once Daphne remembered the last time she had stood so silently, feeling this nervous. It was when they first came to Capella, and Mother Cadenza had questioned them. She had said something strange— what was it?

She had said the mountain fell two years ago.

Two years. Master Thomas had arrived in Melodia two years ago. Time in Lexicon was not the same as time in Daphne's world. A long shudder ran through her, and she knew the curtains were waving. But Master Thomas sat turned away, and besides, Timothy's eyes were blue. Behind his glasses, as she had seen for herself, Master Thomas's eyes were deep brown. He couldn't be the same man.

"How fares her Highness?" Lady Nadia asked.

"She struggles. And to think I once believed that if

anything happened to her Highness, you could step in and save the country."

"I can, I can!"

He paused, and said with extra gentleness, "Nadia, Nadia! How can you think the people would ever accept a murderess?"

Her voice rose into something approaching a screech. "Don't say that word! I would *never*! You told me that powder wasn't dangerous."

"I!" His chair crashed backward, and Daphne risked another peek. Master Thomas loomed over the Lady like a bad dream until she cowered and sank onto her bed. He spoke again, in a voice that pulsed with feeling. "If you persist in implicating me, in implying that I had anything to do with your insane attack, you will face the gallows. Do you understand me, woman?"

She turned her face away and fluttered her hands in denial. "I'm not assigning blame. I know you never meant for me to buy it ..."

"Do you understand me?"

The Lady nodded, dabbing at her eyes.

Master Thomas came away from the bedside, took off the dark glasses, and rubbed his brow. He laid the glasses on the table beside him. "Now, my dear Lady, you know I'll do all I can to clear your name. We will call it a slip, a mistake. The apothecary—who remembers your visit, I warn you—will testify that a simple throat restorative was in the next box, so you might have scooped up the poison by mistake."

Lady Nadia fell to her knees before him. "Master Thomas, you don't know how grateful I—"

"Very well," he said. "Meantime you remain our best backup if her Highness falters. You have been practicing the songs I wrote you?"

"Oh, yes, daily!"

"If worse comes to worst, if the Diva fails and we have to build a new Ice Castle, if we call on you to serve and you become the Diva, I will always advise you. I will stay close to you and never, never, reveal the truth of your jealous error. Do you understand?"

Her lip trembled. "I understand." She bent and actually kissed his foot.

Master Thomas pulled his foot out of her grasp and turned toward the window. His eyes traveled down the length of the curtain, and he froze.

Lady Nadia emitted a little gasp of fear.

Master Thomas strode to the window, threw back the curtain, and grabbed Daphne by the arm. His eyes flashed in the slanting light, and Daphne saw a thin edge to his dark iris. Ice ran down her back. Contact lenses. Itzo Silica, whose specialty was the thinnest and most delicate glass, bragged that he had done some special service for the Palace. The Composer wore dark contact lenses; behind them his eyes might be ice blue after all. Fear coursed through Daphne, and she ducked her head.

"Who is this? Why is she here?"

Lady Nadia stumbled over herself to answer. "A servant girl, Master Thomas. Deaf. Completely deaf and dumb."

"And yet somehow familiar ..."

That voice, the velvet menace of it ... His blindness was only playacting, to make people think he was wise. Cold seeped into Daphne's bones. Plotting, lying, tempting, threatening, all in that smooth voice. He had been Timothy all along. She clutched her hands together, keeping her eyes down. Please, *please* let him not remember me, she thought desperately.

"Jump!" he yelled at her, but she was holding on to herself so hard that instead of jumping, she just staggered a little, as if the force of his breath had pushed her. There was silence, and then he said, "You can go." She was ready this time: it was a game like "Simon Says." She held her body deaf and still until she felt herself yanked and pushed toward the door.

The door clanged shut behind her, but Thomas still propelled her down the corridor and up the stairs. Just as they reached the kitchen, he tightened his grip on her shoulder and leaned on her as if she were guiding him. They emerged into steam and clatter, and he halted and raised his cane in the air. "Listen, all of you!" he cried in a high, clear, voice. "This servant I am holding has been carrying messages for Lady Nadia, messages stirring discontent against our Diva. She is a traitor, and she must be kicked into the streets. She is banished from the Palace, do you hear me? Banished, on pain of death!"

He thrust Daphne among the cooks and kitchen maids, and they parted to let her hurry to the door.

CHAPTER THIRTY-TWO

The Palace Window

Ivan stamped sideways, raised his left arm and shook it, then made a double stamp to the left. Bangles of music metal sounded at his wrists and ankles as he moved. Ivan's notes were C, E, and G. All around him, twenty former prisoners stepped and turned in time, releasing a fountain of notes. In front of them stood Fort, waving his arms to direct them and wincing at wrong notes. Captain Igni's soldiers, who had come over to Fort's side, nodded their heads as they watched.

A miner burst through the cavern entrance. "Wagon coming," he reported.

The dancers jangled to a halt. "Good news," Fort called out. "The third wagon, last one before the Festival. Soon we'll set out for Melodia and revolution. But for now—places, everyone!"

The miners pulled off their bangles and crowded against the cave wall, where they stood shoulder to shoulder with downcast eyes as if still chained together. Fort and some of the soldiers set themselves on either side of the cave opening, just out of view. Ivan stationed himself in the wagon yard, warming his hands over the fire, while nearby, Rocco and Captain Igni directed a handful of soldiers to sit on boxes and roll dice in a picture of idleness.

The wagon slid to a halt at the edge of the snow. Three guards jumped down, and one of them with braid on his shoulder called out for the loafing soldiers to come unhitch the horses. They sauntered over, more interested in displaying their new independence than in maintaining a show of discipline. Captain Igni loped after them, scolding.

The wagon driver stood atop the wagon and surveyed the yard with an air of gloom. "No pile of ingots, I see. Should have known. The mine's given out, no doubt. And the two wagons before me? Loaded 'em with silver, I wager, and the nomads got 'em, every one."

"Buncha nonsense," Rocco growled. "Come inside and warm up. Couple production problems, that's all. Wagons delayed."

The wagon driver climbed down as if his joints were frozen, and Rocco led him to the entrance. "Some hot food'll thaw you out."

The driver hobbled into the cave, and the dice-playing soldiers invited the guards to follow him, promising hot food and drink. Ivan sucked in his breath and trailed after. This part always made him nervous.

As the soldiers entered the cave, Fort and the rebel soldiers fell on them from either side, knocked them the ground, and seized their weapons. At the same moment, Rocco closed his miner's hand like a vise on the wagon driver's arm. No bloodshed. Ivan relaxed.

For the next several hours, while the wagon driver and the guards, now prisoners, ate, drank, and warmed themselves, Fort wooed them. He spoke of injustice and exploitation, the evils of slavery and the benefits of shared ownership. With a flourish, he summoned men to show them finished disks of the music metal, and he launched into a long explanation of what it could mean—equal opportunity, a chance for universal education, economic justice. The new prisoners' eyes glazed and their heads nodded wearily. Before sundown all four had signed on to Fort's revolution.

After dinner, which was loud and raucous—every man celebrating his right to music with drinking songs—Fort came over to Ivan, shaking his head as if to clear his ears. "To be honest, I hoped universal music would sound better than this."

"They haven't had your privileges," Ivan said. His voice came out sharper than he meant. Sometimes Fort annoyed him, the way he drew all eyes, all ears with his scratchy words. "If you wanted lovely music, you should have stayed in school."

Fort flinched, and Ivan, seeing for the hundredth time the scar snaking down his friend's neck, regretted his words.

It's envy, Ivan realized. I'm envious of the way he leads. An unpleasant warmth rose to the roots of his hair. He forced himself to stick out his hand. "Sorry, Fort. I'm an idiot."

Fort shook his hand and grinned. "You're an idiot, and I'm a what?"

"A stuck-up, obnoxious idol. And a snob." Ivan smiled. "There, I've said it. Listen, Fort, at least you remember a time you could sing. Some of us never could. You shouldn't rub our faces in it."

"But you *can* sing, Ivan. You're getting there, you really are. With a little training I bet all these fellows could learn to hold a tune."

"Not well enough to satisfy you. You have a fussy ear, Fort, not like the rest of us regular guys. When I think of my poor old Hermit in his labyrinth, struggling to make musical instruments with his mediocre ear ..."

Fort rubbed his chin and glanced sideways at Ivan. "I meant to say something about your Hermit. We leave the day after tomorrow. Do you think he'd like to come with us?"

"You mean give up being a Monster? Abandon his instruments?"

"No, no. Come out of exile and show the men he's a man like they are, laboring for freedom by building instruments, and only ignorance and prejudice have made him play the Monster."

"He likes being a Monster," said Ivan. "He revels in it." But even as he spoke, Ivan remembered the Hermit cleaning up for him, and he began to doubt.

"As for his instruments," said Fort, "he can bring them along. Don't you see? He can show them off. With instruments, music belongs to everyone. And Melodia has everything he needs to keep experimenting, keep building ..." Fort had the dreamy look in his eye again.

"But isn't it treason to build instruments and play them? He could be hanged."

Fort shook his head. "Today, maybe. Not the day after tomorrow, or the day after that, or ever again, once we change the world."

Fort waited, and Ivan thought about how he'd like to see his crotchety, mad old master again. He kicked a pebble. "Whatever. He can choose. I'll go see him tomorrow."

*   *   *

Daphne sat in the back room of the glass shop, murmuring numbers and writing. Mr. Silica had given her a place to stay after Timothy banished her from the Palace, and in return she had offered to help in the shop. Keeping his books was challenging work, because often he noted transactions on slips of paper that he stuffed in his pockets, and other times he just kept the records in his head—usually, Daphne discovered, when he had charged so little he was embarrassed to reveal it.

She wrote, "Glass bird, medium," and across from that, "21 flats."

Then she gave up trying to concentrate on numbers and pulled out the letter she had just written to Lila.

Dear Lila,

I don't think you've received any of my letters. Remember, if you get one, hang a sheet in the Diva's window. If you can't do that, leave a candle there. Okay, here it is again: Watch out for Thomas. He's not blind. He's plotting against the Diva. He's the one who tricked Lady Nadia into poisoning you both. He wants power. I don't know exactly what he's planning, but warn the Diva!

The door opened, and Mr. Silica entered from the street. He rubbed one ear, a sign that he was worried. "What is it?" Daphne asked.

"I'm sorry, dear. Another octave with no silver delivery." He lowered himself into a chair beside the desk. "I went to the Treasury to inquire. Very odd. New guards there, in ugly brown uniforms. Brown! The most unmusical color. You'll never see brown glinting off cut glass."

"No silver?" Daphne said. "What do you think it means?"

"Thieves, rockslides, rebels, weather, who can say? I walked up to the hill, and the Ice Castle is unfinished. With the Festival starting tomorrow! Who is running this country?"

Daphne hardly listened to him as images came to her of Ivan trapped in a cave-in, lost in a snowstorm, waylaid by bandits. She squeezed her eyes shut, but it didn't help.

"And I ran into Itzo," said Mr. Silica. "He's finished the glass order, five thick sheets, but no one's come to pick it up. He worries they've changed their minds, and he hasn't been paid." Mr. Silica rubbed his forehead. "He cares about that, you see. He's going to visit the Palace and ask."

Daphne shook off her worries about Ivan and stood. "Now you're back, I have to go to the Palace myself."

"Not again. What if you're arrested?"

"I won't be." Daphne picked up a folded letter to Lila and took the cloak folded over the back of her chair. At the door, she looked back at Mr. Silica, who sat watching her and rubbing his ear more vigorously than ever. "Don't worry," she told him, though worry coiled painfully in her stomach.

Outside, she pulled her hood low and stopped to consider. She had to find some new way to get her letter to Lila. She had snuck into the servant's quarters and bribed a kitchen maid; she had tried the regular mail; she had begged a guard at the door for help. Probably Thomas had intercepted the letters, and each visit would be more dangerous than the last. She needed some new inroad to the Palace.

Reluctantly, she thought of Itzo Silica. She didn't particularly like him, and he had refused to help before. But maybe now that he had his own worries about the Palace, he would be more sympathetic.

She turned her steps through the twisting alleys, keeping her hair covered and her head low, trying to remember the way to Silica Glass. There it stood, past the tannery, across that vacant lot, with a huge letter G hanging from its roof. G for glass, of course, but Itzo had still not replaced the S, as if he were ashamed of his family name.

Two men in brown uniforms flanked the door, and

Daphne hesitated. Just as she decided to approach anyway, the door opened and two men emerged, one short and wide, one tall and thin. It was Itzo Silica, talking and nodding, and the man who reached out to shake his hand was bald, wore dark glasses, and carried a cane.

Alarm leaped up inside Daphne's chest. She withdrew into the shadow of the alley. If Timothy spotted her, he'd set his brown-shirted guard on her. But why was he out here, consulting with Itzo? Of course he might just be buying new contact lenses, but Daphne wondered if he was dabbling somehow in the new project, the breakfast room windows. Why would he buy a surprise gift for a monarch he was plotting to overthrow?

Daphne scuttled backward, bending low. If Itzo was dealing with Timothy, she didn't want to ask him any favors. When her feet felt cobbles, she turned and hastened through back alleys to the Palace.

As she reached the main road, citizens scurried to the curb. Boots sounded against stone, and a company of soldiers came marching down the road, stiff arms swinging and eyes fixed straight ahead. She drew back as they strode past, their green uniforms clean and starched, their hair cut in identical bowls around their ears.

"Good thing they're here," a woman said behind her. "Rebels swarming in from the south, have you heard?"

She wasn't addressing Daphne, who stood still, listening, as the woman's friend answered. "Then send the soldiers south where the trouble is, that's what I say. We've never had soldiers marching around during the Festival. Never in my whole stretched-out life. It's a time of sworn peace."

"Peace or not," the first woman said, "look at what's happening. Fruit deliveries way down. No shipments from the silver mine in three octaves. Someone's waylaying them, that's for sure. Rebels from the south stealing our silver!"

"Ours!" the second woman said. "Fat lot of it *we* ever see. But the Palace, oh yes, always building, always primping, best of everything. Let them send the army to patrol the silver road, that's what I say. No need for soldiers in the heart of the city."

The two women moved on, still arguing, and Daphne turned aside, feeling the worry tighten inside her again. Only one day before Spring Festival, foreboding hung over the city. Even here in Melodia, snow lay heavy on the roofs, and icicles dangled nearly to street level. And what if the Ice Castle remained unfinished or the Diva's voice had not healed enough to melt it? Could it be true that spring would hang back and wait for another year? Would she and Lila and Ivan live another year separated by class and prejudice? No, surely it was only superstition; but Daphne pulled her cloak tightly about her as she hurried.

Peasant wagons crowded the entrance to the Palace courtyard. Daphne slipped in among them. At the main door stood two sentries in the new brown uniforms. Daphne ducked into a corner in the shade of the courtyard wall. In front of her a little boy and his sister challenged each other to leap across puddles.

Daphne looked up at the high window of the Diva's tower.

It was blank. Either Lila still hadn't received her message, or she was unable to respond: banished, arrested, imprisoned.

Should I even try again? Daphne wondered. It's the Diva Timothy's after, not Lila. Maybe Lila is safer if I don't interfere.

Then something flickered in the window. Not a sheet or a flame, but the sleeve of a dress, perhaps. Daphne thought she could make out a hand resting on the pane and a pale face framed in dark hair behind. Lila, looking down.

Daphne stepped into the sunlight and waved both hands, jumping up and down. A couple of the peasants turned to look at her and then away. Daphne glanced toward the brown-shirted guards, but they were busy inspecting papers for some delivery. Daphne drew the letter for Lila from her sleeve, waved it in the air, and then with a flourish tucked it into a crack in the wall behind her. There. If no letter could penetrate the Palace to reach Lila, maybe Lila could descend and collect a letter herself.

CHAPTER THIRTY-THREE

Joy

Lila stood at the window, gazing down into the Palace yard. All morning, people had been coming and going—merchants carrying bolts of colored cloth, seamstresses scurrying away with the cloth marked and measured, soldiers in their green uniform coats hastening across the courtyard with rolled messages in their hands. Most often of all came peasants with wagonloads of leftover roots and dried fruit for the feasting to come. All through the three days of Festival, the Diva told her, people feasted on the last and best of their winter food, saved for this day. But she, the Diva, would eat frugally to protect the voice that practice had so recently restored.

"You, my dear, may feast with them if you choose," the Diva had said.

"I'll stay with you, Your Highness."

The Diva had smiled and stroked Lila's hair.

But now, Lila placed a hand against the window and wished she could go out and mix with the ordinary citizens— run free in the city like Daphne, jump over puddles like those two children waiting in the yard for their father to finish his deliveries. Dance like that odd cloaked woman who stepped from the shadows to leap and wave her arms.

The person threw back her hood, and yellow curls sprang free. It was Daphne.

"Lady Lila," the Diva said. "Come place your hand against my abdomen as I sing. Tell me what you feel."

Lila leaned closer to the window. Daphne pulled something out, a sheet of paper, and waved it.

"Lila, I am speaking to you."

Daphne turned and stuffed the paper into the wall.

Lila leaned her forehead against the window to see more clearly, but all at once she felt a sharp jerk on her arm. The Diva spun her around and pulled her close. "Are you listening to me?"

Lila said, "Oh, yes, Your Highness, but I long for a breath of fresh air. May I walk in the courtyard?"

"Child, do you know how many nights I wept with homesickness when first I came to the Palace? How I grew pale and thin that first long winter, and longed to be an ordinary child?"

Lila sighed, because indeed she did know, having heard more than once.

The Diva placed a hand under her chin. "I have heard

you speak of your 'gift' for singing. Here in the Palace of Music, we don't have 'gifts.' We have duties."

Lila nodded and tried to pull away. The Diva's approval was like a lovely garment that you might long for in a shop window. When you put it on it was beautiful and glimmering, and people on the streets turned their heads to see you, but somehow, beneath it all, you were suffocating.

The Diva drew her back. "None of the other Ladies have received what you have, Lila. None of them have received octave after octave of teaching, coaching, and full attention from the Diva in her last year. Yes, her last year." She let Lila go. "It will take all my strength, Lila, to summon the spring this year. And if you are going to be hanging back, longing for something different, you should leave now. I can't afford to have you pulling against me."

"Oh, no!" Lila said, full of remorse. She took the Diva's hand and kissed it. "I will be with you, serving you, every moment until you enter the Ice Castle."

The Diva reached down and stroked her hair. "And now, shall we call the carriage and ride through the city for that fresh air you mentioned?"

*　　*　　*

The Diva kept a hand on Lila's shoulder as they walked to the carriage. "I can't risk twisting an ankle now, dear. Climb up, and help pull me in."

I'll get the letter on the way back, Lila thought.

Citizens stretched their necks to see as the carriage rolled by. They clattered past women arranging dried flowers on their doorsteps and children knocking icicles from eaves. The Diva called a halt in front of a small raised stage beside a fountain where a trickle of water struggled through the ice.

The Diva took Lila's arm, and they descended to the pavement. "Now, Lila, sing for us," said the Diva.

Lila turned to her in astonishment.

"Yes, dear," the Diva said. "It's your turn to sing. Surely you know that all the Ladies sing for the Festival. You will be singing early. No false modesty, now."

Lila felt a strange reluctance to climb the steps to the stage. After weeks of practicing in a closed room, the idea of singing in the open felt strangely exhibitionist. "What shall I sing?"

"Your choice. When Ladies don't have a Composer of their own, they often sing an old favorite from their native town."

Lila mounted the steps, looking around her for inspiration. A show tune didn't seem grand enough for Spring Festival. A shaft of bright sunlight made her shade her eyes, and she looked up at clouds that were dark but edged with gold. Already, in front of the stage, people were gathering. A pair of small children chasing across the cobbles stopped, put their hands to their mouths, and turned to stare. This is what the Diva feels each year, she thought. The people are on the edge of happiness, just teetering there, waiting for her to help them break through.

Only one song could answer. She took a breath, stood straight, and sang the first notes of Beethoven's Ode to Joy.

She sang in German, throwing herself into the song, trying to make the words' meaning come through by the singing alone.

Freude, schöner Götterfunken,
Tochter aus Elysium,
Wir betreten feuertrunken,
Himmlische, dein Heiligtum.

Lila sang in round, warm tones and felt as if she were floating. When she finished, she bowed her head and descended the steps. Around her, wide-eyed people drew back and cleared her path to the Diva, whose face was white. The Diva took Lila's arm with a trembling hand and guided her into the carriage.

The Diva stared with such amazement that Lila feared she had broken some taboo. She slid into the corner of her seat and waited for a scolding, but what the Diva said, in a hushed tone, was, "You never told me you came from *his* country, from the Land of Music."

"Whose country?" Lila asked.

"Zart's. You must know him, the first Composer—you sing in his language. He was only a child when he came, people say. He escaped from his father to visit us, and he sang for the people and taught them to write notes and invented melodies and spoke the way you did just now. He was the first Composer, and he visited us more than once."

"Zart?" said Lila. "You mean Mozart? Speaking German? *Deutsch*?"

The Diva eyes shone. "I felt there was something about you—something different, magnificent. But why did you keep it a secret? Have you been sent to give me strength? To rescue me?"

Lila slid off her seat to kneel at the Diva's feet. "You have it all mixed up, Your Highness. I'm just a regular girl who slid off a roof. I came here by accident. I came to learn from you."

The Diva examined Lila's face, sighed, and then patted Lila's hand as she gazed out the carriage window as they made their jolting way across the cobbles. "Nevertheless, I shall rely on you."

*   *   *

The wagon driver whistled, and the horses leaned back in their harness, bringing the wagon to a creaking halt. The Hermit lowered the recorder he had been playing, and Ivan, who had been sitting with his back to the driver, twisted around to see what was happening.

Wagons and sleds had halted on the road ahead, blocked by two huge bears in harness that struggled to haul a sledge covered in ice blocks up onto the snow-packed road. The wagon had stopped at the edge of a plateau. To the right, the land fell away toward a tree-lined frozen pond with a great gap of dark water at its center. On the pond, men with axes and long saws hacked at the ice. One pair of bears hauled a sledge piled with ice blocks up the zigzagging road, and other bears milled around below, their keepers holding them by flimsy-looking leashes.

"What's going on?" Ivan called to Fort, who had already jumped down from the second wagon.

"They're cutting blocks for the Ice Castle," Fort called back. "I'm surprised they're still at it. The Castle should have been finished days ago. Someone must be paying a lot of silver for these nomad teams."

This was their fifth day of travel; they had meant to arrive in Melodia yesterday, in time for the Festival's start, but stormy weather had delayed them. There were thirty-five of them—twenty miners, nine soldiers, three wagon drivers, Fort, Ivan, and the Hermit with his rudimentary collection of instruments. Their wagons carried a horde of music metal disks and a larger supply of unprocessed ore, with which they meant to demonstrate their purification method. "At the Festival, women set up looms and carpenters bring out their lathes," Fort had said. "We'll show them making music metal is a craft like any other."

The ice bears plodded with their burden, filling the road. No one dared pass the bears. Traffic swelled behind them—sleds, wagons, and people on skis and on foot, dressed in finery, with yellowkin feathers or ribbons or last year's dried flowers stuck in their hair. Then, just as stone towers appeared over a snow-covered hill, the bears turned off, and the traffic surged forward. Even from here Ivan saw Melodia's banners hanging like patchwork against the towers of what must be the Palace. He felt frogs hopping in his belly. Daphne and Lila would be there, in the city, expecting him—Daphne's letter had said they would meet him.

But first he would witness the launch of Fort's unlikely dream—twenty-two ex-prisoners, a Hermit, three wagon drivers and nine soldiers taking the city by music and dance. The plan was so crazy, so full of risk, Ivan felt almost ashamed that he'd helped Fort organize it.

"We're getting close," Fort said. "Let's get the men started."

Fort called the miners to descend from the wagons, and Ivan handed down their collection of metal disks, each marked with a man's name. Fort passed them out, and twenty miners fastened sets of disks to their wrists and ankles.

Ivan watched from the lead wagon as Fort's team—burly men with mine dust ingrained in their faces—made their silent way along the snowy road. They looked so sturdy and determined that Ivan ached with hope for them. Here they marched, prisoners who had wrenched music from the ground and purified it. And he, Ivan, had helped show them the way. With music metal the prisoners had bargained for their freedom, and now they marched as free men, come to offer their findings to everyone in Melodia, from those high in the Palace towers all the way down to those who slept in trash heaps.

Fort signaled for the miners to step into their dance. Back and forth in the wagon's wake they weaved. When they stepped softly, their metal disks stayed silent, but when the dancers stamped, music rang out from their ankles, and when they shook their wrists or clapped their hands, new notes sounded over the old.

Fort had worked out the patterns. Each dancer could play an arpeggio, and together they stomped and shook out simple tunes, but in the purest of ringing tones. The peasants they passed on the road stared in amazement, their mouths hanging open. The miners overtook a high-class family riding in a sleigh behind fine, plumed horses, and the passengers swiveled their heads to see. The mother's sniffs of disapproval faded as her children hummed along with the dancers, tapping their hands on velvet-clad knees.

Ahead, more banners hung from the parapets of Melodia's half-crumbled walls. A guard post loomed beside the gate. Ivan hoped the guards would be drunk already on music and beer, waving everyone through with festive congratulations. He gripped the side of the wagon and waited.

The gateway, when they reached it, was so clogged with people that newcomers on foot swarmed around it, across the snowy fields and over the low city walls. The miners' three wagons crept forward along the road. When guards halted them, Fort stepped up to meet the inspector, who waddled forward with his baton of service and his red-tasseled hat.

"Your purpose here?" the man asked, his head bobbing.

"We're delivering ore."

The inspector humphed and made a note on his paper. Then he marched all the way around the train of wagons, peering under them. He was too short to see inside, but he made a show of looking anyway. "Are you harboring any rebels?" he asked.

Fort regarded him with shining brown eyes. "What are rebels?"

The man gestured with his pen. "Oh, you know, wild fellows. Bloody-minded vandals who want to tear down the Palace of Music and let wolves run savage through the city."

"No," Fort said. "We aren't harboring anyone like that."

*   *   *

As soon as the miners stepped through the gate of Melodia, the air softened, and Ivan removed the torn blanket he had been wearing as an extra cloak. The Festival flowed around them. As the wagons clattered over the cobbles, wood smoke and the smell of burnt sugar wafted toward them. One of the dancers darted to a booth and returned with a pile of almond pastries that he and his fellows tore apart before any morsel reached Ivan.

Ivan's stomach growled. What would it be, to feast on sweets and meat and baked goods again! The wagons paused for a group of children in uniform to follow their choirmaster across the street. Some of the children poked each other into place while others marched straight ahead with the glazed look of stage fright pasted on their faces.

Fort found a corner where the miners and soldiers could climb down. "Don't make too much noise," Fort said. "We're off to negotiate your freedom."

*   *   *

A road wound around the back of the Palace to the Treasury, which was dug into the hill where the Palace stood. Exhausted horses drew the three ore wagons to a halt before the Treasury door, and Fort and Ivan jumped down.

"Brown uniforms," said Fort. "I haven't seen those before." He offered a hand to one of the two sentries standing beside the door. "Friend, we've brought the silver wagons, full of ore."

The sentry did not react. Fort dropped his hand. "Will you open the doors for us?"

The sentry stared straight ahead. "Deaf?" Fort said. "Could they be?" He walked to the great door and turned the handle. Before he could push it open, the sentries' crossed spears blocked his way.

"Now come on," said Ivan, walking up to stand beside the second sentry. "He's not a thief, you can see that. We'll drive these three wagons inside and drive out with them empty. This city's had no silver delivered for three octaves. Who's going to be paying your wages without silver? And we've brought the greatest treasure in decades. Music metal. Do your masters want us to go and strew it about the countryside instead?"

The two sentries stared at each other, and then one of them slipped through the door. A few minutes later he returned with an officer also dressed in brown who hailed them from the door.

"Silver, eh? About time! Was it rebels or bandits held you? You got the Treasurer dismissed for your delay. The army protects the Treasury now. Not that there's much to protect, sad to say. Old junk is all. But what's this? Is this silver?"

"It's much better," Fort said. "It's ore we can purify into music metal."

The jovial officer narrowed his eyes. "Is it, now? Master Thomas will want to see that." He turned to the sentries. "Take hold of them."

Fort tried to shake off his captor, but Ivan said, "And the wagons? You want the wagons to drive away?"

The officer scowled. "Call for the wagons to come inside."

"Sure, if you let us go. You might want us to gather in the music metal we've left in the city."

The officer moved his jaw in a circle, thinking. "One can go, but one stays behind as hostage."

The Hermit climbed down from the lead wagon and hobbled over, rubbing his back. "Hostage, that'll be me. That wagon was rattling my bones to powder. Nothing I'd like better than to get out of this infernal sunlight. Now stand back, young fellow, and let the treasure in."

CHAPTER THIRTY-FOUR

Spring Festival

Mr. Silica bustled into the shop. "Your Lila is well, dear. There's word of the lovely young Lady who sang out joy in a magical ancient language. And Itzo's deal has come through. They paid him in silver and will pick up the order this evening."

"Weird timing," Daphne said.

"Yes." Mr. Silica paused. "It's very odd. They didn't want him to install it, not even to come along. Enjoy your holiday, they told him."

"Well, good for them," Daphne said. Before Mr. Silica could start to worry again, she said, "It's Spring Festival." The words came out flat, because in all her explorations yesterday, she'd seen no sign of Ivan. But maybe he'd be here today. I have faith in you, Ivan, she thought, and to Mr. Silica she said, "Let's go out and see some more performances."

"I'll buy you lemon pastries," Mr. Silica said. He laid his coat aside, stuck one thumb in the pocket of a vest decorated with tiny flowers, and led Daphne out the door.

They followed two men on stilts—how could they manage stilts on cobbles? Daphne wondered—down a street to where a tightrope walker danced along a rope between two roofs, while her partner below sang a mournful love song. A tenor perched on the roof of a butcher shop and sang in praise of meat. In front of the barbershop a group of men sang of nostalgia and friendship in four-part harmony.

Snow melted off roofs and ran in rivulets through the streets. Mr. Silica bought Daphne chicken legs, dried peaches, and cider. Strangers jostling against them fastened ribbons to Daphne's hair. Mr. Silica laughed and tapped his feet. Daphne took hold of his hands to twirl him around, but he stopped her after one swing. "We're not performers, my dear. We must be orderly."

Just then, a rumble of excitement running through the crowd swept Daphne and Mr. Silica forward to the main road. The crowd hung back from the intersection as a group of men—mostly bearded, with grayish skin, sturdy muscles, and dirty clothes—formed themselves into four rows. They began to dance, one at a time, stepping from foot to foot, shaking one wrist or the other. With each step, each shake, a sweet note sounded. An arpeggio, then a chord, and then another man joining. They rang like a carillon, playing what sounded like a hymn.

"A prayer to the goddess," Mr. Silica said into her ear. "Oh dear, men looking like that. I'm sure it's sacrilege." He made a quick pious gesture and kissed his knuckle, but he didn't turn away.

When the dancers had finished, they fumbled for a minute, trading and rearranging bells, until they started something new, a rollicking, merry song.

"It's charming," Mr. Silica said. "It's lovely. But who are they? Who could have given them permission to perform?"

"I could learn to dance like that," Daphne said. "You and I could be part of that. Anyone could."

Now the dancers made motions of invitation, and some of them began to sing. They had quite ordinary voices, but they looked so happy that some of the watchers began, like Mr. Silica not long before, to tap their feet, even to hum.

"It's like the drumming in Capella," Daphne said. "They're miners. I know who brought this. It's Fort and Ivan. Mr. Silica, Ivan has arrived!"

But the townspeople drew back, glancing at one another, putting their hands in their pockets, holding their feet back from tapping. Even Mr. Silica tugged on Daphne's sleeve, saying, "Soldiers are everywhere. Come away, my dear, it's not safe."

"No," she said. "This time I'm not running away." When Mr. Silica still pulled at her arm, she yanked free of him. A few feet away, a boy in a red vest, yellow trousers, and wooden shoes stood with his bare ankles showing. Daphne grabbed his hand and pulled him into the street. "It's music for everyone," she shouted. She threw off her hood and shook out her hair. "Do you hear? Music for dancing, music for singing!" She raised her arms and danced as she had danced in Capella. The mouth of the boy in the red vest made an O; he stumbled and blushed; and then he caught her by the waist, swung her around and whooped, his feet clattering on the cobbles.

Another girl drew a partner into the square, and then another, and soon the cobbles sounded with the drumming of feet.

The music stopped, and Daphne's partner released her. "Fun, isn't it?" a girl's voice said next to her. Daphne looked over and felt her mouth fall open. It was one of the servant girls from the Palace, a girl who had always worn a gray shawl and kept her eyes down.

"You're not deaf!" Daphne said.

The girl giggled and tossed back her brown curls. "A girl has to get work, doesn't she?" She laughed and made a pirouette. "Just think, if they up at the Palace knew, with all their jibber-jabber, what we really think of them!" She twirled away, and Daphne saw her throw her arms around a young man.

The music started again, and a note rang at Daphne's side as a pair of strong arms caught her around the waist. She turned, and it was Ivan, grinning, his face scrubbed but dirty along the hairline, his jacket ragged, and his hair long enough that it flopped over his ears.

"You did it!" she said. "You're here."

"And you got them dancing, just as we were about to flop."

She laughed. "Not bad for a deaf girl." She put her hands on his shoulders and they spun, his bangles ringing in time but out of tune with the others. Ivan, still terrible at music. She wanted to hug him.

The dance music stopped. Ivan bowed to her and walked back to lose himself among the miners. Red-faced, sweating, with wide grins, the miners began to dance another song. It sounded like a folk song, and the people on either side of Daphne rocked from side to side and hummed. A few of them were brave enough to start singing words. Daphne turned in a circle. She could see neither Ivan nor Mr. Silica.

As the people's voices rose, rough and poorly matched, singing in different keys or no key at all, a clatter of hoofbeats sounded on the cobbles. A shout arose, and the hoofbeats rattled closer. The servant girl Daphne had seen earlier ran up and grabbed her arm. "Soldiers! Run!"

But Daphne pulled free, craning her neck to see. Horses trotted down all four streets that converged on the square. Plumes on the horses' heads dipped in time with plumes on the helmets of the cavalry, who wore bottle green coats and blue pantaloons. The horses parted and ranged themselves in double ranks around the intersection, while still more horses clogged the roads.

The servant girl slipped away. On every side, citizens fell back behind the horses, jamming onto sidewalks and pressing against buildings as if they could melt into the stone. The horses sidestepped and backed, pressing people against the walls. At the center of the crossroads, the dancers tried to stand their ground, but Daphne saw them squeeze closer together as the horsemen stationed themselves around the intersection. Then from the midst of the dancers strode Fort, dressed as the miners were, with bangles tied to his wrists and ankles.

"Have you come to dance with us, Captain?" he called to the officer at the head of the first group of horses. "Have you come to join in celebration of the Festival?"

The officer stood in his stirrups and waved a sword over his head. "Disperse! Cease this desecration, or we will mow you down!"

A whimper ran through the crowd, and spectators pressed even more closely against the shop fronts. A stout woman tugged frantically at the locked doors of a laundry; a group of boys climbed over each other into an open window. But Fort smiled. Then Ivan emerged from among the dancers, also, and stood shoulder to shoulder with Fort.

Not again, thought Daphne. She clenched her hands and willed her feet to move, to walk through the line of horses and take her stand with Ivan and Fort. She took two steps forward.

Ivan said in a mild voice, "The people can't disperse with horses blocking the roads."

"Dismount and join us," Fort said. "Sing, dance! Use the voice and the legs the goddess gave you."

"Rebels!" growled the officer. "Anarchists! A trampling is what you need." He raised his sword again.

But then a rustle sounded behind him. Daphne stretched forward far enough to see a carriage pull to a stop behind the second rank of horses. The carriage door opened, and down stepped a lady in a long, gold-spangled gown: the Diva. As she glided forward, the horses sidestepped to make way. The Diva held her dress out of the mud between the cobbles, and supporting her arm walked Lila, her face white but her head high and steady.

When the Diva reached the front rank of horsemen, she laid a long, elegant hand on the mounted officer's knee. "Captain, don't chase them away. These are the days of Festival, after all. I should like to hear once more the songs of our childhood, so many years ago. And look, oh my dear people." She stepped into the street and twirled slowly, one arm indicating the dripping eaves on all sides. "How the ice melts! Sing!"

CHAPTER THIRTY-FIVE

Master Thomas

Lila dropped slightly behind the Diva, letting Her Highness occupy center stage. She looked past the Diva to see Fort bow, turn, and murmur to his dancers, rearranging them for another song.

Lila's chest constricted at the sight of Fort and Ivan here, free. Did Daphne know? She wanted to break free, too, and run to greet Ivan, but she was still the Diva's servant, whom dignity required to stand, impassive.

Ivan's eyes locked on hers, and for just a moment his face broke into a grin. He shook melting snowflakes out of his eyes, and as the dancers began to sway and stamp, he crept around the rear ends of a line of horses to stand beside Lila. The Diva remained in front of them, surveying the dancers.

"You've risen high," Ivan said in Lila's ear.

"I'm the Diva's favorite," Lila said. She said it in a matter-of-fact tone, because it was the truth. She hoped it didn't sound like bragging.

"How do you like it?"

"It's lonely," she said, surprising herself.

He gave a small nod. "Listen. I've invented a way to purify the music metal from rock, and your leaves showed me how. We left the ore in the Treasury with a man I've told all about it, but the guards are very suspicious. Once everyone realizes what we've found—well, I'm hoping they'll be grateful enough to help us get home."

For the first time in months, home sounded good to Lila. "Have you seen Daphne?" she asked. "I used to see her every day, but Master Thomas banned her from the Palace. She left me a letter in the wall, but when I got there it was gone. I don't know if she's still pretending to be deaf and dumb."

"She's not. She's here."

The song ended. This time, perhaps intimidated by the Diva's presence, none of the citizens had sung along. Fort bowed his head. "Forgive me, Your Highness, that ends our repertoire. We had only two octaves to prepare."

The Diva's voice held mild reproof. "And thus, despite the freshness of your presentation, your performance is full of errors and infelicities."

Lila felt Ivan wilt beside her.

The Diva continued in a softer tone. "To achieve perfection, to achieve Art, requires months, nay, years of dedication. But during these three days of Festival, on this one year of years, we shall accept enthusiasm in its place."

The Diva turned around with a rustle, her chin high in the air. "Come, Lila, we have other performances to bless."

Lila lowered her eyes and lifted her skirt, ready to follow. But the sight of Ivan, standing aside and making a face, prompted her to speak. "Please, Your Highness, could they visit us? The leaders, could they ride with us and tell us how they did it, how they taught music and dancing so quickly to such rough men?"

The Diva looked down, and Lila saw the drooping skin around her eyes and mouth. Behind her gaiety, she looked weary, even a little uncertain. Lila said, "They have left us a great surprise in the Treasury, and we should talk to them."

The older woman reached and tugged gently on a strand of Lila's hair. "Let them come to the Palace once the Festival is over," she said. "Let them speak to us after we have rested."

$$* \quad * \quad *$$

With the singing over, and after Ivan had relayed the Diva's invitation to Fort, Daphne led Ivan back to Mr. Silica's glass shop. Mr. Silica, with sidelong looks at Ivan, brought the cousins sandwiches and lemon drinks, and then withdrew.

Ivan told Daphne about the mine, about his search for the music metal that was more valuable than silver, and about his apprenticeship with the Hermit. He took paper from Mr. Silica's desk and sketched out the instruments he and the Hermit had improvised, and how they had solved the secret of how to space the notes. As he talked, Mr. Silica drew nearer, until he was sitting beside them, laying his finger on the paper and asking questions. On the other side, Ivan outlined his method for separating the music ore into pure tones.

"This is amazing," Daphne said, studying the paper. "You're a genius, Ivan. An inventor."

He tipped his chair back and ran a hand through his hair. "We just took bits and pieces and put some ideas together." But she had never seen him look happier. "Fort thinks we can restore the country by bringing music to everybody. Give them instruments, he says, and they can all make music, their own music. Everything will turn upside down, and rich people won't be able to lord it over the poor anymore."

Daphne thought of the dancers huddled together in the intersection with the soldiers on horseback lined up against them. She shifted in her chair. "I don't know, Ivan. Think of Allegra's father and the Ladies in the Palace—they're not just going to step aside for the rabble." She pushed her chair back and stood. "Don't you know what happened to the music metal in the past? Officials confiscated all of it and melted it down for official bells in schools and town halls. They created a monopoly. For regular people to own it was against the law."

"I know." Ivan stood, too, and walked back and forth, gesturing. "But the supply of it was limited then. Don't you see? Now we know how to make enough for everyone. The whole country can sing and dance, Daphne. Who knows, that might make summer last longer, and maybe this whole Ice Age or whatever it is could come to an end. Anything can change, Daphne."

She shook her head. "Fort's got to you. You've become such an idealist you're blind to the dangers."

He stopped in front of her. "We just have to convince the Diva. And Lila got us an audience."

Daphne sighed and looked away. "The Diva's position isn't that secure right now. People say she's too old, that she can't lead anymore. They're waiting in the wings to sweep her aside."

He frowned. "She seemed pretty much in charge today."

"Today, yes. But the day after tomorrow, the Diva has to sing herself free of the Ice Castle. She goes in tomorrow night, and they wall her up in a tower of ice, and she has to sing herself free. If she doesn't find the strength—if her voice was too badly damaged by poisoned tea—why, then the Composers have to choose someone stronger before the people riot and chaos sets in."

He looked at her. "Poison tea? What kind of place is this?" When Daphne shook her head, he said, "Do they have a new Diva picked out?"

"Oh yes, they do. At least the Chief Composer does. And Ivan, this is the worst of all. I meant to tell you right away: the Chief Composer is Timothy. Somehow he got himself here, and he pretends to be blind and sticks close to the Diva, and he tricked one of the Ladies, Lady Nadia, into trying to murder the Diva. If not for my yellowkin, Nadia would be Diva already, and in his power. If Lila's Diva fails and Timothy sets Nadia up as Diva, he can blackmail her and basically control her."

Ivan scratched his head. "Has anyone warned the Diva?"

"I've sent messages to Lila but they don't get through. I'm banned from the Palace on pain of death, even though Timothy still thinks I'm deaf and dumb and doesn't recognize me."

"Maybe his vision really isn't that great. But why do you think he wants control?"

"I don't know. He has soldiers marching through the streets. He's expecting some kind of trouble, or else he's stirring it up. Remember how he wanted to control everyone in Origin, Ivan, but he seemed as if he meant well? Now he doesn't bother to act kind at all. He wants power, Ivan, and silver, and he's scarier than ever."

*   *   *

"Is Her Highness in?"

Master Thomas's voice outside the chamber door had a cool edge. The Diva took the hairbrush from Lila's hand and made pushing motions with her hand. Lila drew back to hide the way Daphne used to among the curtains that hung from the Diva's bed. Master Thomas was irritable lately; he didn't like to find the Diva wasting her time on Lila.

Master Thomas tapped forward, heading slightly the wrong way as usual, until the Diva called out to correct him. She gave him her hand to kiss.

He held onto her hand instead of letting it go. "What's

this I hear, Your Highness, about you letting an unauthorized performance proceed in your presence?"

The Diva replaced her hand in her lap. "The people enjoyed it, Master Thomas. And do you know, the snow melted from the eaves."

He shook his head. "Hot bodies, nothing more. And your attendant sang in some unearthly language."

"She calls it German. Master Thomas, she comes from Zart's country."

Master Thomas looked confused, and then he gave his head a shake. "I must ask you, Your Highness, at this particular time of threat, when all sorts of hoodlums and revolutionaries threaten our country, do you think such irregularities are wise?"

"Yes, Thomas." Her back grew straighter. "Yes, I do believe them wise."

"And what if I told you"—he leaned closer—"that those dancing men are convicts, every one of them, escaped from the mines?"

The Diva spoke firmly. "Then I would remind you, Master Thomas, that the Festival is a time of amnesty, when the Diva may pardon whom she pleases."

"*After* she brings the spring," he reminded her. "Or should I say, *if* she brings it." He leaned over the Diva, and his voice grew gentle. "You grow older, Your Highness. You are not fully recovered from the poison. Let another singer carry the burden this year."

The Diva stood, and her voice shook. "How dare you

suggest such a thing—that I abandon my people, that I surrender my sacred charge!"

Lila took three silent steps to the Diva's side, and slipped her hand into the Diva's.

Master Thomas seemed to twitch, and for a moment his face turned from the Diva toward Lila. How could he have heard her? She was sure a mouse made more noise.

His face smoothed, and he turned back toward the Diva. "You know I care for nothing more than your welfare, Your Highness."

The Diva frowned. "I believe sometimes you care a little too much, Master Thomas. On my return I visited our Treasury, only to find it sadly depleted of silver."

"There has been mutiny in the silver mine, which will be stamped out as soon as the Festival is over." His voice grew even more soothing. "And yes, it is true, we have raised an army to protect you, and Melodia, against attacks by the southern rebels."

The Diva sniffed. "The accounts suggest an army far larger and more expensive than we ever discussed, Master Thomas. Nor do I remember ordering brown uniforms."

Lila watched him closely. Over time, she had grown to distrust Master Thomas for the way he always smiled the same pinched smile and always spoke in the same smooth tone. He gave the slightest laugh. "Oh, Your Highness, you shouldn't be worrying yourself with accounts and tailoring the day before you enter the Castle."

"No, I should not."

Her tone, Lila thought, would not melt any ice.

Master Thomas cocked his head, as though waiting for more, and then he waved a hand as if erasing marks on a whiteboard. "Your dear Highness, new intelligence tells us the southern rebellion is much more serious than we first imagined. Even now, a ragtag battalion marches toward us, intent on disrupting the Festival. Worse, the rebels have infiltrated supporters into the city, to foment unrest among your citizens." He clasped his hands. "I have selected the most loyal troops for your personal guard and supplied them with special uniforms. Overall, the need for troops has been greater than you initially authorized, but I have proceeded with your safety uppermost in mind."

The Diva eyed her Chief Composer as he stood waiting, his head slightly upturned in an attitude of meekness. Then she spoke, and her voice rang with the certainty and power of command.

"Here are my express orders. There is to be no violence during the Festival. I want those brown-clad soldiers out of sight. What use are special guards at the Treasury once it has been emptied? I have set my own guard there. Post our soldiers along the remnants of our walls, and if this rebel army arrives, hold it there with threats, not force itself."

She waited until Master Thomas nodded his assent before she continued. "When I have sung this land free from the grip of winter, I will lead the people of the city to the walls and address the rebels. Do you hear me? Robed in the majesty of the goddess I will persuade them to lay down their rude arms and rejoin the proper order of their lives."

Lila felt the Diva tremble, but her trembling had nothing to do with fear. It's righteousness, Lila thought. Righteousness is making her tremble. This strength, this sureness, her dedication to her music—they're all part of the same thing.

Master Thomas bowed, and the Diva gazed down on his bald head. "After the Festival, I will turn my attention to financial and military matters. I shall expect to find everything in order. Meantime, I am concerned to hear that the Ice Castle, whose construction you begged to be allowed to oversee, is not yet completed."

He clasped his hands in front of him and spoke in his silky voice. "Your Highness, I am monitoring the work very closely. Tomorrow evening, when you enter the Castle, you will find everything ready for you."

Her nostrils flared. "Master Thomas, I expect no deviation from tradition. No thinning of the chamber walls to make my task easier. I will not have my people or the goddess shortchanged."

He looked shocked. "No thinning of the chamber walls, Your Highness, I assure you."

"As for any weakness that remains from my poisoning," the Diva said, "tradition allows me an attendant."

He raised his eyebrows, and the Diva said, "Lady Lila will keep watch beside me in the Castle."

An odd smile touched Master Thomas's lips, and he bowed. "So be it." He backed away, still bowing, all the way to the door, where he turned and, upright, exited without using his cane.

The Diva sighed and sank into a chair. She pulled Lila close. "That man has been so attentive to me in every way. Why, child, do I begin to doubt his loyalty?"

CHAPTER THIRTY-SIX

The Ice Castle

At sunset the next evening, Lila walked at the Diva's side as the procession left the Palace. The Diva swept along after the prize-winning choruses, wearing a long gown embroidered in green and gold thread. Lila followed, wearing her own green coat, mittens, and boots, and carrying a basket of food and supplies. Four guards flanked them, and all seven Composers followed, their black overcoats edged with ribbons of green and gold. Six of them, even the blind ones, turned their heads as they walked, smiling and chatting. Only Timothy, last in line, marched with his head down and his lips tight.

Tanners and cheese makers, schoolchildren and mothers clutching toddlers cheered and waved on either side as they marched through the streets and out the west gate. Lila heard comments and exclamations.

"Who is that young girl?"

"Why, didn't you hear her sing the other day?"

"But why does she march with the Diva?"

"The Diva is allowed an attendant."

"That child doesn't look strong enough. See how pale she is!"

They passed town choruses, the children ranked in order of age, dressed in neat uniforms. A patch of sky blue and yellow attracted Lila's eye. When she turned, she saw familiar faces, and in a back row, astonished eyes gazed at her from amidst a blaze of fiery hair.

At a bottleneck by the west gate, a pair of sturdy-looking workmen grumbled without taking note of who walked behind them.

"The Castle was so slow to go up this year."

"Because they wouldn't let us common folk help, like has always been our right."

"Soldiers chasing us off, cheating us of a chance for silver. Then this morning I figure they'll be desperate for help, so up I go first thing, and guess what? They wrapped the job up in the dark of night. With soldiers!"

"Who's running things, that's what I want to know?"

Master Thomas, Lila said to herself. Master Thomas is running things, and Daphne never trusted him.

A path cut in steps of snow wound up the hill beyond the west gate. At its top, Lila saw the Ice Castle with the setting sun glinting off it in a fierce orange color. Blocks of pond ice set atop one another rose to a tower thirty feet high. Along the outside of the castle wall, all the way to the tower, ran a set of ice stairs, which the Diva would descend victorious as soon as she sang herself, and spring, free from the icy fist of winter.

Lila gazed up at the Diva's singing chamber, a block of translucent ice atop the tower. It looked so solid that her heart sank. The ice of its walls had to be as thick as the length of the Diva's forearm, that was the tradition. Who could sing her way out of such a prison? Lila had learned enough of warm singing to warm herself for a few minutes outside on a cold night, but even in Capella, field workers cleared away the snow before the singers came. To melt through more than a foot of ice! That she couldn't fathom.

When they reached the hilltop, the Diva led the way through a door carved in the Castle wall. In the cold hush within, her Ladies and their servants waited in gowns of pastel colors, strewing dried flower petals in her path. Three Ladies led the Diva and her attendant up the internal stair to a second story of ice, and beyond that to a small platform. From there, an ice stairway, only a foot wide with no railing, led to a hole in the floor of the tower room.

What if the Diva slips? Lila thought in a panic. But the Diva lifted her skirts, which extended far beyond the width of the stair, and climbed with sure steps until she disappeared into the chamber above.

Now it was Lila's turn. She handed her basket to a soldier standing by with an axe, lifted her skirt as the Diva had done, and took the first step. Someone had sprinkled the steps with sand so they weren't slippery at all. It's like climbing up to that funny room at the top of the barn, Lila thought. I'm about to enter another new world.

Lila stepped up through the hole, knelt on the ice, and reached back for the basket, which after a couple of unsuccessful tries the soldier tossed up to her.

"Replace the block of ice now," the Diva said in a quiet voice.

Lila knelt, braced her feet against the wall, and slid a wedge-like block of ice a foot thick into the hole. Only a crack of daylight appeared around the block. Lila reached into her basket, drew out a leather bottle, and poured water all around the block. The water froze almost on contact, sealing off direct light, and suspending them in darkness lightened only by a faint orange glow—the last glimmer of sunset penetrating the western wall.

Lila looked around the room, a cube about eight feet wide, with ice a foot and a half thick on every side. Except the floor, she reminded herself. The floor was only a foot thick.

The room shook to a series of distant thuds. Lila tried to dig her hands into the floor. "What's that?"

"They're cutting the inside stairs away," the Diva said, "so we can't turn back."

With the stairs gone, they would be suspended over empty air, with only one way out. Lila shivered, and at the same moment, she heard a muffled crash, and the tower quaked again. The stairs were gone.

"Now, daughter," the Diva said, touching Lila's shoulder,

"the vigil begins. Tonight we sing simple prayers, enough to warm us and no more. Only when dawn arrives do we begin to warm our way free." Her grip on Lila's shoulder tightened, and she lowered herself to her knees. She placed both hands over her face and bowed her head. Then, as full darkness fell, she lowered her hands and began to sing.

The Diva touched Lila's arm and Lila let her voice merge with her teacher's. The Diva had taught her that this song must be sung as softly as possible, but still with fullness of tone, round vowels, vibrato in the right places. The song praised the earth and praised the goddess for her care of it, then begged her to return, bringing warmth and color and new growth. The song-prayer cycled between praise and lament and a plea for return, with the melody shifting slightly at each verse. The Diva had urged Lila to make up her own variation, and when the Diva paused for a drink and to breathe for a while, Lila sang her verse about the yellowleaf trees with their feet in a streamlet that ran murmuring down the slope.

Their song weaved a cocoon of warmth around them through all the long hours of darkness, and even when Lila nodded off, the Diva's voice made her bed of ice feel almost like a bed of satin.

*   *   *

After another day of Festival spent performing with the miners and persuading people to sing and dance, Ivan joined Daphne to follow the procession through the evening streets of the city. Atop the hill they listened to the sounds of chopping as Lila and the Diva were sealed into their cell. But with nightfall came silence, and the only people who remained on the hilltop were a few guards and some pious citizens praying with their faces in their hands.

"What now?" Ivan said in Daphne's ear.

She tilted her head. "I guess there's nothing we can do for them right now. They should be safe enough. We can return in the morning, like everyone else, and hope she sings them free."

"I'll see you back here then. I need to go check on the Hermit."

*   *   *

The green-clad soldier at the Treasury door let Ivan into an underground room with dark nooks and piles of gear that reminded him of the Hermit's quarters at the mine. In the first room, counting tables covered by leather-bound account books stood at neat intervals, and chests empty of all but a few silver coins lined the walls. But the second chamber resembled twenty of the Hermit's workshops crammed into one, with equipment and old mechanical devices piled one on top of the other. Ivan found the Hermit pulling to free a wooden frame and a tangle of strings and wires.

The Hermit didn't bother to greet him. "Help me pull this out. What is it?"

Ivan tugged on the frame, couldn't free it, and stooped to clear away the objects that stood around it. "A harp, I think. A really old, really broken one. Haven't you been out to see the sights at all?"

The Hermit growled. "People, noise, infernal sunlight! I don't know why I ever let you drag me along. Sing for the goddess: superstition and nonsense!"

Ivan pulled aside a rocking chair inlaid with some sort of green jewel and dragged the frame out of the rubble. It did look like a harp, or the top piece of one, with the swooping curve and strings sprouting from the inside edge. "But I brought you to this treasure house, Master, so how can you complain?"

The Hermit cleared his throat, and Ivan helped him carry the harp fragment over to the light.

"Not bad, not bad," the old man said. "You'll have to help me rebuild it, boy."

Ivan stepped away. "I'm sorry, sir. I just meant to check on you. I need to stay tonight with Fort and the men. Tomorrow the Diva sings in the Ice Castle, and I want to be there first thing."

"And just when I had a gift picked out for you, too," said the Hermit.

Ivan hesitated, and the Hermit handed him a flat object in a round brass case. Ivan opened it. "Another compass. Master Hermit, thank you so much. But wouldn't it be stealing?"

"Naw, she said I was welcome to take some souvenirs. And maybe to stay. She hasn't decided."

"Who hasn't decided?"

"The Diva," the Hermit said. "She visited the day you brought me here. I told her stuff, and she's thinking. But she said to keep quiet and keep my head down for now, so that's what I'm doing. But as for the Ice Castle melting, balderdash! Buncha superstitious nonsense."

*   *   *

Lila woke, hungry and thirsty and needing to use the chamber pot. The darkness was less than complete now, and the Diva knelt in her same spot, still praying in low song. Lila scrambled up, did her business, stowed the chamber pot under a cloth in the corner, and poured a little alcohol over her hands. Then she prepared a cup of cold tea for the Diva and laid out a picnic of meats and cheese, pickled vegetables and rolls.

"A long night," the Diva said, in that new, soft voice of hers that seemed to be saving its force for later. "And your watchful attendance was short."

Lila bowed her head in apology, and the Diva said, "How little the young know of sacrifice! To think I believed you might bring me some special power. Here, child, lend me your arm."

With her knees creaking and Lila pulling hard, the Diva managed to rise. She accepted the drink Lila gave her, but shook her head at the food. "Dawn arrives, child. I begin."

She embarked into song, and though Lila had heard her practice many times, she had never heard anything like this. The song began with the smallest of ripples, like the smooth water of dawn as a canoe slips by; it shimmered, brightened, and took on color and warmth, until it seemed as if sky and water shone in sunlight. Without raising her volume, the Diva suffused her song with warmth. Warmth rose from the resonance of her vowels, the dignity of her stance, her breathing. Temperature within the ice chamber began to rise, and before long the Diva removed her cloak and Lila laid her green coat aside.

The Diva paused, drank more tea, and began a forest song, one of Lila's favorites, written by an ancient Composer, not Master Thomas. The song was subtle, full of shadows in place of the Dawn Song's clarities. There were sections in minor keys, changing mid-phrase, until merry intervals broke in and reminded Lila of laughter and the yellowleaf trees.

The song wound on and on, and the ice chamber began to feel like a steam bath. The walls grew slick with moisture, and puddles expanded on the floor. The Diva paused to steady herself with a hand on the wall.

Lila put an arm around her waist to support her. "Do they hear us outside, my Lady?"

"A little," she said. "Listen."

Standing absolutely still, Lila heard the faint echo of a chorus. "Listen! They're singing, too."

The Diva ran a sleeve along her hairline. "They like to believe they are helping me. Of course their voices, so far below, so undirected, do little to the ice, but it heartens me that they seek to share my burden."

She began again, a song of fields and flowers, then one about rainbows amid summer showers, then one about white clouds sailing overhead. The walls of the chamber dripped all around them, and they stood up to their ankles in warm water.

The Diva paused, panting. "He thought I no longer had it in me." She smiled, showing her teeth. "What do these Composers know of dedication and training?" She returned to her song.

Her voice resounded in the chamber, as pure and beautiful and strong as ever, but Lila, offering a shoulder for her to lean on, handing her a cloth with which to dry her sweaty brow, worried. It was hard to tell time here in the sealed-off chamber, but the room seemed bright with filtered daylight, and brightest at the ceiling, as if it were already noon. By tradition, they should be almost free by now. When Lila pushed with her hand at the ice wall straight in front of the Diva, it seemed to give only a little. Underfoot, on the other hand, the ice felt more fragile. Twice, Lila's foot broke through a crust and fell an inch deeper into the floor.

Walls eighteen inches thick, she thought, but only twelve inches for the floor. And nothing below. Yet the Diva was directing her voice well.

With a crack, Lila's left heel slipped deeper. She squeezed the Diva's hand, and the Diva, finishing a phrase, looked down in question.

"Please," Lila said. "The floor seems to be thinning fast."

The Diva's eyes came into focus, and she looked around. Like Lila, she prodded the wall and dug her heel into the floor. Her eyes widened.

"It's the problem we feared, child. I am not directing my voice well enough."

"I think you're doing fine," Lila said. "If I put my hand

between your mouth and the wall, the heat makes me pull it away."

The Diva frowned. "And yet it's too hot in here. Too hot near the floor."

"What if ..." Lila said, and hesitated.

The Diva peered at her. Her left eyelid drooped; her shoulders were not quite so straight as before.

"What if I sang a cooling song, down by the floor? Like I used to do for your fever. I can't make it freeze again, but maybe I can make it thaw more slowly."

The Diva nodded. "Thank you, Lila."

Lila got to her hands and knees in the water and leaned to put her mouth next to the surface. She sang the songs she had sung to cool the Diva's fevers in the afternoons. She sang of mountain streams and ice-skating, a quarter moon sailing high in the darkness, and cool lemonade on a hot day. It wasn't just the words that made the song cool, but the notes themselves, their sequence and mostly their tone. She sang as simply as she could, without flourish, and the water seemed to grow colder, until she had to sit back and dry her frigid hands.

The Diva kept singing. Her hair pulled free of its bindings and stood like flames around her head. For the first time since they had recovered from the poison, Lila heard strain in the Diva's voice. The Diva staggered and steadied herself with a hand against the wall.

"Rest for a minute," Lila urged her. "Take some tea."

The Diva shook her head. "The singing must not be interrupted."

"Then I'll sing," said Lila, and as the Diva sank to her knees, Lila took her place before the wall. She summoned thoughts of daffodils, of birds' nests, and of bicycle rides along the river, and she sang Beethoven's Ode again. The song swelled in the little space of the ice room, and Lila felt the heat flowing out of her toward the wall. But her strength leaked away from her, and to her amazement, she found her legs weak by the end of the song.

The Diva pulled herself to her feet and put an arm around Lila. "You see what it takes to be the Diva. Pretty singing is not enough. But you gave me respite, and I can go on." Throwing her head back, she projected the warmth of her voice once more.

Lila rested, regaining her stamina in the cold, shallow water of the chamber floor. The water had a faint orange glow and Lila's throat tightened. Not sundown, not so soon. With a splash, she climbed to her feet.

But no, the light slanted in from the south-southwest, halfway down the sky, neither low enough nor far enough west to be terribly late. It was the ice itself that seemed to be tinted slightly orange, instead of the faint green-blue she expected. Lila turned around, surveying all the wet walls. In the northeastern corner she saw something odd: the faintest hint of a rainbow.

The rainbow reminded Lila of the rainbows cast on Allegra's wall by light passing through her collection of prisms. Lila traced back along the path of the light with her eyes. Halfway up the southwestern corner of the chamber, she discerned a glint of sunlight. The surface of the ice there was clear and smooth, almost too clear and smooth for ice. Almost like glass.

Glass. It was glass that split the light in Allegra's room and threw a rainbow against the opposite wall.

Lila tore off her shoe and dug its heel into the southwestern corner, near where the Diva had concentrated her singing. The Diva exclaimed and pulled on her shoulder, but not before Lila had loosened a chunk of softened ice and thrust her hand inside the hole it left. Smooth, hard, cold. "It's glass," she said. "They've walled us in glass."

"No." The Diva pushed Lila aside and reached into the burrowed hole. Her eyes shut, and she sank to the floor. "Thomas," she said.

Lila pushed her hand back into the hole and tugged at its edges, trying to enlarge the space. If she could clear enough glass, they could signal for help. She put her face to the hole and saw the glint of glass, but beyond it stood a solid wall of translucent blue-white: ice. They were trapped within a wall of glass coated inside and out with thick walls of ice. The outside layer of ice would be so well insulated that all the Diva's singing could never melt it.

Lila's fingers throbbed, and she was shaking. She turned to the other walls, to different heights, different distances from the corners. With her own shoe, with the heel of the Diva's shoe, she drilled holes in the softened ice, and each time, she ran up against the glass barrier.

And below them? She hesitated, holding her shoe near the corner of the floor. The Diva nodded, and Lila dug. She found no barrier. Four inches down, her shoe poked through to open air, and the water where Lila was kneeling drained out in a rush, tearing the hole to the size of her foot.

Lila scuttled backward. If the Diva kept singing, they would fall. Panic moaned in her ears.

No, not panic. The Diva moaned. "Oh, he has betrayed me. He has betrayed my people!"

Lila struggled to think clearly. Like Daphne solving the logic problem to save Fort, she knew she had to spread the possibilities out in front of her. She and the Diva had no way to melt the glass, no way to mark it so the people could see it through the ice. They had nothing to thrust against the glass to break it.

No, they were meant to fail. Master Thomas, who had overseen the construction of the Ice Castle, wanted them to fall to their deaths. Lila didn't know his reason, but it must have to do with the missing silver and the soldiers marching through the city. She imagined Master Thomas taking charge, making all the schools stricter and more exclusive than ever. The Palace would be ruled by poison and fear. His soldiers would march Fort and Ivan back to the silver mines and whip the prisoners to make them work faster. Silver would disappear from the treasury while children in towns like Capella scrabbled in the dirt for scraps of food.

No! Lila thought. She couldn't remember ever feeling a stronger NO. "We'll call for help," she told the Diva. "We can call through the hole in the floor."

The Diva shook her head. "No one will hear us. The Castle door is closed. Our cries will sound through three levels of empty space and no one will hear us."

The Diva slid to the floor in the corner farthest from the hole and huddled there, her hair wild and her head slumped on her knees.

Lila didn't have time to comfort her. She put her mouth to the hole. "Help us! We're surrounded by glass! Bring ladders! Help us!"

Her voice swirled in the void below and returned in weak echoes.

"No one will hear," the Diva repeated, shaking her head.

Lila shouted until her voice began to break, until the edge of the hole collapsed and one of the hands she was leaning on fell through. Her head and half her chest followed, but the Diva grabbed her ankle, and Lila crept backward out of the void. She sat next to the Diva, shaking. "But you said they could hear us singing."

"Faintly. They hear the tones. No words."

The tones. Lila squeezed her eyes shut, thinking. There must be some way to get a message out.

CHAPTER THIRTY-SEVEN

The Glass Factory

Choirs murmured and stamped their feet in the cold. Daphne glanced in all directions. Fort wrinkled his forehead, Ivan opened and closed his hands, and a woman farther along the line clutched the edges of her skirt and moved her lips with eyes tightly shut. On all sides people jostled, rubbed their necks, and muttered to one another. The ritual was taking far too long. The sun was sinking below the treetops, and all the prize choruses had finished their songs and their tours of the Ice Castle walls hours before.

"I don't even hear singing anymore," Ivan said.

"Do you suppose they're freezing?" Daphne asked.

Fort shook his head. "The Diva won't freeze."

"But I don't hear singing," Ivan repeated, and then they did.

Instead of a song this time, it was one note, faint and pure and distant. Lila's voice, Daphne was sure of it. She gripped Ivan's arm and he, too, stood still, listening. Lila's voice, and then another with it, richer, singing the same one tone.

"G," Fort said. "They're singing a G."

"But why?" Ivan asked. "Have they run out of songs?"

Fort shook his head. "The Diva doesn't run out of songs."

G, thought Daphne. G, last note in the cycle before you turn to A again. Maybe it meant something. Maybe it meant the Diva was nearing the end of her strength. No, surely not. She pictured it, a G in swirling script like the G clef, or like the G atop Itzo Silica's factory.

Then she knew.

"Glass," she told Ivan and Fort. She grabbed Fort by the arm. "It's G for glass. Someone stuck glass up there in the ice, and they can't sing their way out. It's Timothy, Ivan, I'm sure of it!"

"How—" Ivan began.

"Listen. Mr. Silica's son got this secret order. Five thick, square sheets of glass, to be ready the second night of the Festival. Timothy ordered it. I'm sure of this, Ivan."

"Five sheets," Ivan said with infuriating slowness. "Four walls and the floor. We can go in by the ceiling."

"Not the floor," Fort said. "They get in by the floor, through a hole in the ice. It must be four walls and a ceiling."

The implications of his words sank into them. Ivan said, "That means only the floor can melt through."

Fort said, "We need to go up there with ladders and axes. My miners—"

"Wait," Daphne said. "If you rescue them that way, Timothy will win. The Diva will have failed. He'll retire her and put Nadia in her place, and then he'll take over."

"People will find the glass," Ivan pointed out. "When spring comes and the Castle melts ..."

"If spring comes," Fort said.

Ivan threw his hands up in exasperation. "Of course spring will come. And even if it doesn't, we'll take the Composers up on ladders and show them."

"By then," Daphne said, "Timothy and his army will be in control."

Ivan slammed his fist into his hand. "Daphne! Are you saying we should let Lila fall?"

"Of course not!" she yelled back at him. Around them, people turned to stare. "Get a net, get something, and stand in there ready. Figure something out, Ivan. Just don't rescue them yet. I have an idea for how we can still let them win."

She turned and pushed her way among people who pointed at her gray shawl and scolded. Skidding and slipping, she hurtled down the snow steps of the hill, and as fast as her breath allowed, she ran along the stretch of road to the west gate. The soldiers had left their posts: what did that mean? Through the lanes she ran, slowing only when she needed to hold her side and catch her breath. Was it worth checking Mr. Silica's shop? She took the detour and beat on his door.

No good. Empty. For a moment she doubted herself. What if he and his son were at the Castle like everyone else? But no, she had looked for them there all day.

She ran again, trying to keep a steady pace this time, through the alleys, past the tannery. In the distance she heard shouts and hoofbeats. But here at last was the vacant lot and on its far side the glass factory, with the great G hanging from the roof. She sprinted across the field, her thoughts full of Lila and the Diva crouching on a melting floor.

Daphne flung open the factory door. On a stool near an empty cauldron sat Mr. Silica with a bottle in his hand, and next to him sat Itzo eating pastries.

"Ah, Daphne," Mr. Silica said as she approached. He waved the bottle. "Welcome to Silica Glass. On this one day of days I thought no one would mind me visiting my old factory. Did I ever give you the tour, my dear? Have some wine!"

Daphne ignored him and went to stand in front of Itzo, her hands on her hips. "That glass Timothy ordered," she began.

He looked confused.

"I mean Master Thomas," she said. "Those five sheets of thick glass."

Now he looked frightened. "I finished them," he said. "There should be no problem."

Mr. Silica shook his head, looking more alert. "Your order came from Master Thomas?"

Daphne seized hold of Itzo's sweater and yanked him

to his feet. "Listen. They've locked Lila and the Diva in a chamber of glass encased in ice. That's your special room."

Itzo's eyes widened, and he tried to pull away. "Not my room. I had nothing to do with that."

"It's your glass."

"I would never—I didn't know, I swear!"

Daphne tried to shake him. "What's the weakness, Itzo? How do we break the glass?"

Itzo shuddered. "You can't break it. Six men with axes, maybe. But they can't fit on the stair."

Daphne let go of him and took a step backward. "But you came to see your father about some weakness. Something you added was going to make it breakable."

Itzo looked wildly from Daphne to his father. "I don't know what she's talking about."

Mr. Silica, on his feet now, too, spoke softly. "What color was the glass, son?"

"It was clear, transparent! Perfect, the way they ordered!"

Mr. Silica fixed his son in his gaze, and after a moment Itzo lowered his eyes. "Orange. The glass had the faintest orange tint. When they picked it up they thought it was just the torchlight."

"What note makes orange glass break?" Daphne demanded.

"Oh, it won't break," Mr. Silica said. "It's much too thick to break."

"What note?" Daphne repeated.

He shook his head. "For orange? That I don't know. Son?"

Itzo shook his head, too.

Daphne clenched her fists. "What *do* you know? Tell me anything."

When Itzo trembled, his cheeks shook. "The ore ... the impurity that turns the glass orange, it comes out, yes, it melts first. Yes, yes, I'm sure now." Itzo's words tumbled over each other. "Just orange, and the rest of the ore left over."

"That's right," said Mr. Silica. "Orange comes when the ore first starts to melt. The lowest temperature melt."

"Ivan will know what note that is," said Daphne. "From purifying the music metal, he'll know."

Itzo said, "Yes, yes, first melt, leaving chunks of unmelted ore, do you want to see?"

"No," Daphne said. She turned to Mr. Silica. "We're going to sing them free. The whole city needs to help. Every voice. Do you understand?"

"Yes, child. I'm coming with you. Itzo, gather more people."

"As fast as you can," Daphne said. "I'll run ahead." Without saying good-bye, she made for the door and ran across the empty lot.

*　　*　　*

The sound of stamping horses and shouted orders rang out louder now. Ahead, just off the main street, horsemen waited in a file. Timothy's army.

Daphne doubled back, turned south, and slipped through the alleyways. She must have passed the horsemen now. She veered again toward the main road, and ran softly across the cobbles. Ahead, she heard shouts and curses. She wondered if the citizens were already giving up on the Diva, drifting away from the Castle only to find Timothy's soldiers awaiting them. He would call the people rioters and rebels, and he would put them down. She had to head them off, turn them back to help the Diva. She rounded a corner and came face to face with a mob of men waving shovels and pitchforks. They surged and roared like surf in a storm, and she needed their voices. She waded into the mob, calling, "Wait, wait, you can help!"

Men in overalls and patched trousers turned to stare at her, and even as her momentum and their turning bodies swept her deeper among them, she realized her mistake. These weren't citizens of Melodia. She pulled up, trying to paddle backward out of the crowd, but a hand reached from behind her and grabbed hold of her collar. "So, we meet again," said Timothy's voice in her ear.

CHAPTER THIRTY-EIGHT

The Diva

Daphne squirmed to get free of Timothy's grip. "He's not blind!" she shouted. "Don't trust him! He's not blind!"

With a vicious wrench at her collar, he twisted her around to face him. "No, not completely blind," he said. "Still, it took me a while—you'd vanished by the time I remembered you: the girl who tore down my paradise."

He meant the City under the Mountain, golden, fragile, built on deception. "I didn't tear it down! It was falling down already. You just wouldn't see."

"Not a crumble," he said, giving her collar a shake. "Not a flake fell until you and that boy came, bringing discord. And now here you are again, raising suspicions, arousing fears. Blundering in with all your ignorance to interfere once more." He turned her to face the mob of farmers, who watched in puzzlement, occasionally shaking their pitchforks. "Behold a spy!" he told them. "She pretended to be deaf and dumb so she could sneak into the Palace and plot for the Diva's death. She tried to serve poison to our Diva. And now that you have come to rescue her Highness, this spy means to betray you to the very soldiers who have mutinied and locked our Diva away!"

The mob roared and thumped their makeshift weapons on the cobbles.

"I called the army down from the walls," Timothy said. "I made the way safe for you to enter. Otherwise, this conspirator would already have summoned the soldiers to crush you." He held Daphne's collar, looking from face to face, "I have no time for her now. You men can take care of this parasite. She's yours. Don't let her get away." He thrust her into the mob. "This traitor and vicious spy, she is yours."

Rough hands grabbed Daphne, and a gaggle of hecklers closed around her. One of the men poked at her stomach with the edge of his shovel, and another lifted her shawl with his pitchfork. "Yellow hair," he said. "Look at that yellow hair. Like a bird, she is. Make her sing!"

Daphne tried to gulp down her panic. She felt tossed among waves with no sure sand beneath her. These men must be the fearsome southern rebels, and Timothy had let them into the city. But Timothy had said they meant to rescue the Diva. Maybe they were innocent men after all, simple men, men he had tricked the way he had tricked the

Diva, Nadia, his and fellow Composers—the way he had manipulated them all. Soon he would call his horsemen to fall on these men and crush them, so he could say he'd saved Melodia from rebellion. Grateful townspeople, their Diva fallen, would hand him all the power he desired.

A bearded giant in overalls leaned over her. "Where shall we put you?" He lifted her onto a stone marker set in the middle of the street. "Now sing." The men pressed close, prodding at her with their farming tools.

She tried to lick her lips, but her mouth was too dry. Even if she sang, if she could gather enough moisture to sing, they would only hate her as one of the privileged. "Don't believe him," she said. Her voice came out in a croak, almost like Fort's. "He has soldiers lying in wait to attack you. He has put the Diva in danger."

"You liar!" said a man with a broad face and flattened nose. "Paid us good money, he did, good silver, to come here and help the Diva. But you!" This time the pitchfork poked hard enough to hurt. "Sing!"

"I'm on your side," Daphne said in desperation.

"Liar! Look at you," the man jeered. "What do you know about being poor?"

"Listen," Daphne said. She closed her eyes and rocked back on her heels, fishing for the words of Fort's poem, the words Ivan had written out for her. She recited:

Now who gets to sing when the winter comes?
Who has to dance when the sun goes down?
Who eats at home in a house of stone?

Who huddles in mud while the children moan?
Why have they stolen your music?

She paused. The men nudged each other. "I've heard that one before. Have you heard it? There was that fellow ..."

"The drummer in the scarlet cloak," Daphne said. "Fort. He's my friend."

They looked at her differently now. Their weapons drifted lower.

She took a breath. "I saved him from execution."

Whispers, narrowed eyes, heads shaking in doubt. "Why should we believe her?" someone growled.

Daphne turned toward the giant who had lifted her and held out her hands in supplication. "Ask him, ask Fort. He's here now, out by the Ice Castle, working to save the Diva. I'm trying to get to him. I need to find some strong men to help him."

A rumble of confusion ran through the crowd of farmers. "He's here? That fellow's here already? Save the Diva, she says? Needs some strong men, do they?" Others said, "Watch out, she's a tricky one. We should stick with Master Thomas."

She recited in a voice that swelled with indignation,

Why have they stolen your music?
Why have they stolen your music?
The day comes, goddess, when your people rise,
When all of your people rise and sing,
When they dance and they sing and stand up like men,

And all the ice prisons come tumbling down.
Stand up!

The giant who had lifted her to her spot nodded, chewing on his beard. "Not bad." He swiveled to survey the crowd. "Neighbors, I'm going with her." He lifted her down, and a number of other men shouted their assent.

"Hurry," Daphne said. "But quietly, so the soldiers don't hear us."

She led them south a little farther, then west and north and west again, twisting through the alleys, darting across intersections. The west gate still stood unguarded. On the road, she broke into a jog, and the rabble of farmers thundered behind her, their heavy boots striking the cobbles. She heard their gasps of awe as they caught their first sight of the Ice Castle. The shadows were long now, but atop its hill, the Castle glimmered in orange light.

"Ivan, Fort!" she cried as she crested the hill. Choir members turned to stare, and they drew back at the sight of her wild hair flying and the ragged mob of impassioned farmers lifting their implements of war.

Ivan ran up to her. "Fort's in the castle with his miners, rigging a net."

"Get him out here. These men will lynch me if he doesn't come tell them I'm a good person."

Ivan shouted instructions to a boy who trailed him. Glancing around, Daphne saw the citizens waiting in small groups, like spectators at a disaster, wanting to help, not knowing what to do. In a cluster at the edge of the crowd huddled six of the Composers, probably discussing who should be the next Diva. She wondered what they knew of Timothy and his plans.

"Ivan, what note melts first? In the music metal. What note melts at the lowest temperature?"

"D," he said. "Why?"

"The glass has an impurity in it to give it strength. But if a pure enough, strong enough D note sounds, it might shatter."

"What would happen to Lila?"

She stopped short. She had assumed the glass would shatter into a thousand dull pieces, like a car window. But what if it shattered into knives? "I don't know," she said.

Mr. Silica's voice spoke beside her. "It will collapse everywhere at once." He bent forward, resting his hands on his knees, breathing hard. "Tiny pieces—almost harmless—stand away from the walls." He looked at Daphne. "I thought you'd be done by the time I got here."

"Detour," she said, waving at her followers, who shifted from foot to foot, glaring around in suspicion.

"Daphne," Fort said behind her. "What do you need?"

She turned, and because it seemed simplest and quickest, threw herself toward him with outstretched arms. His arms wrapped around her, and he swung her around with his cheek pressed against hers.

"That," she said, once he set her down "Thank you. And a D."

"You want a D?"

"The biggest, purest D we can make, to shatter the glass."

Fort fished in the pouch that hung from his belt. "Here, D." He took a pair of disks and, on inspiration, handed them to the giant farmer. "Clash them together like this, see? That's the tone we need. Get people to sing it."

"All your dancers," Daphne said. "They can get the people singing."

"They're holding the net," Ivan said. "Here, men, I need volunteers for the net!" He counted off farmers and citizens.

Daphne saw one of the prize-winning choruses, a group of teenagers, sitting off in the snow, slumped and obviously bored. She ran over to rouse them. "Please, a D, I need you all to sing a D for the Diva, to free her from a glass prison. All of you stand here and sing up at the tower. Sing for her as she has sung for you all these years!"

The chorus members stared at her, but then one stood up and flourished a baton. "Come on, chorus members, you heard her. It's time again. Give it your hearts, team!"

Daphne found children sliding down the snowy hill, choruses in back of the Castle breaking out a picnic, the tenor from the butcher shop kissing a lady behind a tree. Daphne dragged and begged and cajoled, and soon she didn't have to any longer, because they all heard the single note rising and came to see why.

At the front of the Castle, Fort's dancers wove among the citizens, sounding the D of their bangles, and Fort followed, urging everyone to sing, not just the choruses but the citizens, too, shopkeepers and laborers, mothers and tavern keepers, cheese makers and tightrope walkers and farmers. "Just listen," he told them, as they shrank back,

protesting that they couldn't sing, never had been able to. "Listen, and join your voice in, make it match and then give it your heart—for the Diva, for spring."

Even Ivan stood with his mouth open, and as she approached, Daphne made out his voice—sure, strong, and in tune for once in his life. She stood beside him, and when she opened her mouth and began to sing, she felt her voice join a river of sound.

*   *   *

Lila heard it, faintly, then louder. How odd, one note, one single note in different octaves. So many voices. What did it mean? Was it a reply to her signal, *glass*? What began with D? Daphne, down, drama, double? Diva, of course.

She knelt beside the crumpled Diva. "Listen, they're singing for you. The people are singing their love for you."

The Diva lifted her head. "So many of them," she said. "So many voices!"

"Get up," Lila urged. "Sing back to them. They deserve to hear you sing back. I'll do it, too." She helped the Diva to her feet, brushed the frost off her dress, and neatened her hair. "Together, Your Highness, our very best D."

They sang, and their voices blended, Lila's cool voice with the Diva's rich warm voice that brimmed with a lifetime of devotion and study. They sang, and the walls vibrated. It's more than just a message, Lila thought. Singing as if her heart could burst free of her ribs, she reached to draw the Diva into the center of the room.

Standing beside her, the Diva drew a new breath and sang with full force. The floor held as the walls quaked.

The room exploded.

Lila threw up her hands to protect her face as a shower of glass fell around her. The Diva collapsed on the floor, weeping. When Lila knelt in the pebbles of glass to tug on her shoulder, the Diva lifted her head. Tears streaked a face pocked by tiny cuts, but she was smiling. Lila crawled to the edge of the platform and looked out at the evening. People stood with their heads thrown back in awe, shielding their eyes as glass crystals fell among them like snowflakes swirling in the sunset, casting rainbows and flashes of orange and yellow as they fell.

CHAPTER THIRTY-NINE

A Barn in the Snow

Spring burst into the Land of Winter.

Almost too fast, Daphne thought, as she and Lila and Ivan crossed the vacant lot to the old glass factory, which had become a metal works. In place of icy puddles, tulips peeked from the earth. A scraggly tree had sprouted leaves, and a robin flew toward it carrying a bit of string. Daphne and Lila walked without their shawls, and Ivan wore short sleeves.

They had come to say good-bye. As they stepped through the open door, where an S now hung beside the G, Mr. Silica hurried to shake their hands, while Fort waited beside the furnace, smiling.

"I wish you'd stay," Mr. Silica said. "Daphne, I'll make

you chief accountant. Ivan, you can be production engineer. Lila, you—why, you can teach the metal to sing."

Daphne said, "If Lila stays, I think the Diva will keep her to herself." She meant it as a lighthearted compliment, but Lila bit her lip, and Daphne was sorry she'd said anything. The Diva had asked for an interview with Lila at noon.

"Let me show you our latest." Mr. Silica ushered them into the heat of the factory. "Our largest batch yet of F sharp, with a perfect tone!"

He spoke with forced merriment that didn't fool Daphne. Since his son's arrest after the Festival two weeks ago, Daphne had seen him many times sitting in a corner, staring at nothing and looking old. She said, "Mr. Silica, I have news."

His eyes flew wide in alarm and he sank back. Everyone knew the penalty for plotting against the Diva was death.

Daphne smiled. It had taken all her persistence and all Lila's charm to bring him the gift she was about to offer. "Itzo's been pardoned."

Mr. Silica gave a cry and gripped her arms. "How did you—"

"I finally convinced the Diva he didn't know about the plot. I told her Itzo gave me the key to her rescue." She patted the old man's hand. "He'll be released, but he's assigned to take a new batch of volunteers to the mines—not slaves, real miners who get paid. He's supposed to mine ore and learn the business from bedrock up."

Mr. Silica kept hold of her hand until Ivan said, "Let's show the girls what we made for them."

Mr. Silica stepped backward, wiping his eyes. "Master Fort, produce the medallions, if you please."

Fort wore the dark uniform and embroidered badge of a Composer now, the youngest in a generation. The Diva had selected him to replace Timothy, who had fled the evening she and Lila escaped the Ice Castle. Fort still had the visionary shine in his eye, and whenever he smiled, Daphne felt a fluttering in her chest. He reached behind him and brought out a handful of metal. With a flourish he handed a medallion to each of the girls. "Our own manufacture, with Mr. Silica's artwork."

Peering up round-eyed from Daphne's medallion was the embossed figure of a bird holding its beak open as if the artist had caught it mid-song. She ran her finger over it, stroking it. "A yellowkin."

"And a D," Fort said. "Go ahead, strike it."

Daphne flicked her fingernail against it. "The note that brought the spring. I'll always remember." Tears blurred her eyes, and she looked toward Lila. "What did you get?"

"A treble clef," Lila said. She struck the medallion. "And a G, to remember my cry for help."

Ivan shook his head. "To honor your courage and cleverness, Lila, in solving the mystery and letting us know."

Lila smiled.

Ivan took another medallion from Fort. "We chose medallions for ourselves, too, while we were at it. Take a look. Mine's an E, for the first step I took across the Hermit's bridge." He showed them the medallion, with the image of a bridge. "Bridges are my fate, I think."

"Mine's not finished," Fort said. "It's going to be an F, not for Fort, but for Freedom, to remind me where I came from. And Mr. Silica's going to stamp it with a pair of broken manacles."

"Wow," Daphne said. "You could make a business of this."

"No," Mr. Silica said. "Four medallions only, in honor of this year's spring, when four brave young people set music free."

They fell silent for a moment. Then Fort said, "All right, let's head for the gate. Mr. Silica, I'll be back in a few days."

Daphne hugged Mr. Silica, her arms reaching only partway around him. He staggered in surprise, then steadied himself enough to pat her on the back, murmuring, "There, there. Always friends. Always grateful. Always ..."

Ivan shook Mr. Silica's hand. "Good luck with the Hermit. Don't let him bully you."

As Fort and the cousins crossed the vacant lot, Lila caught at Daphne's arm. "Wait." She had dark shadows around her mouth and eyes. "I still need to have my conversation with the Diva."

"We'll wait for you by the gate," Daphne said, trying to sound matter-of-fact, as if even though she had become a beloved heroine, of course Lila would join them, leaving the cheering, the adoration and praise behind.

"Courage," Fort said, and he hung Lila's medallion over her head.

*   *   *

"My dear child," the Diva said, turning from the window. "You must not go." She looked younger. Her eyes were bright, and her hair had been newly colored—gold, with just a hint of orange.

Lila curtseyed. "Thank you, Your Highness, but I need to get home."

The Diva glanced at the mirror, touched her hair, and turned back to Lila. "You misunderstand me child. This is not false politeness. You *must not* go. You owe it to yourself, and to me, to stay."

"I'm sorry," Lila said, lowering her gaze.

"I insist that you heed me. You have talent, child, rare talent. I have not said this before. With the right training, you can be remarkable. Memorable." The Diva gazed at her with a look halfway between cool assessment and parental pride.

Lila felt herself glow in the Diva's approval.

"You could be Diva someday, with the power to rule, to teach, to protect. You could make life safer and more beautiful for all your people. There is no higher calling, Lila."

Lila's legs quivered. The Diva was offering her a glimpse of success greater than any she had imagined: garlands, parades, applause, good deeds, and fame.

But not home. She thought of the children she had seen playing outside the Palace window, and she lowered her gaze. "Thank you, Your Highness, but I need to go home."

The Diva leaned over her with piercing eyes. "You thank me? Like this, you thank me—for giving you my time, for watching by your sickbed, for sharing my secrets, for bringing you with me into the Ice Castle? No one else has received such privilege, such attention. And you say, 'Thank you, but I'm leaving now'? Back to some run-down, unmusical hovel beyond the mountains?"

Lila lifted her head. "Back to the land of Mozart and Beethoven."

The Diva frowned, the white dents deepening at the corners of her nose. "That was a sham, a cry for attention, though I forgive you for trying to impress me. Somehow you learned a song in Zart's own language, but in the tower of ice, when I was in need, you had no special magic. You proved yourself a very ordinary little girl. But stay with me, and I will make you extraordinary."

Lila thought, I saved you in the tower. She said, "I have my own life, my own world. I want to go."

The Diva threw up her hands and swung away. She paced faster and faster around the room, then hurled her chair aside and pointed a long finger at Lila. Her eyes narrowed as her voice rose. "Ungrateful, unworthy child. If you leave me, you will never have my blessing."

Lila flinched, but this time she managed to look the Diva straight in the eye. "I'm sorry to leave without it." She pivoted and walked for the door.

Sobbing sounded behind her. Lila faltered, but she didn't turn.

*　*　*

The cousins and Fort walked northeast through a land

sliding into spring. Melting snow left boggy ground where tiny wildflowers grew. In ponds edged with rushes, ducks landed in a spray of water. Birdsong trilled on the breeze.

They camped the first night on a bluff, on dry ground among pine trees. Ivan used his new compass and marked the site on Lila's homework map from their Capella days.

Settling beside Lila, who had been silent all day, Daphne laid a handful of tiny blue forget-me-nots in her lap. "It's because she loves you that she made such a fuss, Lila. In a month, a year, she'll think back on how you stood by her and saved her, and she'll bless you in her heart."

"Maybe. Thanks for saying so, Daphne," Lila said, and she got up to gather twigs for the fire.

Daphne looked at the forget-me-nots scattered on the ground and wished she'd been brave enough to give them to Fort.

*   *   *

As the three cousins walked abreast on a wide path through the forest on the second day, Lila, who had been silent for almost an hour, said, "It was like an orchestra, wasn't it? More an orchestra than a chorus."

Daphne asked, "What was?"

"Us. You were a servant and Ivan was a slave, and I was living a fancy life up in the Palace, but we each had a part. It was like the theme of a symphony going from the strings to the woodwinds and then the brasses. Or it's like the melody getting all the attention—me—but it wouldn't sound nearly as good or even stand on its own without the rhythm and harmony propping it up."

She looked from Ivan to Daphne, her face pink. "I'm sorry you had to be my servant, Daphne."

Startled, Daphne laughed. "I hated it. I really resented being a servant at first. I kept thinking, 'Why me?' But then I saw the other servants and wondered, "Why should I be so high and mighty?' After that I tried to have my own free thoughts but be a good servant all the same. I grew more humble, and it wasn't so bad."

The two girls looked at Ivan. He wriggled his eyebrows and said: "Okay, my turn for the big self-revelation. If we were an orchestra, I'd be the buffoon."

"The bassoon," corrected Lila.

"Write it in that old English way where the s's look like f's, and it's buffoon. The big funny-looking one with the awful sound."

"But it's a beautiful sound," said Lila, and they fell to arguing about the sounds different instruments made, and what instruments played well together, with Lila humming examples from musical pieces the other two had never heard of. Fort walked beside them, head cocked to listen.

* * *

Late in the afternoon of the third day, they emerged from the northern edge of the forest, their footsteps crunching through remnants of crusty, wet snow. Daphne walked to the top of a rise, where she shouted and jumped up and down, pointing off to the left. Ivan and Lila tore up the slope after her and saw a distant building, dark red, rising from the snow. Ivan threw himself into a cartwheel of celebration. When he came upright, he caught hold of Lila and Daphne in a double hug and then dragged them with him at a lumbering run toward that distant building.

"What are you doing?" Fort shouted after them. "I don't see anything."

Ivan reached the barn first. It was Aunt Adelaide's barn, all right. He recognized the drooping gutter and the broken downspout.

He ran around to the sliding door, but no matter how hard he put his back into it, he couldn't make it budge.

Fort came up panting and asked, "Do you really see something?" Instead of answering, the girls stood looking up the high straight walls to the roof.

"There's a barn," Ivan told Fort. "We have to get up to the roof. This is why I had you bring the axe." He led Fort back to the edge of the forest, where they selected a young pine.

Fort felled the tree, and Ivan trimmed back the branches, leaving only stubs on either side of the trunk. They carried it back between them, Fort still looking skeptical. Ivan and Daphne leaned the tree ladder against the eave.

"There's really something there," Fort said in surprise. "I can hardly see it, but it's holding the ladder up."

"Yep," Ivan said, grinning. He hated to leave Fort, but it was fun to see him all amazed like this. He turned to the girls. "Who goes up first?"

"I guess I do," Lila said.

Daphne turned and flung herself into Fort's arms. He swung her around the way he had that evening in front of the Ice Castle. He even kissed her, making her feel as if a flock of birds had taken wing inside her, even though it was only a kiss on the corner of her mouth, and the bristles on his chin scratched her face

The kiss gave her the courage to say what she'd been mulling over all during their walk. "Come with us, Fort. Visit the land of Mozart. We can show you so many things, all kinds of music and weird instruments. Even if you stay an octave or two, when you come back only a day will have passed."

Ivan shook his head and laid a hand on Daphne's arm. "We don't know how it works in the other direction. For all we know, Fort might come back to the Land of Night and find that months and months have passed."

Daphne shook off Ivan's restraining arm.

Fort smiled down at Daphne, looking only at her. "What an adventure that would be. Can we save it for next time? I can't risk leaving now, not with instruments to build and new music to write and schools to set up for the poor. Too many rich old men are still lurking in the background waiting for the Diva to change her mind and shore up the old divisions again."

"Okay," Daphne said, looking down and feeling that her wishes were puny compared to such great purpose.

Fort placed both hands on her shoulders and gave her another kiss, very light, on the forehead. "Come visit again, Daphne," he said.

She had to be satisfied with that as Lila and Ivan each gave Fort a swift embrace. Then the three cousins mounted the tree, shouted their good-byes, and maneuvered onto the roof.

"I still see Fort," Lila said, waving. "But he doesn't seem to see me."

Ivan looked back at Fort standing there, his face wrinkled in puzzlement. "I know. It's funny. For them the border seems to be the barn itself. For us it's the cupola." He turned to Daphne. "He's too old for you, Daphne."

Daphne wanted to shove him off the roof.

"Cupola," Lila said. "So that's what it's called."

Daphne waited until Fort, below, turned toward the woods. His shoulders drooped a little. He would have been hard to explain to the grown-ups, Daphne thought. It hurt to think so, but Ivan might be right after all.

"One last breath," Ivan said, and together they inhaled the air of Lexicon, sweet with fir needles and melting snow, the distant tang of bear pelt and reindeer milk, the shivering tinkle of new leaves and the scent of flowers poking through the mud. Daphne's heart squeezed. It was hard to leave in the surge of spring.

Ivan let his breath go. "Ready."

CHAPTER FORTY

Great Aunt Adelaide

Across from Daphne, Aunt Leonora laid down her fork. "How *could* you get your coat so dirty?" she asked Lila for the tenth time. "I don't see how you could possibly have done so much damage to your boots overnight. If you haven't caught pneumonia, I don't know why." She swept a look of scorn across Ivan and Daphne, who were far more ragged-looking than Lila.

"We're just so glad to have you back, kids," Daphne's mother said. "And whatever voodoo you were doing over there—when John checked he said you were just playing checkers and listening to your iPod—but whatever you were doing, it must have worked. The operation went well, and Aunt Adelaide rested quietly all day."

Leonora broke in again. "Your fingernails, Lila. Chipped like a bricklayer's. What will your director think?"

"I'm a mistreated servant, Mother. A poor servant can have chipped fingernails."

Aunt Leonora recoiled as if she'd been slapped. Then she stood and leaned over the table to address her daughter. "Now listen to me. You had no business out there. It's time you grew some backbone instead of blindly following those who are older and supposedly wiser than you."

Daphne rolled her eyes at Ivan.

"I see you." Aunt Leonora glared at her. "Don't think I can't see you. Show any more attitude like that and I'll rescind my invitation for you to visit Lila in the city this summer." She rounded on Lila again. "It will be a miracle if you haven't ruined your voice by huddling in the cold, breathing moldy old hay dust, and neglecting your practice."

"I practiced." Lila said. She stood, threw back her shoulders and sang in Italian, a lament so sweet and tremulous and then so full of resignation and forgiveness that the curtains wavered before the windows and Daphne felt a longing swell within her to do great and noble actions.

Aunt Leonora sat down, her mouth open. The other adults applauded, and Leonora said, "Mozart? You learned Mozart in a barn?"

"About the summer, Mother," said Lila, "I've been thinking. I don't think you should invite Daphne to visit the city. Instead, I'd like to go to Oklahoma and spend the summer with Dad."

Aunt Leonora's eyes looked ready to pop out. She opened her mouth, closed it, and opened it again like a fish. "But

424

your voice lessons! Your auditions! Just as you're emerging! After all my arrangements, all I've sacrificed!"

"I appreciate all you've done, Mother, I really do. I love to sing. But I think I want to take some time off once the show's done. I'd like to play outside, go to the movies, learn to rollerblade, you know? I'd like to have friends for sleepovers and go hang out at their houses. Maybe I'll learn to play the trumpet."

Daphne glanced around the kitchen. Ivan was trying to hide a grin with his hand, his dad looked as if he might burst into laughter, and Daphne's own mother had her hands poised as if she were about to break into applause again. Daphne sent Lila a look of encouragement.

Aunt Leonora looked as if a falling rafter had hit her on the head.

Ivan's dad stood up. "Well. Who's doing the dishes?"

*　*　*

Ivan's father showed the three cousins into Aunt Adelaide's room. "Just a few minutes, kids. I'll be down the hall if you need me."

They approached the bed and took stations around it. Aunt Adelaide looked up at them, pale and bleary-eyed. One tube fed into her arm, and another drained from her abdomen.

"How are you?" Daphne asked.

"I am minus most of a pancreas. And I hear you spent the night in the barn."

"Not exactly," Ivan said.

A smile spread across her face. "How I envy you."

425

"Don't be so sure," Daphne said. "It was the Land of Winter."

Lila moved closer and touched Aunt Adelaide's hand. "Is that where you got the ideas for your books?"

Ivan and Daphne stared, and Aunt Adelaide let out a weak laugh. "Oh, yes, children, Leonora ferreted out my secret identity years ago. I write books. And she forces you to read every one, doesn't she, Lila dear? So you can talk about them and impress me."

"The last one really helped me. It helped me see how beautiful the winter was."

"The stories don't come from Lexicon, Lila, but the inspiration does."

Aunt Adelaide turned her glance to Ivan, who brought his hand in front of her and opened it to reveal the Astronomer's medallion. "We brought it back. It was really helpful, but now we each have our own."

Instead of answering, she lifted her head off the pillow, and he slipped the medallion over her head.

Daphne stepped forward. "Aunt Adelaide, I wish we could have found something to bring you—some magical potion that would cure you. But it didn't work out that way." Tears filled her eyes, and she blinked fast so Aunt Adelaide wouldn't see them.

"Oh, Daphne," Aunt Adelaide said.

"So all I have for you," Daphne continued rapidly, "is this feather. It's from a bird with the most beautiful voice." She handed Aunt Adelaide the yellowkin feather.

Aunt Adelaide brushed the feather against her cheek and

held it to her ear. "I think I hear the singing." She fumbled to put it in her hair, and Daphne bent to help her.

Aunt Adelaide beckoned them to come closer. "Ivan, I've talked to your father. Now you must all tell me if I've done right. Daphne and Ivan, I've left the farm to you. It's a big responsibility, I know. Ivan's father has agreed to be trustee until you two come of age." She turned to Lila. "And to you, dear, I've left the rights to all my books. They're not worth much now"—as Lila protested, Aunt Adelaide shook her head—"but someday they may come back. And you know, when you're older ..." She broke off and looked dreamy for a moment. "I'd love to see one or two of them made into musicals, just for fun."

Lila nodded her head, smiling, and squeezed Aunt Adelaide's hand.

"I loved writing those books," Aunt Adelaide said. "That's what Lexicon taught me, Lila. To follow my heart." She drooped back against the pillow. "I want to hear more, but I'm tired, children. I never knew surgery could make one so tired."

"We'll come again," Daphne said. "Maybe not for a little while, so you can rest. But we'll come, all of us together, and we'll tell you everything."

"One last thing," Lila said, "before we go ..." She stood at the foot of Aunt Adelaide's bed and opened her mouth. Very softly, adding her own turns and trills, she sang the Diva's hymn to spring.

Chart of the Three Gates

What the gates say	I. Slavery	II. Banishment or Execution	III. Banishment or Slavery
If all are true	Slavery	Execution	Banishment
If two gates are true	True (S)	True (B or E)	False (not B or S)
	Slavery	Banishment	Execution
	True (S)	False (not B or E)	True (B or S)
	Slavery	Slavery – doesn't work	?
	False (not S)	True (B or E)	True (B or S)
	B or E	B or E – can't tell, doesn't work	The other two are B or E, so this must be S
If only one is true	True (S)	False (not B or E)	False (not B or S)
	Slavery	Slavery – doesn't work	Execution
	False (not S)	True (B or E)	False (not B or S)
	Doesn't work	Banishment	Execution
	False (not S)	False (not B or E)	True (B or S)
	Execution	Slavery	Banishment
If all are false	False (not S)	False (not B or E)	False (not B or S)
	Banishment	Slavery	Execution

Questions to Think About

Ask a few of these and let the conversation begin!

- In the Land of Winter, high social status and opportunity are reserved for those born with musical talent. Do you think musical talent is fixed or changeable? Do all children in the Land of Winter have the same opportunities to show and develop their talents? What determines status and opportunity in our world?

- Early in the book, Lila is rehearsing the part of Cosette, a character who is "sent away as a child and forced to be a servant while this other girl her own age gets treated like a princess." How is this story from the musical "Les Miz" echoed in The Ice Castle? Can you find other connections to that musical story?

- The Diva tells Lila, "I have heard you speak of your 'gift' for singing. Here in the Palace of Music, we don't have 'gifts.' We have duties." In what ways is Lila's singing a gift and in what ways is it a duty? Does Lila's sense of duty change over the course of the book? Do you have particular gifts, and do they bring duties with them?

- Who was Zart, and what does he have to do with the Land of Winter?

- At one point Ivan writes, "I hate to say it, Daphne, but did you ever think that maybe this one is Lila's adventure, and we're just along for the ride?" What do you think? How do the three cousins' journeys of adventure differ? Does one cousin grow and experience more than the others?

- In chapter 13, Daphne appears to accept the social structure of Capella, while Ivan rejects it. Why do you think their reactions are different, and how does Daphne come to change her views?

- The Hermit is a frightening, monster-like character when Ivan first meets him. How does Ivan handle him? In what ways is he a mentor to Ivan? Does the Hermit change, or is it just that Ivan's attitude and understanding change? Explain.

- Fort went from a life of privilege to a life as a rebel and outcast. How has the experience affected him? Is he dangerous? Do you think he has the character to be a good Composer?

- What does Lila learn from the Diva? How does Lila's relationship with the Diva compare to her relationship with her mother?

- If you were making a medallion of music metal for yourself, what note and symbol would you choose?

Musical Challenge Activities

- Pass out paper and drawing materials and challenge kids to draw a picture of a musical instrument in a way that clearly demonstrates how the instrument works. Ask the kids to explain the instruments to one another in a way that would allow the Hermit to reproduce them accurately.

- Hold a singing audition, and based on the results, assign each child a class within the Land of Winter—laborer, middle class, or upper class (noble or high official). Players stay in class character as they discuss aspects of the book.

- Invite twelve kids to play the interval game Fort describes in chapter 20. Each player is assigned a note (played on a piano or other instrument). They stand in a circle arranged in the order of their notes. One player starts with a ball or beanbag and announces a particular interval. To the accompaniment of the piano, which starts at the given note and advances by the given interval, players toss the ball by intervals around the circle with players who catch the ball naming or singing their notes.

- Participants design their own medallions by choosing a favorite note and symbol. They draw and cut out or otherwise manufacture their medallions.

- Working together, kids design a new musical instrument and collaborate on building a prototype.

Looking for more fun activities?

Head over to http://www.lostinlexicon.com/games.html

Look for the *Lost in Lexicon Musical* coming soon! You can catch previews of the music by contacting the author on her website at http://www.lostinlexicon.com.

About the Author/Illustrator

Pendred (Penny) Noyce is a doctor, education reformer, and writer. She grew up in Silicon Valley, California, surrounded by apricot orchards and fields of mustard. Along with her brother and sisters, she rode ponies, put on plays, and explored the rapidly changing countryside.

As an adult, Penny has practiced internal medicine, supervised medical residents, and become a leader in Massachusetts mathematics and science education reform. She serves on a number of nonprofit boards, including that of the Noyce Foundation, and she chairs the boards of Maine's Libra Foundation and the Rennie Center for Education Research and Policy. She loves to give talks to teachers and kids.

Penny is married with five children who all love to read, travel, ski, and seek out adventures. She has yet to visit Australia and Antarctica. She lives in the western suburbs of Boston with the parts of her family that haven't already grown up.

Joan Charles lives in Santa Monica, California. As a child she put on plays and puppet shows, wrote and illustrated a family newspaper, and played endless games of Parcheesi with her sisters on rainy summer days. Her favorite thing to do was draw and make up stories, and that's still true today.

What's coming next in the *Lexicon* series?

The Floating Harbor: An Adventure in Art

by Pendred Noyce

When Aunt Adelaide, weakened by cancer surgery, asks Ivan and Daphne to give her one last glimpse of Lexicon, they end up tossing in a rowboat on a darkened ocean. Stormy weather, a volcanic eruption, and marauding pirates separate them. Daphne confronts an old enemy and makes an intriguing new friend who offers fame, fortune, and a very different future for Lexicon. Ivan, helping Aunt Adelaide travel among the floating islands in search of a lost love, finds himself working to scuttle Daphne's plans. Geological upheaval, family secrets, and the threat of Lexicon lost forever propel the cousins into a frantic exploration of the meaning of art, forgiveness, loyalty, love, and impending death.

To learn more about Lexicon, visit

www.lostinlexicon.com

Keep in touch with Daphne and Ivan by following their blogs at www.daphneswordblog.tumblr.com and www.ivansnumberblog.tumblr.com.